Keeping Secrets

Alyson Noël

D0067291

St. Martin's Griffin ⚇ New York

KEEPING SECRETS: FAKING 19 © 2005 by Alyson Noël, L.L.C., and SAVING ZOË © 2007 by Alyson Noël, L.L.C. All rights reserved. Printed in the United States of America. For information, address St. Martin's Press, 175 Fifth Avenue, New York, N.Y. 10010.

www.stmartins.com

ISBN 978-1-250-01862-5 (trade paperback)
ISBN 978-1-250-01863-2 (e-book)

10 9 8 7 6 5 4

Keeping Secrets

Also by Alyson Noël

Fated

Everlasting

Night Star

Dark Flame

Shadowland

Blue Moon

Evermore

Whisper

Dreamland

Shimmer

Radiance

Cruel Summer

Kiss & Blog

Fly Me to the Moon

Laguna Cove

Art Geeks and Prom Queens

For Sandy, who believes in blue hippos

Chapter 1

FIVE CELEBRITIES I'D SLEEP WITH IN A SECOND

1. Richard Branson
2. Tobey Maguire
3. Edward Norton
4. Jake Gyllenhaal (sp?)
5. That guy with the dark hair and sunglasses that I saw at
   Java Daze that time with M that I know is famous but I just
   don't know what I've seen him in.

Okay, so maybe my list isn't the same as yours. You're probably going, "What's with all the old guys?" or "Richard who?" or "What about Justin Timberlake?" or maybe just, "*Eww!*" Well, technically, I'm a virgin, so the whole list is sort of hypothetical anyway. My best friend M thinks the Richard Branson thing is really sick. She thinks I'm obsessed and swears I've gotten all Freudian since my dad abandoned me. Personally I think M is taking her psychology class a little too seriously.

My parents divorced when I was twelve. I knew it was over when my dad mumbled something about having to find himself as he walked out the door. I swear he was just like Burt Reynolds in *Boogie Nights*. I wish I could tell you about how much I miss him, but the truth is I just wasn't sorry to see him go. That was five years ago, and now at seventeen and a half I can honestly tell you that the only real difference is that these days we're kind of poor, when before we had stuff. Really, that's it. Sometimes it sucks, but for the most part it's totally worth it. I mean, nobody screams in the middle of the night anymore. There's just nothing worse than living in a house where people scream.

I don't remember much about being a little kid. I guess it was an average California childhood. I mean some days I was in trouble and other days I was riding the Matterhorn at Disneyland. I just wanted to go to school, see my friends, ride my horse, eat dessert, and stay up past my bedtime. Those were my goals. Then when a few years passed, and I got a little older, I would just burrow deep under the covers when the screaming started. My sister swears it was really good once. Really happy, just like the Nickelodeon channel. But I can't remember that part. She's eight years older than me, so I guess all that happiness was before I was born. I've pretty much always assumed that I'm a product of make-up sex.

Having divorced parents isn't so bad; when you grow up in Orange County it just makes you normal. Nearly everyone's parents are split, and those who aren't, are like totally on the verge. People here are stuck in a state of permanent adolescence. Most of my friends' mothers take yoga classes and raid their daughters' closets for cool stuff to wear, and their dads watch us a little too closely when we swim in the pool. It's like a continuous midlife crisis, and the parents are like teenagers with credit cards and no curfew. California is like a high school where no one graduates. I'm not kidding.

Anyway, getting back to my "Branson thing," it's not problematic like M says. I'm not obsessed. I just really like him, admire him, and yeah, I think he's sexy. I mean who's supposed to make the list? *NSYNC? The Backstreet Boys? I'm sorry but I just can't go for that prepackaged, focus group, made-for-teens junk. Those guys are like shrink-wrapped with a Mattel stamp on their ass.

I like to think I've developed a more mature, refined taste, but M just swears I've got a daddy complex.

It all started one day last year when M and I were shopping around in this thrift store in Los Feliz (that's in LA). M was in the fitting room squeezing into a pair of old wrecked Levi's and I was just trying to entertain myself when I noticed this book titled *Losing My Virginity* displayed on this gruesome, green coffee table. Thinking it was some kind of "how-to" guide, I eagerly picked it up and started to read. But halfway into the first paragraph I realized it was just a clever title. It's actually Richard Branson's autobiography.

It's not like I hadn't heard of him before, 'cause I think he was on a *Friends* episode or something, but before I saw the book I guess I never really gave him much thought. Well, M decided not to buy the jeans, but I bought the book and I finished it in like a night or two. I guess you could say I'm like a Branson expert now. You could probably ask me anything you want about Virgin Records or Virgin Airlines and I'd know the answer. I know it seems kind of weird, but I can't help it, he's just *so cool!* I mean, he totally sucked at school (like me), so he dropped out and became an entrepreneur. But even though he's worth like billions of dollars now, he's not just some boring business guy that's all about work. It's like, when he's not busy running the Virgin empire, he spends his free time either flying around the world in a hot-air balloon, or hanging out on *his very own* Virgin Island with all of his rock star friends! And he keeps it all organized by making lists every day (also like me), *and* he's a total hottie! (Well, for an old guy.)

But one more thing about Richard Branson, before I forget, I want to make it clear that I don't love him because he's one of England's wealthiest, most famous, men. I'm really not that shallow. I love him because he has the guts, freedom, and imagination to do whatever the hell he wants and that, to me, is incredibly sexy. I guess because sometimes I feel so trapped.

So I daydream, and I admit, sometimes it's a problem. I have a hard time paying attention to boring stuff like economics and all the other senior-year required courses. I used to think that meant

I had attention deficit disorder. I mean, I was seriously worried about that for like six months. So one day I finally bit the bullet and made an appointment with my guidance counselor at school. After what seemed like extensive testing, trying to stay in the circles with a number-two pencil, she told me that I'm okay, I'm just extremely undisciplined, that's all. She also told me, that it's quite possible that I'll never amount to anything if I don't start doing better in my classes. Never mind that, I was just relieved that I wasn't going home with a prescription for Ritalin.

One of my favorite fantasies is about Richard Branson and me in Paris. Just because I've never been to France doesn't mean I can't imagine it. So sometimes during a really long, boring, AP History lecture, I'll sit staring at the chalkboard so my teacher thinks I'm listening. I'll even nod occasionally and scribble stuff on paper like I'm actually soaking in real knowledge, but what I'm really doing is imagining myself, in the Virgin Megastore café in Paris.

I'm seated at a small table in the back and I'm wearing a devastatingly sexy little black dress, strappy high-heeled sandals and black Gucci sunglasses, which are like completely "de rigueur en Paris." I'm delicately sipping a glass of champagne, nibbling on a salmon burger, and reading Paris Match *when Richard Branson walks in. I look up, our eyes meet . . .*

But the truth is, I'm nowhere near Paris. I'm at school, standing in front of my vomit-green locker and I've got exactly three minutes between now and my lunchtime appointment with my mom and my guidance counselor, Mrs. Gross (I swear that's her name). You see, Mrs. Gross wants us all to meet and discuss my "academic goals," that's how she worded it, and I'm wondering if I should tell her that I really don't have any.

Well, my mom is pretty unhappy about having to take time off work 'cause I screwed up, and I know this because she doesn't even want me to meet her in the parking lot and walk her to the office. This morning when I was leaving for school she just gave me that look, the one that tells me she's "this close" to giving up on me, and said, "I'll see you in the office at noon, Alex." Then she lifted her coffee cup and fixed her gaze on an earlier disappointment of mine, a faded, red circle in the middle of the kitchen table, the result of a spilled bottle of Revlon Cherries in the Snow nail polish.

I slam my locker shut and head for the administrative offices, and when I pass the student parking lot I briefly contemplate making a run for it, even though I know I can't really do that. So I tell myself I'll just go in, sit down, let the adults talk, nod my head a lot because they always read more into that than there really is, and soon it will be over.

I see my mother as I'm entering the building but I just glance at her nervously and follow her inside. I mean, we don't smile and hug or even say hello because it's not like I'm about to receive an award or anything.

When we go into the office I just stand there all nervous as I watch my mom and my counselor exchange names and shake hands. Mrs. Gross says hello and motions to two chairs facing her desk. And as I sit down and look around, I give myself a mental lecture for letting it get to this point.

It's your basic school administrator's office. You know, sickly looking plant in the corner, college degrees in gold shiny frames on the wall, and an obsessive-compulsive, fake walnut desk that holds a picture of what looks to be a very happy, if oddly posed family.

Mrs. Gross walks over to a filing cabinet and I watch her fingers deftly crawl over several manila folders until she comes to a big, overstuffed one that she lifts with both hands and places solidly in the middle of her desk. It has my name on it and it lies between us, heavy and foreboding. And I can't stop staring at it while I wonder what I had possibly done up until now that could fill up a folder like that. I mean, I'd always considered myself and my high school experience as pretty mediocre.

She starts leafing through it, giving us a briefing on my entire academic career, and it feels like the moment right before you die when your whole life flashes in front of you. The beginning is all good.

"Well, as I'm sure you know," she says, mauve finger nails scraping between the layers of papers, "Alex was maintaining an A average, even with a challenging schedule of AP classes and several extracurricular activities such as ninth-grade-class vice president, tenth-grade-class president, homecoming princess, French club member . . .

Blah, blah, blah. I can barely recognize the overachiever she's going on about.

"But lately," she says, "I've noticed a disturbing trend."

My mother leans in closer but I just sit there crouched in my chair, staring at Mrs. Gross's sensible shoes peeking out from under her desk.

"Alex's grades are dropping at an alarming rate. During her junior year she slipped from A's to C's. Last semester she had C's and D's, and I'm afraid her current midterm results are much, much worse." She flips through a couple of papers and shakes her head. "And I'm not aware of her currently participating in any school-sponsored, extracurricular activities." She removes her glasses and rubs the area on the bridge of her nose where they've branded her pink, then puts them back on and continues. "Because of the drastic drop in her grade-point average, her lack of involvement, and her troubling attendance record, Alex is no longer eligible for any of the scholarships she applied for." She looks from my mom to me to see if we are comprehending the weight of all this. I sink down even lower in my chair, and I can feel my mother's refusal to look at me.

"But she was doing so well! Why wasn't this brought to my attention earlier?" My mother asks, shifting the responsibility to the school when the fact is she hasn't asked to see a report card of mine in way over a year.

Mrs. Gross clears her throat and says, "Well, as report cards are mailed to the home on a quarterly basis, I assumed you were aware of Alex's grades." Then she drums her fingers on a pile of papers, and it's my mother who starts to squirm now.

"I'm afraid that Alex is running the risk of jeopardizing all of her prior accomplishments," Mrs. Gross says as she lines up the corners of the papers that reside in my file. "You must understand that those first two and a half years are not enough. It is imperative that she gets her academic record back on track. A scholarship is out of the question. College will be out of the question as well, if we don't see immediate improvement in her grades." She pauses, then looks right at me and says, "I'm afraid that if your grades continue dropping like this you run the risk of failing your senior year and not graduating with your class."

I can feel them both staring at me now, waiting for a reaction. But I just wrap my arms around my waist, making myself smaller, less visible. And even though I heard what she said, I just continue to stare at the ground. I refuse to react because there's no way that could be true. She's just totally trying to scare me, and I won't let her.

I hear Mrs. Gross take a deep breath and say, "I'm not sure how to say this, and I don't want to overstep here, but Alex's behavior patterns, with the dropping grades, and the lack of interest in school activities, well, these are all indicators of chemical abuse."

"But, I've never done drugs!" I shout, forgetting my vow to just wait it out calmly and quietly. I'm out of my chair and I'm facing Mrs. Gross and I just can't stop myself as I say, "Look, maybe I lack involvement or whatever. Maybe I've let things slide. But I don't do drugs, and I never have! I can't believe you just said that to me!"

I'm standing in front of her, frantic and desperate, but she just sits there, regarding me calmly, and I realize that she doesn't believe me. That she's already made up her mind. How can I explain to this sensible-shoe-wearing, Sears-family-portrait-posing, textbook-loving, middle-aged woman that I don't do drugs because I can't lose control. Because my life is so unsound that if I lose control and end up in the back of an ambulance or a squad car there is no one around to bring me back to a safe place. My family is not financially or emotionally equipped to deal with a crisis like that. The only safe place I have is the one I built myself.

I sink back into my seat, cross my legs, and stare at a dirty spot on the floor in front of me. I start to gather my long brown hair into a nervous braid.

"Mrs. Gross," my mother begins, "I assure you that Alex doesn't have a drug problem." She says that with a real tone in her voice. The same tone my sister and I used to get in trouble for (as in "don't take that tone of voice with me, young lady!"). "Now as far as her grades are concerned, I'll keep a closer eye on that and see that she does better." Then she nods her head and looks at her watch, and taps her foot impatiently against the worn tile floor.

Mrs. Gross looks from my mom to me, then leans back in her chair and drops her shoulders in a way that means defeat. And I wish I didn't see that because it makes me feel even worse.

"Okay, Alex," she says. "I want to see some immediate improvement. And let me remind you, once again, that this is a very crucial time where college is concerned. You have to have a plan for where you want to go."

The only place I want to go is *away*. And so I nod my head, so she'll think that I'm already taking action against my sorry self, and follow my mom outside.

The day seems brighter than I remember but maybe it's because everything in that office seemed so dark. I walk behind my mom, struggling in my platform shoes to keep up with her clicking heels and rapid pace, and I'm hoping that she'll stop, and turn, and say something to me, something positive to show that we're still okay.

But when we're halfway to the parking lot the bell rings, and without turning around she shouts over her shoulder, "Alex, go to your next class. You can't afford to be late. We'll talk later."

So I stop and watch her cut through the tide of students until I can no longer see her.

Chapter 2

On my way to AP English I realize that today is the absolutely last day to hand in the *Anna Karenina* critical essay that was assigned exactly eighteen days ago. And suffice it to say that even though Anna, Vronsky, and the oncoming train all made for a pretty good read, I didn't feel like writing about it. So I didn't. I guess that's just the sort of thing that landed me in my counselor's office.

And even though Mrs. Gross says I blew my chances at a scholarship, I know there's just no way this school can flunk me. I mean, so what if I've picked up a bad habit of cutting certain classes. They've got an entire folder full of all the good stuff I've done, and they just can't go failing people for a few C's, some random D's, and a perceived lack of involvement.

I'm gonna go to my English class, make up some excuse for not having my *Anna K* paper, then just sit there and get through it. Just like I did in Mrs. Gross's office (except for that one unfortunate outburst). Then tonight I'll go home and write that stupid paper. And when I'm done with that I'll call my dad and ask him to pay for college. After all, he paid my sister's tuition, and it's the least he can do for me since he never pays child support.

I'm three steps from the door when M runs up next to me and says, "Cool outfit, Alex."

I'm wearing faded, old 501 Levi's that I've decorated with paint and rhinestones and they look just like the ones they sell in trendy boutiques for two hundred dollars. I've paired them with these three-inch platform sandals I can barely walk in, a white, little-boys' tank top, and a vintage, pink cashmere cardigan with a capital *A* embroidered on it. M and I are totally into clothes. It's a hobby we both take very seriously.

"Did you write your paper?" She's peering at me intently but I don't answer. I don't even look at her. I won't incriminate myself. "Oh my god, you didn't!" She grabs my arm. "Jeez, Alex! What are you gonna do?"

Sometimes I cannot believe that M is my very best friend. I mean, a little support would be nice. I smile at her brightly, and push into class in front of her, but all the while I can feel her eyes watching the back of my head, judging me.

As I walk into class, I avoid eye contact, and sit at my strategically chosen desk. M and I don't sit next to each other. She likes to sit front-row center so she can raise her hand a lot and give correct answers. I prefer to be somewhere in the nether regions of the room, but not too far back. It's not like I want to broadcast my intent to go unnoticed.

Everyone around me is nervously shuffling papers and making last-minute requests for the stapler. And when I look around I realize that none of them will ever be made to suffer the humiliation of a parent/counselor conference because they're the kind of people who do all of their homework, and get good grades, and care deeply about Tolstoy's use of symbolism.

I sit in my wobbly chair, hunch over my desk, and stare at the graffiti etched on it. Someone has carved "YOU SUCK" and I'm wondering if I should take it personally. I don't mean to sound paranoid, but I don't remember it being there yesterday.

I rub my index finger over it again and again, as though that will somehow erase it and make it less true, and when I look up, Christine "the Collector" is standing right next to my desk. So I just watch her stand there, arms heavy with papers, acting like this little extracurricular activity of hers is gonna go on her résumé or something. She taps her creepy, pale pink, acrylic nail against the stack of papers and says, "We're one paper short." She just stands there waiting. "Yup, we're one paper short." She doesn't even blink.

I glance at the headband she's been wearing since she was the hall monitor in fourth grade, and then I look right into her beady, preppy, little eyes, but she's impossible to intimidate, and the only way to get her to leave is to give her something to collect. So I reach into my fake Prada backpack that my sister bought for me in New York and retrieve the short story I worked on all night. It's about a girl who goes to Paris and meets up with an older, English businessman. It's titled "Holly Would." When I hand it over she snatches it, scrutinizes my hand-scrawled mess, and smirks. I'm telling you, she's a total bitch.

I sit there frozen, just waiting for Mr. Sommers to sort through the papers looking for mine, but instead he leaves them in a haphazard pile on the upper-right-hand corner of his desk, puts on a Mozart CD, and begins a discussion about existentialism. M eagerly raises her hand and I relax and sit up a little bit straighter, knowing I'm off the hook today. But tonight he will go home, put on his slippers and start grading papers. By tomorrow he'll know.

"What was that I saw you hand in?" M gives me a suspicious look. "Don't tell me you actually turned in one of your Richard Branson fantasy stories instead of the Tolstoy paper!"

"Okay, I won't tell you." We're walking toward the student parking lot.

"How long do you think you can get away with this?" She looks at me, her face full of concern, mouth twisted with disapproval.

I lean against her car, give her a bored look and say, "At least until tomorrow."

"You're out of control." She shakes her head and opens the car door. "You working tonight?"

I think about how I promised myself I would go home and write my paper and call my dad, and start planning for my future, but for some reason I just shake my head and smile for the first time in two hours.

"Good, let's go into the city."

We get in the little, red BMW Z3 convertible that her parents gave her on her sixteenth birthday. Tan leather interior, marbled wood dash, shiny spoke wheels: I covet this car, but I don't resent her for it. We put the top down, crank the stereo, and put on our faux Gucci sunglasses (okay, M's are real), and head for LA.

Chapter 3

M and I have been friends since I moved to Orange County two weeks before my eighth birthday, and I have to tell you that even at that young age I suffered from culture shock. I had come from a nice, middle-class neighborhood where all the kids played together during the summer and anyone's mom would give you change for the ice-cream truck. Our new neighborhood was totally different. It was all about big houses, big yards, and big gates. There were no block parties, no neighborhood games of kick the can, and definitely no one hawking Popsicles from a musical truck.

On the first day of school I stood in front of the class, nervously chewing on a strand of hair, as my teacher introduced me as the new kid. Everyone just sort of looked me over and ignored me. But M gave me a big smile and invited me to sit with her during lunch, and from that moment on we've been best friends.

I know that on the surface we seem really different. I mean, M's family is rich, mine used to be. M is popular, I'm totally B list. M is a perfect, California blonde, in that, long-haired, blue-eyed, lightly tanned, Kate Bosworth kind of way. I'm dark haired, dark eyed, and kind of quirky, in an Alyssa Milano way. M writes all of her essays, I read the books but rarely complete the assignments.

M just has this amazing ability to totally compartmentalize her life. I mean, on the weekends she can be pretty wild, but during the week it's all about homework and student body activities. I'm not as wild as people think, but I just can't seem to care about school.

But we definitely have things in common too, like we're both totally into clothes, we like the same music, and we're both "gifted." I mean, we scored the exact same numbers on our IQ tests. We just have all this history together and it's a pretty great feeling when someone knows you that well and they still want to hang out with you.

So we end up at our favorite sandwich shack in Venice Beach. There's this really cute guy who works there that I used to have a mad crush on. But he's not into me, because he has a mad crush on M. But she's not into him because she would never date a guy that works in a food stand. She just totally plays him for the free-bies. I mean, it's not like she can't afford to buy her own veggie rolls, she just really loves the game.

So she walks up, leans on the counter and goes, "Hey."

That's all she says and he's grinning like a lottery winner. "What's up?" he asks, all excited. His eyes flicker to me briefly then rest on M.

"Well, I'm kind of in the mood for a beer." She lowers her sunglasses and leans on the counter. I think I saw her flutter her eyelashes.

He looks around nervously and says, "Okay, but you've gotta show me some ID or my boss will kill me."

"But you know me, I'm here all the time," she gives him her best smile, the one she saves for school portraits and cheerleading tryouts.

The poor guy just shrugs and I admire him for maintaining some integrity in her presence.

"Oh, all right," she says, making a big show of flipping through the stacks of pictures and little pieces of paper in her wallet. "Damn!" she shakes her head. "You know what? I lent it to Ashley Olsen and that bitch never returned it."

He totally cracks up and puts two veggie rolls and two bottles of water in a bag and hands it to M, free of charge. I mean, the truth is we do have fake IDs, and pretty good ones too, but who wants a beer at three-thirty in the afternoon?

As we're walking away I turn around and I see him looking at her with the most wistful expression. And it makes me really sad. So I promise myself that next time I won't look back.

We find a spot on the sand where we can sit and eat and watch all the stoners and freaky people. That's why we come here. I mean, the shops along the boardwalk are kind of cheesy and the beach itself isn't so great, but the humanity parade is always entertaining.

The boardwalk's pretty crowded today with people strolling, blading, mostly just trying to stay vertical. M takes a sip of her water and goes, "Hey, check out that old guy with the lizard."

I follow the direction of her finger and see some guy walking around in a tie-dyed Grateful Dead T-shirt with this huge iguana perched on his shoulder. He's so weather beaten it's hard to tell how old he is. "You mean the whacked-out dead head? I think I saw him here last week." I squint into the sun.

"Yeah, him. Hey, Jerry's dead!" she yells at him; that really cracks her up. "Man, I love LA," she sighs. "You just don't get this kind of scene back in Orange County."

I nod in agreement. We come from a pretty sterile suburban neighborhood, nothing but minivans and jog-bra moms, a library named after a disgraced ex president, three hundred churches, and not one decent place to get a drink. Our trips to LA have become legend at school. Everyone always wants to come with us but we're very select about who we invite; we usually just hang with each other. My mom probably wouldn't like it if she knew I was coming up here all the time, so I usually tell her that I'm going to the mall or something. I mean, it's not like it's a total lie because we usually do go in shops when we're here.

I watch the iguana man weave down the boardwalk wondering where he's going. He looks so alone that I hope he didn't hear M making fun of him. Then I tear my sandwich into little strips and throw them to a depraved-looking seagull. He spits out the veggies but swallows the bread, another carbo addict. I close my eyes and lie back on the sand; it feels warm and grainy against my skin.

I'm on the French Riviera. I emerge from my lavish cabana wearing a tiny black-sequined, string bikini and a very large-brimmed straw hat. This is a fantasy, so of course I give myself amazing cleavage and a rock-hard ass. Next to my lounge chair waits a turquoise drink with lots of plastic monkeys, paper umbrellas, and a big wedge of watermelon hanging on to the rim. I lie on my belly and take a sip. Suddenly, I feel a warm hand creeping along my spine; I lift my Versace glasses and turn—it's Richard Branson . . .

"So what do you say Alex?" M asks, interrupting my daydream.

"What?"

"You wanna go shopping on Melrose?"

I sit up and shake the sand out of my hair. "Yeah, let's go."

Chapter 4

I f you've never been to LA then let me tell you that it's not a big city like you probably think. It's more like a bunch of suburbs connected by freeways and boulevards. Different areas mean different things, like, Beverly Hills is rich but not as obnoxious as the TV show, and Melrose is way cooler than Heather Locklear.

M squeezes into the world's smallest parking space and we get out of the car and start walking down the street. Hanging out here is the best; sometimes we see famous people. But we don't get crazy about it, we act bored like we're used to it. Just two weeks ago we saw Steven Tyler, you know, that old guy that sings for Aerosmith? Liv Tyler's dad? I mean, you can't miss him, he's all big hair and tattoos, major flamboyance. But when we walked past him we just said "Hey" and kept walking.

"Oh, I love this store!" M says as she walks into some upscale boutique.

I take a deep breath and follow behind wondering if she's gonna have one of her scenes. Every now and then when we go shopping together she'll glide through the store touching all the merchandise and making comments about how she could buy anything she wants, because Daddy's platinum card knows no limits. I guess sometimes she likes to remind me of the economic gulf that divides our families, but I try not to let it get to me. Just because M's parents are like some sort of endangered species still on their first marriage doesn't mean they're happy. I know way too much about her family to be upset by stuff like that.

So I go off on my own and I just sort of meander through the store. There is some seriously cool stuff in here but nothing I can afford. It's weird, because when I'm with M the salespeople are all over us, but just wandering on my own they totally ignore me.

I spot these really cool jeans, they look old and faded and used, and it's amazing how much it costs to buy jeans that some-one else has trashed. I take them over to the mirror and hold them against my own, and I run my hand through my hair even though it looks okay. I have pretty decent hair, I mean it's long and dark and wavy, kind of like Alanis Morissette's before she cut it, but my nose is perpetually shiny. I discreetly rub the back of my hand over my nose and adjust the position of the pants.

"Brilliant!"

I look up and there's this really cute guy smiling at me. He's got that kind of messy, brown, Hugh Grant hair, cool clothes, and he's carrying a big shopping bag with the name of this store on it. And I think I heard an accent.

"You like them?" I ask.

"You should get them," he says, nodding.

"So I guess you're not from here," I say, "Are you British?" I clutch the jeans tightly against me. He's so cute it's making me nervous.

"English," he says.

"Do you know Richard Branson?" I blurt out before I can stop myself. God, why did I do that?

"I met him at a party once. Why? Do you know Richard Branson?" He looks at me and smiles.

"Me? No. But I'd like to." I can feel the heat rising to my face. "What's he like? Is he nice?" I ask, noticing how his blue eyes crease up a little bit in the corners when he smiles and wondering how old he is. Definitely not as old as Richard Branson, probably more like twenty.

"Wait a minute." He laughs. "I don't even know your name and I'm already competing with another guy?"

"Oh, I'm Alexandra, but I go by Alex." I smile nervously.

"Alexandra the Great," says M as she walks over eyeing the Brit with interest.

"And your name is?"

"M. Just M."

"Well, I'm Connor, Connor Firth."

He said "Firth" in a way that sounds like "First" and I'm wondering if I'm supposed to know him or something since he gave his first and last name, like maybe he's famous. But it's not familiar so I assume that's just how people in England introduce themselves. You know, like all proper and everything.

We shake hands all around, mine are always so sweaty, but he doesn't seem to notice. "Well, what are you guys doing?" he asks.

M holds up a stack of clothes she's been carrying and goes, "Uh, shopping?"

It sounds kind of rude and I cringe when she says it, but Connor just laughs and goes, "Well, there's an opening at a gallery down the street. I'm headed there now. Would you care to join me?"

I watch M drop the stack of clothes on the nearest rack and go, "Okay." And the way she just said that and the way she's looking at him, gives me this awful feeling that she's really gonna go for him and then I won't stand a chance. I mean, M is beautiful and rich and funny and smart. She's a hard act to follow. And even though I found him first, it definitely won't matter to her. She's used to getting what she wants.

Chapter 5

So we're walking down the street toward this gallery, with Connor in the middle and M and I on either side, and M is walking all lopsided, like she keeps losing her balance and has to bump into him or grab on to him, but I can totally tell she's doing it on purpose. And it makes me wonder if she really does like him, or if she figured out that I might really like him, and so then she decided to like him just because of that.

When we get to the gallery it's filled with all these trendy people sipping apple martinis and checking out all the other trendy people. The Moby CD they're playing is practically shaking the art off the walls and as I look around I'm pretty sure M and I are the youngest ones here. I mean, everyone else looks like they're pretty sophisticated, you know, like they're in their late twenties or something.

M really gets into this scene. She doesn't know anything about art but then again neither does anyone else. As long as you hold a cocktail, keep circulating, and make really vague comments, no one can tell.

So she's standing really close to Connor now, like she's his date and I'm just some dorky tag-along, and then she squeezes his arm (again) and goes, "Connor, do you think you could get us some wine or something?"

He looks at both of us and says, "Sure, any preference?"

And M (still touching his arm!), smiles and says, "Oh, chardonnay please."

Connor looks at me and goes, "Alex?"

And I go, "Um, red?" like it's a question not an answer. What a retard.

We watch him walk away and then M looks right at me and goes, "Wow, what a hottie. Way to go, Alex."

"What?" I squint at her. I mean, is she kidding? She's been acting like Columbus crawling all over a newly discovered continent and now she's giving me the finder's credit? "Are you kidding?" I ask her.

"What?" she says, and looks at me innocently.

But I just shake my head and don't say anything because I'm not sure what's going on anymore, or what I'm even doing here in the first place. I should be home writing a paper, not hanging in LA, in a scene that I clearly have no part in.

When Connor comes back he's juggling these three glasses of wine and M grabs the white one and goes, "Don't wait up!" then disappears into the crowd, just like that.

I look at Connor and shrug and I hope that he's going to be a little better at the small talk than I am.

We're wandering around the gallery, looking at these big huge oil paintings of what appear to be floating body parts on a sky blue background. And I'm wondering if he understands it any better than I do. Then he turns and looks at me and asks, "What do you make of all this?"

And I go, "Well, um, I think it's really LA."

"What do you mean?" He looks at me intently.

"Well, you know, it's about body parts, and LA is about body parts, for the most part." Oh god, do I sound stupid or what? "I mean, I think it's lonely, really. Like there's an arm over there on that canvas and a knee over on that one and they are all alone because someone has deemed them too imperfect to join the other body parts." I can barely breath.

And then he looks at me, smiles and says, "Thanks for explaining that, I'm always a little confused by modern art."

And I feel totally relieved since I was just talking off the top of my head and I'm not really sure what any of it means either.

So we're just standing there looking at the paintings and I'm desperately trying to think of something to say to fill the growing silence, when I hear someone yell, "Connor! Hey!" And over walks this kind of short, kind of strange-looking guy. And I don't mean strange looking in a genetic way, I mean like he's dressing that way on purpose. You know like black-frame geek glasses, vintage metal band T-shirt, jeans dyed to look dirty, silver Puma tennis shoes, and a black, nylon, man-purse slung over his right shoulder that he probably thinks is a "messenger bag," but it's not. Oh yeah, and his curly, dark brown hair is all brushed and frizzed like Jack Osbourne's.

So Connor goes, "James, hey!" And they both shake hands and then James smiles at me expectantly and I have this momentary fear that Connor might have forgotten my name. Because you know how easy it is to do that when you've just met someone and you're all nervous and you've only heard the name once anyway, but then he goes, "Oh, Alex. James. James. Alex." And I'm totally relieved.

We say hello and I'm expecting to shake hands or something but James leans toward me with his eyes closed and his lips all puckered up. And right when I'm thinking there's no way I'm letting this guy kiss me he makes this loud smacking noise somewhere in the vicinity of my cheek, and I just stand there frozen, wondering if I'm supposed to reciprocate, in this pseudo-European greeting even though we're both American. But then he starts talking about business and stuff so I just try to look involved even though I have no idea what any of it means.

Finally James looks at me and smiles then says to Connor, "Well, I don't want to keep you from your date. Let's do Ivy next week."

And Connor says, "Definitely."

I watch James walk away and ask, "What is 'doing Ivy'?"

Connor shakes his head and laughs and says, "It's a restaurant."

Oh. I guess that's one of those places you're just supposed to know, and not knowing makes me feel like a total outsider and a big loser. "Is he a good friend of yours?" I ask, trying to save myself.

"Not really. I don't mean that he's a bad guy, he's just more of an acquaintance I guess. He owns this gallery. Actually I'm looking for another friend of mine, Trevor. He said he'd be here but I don't see him anywhere." Then he looks at me and smiles and says, "But that's okay, 'cause you're here and you happen to be way better looking than Trevor."

I just sort of stand there and I probably blush, but I don't say anything because when someone tells me I'm attractive I never really know what to say. Not that it happens all the time or anything.

So then Connor starts talking about some of the people who are here tonight. Stuff like, that guy over there works for Maverick records, or that girl with the pink hair is a makeup artist. And even though it's interesting I sort of stop paying attention to the actual words because he's looking at me in the sexiest way and it's making me feel really nervous again.

I start thinking about my virginity. I mean, it's not like I'm very religious, or moral, or even scared (well maybe a little scared). I guess I just never had an opportunity that I could take seriously. Last summer I had this boyfriend for like, a month. I met him on a weekend sail to Catalina with M and her parents. At first I thought he was exotic, you know, from somewhere else, but it turned out he lived in the town next to ours and was still in high school too. So we used to make out and stuff, and at first I was really into him, but it wasn't long before I noticed what a major knuckle dragger he was. You know, like a total caveman. M used to call him Thor. He was really jealous and used to get mad when other guys talked to me. So I had to let him go. I won't have any guy telling me who I can talk to. After that I just figured I would hold out until someone glamorous comes along. I just hope I don't get hit by a car or something first. It would be just my luck to die a virgin.

So I look at Connor and realize I have no idea what he's been saying. I swear my glass of red wine is still half full but my stomach is feeling all queasy and I'm getting kind of dizzy. There's just no way I'm gonna let myself vomit in front of him, so I thrust my glass into his free hand and tell him I've got to get some fresh air.

I push my way through a crowd of people and when I get outside I'm surprised at how cold the night is, but I take off my cardigan anyway and let the cool air just wrap around my shoulders. I look down at the ground and breathe deep and slow just like they taught in the yoga class I took that one time, and I try to convince my mind to convince my body to not puke. To not totally humiliate me in a public place, in front of a totally cute, sexy guy from England, who met Richard Branson at a party once.

When I start to feel better I lift my head and look at the night, and even though I search I cannot locate one star in this polluted LA sky. So I close my eyes and roll my neck and sort of sag against the glass brick wall. Suddenly Connor is there and he's kissing me. At least I think it's Connor. I mean, my eyes are closed so I can't be too sure. It's the most amazing kiss. I just let it linger as long as possible. After awhile I open my eyes and Connor's smiling at me. He brushes his fingers lightly across my cheek and asks me if I'm feeling better now and all I can do is nod, because I'm totally breathless. Then he grabs my hand, entwining his fingers around mine and walks me back into the gallery. That's it. No struggle, no date rape. Sometimes guys surprise me.

I look around the room for M and I see her in the corner talking to some guy in plaid pants. He's completely focused on her and I'm wondering what it is that she's saying. But I guess it doesn't really matter, because there's just something about M that keeps people standing there.

Connor squeezes my hand and says, "I've got to take off soon 'cause I've got an early meeting tomorrow, but I'd really like to see you again. Can I call you?"

So I say "Okay" and act really nonchalant as I'm writing my number down on the back of his card, but inside my chest my heart is hammering and my hand is a little shaky and I really hope he doesn't notice.

He kisses me on the cheek then walks out the door, but I don't turn around to look after him because I don't want to know if he's looking after me, or if he's already moved on to the next big thing. I mean, this night has been practically perfect and I don't want to wreck it by seeing something that might upset me.

On the drive home I ask M about the guy in the plaid pants that I saw her talking to. She just laughs and says that she can't remember his name but that he's British too.

"Do you think he knows Connor?" I ask. I like saying his name.

"I have no idea." She yawns and cranks her new Strokes CD and starts singing at the top of her lungs.

When she turns onto my street, I start to panic because I didn't do what I promised myself I would, and now it's too late to write twelve pages about Tolstoy's technique. And you can bet there will be hell to pay, if not tomorrow then someday soon, because if there's anything I got out of that meeting today, it's that they're watching me now, and I won't be getting away with much.

M drops me off at the bottom of my driveway and asks, "What are you gonna wear tomorrow?"

I open the car door and reach for my backpack that got wedged into the tiny space in the back. "I don't know," I say. "But definitely not denim, I did denim today."

She nods her head and pulls away with a loud screech and I can hear her car all the way to the end of the block.

As I walk up the slope of concrete that leads to my house, I look at the moon and try to determine if it's a man or a woman or something else all together. And I remember how when I was a little kid my mom used to hold my hand and point at the sky and show me how all the dents and craters and shadows could create the illusion of a changing face. I thought there was magic in the moon and we could stand there for hours. But that was back when I believed in things like that, and she believed in me.

I go into my room, throw my purse onto a furry leopard chair, and pick up my phone to check my messages, but I'm greeted with a steady hum so I know no one called. I guess I just couldn't help hoping that Connor had phoned to say how much he enjoyed meeting me, even though I know how totally improbable that is.

But there's a call I have to make, and I glance at the glowing numbers on the alarm clock next to my bed and wonder if 10:52 is too late. It might be, but I call anyway. While I listen to it ring I rehearse what I'm going to say. But on the fourth ring it goes straight into voice mail so I just go, "Hi Dad, it's me. Um, Alex. Can you give me a call? It's important. Thanks." And then I hang up feeling kind of relieved that I didn't actually have to ask him because he's my only hope now and I'm not really sure what he'll say.

I wash my face, brush my teeth, and put on this soft, pink, vintage slip that I like to sleep in. I climb into bed and the sheets feel cool and the blanket is warm, and I know that when I wake up I'm going to have to face Mr. Sommers about the paper I didn't write, but I don't want to think about that now. So I try to think about dining with Richard Branson at the restaurant at the top of the Eiffel Tower, but Connor's head keeps appearing on Branson's body.

Chapter 6

The next morning my mom peeks her head in my room to make sure that I'm up and thinking about getting ready for school. I assure her I'm wide-awake, then roll over for another ten minutes.

She's back. "Alex, I'm not kidding. I'm leaving for work now and you better get up or you'll be late for school."

"Is that the worst that will happen?" I ask her.

"Alex, now!"

"I'm up."

I wait until she leaves my room then I crawl out of bed and go into my bathroom and turn the shower on high and hot. I sit on the closed lid of the toilet seat and watch the room get all steamy. The dream I had last night is still lingering but it wasn't about Richard Branson or even Connor. It's that same old recurrent nightmare about when my horse died.

I was in the seventh grade and it was a terrible time. It was not long after my dad left, and next to M, my horse, Lucky, was like my best friend. One day when I went to feed her I found her in her stall just lying there. I got scared and called the vet. He gave her shots and vitamins, he did everything he could, but after three days he said he just couldn't help her and he'd have to put her to sleep.

I really hate that term, "put to sleep." Sleep is when you get to wake up. And it didn't help knowing that my dad had just bankrolled some gorgeous thoroughbred at some cushy stable for his latest girlfriend. I think my horse died of poverty, exposure, and depression, just another casualty of the divorce. I tried to love her enough to keep her alive, I really did. But she died anyway. I guess it's just as well since we could barely afford to feed her. Horses really eat a lot.

I climb into the shower and lather up. I'm big into grooming. In an average shower I use shampoo, conditioner (deep conditioner in the summer), lavender-scented shaving gel, facial cleanser, facial scrub, and body cleansing gel, followed by body scrub. While my skin is still damp I spray on body oil, which I let soak in for about sixty seconds, then I lightly pat my skin dry and apply body lotion, deodorant, astringent, lip balm, leave-in conditioner, and a tiny bit of some perfume sample. This month it's Gucci Rush because I like the name. I'm a total product whore.

With a towel turban around my head and a robe wrapped tightly around me, I stand in front of my closet looking for something to wear. I mean, I've spent the last three and a half years building a fashion reputation and now everyone expects me to show up in something cool and unusual and sometimes it's a real burden.

And I'm thinking maybe that was the wrong approach, drawing that kind of attention to myself. Maybe I should tone it down a little, you know, work a little harder at blending in. So I slip into the safety of some faded, denim overalls, a lacy camisole, an antique-beaded cardigan, and my split toe Nikes. I quickly brush on a little mascara to accentuate my brown eyes and grab two rubber bands and braid my wet hair during the red lights on my way to school.

I see M in French class. And I don't mean to be rude but she's got a pretty major zit on her chin, and I can't stop staring at it. You know how trying not to look at something just makes you obsessed with it? Well, that's what it's like with M's chin. At least she didn't try to cover it with makeup like some girls, 'cause that never really fools anyone. But it's still kind of funny to see M looking less than perfect.

She sees me staring so I go, "Rough night M?"

"Very funny," she rolls her eyes. "I thought you said absolutely no denim today."

"I almost wore my pajamas," I tell her.

"I know what you mean. I'm feeling a little sleep deprived, but it was totally worth it, don't you think?"

"Totally." I look around the room to see if anyone's listening. I have to admit we usually talk loud enough so everyone can hear, but then we get annoyed when we catch them.

M leans in and says, "That guy in the plaid pants called last night. He must have dialed right after we left 'cause there was a message from him when I got home."

"No way." I look at her in amazement. Even though I'm used to M always stealing the show, I can't help feeling a little jealous. "Did he leave his name?"

"No. He just started talking so I still don't know it. Oh, and I got accepted into Princeton! The letter came yesterday when we were in LA. The maid put it in my room."

I'm staring at M with my mouth wide open when Mademoiselle walks in. "Bonjour!" she says.

"Bonjour Mademoiselle!" I hear my classmates answer, but I can't concentrate now because all I can think about is how my life totally sucks compared to M's. She's got a new boyfriend, and she's going Ivy. I've got an empty voice mailbox, and I may not get out of high school. I mean, I'm happy for her, really I am, but there's a part of me that feels like vomiting.

I manage to slide through the rest of the day. Partly because we have a sub in Economics (I hate that class), so I don't even pretend like I'm paying attention, and partly because Mr. Sommers makes absolutely no mention of the paper I didn't write. It's like he still doesn't know or something, and I'm hoping that will buy me an extra day or two since that's all I really need because I'm totally gonna do it tonight, after work. I promise.

After school I go to work for four hours. I've been working in this department store for like a year and a half. I entered this contest where they picked one student from each local high school and the winners got to be in what is called Teen Board. It involved in-store modeling, fashion shows, charity events, and a job for anyone who was interested. I was really nervous at the interview and totally didn't expect to be chosen. I mean, all of the usual suspects showed up, you know, the cheerleaders and supermodel wannabes, everyone clutching their portfolios. I didn't have a portfolio, just the application and some majorly sweaty palms.

I was only there because I needed a job. Those child-support checks were getting few and far between, and quite frankly, I was sick of begging for them. Believe me, I never took the modeling part seriously. I'm not like all the other girls in my school carrying around composite shots and taking voice lessons. That's the funny thing about California, life somehow becomes one long audition. Anyway, for whatever reason, they picked me and I've been working here ever since. The modeling part was fun, I'll admit, but when it was over I didn't really miss it. This isn't the most exciting job, but it's decent. I mean I get to work with nice people and I get a good discount on clothes.

Well, a couple of months ago the managers here transferred me from the Junior Department over to Women's. They told me they thought I was very mature and could handle a more professional group. That really cracked me up. I mean, I never really think of myself as being mature. But I have to admit I like being over here. The women I work with are really nice. They worry about me and give me advice. I usually don't like it when people act like that with me, like I need help or something, but it is kind of nice when these ladies try to make it easier. The other difference about working over here is how these customers, who are like my mom's age, talk so freely about their cheating husbands and plastic surgeries. I just give them a sympathetic look, and vow to never grow old.

The store is dead on Friday nights. I guess most people have better things to do than shop. So after I refold all the cashmere sweaters and try on a few leather jackets, I pretty much spend the rest of the time making a list of the five things Richard Branson and I would be doing during a Virgin transatlantic flight. Canoodling is at the top. I don't really know what it means but they're always accusing Julia Roberts of it in *People* magazine so I figure it must be good.

My phone rings and it's my friend Blake calling from the Men's Suits Department where he works. Blake was on the Teen Board the year before me, he's the one that got me into this. He's also gay, but he's way open about it so he's definitely not going to mind my mentioning it.

"Alex, what are you doing?" he asks.

"Oh, just leaning on the cash register, staring into space, making lists. Hey, what does *canoodling* mean?"

"It's sexual."

"Yeah, but what exactly?"

"Cuddling?"

"Oh, is that all? Are you sure?" I ask.

"No, I let my subscription to *Teen People* expire. Hey, what are you doing later? Do you want to get a coffee or something?"

"Well, I told M I'd meet her at the baseball game tonight." I lean against the cash register and look in the mirror.

I can practically hear Blake rolling his eyes when he says, "You did not just say that. A baseball game?"

"Yeah, it's a night game, but it should be over by the time I get there. God willing. Wanna go?" I ask.

"Honey I am never going back to that place."

Blake graduated a year ago.

"And I can't believe you'd choose sports over me. C'mon, I'll even pay."

"Really?"

"Yes, really."

"Well in that case . . ."

At about ten minutes to nine I start closing out my register. I count the change as quietly as I can because the management here doesn't like it when you start early. Then I just stand there until exactly nine o'clock and then I bolt upstairs to deposit the money. I see Blake on my way up. We both look at each other and then we start tearing for it, I mean, really running. I'm gaining on him big time until my heel catches on something and I go soaring and crashing. But I'm not hurt. I just lay there laughing on the floor, right next to some home furnishings display. Blake feels bad for me so he comes over to see if I'm okay. I give him my hand so he'll help me up, and then right when we touch I pull him down and I jump up and beat him to the deposit spot.

He walks up behind me, rubbing his elbow, and saying, "I can't believe you'd cheat like that."

And I go, "Yeah, well, I really do have ambition, it's just usually about all the wrong things."

So we end up in this generic coffee place somewhere between work and home. It tries to be hip but it's really not that cool, and I'm not even going to mention the name because there's already one on every corner and they don't need me to advertise for them.

I order a decaf latte, and try not to feel bad about ditching M. But let's face it, I barely go to school during the day, why would I go at night?

"So what's new with Ronette?" I ask as we sit down. She's the manager of the Men's department. Her real name is Rhonda but we secretly call her Ronette, because she has totally retro hair, and, well, she's kind of a bitch.

"Honey, I can't wait to give her my two weeks notice," Blake shakes his head and takes a bite of his almond biscotto.

"When are you leaving for Parsons?" It's a question I've avoided asking.

"Soon. June."

"What?" I practically choke on my latte, that's only three months away.

"I want to spend the summer there. You know, find an apartment. Get settled in, check out the scene."

I sit there staring at him. "Um, not to be selfish or anything, but what am I going to do without you?"

"Come with me." His oversize coffee mug hides most of his face, but his eyes are right on mine.

"If only." I look down at my cup and put my head in my hands. I don't have the talent for design like Blake does. I don't have any talent. It feels like everything is creeping up and closing in. I wish I could just stop time until I was ready for it to happen.

"Have you been accepted anywhere yet?"

I don't answer.

"Are you okay?" he asks, concern in his voice.

"Yeah, yeah." I look up at Blake and give what I hope will come off as a confident smile.

"Alex, you're smart and talented. You can do anything you want," he says.

"Oh, please," I shake my head. "Nobody wants me. Well, that's not entirely true. There's one loser school that kind of wants me, but yesterday I found out that my grades suck so bad that I no longer qualify for a scholarship. And if they don't get better then I won't qualify for admission. And they're even trying to tell me that I might not get out of high school, but there's no way that's true. They're just trying to freak me out. Oh yeah, and I called my dad to ask for help but he won't call me back."

"Why won't he call you?"

I shrug. "I guess he's just really really busy."

"So, why don't you visit him at his office or something?"

"Because if he says no, then what will I do?"

"Why would he say no?"

"Because, for the seventeen and a half years that I've known him, he's said it an awful lot." I stop and take a sip of my coffee. "But he owes me this, he really does."

"Alex—"

I hold up my hand. "Could we please not talk about it?"

"All right." He gives me a concerned look and says, "I just want you to know that you have more options than you think."

Chapter 7

So instead of going home and writing my paper, I stop by M's to see if she's there because I feel kinda bad about not showing up at the baseball game. And as I park on the street and get out of my car, I wonder why the promises I make to other people always become more important than the ones I make to myself.

As I walk toward the front door I hope that her parents aren't home. I guess they're not that bad, but it's always better when they're not around. I mean, M's mom really doesn't do much except think about her weight, it's like she's a professional size two or something. And M's dad makes me call him "Doctor" because he is one. Still, what an ego. I mean, he's a plastic surgeon doctor, not a real doctor. He saves noses, not lives.

So M opens the door and says, "Hey what happened? You weren't at the game."

"I had coffee with Blake," I tell her as I walk inside and head for the living room 'cause that's where we always hang out. When I hear a voice I stop and look at M and whisper, "Are your parents here?"

M shakes her head, "No, it's just Tiffany."

"What? Why?" I stand in the hall. Tiffany is my least favorite of all of M's fellow cheerleaders.

"She had to pick up a sweater I borrowed at the game last week, and now she won't leave. She's wasted too, you've gotta see it," M says as she pushes me into the living room.

"Hey Alex!" Tiffany waves at me from the couch.

"Hey Tiff, what's up." I plop myself onto an overstuffed armchair and grab one of the beers sitting on the table.

"Well," she slurs, "I was just telling M that I'm totally considering breaking up with Dylan, even though I totally love him."

M shakes her head and rolls her eyes, and picks up the remote control for the stereo. And I'm left with no choice except to ask, "Why are you breaking up if you still love him?"

"Because I'm so sick of him flirting with other girls." She starts crying then and I look at M totally alarmed, but she has her eyes closed, singing along to some Alicia Keys CD.

"He was totally flirting with Amber tonight, you should have seen him. And I got so mad I just left without him. I even fell off the top of the pyramid, but he didn't care."

"Are you okay?" I ask her. For some reason I'm genuinely concerned.

"My arm kind of hurts, but the point is he didn't even notice! And I love him. I love him so much, and I don't understand why he always flirts with her. She's not that pretty!"

I just look at Tiffany and I want to tell her that life really isn't one long beauty contest. That everyone's just trying to find what makes them feel good, but I don't say anything. I just hand her a tissue, and wish she'd stop talking because she's really starting to depress me.

Then she clutches her stomach and says, "Oh, I don't feel so good." And I watch her run for the bathroom.

M opens her eyes and goes, "Dammit. She better make it in time, 'cause I'm not cleaning that up."

"How much did she drink?" I ask.

"Three of those empty bottles are hers. I've been putting up with this shit for like an hour now and I'm totally over it." M sits up and puts down the remote and looks at me. "Tiffany is such a loser. She's all upset over some retard jock. I swear, high school is so small time. I am so over it." She shakes her head and takes a sip of her beer.

I look up then to see Tiffany standing in the doorway and at first I'm afraid she might have heard us. But she just goes, "M will you take me home? I don't think I should drive."

Tiffany's clutching her stomach and she looks pretty bad, but when I look at M she looks really mad, so before she can say anything I go, "I'll take you home Tiffany. I was just getting ready to leave anyway."

I take one last sip of my beer and grab my purse and guide her out the front door to my old Karmann Ghia that used to belong to my sister. I put her in the passenger seat and buckle her in and she just sits there with her eyes closed. And even though throwing up didn't make her sober, I'm thankful that it made her quieter.

When we get to her house her eyes are still closed and I can't tell if she's passed out or dead of alcohol poisoning. So I tap her softly on the shoulder and say, "Tiffany, wake up. You're home."

And then she opens her eyes and bolts out of my car and runs straight for her mother's prized rose bushes where she vomits orange all over them for like the next five minutes.

I get out of my car and watch her and I'm torn between being totally grossed out, and hoping that her parents don't wake up, see this mess, and hold me responsible.

When she's finished I hand her another tissue and walk her to the door and assure her that she'll feel much better in the morning, which is a total lie because once the hangover sets in, it will be much worse.

As I'm driving home I look at all the sleeping houses, all locked up and tidy until morning. And from the outside everything looks so protected, so safe. But you just never know what kind of lives are being lived in those houses. I mean, you just never really know anyone. Like Tiffany, it was weird watching her break down like that. It's not that I thought she was without feelings, it's just that at school she always acts so perfect and together, like nothing bad ever happens to her. So it was really surprising to see her crying over some guy and heaving in the rose bushes.

And I remember how I used to be like Tiffany. How I used to care about the things that happened at school. How I used to be part of that ruling class of cool kids that spend most of their time making everyone else feel bad about not belonging. I used to take it seriously too. But then my parents started regressing, and messing up at all of the things they were supposed to be guiding me through, and it forced me into a whole new set of problems. I mean, once you start worrying about your mom's mortgage payment, you can't really worry about Sadie Hawkins with the same intensity that you used to.

So when I get home the first thing I do is go into my room and check my messages: nothing. No one called. Not even Connor. But it's only been a day. Usually guys wait longer than that, right? Well, unless you're M. When you're M, they're dialing your number before you even get home.

But my dad didn't call either so that means I'm gonna have to call him again. And I can't believe it's gotten to the point where I'm dependent on the one person I could never depend on.

I dial his number with a shaky hand, and when it goes into voice mail I leave the same stupid message as last night.

Then I put on an old T-shirt with a faded picture of Lisa Simpson, and instead of starting my paper, I lie on my bed and look at this month's *Vogue*. I fall asleep wishing I looked like Gisele Bundchen.

Chapter 8

Saturday afternoon I'm staring at the cover of *Anna Karenina* and a blank piece of paper when M calls. "Alex, did Tiffany barf again on the way home?"

"No, she was fine," I lie. For some reason I don't feel like telling her about the rose bushes.

"Well she missed the toilet, and the poor maid had to clean it up."

"So why didn't you do it if you felt so bad for her?" I put down the book and pick at a hole that's forming on the knee of my sweatpants.

"Yeah, right. Oh my god, I forgot to tell you. Tiffany totally fell off the top of the pyramid last night!" M is cracking up. "You should have seen it! She just went flying off the top and hit the ground!"

"Yeah. She mentioned it. But she seemed fine," I say.

"She seemed fine because she was so drunk she was feeling no pain."

"You mean she was drunk at the game?"

"Big time . . . Amber brought these little water bottles full of vodka for everyone, and they were all like totally guzzling in the parking lot before the game. But I gave mine to Tiffany because

I don't like vodka without juice, and she totally downed that too. Everyone was fine except her. She can't handle drinking. What do you bet she shows up Monday morning in a neck brace or something? I swear she did it on purpose."

"That's ridiculous."

"Not really. I think she was trying to get Dylan's attention, but he didn't even notice."

"Why are you guys doing pyramids at a baseball game anyway?" I ask. Everything cheerleaders do is a mystery to me.

"Because school's almost over, it's our last chance. So anyway, listen, there's a major party tonight in LA and we're invited."

"Really?"

"Yeah, that guy that I met at the gallery, the one in the plaid pants? It's at his house."

"Did you remember his name yet?"

"As far as I'm concerned it's Plaid Pants because I still don't know it."

"You're kidding?"

"No, really. When he called he just said, 'Hey,' and I went, 'Hey,' and I totally missed my chance to say 'Who is this?'"

"Well, how did you know it was him?"

"The accent, he's British. Anyway he's having some big bash and he told me to bring a friend if I want. Are you in?"

"I guess," I walk across my room, peer into the mirror, and hold up the back of my hair, wondering if I should cut it.

"What do you mean? You've got something better to do?"

"Well, I really should write that stupid paper for English," I say.

"Do it tomorrow. C'mon Alex, it's gonna be great."

"Well," I twist my hair back really tight and try to imagine what I'd look like with a pixie cut, "I was kinda hoping that Connor would have called by now."

"He hasn't called yet?"

"No."

"Well forget him. There's gonna be tons of hotties at this party tonight, we'll find you a new one. Are you in?"

"Yeah, I'm in." I drop my hair and watch it fall, stopping just short of my waist.

"Good. Apparently it started at noon, but I'll pick you up at seven, we don't want to look too eager."

When I hang up I'm in a total panic about what I'm gonna wear. M will just grab daddy's plastic on her way to the mall, but I don't have that luxury, so I have to come up with something hip with what I've already got. I'm usually pretty good at this, you know necessity being the mother of invention and all. But today I'm a little short on inspiration. I put on a Hole CD and listen to Courtney scream about wanting the most cake. Yeah, me too. I crank up the volume and head down the hallway to my sister's old room.

Every time I look in her closet I'm amazed at all the clothes and shoes she left behind. I mean, it looks like she was in such a hurry to bail out of here that she didn't bother to pack. I come across a slinky old prom dress of hers that still carries the faint scent of Obsession perfume, and run my fingers over the silky fabric remembering how she always used to spray that on her clothes so my parents wouldn't know she'd been smoking.

I pull off the sweatpants and tank top I've been wearing all day and slip the dress over my head. I'm the same size now that she was then so it fits perfectly. I stand in front of the mirror and gaze at my reflection. I like the shiny cream color and the deep V-neck and spaghetti straps. The only problem is the length, which is nearly to the floor, and since it's not my prom night, that just won't do.

I gather the fabric around my waist, then I go back into my room where I put on these really cool, strappy, high-heeled sandals that I bought at a thrift shop last year and glued tiny silk flowers all over. I know it sounds kind of overdone, but trust me, it works. On top of my dresser is a little tiara barrette I bought in the children's department at the store where I work. I pull the top part of my hair back, like J Lo does, and secure it. It might be a little too fairy princess, but I like it. So then I take everything off and lay it on my bed and get to work on hemming the dress.

I like to sew. I learned how in my fourth grade Girl Scout troop. It's probably the most useful skill they taught me besides making s'mores. I mean, since I love clothes and I don't have much money, I mostly go to thrift stores, buy stuff cheap, then bring it home and tweak it. That way I never look exactly like everyone else because mine is one of a kind. I also find it calming. I like the hum of the machine when I do a really long seam.

I start thinking about Connor even though I promised myself I wouldn't. I just can't figure out why he hasn't called yet. It seemed like we were having such a great time together. But since I didn't get his number it's not like I can call him. Not that I would anyway.

My mom talks about the giant steps that women have taken since she was my age, but I just don't see it. I mean, maybe we can vote and stuff but there's still these really burdensome social rules that just won't change, like sex. It may seem like everybody in your school is doing it, and most of them probably are, but let's face it, girls that experiment get labeled as sluts, while the guys get the stud trophy. And that's why there will be no sweaty high school stuff for me. No getting biblical in the backseat with some icky senior. And as far as calling guys first, I won't do it. I truly believe they still want to go out and hunt and conquer and drag you home by your ponytail. We may live in the suburbs, but we act like a bunch of cave dwellers.

When I'm finished hemming the dress I press the new seam with a warm iron and put it back on. It looks pretty good. I have about twenty minutes left so I apply a little makeup (with an outfit like this you don't want to go overboard), flip my hair a few times, put on some glittery nail polish, and then dance around with my arms in the air until it dries.

When I hear M's car pulling into my driveway I jot off a quick note to my mom telling her that I'm spending the night at M's.

I feel bad about lying, but I don't want her to worry. The truth is, these LA parties usually go on until the next morning.

M sees me and says, "Cool dress!"

I pirouette on my driveway then climb into her car. I turn down the vintage David Bowie CD she's got blasting and say, "Okay, details."

She looks at me and smiles. "This could be it, the most important party so far. The one we've been working toward."

"What?" I have no idea what she's talking about.

"Okay, get this. Plaid Pants is a film student at USC and his parents are like producers or directors or something in the industry, but apparently they are very conveniently tucked away on vacation or location or whatever in Europe. They've got this fully loaded house. You know like pools, a guest house, screening room, the works."

"Who's gonna be there?" I ask, wondering if Connor could possibly show up, but I don't ask it out loud because I don't want to jinx it.

"Probably like tons of rich, young Hollywood types, because of his parents and film school and all. We might even get to see a celebrity or something."

"You mean like Richard Branson?" I ask.

"No. Probably more like that girl who plays Sabrina the Teenage Bitch."

I look at her to see if she's kidding but she's totally serious and I suddenly start to feel really intimidated and sick to my stomach. It's not about some minor TV star, it's just that all that wealth sometimes makes me feel totally inadequate. I remember reading somewhere that no one can make you feel intimidated without your permission. Well, Plaid Pants has got my full consent. I mean, I'm just not so sure I can blend with this crowd. People with that much money always make me feel like an outsider.

M looks at me, and knows what I'm thinking. "Relax," she says, "it's gonna be fun."

And I look at her and wonder again, as I often do, just where her endless supply of confidence comes from. Is it the birthright of the wealthy, of having the security of two parents and a team of lawyers who will always be there to clean up your mess?

Chapter 9

When we finally get to the house, M drives right past all the cars lining the street, swerves around the Mercedes spooning the Porsche in the driveway, and goes right onto the front lawn where she hits the brake and kills the ignition. She double-checks her lip gloss in the rearview mirror, then smiles and says, "We're here!"

There's a rose bush banging against my window and I think there's another one under the car, but this is classic M, she always makes it easy for herself, and she always gets away with it. I look at her and say, "Jeez, why didn't you just drive into the living room and park next to the sofa?"

She pulls the key from the ignition and shrugs. "I'm not about to walk all the way down the block in these boots."

She holds her foot up for inspection and I can't say I blame her. She's wearing her wicked witch boots, the sleek, knee-high, black, pointy-toed ones, with heels so high it must be like walking on stilts.

We walk the three steps to the front door and when we open it we are confronted with a wall of bodies. I mean, there's like, hundreds of people here, and we just stand in the entryway trying to get a handle on the scene, but I don't see any celebrities, just a lot of people who want to be celebrities. There's a group of tall, blond, tan girls wearing bikinis and Ugg boots, they look like quintuplets, and another group wearing low-cut jeans and newsboy caps, total Britney clones.

There's even some guy walking around in a silk robe, but it's not Hugh Hefner. And even though I can kind of make fun of them in my head, the truth is, that everyone here looks like they belong, and I start to feel kind of stupid in my old dress and tiara. I mean, I might have looked okay in Orange County, but here, around all these hip, rich people, I feel like a dork.

I reach up and touch my stupid rhinestone barrette and contemplate yanking it out when, M looks at me and goes, "Don't. Leave it. You look great."

And I stop, and I leave it, because she's right. I have to be comfortable just being me.

"Come on," she says, "let's grab a drink and find the screening room."

We grab some champagne from a passing waiter then follow the scent of popcorn down a long hallway. We enter a dark room with a big screen and plop into some vacant seats. They have the same seats as the good movie theaters, you know, the plushy kind that rocks back and forth, with cup holders. I place my drink in the little hole and lean all the way back and look at the high, vaulted ceilings. It must be so cool to have a room like this. I mean, at my house it's just an old TV with a broken remote and no cable. It's amazing how other people get to live.

There's like, six guys and one girl in here, and they're all watching some really violent movie. M gets up to get popcorn but I'm ready to leave. I hate gratuitous violence. I mean, isn't there enough of the real thing out there? Like in Afghanistan, and Africa, and that school in Colorado, and the house next door?

I follow her and go, "M, are you gonna watch this?"

She whispers, "Yeah, at least until I finish this popcorn, why?"

"Well, I think I'm gonna leave and walk around some more."

"Okay," she says between bites. "Listen, if we lose each other, meet me by the front door at midnight."

I squint my eyes to adjust to the light of the hallway and wander down it, unsure of my destination. I figure I'll just walk around until something interesting happens. At a party like this, it shouldn't take long.

I'm just walking along, looking at the art on the walls, when all of a sudden a door right in front of me opens and I'm face to face with Connor. My heart skips, my stomach drops, and I stop dead in my tracks. I just stand there staring at him like a major dweeb when he looks up and goes, "Alex!"

"Oh. Connor. Hi." I'm trying to pretend that I didn't see him first, but it's not very convincing.

"It's brilliant to find you here." He's hugging me now and he smells so good, and even though I dreamed of this every night since we met, now that it's happening I can't remember any of my lines.

So I'm just standing there staring at him, trying to think of something to say when this really pretty girl who looks just like Ray of Light Madonna comes out of the same room he just vacated and goes, "Connor, there you are!"

When I watch her slither up next to him and put her hand possessively on his shoulder, I start to feel sick and nervous and I don't know what to do, so I just continue to stand there like a big retard and then I smile at her. Only she doesn't smile back.

Then Connor goes, "Sam this is Alex. Alex, Sam." And since nobody got a title like, My Girlfriend Sam, or, The-Best-Thing-That-Ever-Happened-to-Me Alex, it's hard to tell how either of us rates.

I just stand there and say, "Hi." Giving another go at a smile.

But she just presses her lips together in a failed attempt at a pleasant expression and says, "So how do you know Trevor?"

"Um, who's Trevor?" I ask, looking from Sam to Connor and wondering if I should have just faked like I knew him.

"Uh, your host?" she says, and rolls her eyes, and shakes her head, and looks at Connor like, "Who is this loser girl you found in the hall?"

But Connor just smiles and says, "He's the guy I was looking for at the gallery the other night. I think M met him there."

"Oh, I didn't realize that was his name," I say. But I don't mention that up until now we've been calling him Plaid Pants.

"You know I was wondering if you'd be here."

"Really?" I'm trying to not sound too excited by that.

"Yeah." He smiles and his eyes travel over me, coming to rest on my chest. "Where's M?"

"Watching something violent in the screening room," I tell him. Then I look over at Sam but she's busy inspecting her wavy, long blond hair, looking for split ends or something, and not at all trying to hide the fact that she's bored, and mad, and everything else.

"Uh, Connor, excuse me," she says tugging on his sleeve, "Are you coming back in, or what?"

I just stand there and look from her to him but he just shakes his head, and goes, "No, I'm taking Alex on a field trip. I'll catch up with you later." Then he looks down at me and smiles and I feel like I've been thrown into the deep end of the pool.

Connor puts his arm around my shoulders and walks me down the hall, and I look up at him and say, "I have to warn you, M has given me a twelve o'clock curfew."

"Great. That leaves us with . . ." He stops and looks at his wrist but he's not wearing a watch, "Well, lots of time, I hope."

Then he leads me through some French doors out to this beautiful garden. It's one of those wild, untamed, English-style gardens that make you feel like you're in *Wuthering Heights* or something. He points out all the different varieties of flowers, then stops to pick a really beautiful pink peony. When he hands it to me I wonder how he knew that's my favorite.

We walk by the pool but there's some people splashing around in it, so instead we go inside this really cool cabana. The walls are a dark, smudgy, salmon color and it's stuffed with pillows and hammocks and mosquito nets and lanterns and loads of colorful mosaic tiles, and it looks just like a movie set version of Morocco. I sit on this woven mat and lean back against these giant, over-stuffed pillows, and watch Connor light a few candles and look through the fridge for something to drink.

"Is this a guest house?" I ask, rubbing my fingers over a se-quined pillow.

"No, it's just a cabana, the guest house is farther down," he says.

I watch him walk toward me carrying a bottle of champagne and place it on a low tiled table. The way he just answered me so casually makes me wonder if he grew up like this too. I mean, it's hard to be that blasé about homes like this unless you're used to it.

"You don't think they'll mind?" I ask, eyeing the bottle of champagne with the label I can't pronounce even after four years of high school French.

"Mind what?"

"If we drink their champagne?"

"Not only will they not mind, they won't even notice."

I watch Connor expertly pop the cork, refill my glass, and grab a pillow and lie next to me with his head propped on his el-bow. He's looking at me intently and the fact that he's a total babe, along with the fact that we're completely alone is making me in-credibly nervous. Also, the silence is growing thicker and it's mak-ing me feel like I've got to say something interesting right exactly now but I can't think of anything. Then I remember this article I read in *Cosmopolitan* that said you should just let them go on and on about themselves. Not that I'm used to following that kind of advice, but right now, when I'm feeling this shy and nervous, it does come in handy. So I go, "How do you know Trevor?"

"I've known him since we were kids. We were schoolmates in London, until his parent's packed it up and moved out here.

"When was that?" I ask.

"I don't know, fifteen? Sixteen?"

He looks at me and smiles and I nod my head and take a sip

of champagne as I desperately grasp for something to say next. "So, tell me about your record company? How'd you get started?" I ask. Oh god, I sound like Oprah.

"Well, it started with piano lessons."

"You're kidding," I say.

"No really, didn't you take piano lessons?"

I shake my head. "No, that's kind of like a rich person's sport. I did stuff that was free, you know, community soccer, Girl Scouts, stuff like that."

"You're lucky," he laughs. "It was torture, mainly for my teacher. Finally Mr. Leonard, that was my piano teacher, finally he told my parents that he just couldn't take their money anymore."

"Were they disappointed?" I kind of slide down on the mat so that we're level. It felt weird to be looking down at him.

"Probably, both of them are natural pianists. I guess it skipped a generation. But, the lessons did spark my love of music and they ultimately financed my vinyl buying habits."

"You mean albums?" I take a sip of my champagne.

"Yeah. There's some great stuff out there that can only be truly appreciated on vinyl. Anyway, when I finished college, they really pushed me to go on to law school. But I had already started this small label with a friend, so we made a deal. I told them that if the company didn't start going somewhere within a year, I'd go back to school. But if it did start to grow, well, they had to wish me well."

"So where are you in all that now?"

"Two years, growing, and I don't have to go back to school. What about you, what do you do?"

I just sit there. I'm not quite prepared for this question.

"Alex?"

"What do I do?" This question is like, one for grownups or something and I'm not sure how to answer it. "Well, I'm a student." I smile brightly and sip my champagne but my glass is empty so I end up swallowing air.

"Really?" he nods, seemingly intrigued. "Where are you going? What are you studying?"

Oh shit. He's staring right at me and I know I have to say something but definitely not the truth, so I go, "I'm just doing general studies, you know."

"Where?"

Shit. He's waiting for an answer and I'm totally trapped so I take a deep breath and I mention the name of the town that my high school is in. There's a state college there that goes by that name so I figure I'll just let him draw his own conclusions.

He knows something's up. I can tell by the way he's looking at me.

He leans in closer and goes, "How old are you?"

I'm sweating like a suspect on *NYPD Blue*. "Um, nineteen," I mumble.

"Nineteen? Is that even legal?"

"Legal for what?" I ask defensively, "Voting?" God, I'm lying by a year and a half as it is! "Well, how old are you?" I ask.

"Twenty-three."

"Oh, wow."

We just look at each other and then I start laughing. I do that when I get nervous.

Then Connor runs his hand down the length of my cheek and says, "Okay, I guess nineteen is a little young, but you happen to be nice and cute and I like hanging out with you. So maybe that cancels out the age difference?"

He's looking right at me and I can barely breathe. Then he leans in and starts kissing me and it's awesome and I just sort of follow his lead. I mean, it's not that I don't know how to kiss, I've been doing it since sixth grade, but since he's twenty-three, he's been doing it longer so I figure I could maybe learn something.

We kiss for a long time and I don't remember it ever being like this before. I can feel his fingers sliding inside the straps of my dress and pulling them down my shoulders. I'm not wearing a bra and part of me is thinking that I absolutely have to stop him, but the other part of me doesn't even try. He kisses me everywhere and I just lie back with my eyes closed, thinking I could do this forever.

He slides my dress all the way down to my waist and kisses my belly until he gets to my navel ring. He spins it between his fingers and says, "This is sexy."

I move my hands all over him. He's got a great body, muscular, but not too much, but I keep my hands mostly above the belt. It's not that I've never touched a penis before, because I have, but I just don't want to be the one to start that.

I'm not sure when, but at some point he has removed my dress and his jeans and now the only thing separating us is two cotton crotches. He starts moving south again and right when he's about to kiss me even lower, like way past my belly ring, I immediately sit up and shout, *"Stop!"* And then I feel like a total retard.

I cover my breasts with my hands and scramble for my dress. I can't even look at him, I feel so stupid. I'm some kinda nineteen year old.

He looks at me surprised and asks, "Are you okay?"

And I go, "I'm sorry but I can't do that. I'm menstruating." That's what I said. *Menstruating!* I sound like my sixth-grade health teacher. And I don't know why I said it because it's not even true. But it's just too soon for me, and there's no way I'm gonna tell him I'm a virgin. I pick up my dress from the floor and I'm just waiting for him to say, "Thank-you and good night."

But instead he looks at me and says, "It's okay. Really."

"It is?" I look at him suspiciously, unsure if he means it.

"Yeah, it's your call." He reaches down for his jeans and I watch him step into them, one leg at a time.

I'm standing in front of him half naked with my dress held tightly against me. I feel like such a loser, such a big baby. And no matter what he says I know I totally blew it. But it's too late now, it's not like I can take it back. I turn away from him and pull my dress over my head. When I face him again he's buttoning his shirt and smiling at me.

"You're not mad at me?" I venture.

He shakes his head. "Not at all. But I was wondering."

"What?"

"Well, how long will this take?"

"What?"

"I'm kidding." He looks at me and shrugs. "Well kind of."

I follow Connor outside and I'm just waiting for him to ditch me, to go in search of a more mature, accommodating girl, but instead he reaches for my hand, wraps his fingers around mine, and pulls me up alongside him.

Chapter 10

When we go back inside the house I'm surprised to find the party just as we left it. It seemed like we were in that cabana forever, like something monumental had happened. But now, seeing all these people slightly drunker, but basically unchanged, makes me feel like maybe it wasn't that big of a deal. I mean, Connor is still here, and I have every right to say no, right? I remember reading somewhere that your body is your temple and only you can choose who comes to worship. Whatever. All I know is that eventually I will lose this virginity of mine, but it's gonna be on my terms and it's gonna be glamorous.

We find M lounging on a giant-size beanbag chair, holding a drink in one hand, and a pool cue in the other. The room smells kind of weird like someone's been smoking pot or something but I'm sure it wasn't M 'cause neither one of us does stuff like that. When she sees me standing in the doorway she shouts, "Oh my god! I've been looking all over for you!"

I watch her struggle to get upright without spilling her drink. "Help me out here, would you?" she says.

I give her my hand and help her up. She rearranges her

Burberry plaid miniskirt that has risen up and twisted around, says hi to Connor and goes, "Hey Trevor come here, this is Alex."

I watch Trevor make his shot, and then scowl as he narrowly misses his pocket. He looks up and smiles and gives me a half-hearted wave. And I'm not sure if his lack of enthusiasm is because of the missed shot, or if he's already bored by me.

"I can't believe you missed that shot," Connor says, walking around the side of the pool table.

"I suppose you could do better?"

"You know it."

Connor looks around for a cue stick, and M goes, "Here, take mine, I'm bored with this game."

"We just started!" Trevor says.

"Yeah, well," M just shrugs and takes another sip of her drink.

I settle onto a velvet beanbag chair next to M and watch Connor and Trevor play pool, and I try to think of what celebrities they resemble. Trevor is kind of skinny and not very tall, with hair that's all dark roots and bleached tips. And with his dark brown eyes, and pale, English-schoolboy skin, he looks kind of like a guy version of Gwen Stefani. And Connor with his dark, wavy, tousled hair, swimming pool–blue eyes, hot body, and that one, slightly crooked, front tooth, makes me think of what Hugh Grant and Elizabeth Hurley's kid would have looked like if they hadn't broken up and she hadn't gotten knocked up by that other guy who thought he wasn't the dad but then it turned out he really was.

"Where were you guys?" M asks, giving me a suspicious look.

"We took a walk." I look at her briefly, then back at the guys.

"Where to?"

"Outside," I say, still not looking at her.

"Front or back?"

"Why?" I ask. I mean, god, she's practically leering at me.

"Because you're being so secretive that it makes me want to know."

"We were outside, in the back, in the cabana, by the pool. Okay? Happy now?" I look right at her.

"What were you doing in there?" She leans in and stares at me.

"Jeez, M!"

"Well?"

"Nothing, okay. Just talking." I fidget with the hem of my dress.

"Why so sensitive?" she asks.

I look over at Connor and Trevor, but they're into the game, they can't hear us. "Listen, we almost did it but then we didn't."

"Did you get coitus interrupted?" M laughs.

"Yeah, by me."

"What?"

"I just wasn't ready, I couldn't go through with it."

M looks at Connor who just made his shot and is pumping his arm into the air. "Well, he doesn't seem too upset about it. But I'm telling you, you really need to get it over with and put it behind you. You act like it's such a big deal, and it's really not."

I just look at M and shrug. Our realities are so different. She lost her virginity last summer to some hot surf instructor during a family vacation to Maui. She called me like the minute it was over to give me all the details. It's like, she just breezes through life never worried about the consequences. I wonder what it's like to always feel so safe.

"Well, there's one more thing," I tell her.

"What's that?"

"I told him I was nineteen," I whisper.

"*What?*" she shouts.

"Shhh." I look around frantically. "You heard me," I whisper.

"Does that make me nineteen too?"

"I guess."

"Cool." She takes a sip of her drink and leans back.

"What about you, what have you been doing?" I ask.

"Nothing. I watched that movie for a little while, then I bumped into Trevor and we've just been hanging out."

"Is there anyone famous here?"

"No, just a couple of Bachelorette wannabes." She sets down

her drink, then stands up and walks over to the pool table and leans against the far-left-corner pocket, the same one Connor is shooting for, only now he misses.

"Oh, and you almost had it," M says, giving him a flirty smile.

"I did have it. Until you distracted me," Connor says in a joking way, but I wonder if he's partly serious.

"Yeah, well you seem to be easily distracted," she says.

"What does that mean?" He leans his weight on his cue stick and looks at her, while Trevor lines up his next shot.

"Well, like how long did it take you to call Alex?"

Connor just stands there looking at her, and I'm sinking deeper and deeper into the beanbag chair, wondering where she's going with this and wishing she'd stop right now.

"Oh, that's right, you never did call her did you? See what I mean by easily distracted?"

M just stands there smiling and I'm completely frozen. I can't believe she just said that. I'm just about to say something, anything, when Connor goes, "Well, actually, I was waiting for Alex to call me. I thought that's how you do it in America. Lucky for me I found her in the hallway." Then he looks at me and smiles and winks and even though it was really nice of him to do that, I still want to kill her.

Then out of nowhere she goes, "Hey, is anybody else hungry? 'Cause, I'm starving. Do you think we could get some breakfast?"

"You want me to make you a waffle?" Trevor drops his stick and grabs her around the waist and nuzzles her ear. It's the second time he's seen her and he's already gone. It never fails.

"No, let's go somewhere," she says.

And so we leave all the guests to continue the party on their own, and pile into Trevor's Hummer and end up in some funky old diner with sticky, illustrated menus.

The restaurant scene is surreal. It's like being trapped in that Tori Amos video where she keeps morphing. The waitress looks like she's trying to morph into Christina Aguilera but that's not why I feel sorry for her. I mean, I can't imagine working here at this hour. Nothing but drunk people trying to sober up and not throw up before the long drive home.

When Connor slides in the booth next to me, he moves in so close that our legs are touching. He opens his menu and leans his shoulder into mine, and when I look up I catch M watching us with an expression I can't quite read.

Then Trevor picks up a menu and goes, "Okay, you guys just order anything you want, it's on me. But not you Connor, girls only, you're on your own."

So I go, "Well thanks, Trevor, but I think I'll just have coffee."

"No really, I mean it. You want this burger here," he holds up the menu and points at a picture of a greasy-looking burger, "You just say the word and I'll make it happen."

"Well, as generous as that offer is, I think I'll stick with coffee," I say.

"Okay, last call M, how 'bout it?"

"Well . . ."

So then the pseudo-Christina waitress comes over with her notepad, ready to take our order. I stick with coffee because every time I eat this late at night my dreams get even crazier than usual. Connor gets coffee and pancakes, Trevor taps his finger on the picture of the greasy burger and says, "This. I want this."

And M goes, "Okay. I'll start with a small garden salad with ranch dressing, on the side. Then I'd like a grilled cheese sandwich, but use very little butter please. I'd also like some peach cobbler warmed up with some vanilla ice cream, but if you could put the vanilla ice cream in a separate bowl, I'd appreciate it, because I don't like it when it gets all warm and runny. Oh, and a Diet Coke. Thank you."

The waitress doesn't even flinch. She just takes her tan, hair extensions, and notepad back into the kitchen to place our orders.

Trevor retrieves a pack of cigarettes from his shirt pocket and offers them all around, but Connor shakes his head and says, "Not me. I quit."

Trevor holds the pack in front of me and goes, "He'll never quit. We've been smoking forever."

I look at Connor and he just shrugs, then I push the pack away because M and I don't smoke. Not to mention that it's illegal to smoke in restaurants in California and I wish that Trevor would just stop because I'm kind of a wuss about rules like that. But then M grabs the pack from Trevor pulls one out, taps it on the table like a professional smoker, and holds it up to her mouth, waiting for a light.

I look at her totally shocked because we gave up smoking after three tries in junior high when we realized it didn't make us look cool, it just made us smell bad. But now Trevor gives her a light and she's smoking it, and I can't believe she's doing that but I don't say anything.

When our food arrives M and Trevor finally put out their cigarettes and everybody just sort of digs in. There isn't much in the way of conversation, which is fine by me 'cause I sort of shut down when I get tired and it's hard for me to act all vivacious. Trevor and M are sharing off each other's plates and whispering back and forth. Then suddenly they both get up and say, "We'll be right back."

I watch M walk away and wonder what they're up to. Normally she'd drag me into the bathroom with her so we could talk about the guys and stuff. But I guess she's not going in there with Trevor so they can have a conversation.

I take a sip of my coffee and lean my head back and close my eyes. I feel Connor squeeze my hand and then lean over and kiss me softly on the cheek. I open my eyes and smile at him.

About fifteen minutes later Trevor and M come back and want to go. She's acting all hyper and fidgety and weird, and when I try to catch her eye she purposely looks away. And I'm really starting to wonder what went on in the bathroom just now. I figured she probably went in there to fool around with Trevor, but now I'm thinking there was more to it, like maybe they were doing drugs or something. I mean, earlier, when she was playing pool and the room smelled like pot, I was so positive it wasn't her. But now watching her act all strange and secretive, I'm no longer sure.

When we walk outside I'm surprised to find that it's still dark. I mean, it feels like it should be the next afternoon or something. But technically it's Saturday morning and I remember that I'm scheduled to open the store today.

"So where to now?" M asks bouncing up and down in the backseat of the Hummer.

"Wherever you want." Trevor looks at her from the rearview mirror and smiles.

"Alex, what do you think?"

I look at my watch and then I look at everyone else, and I don't want to be a major party wrecker but I really need to get back to Orange County so I can sleep, shower, and change before work. "Well, I hate to say it, but um, I really have to go home soon." There I said it, peer pressure be damned.

"No!" M whines. "The night is young!"

I look at her and I can't believe she's whining like that, but I just say, "I'm sorry, but I have to work tomorrow."

"Call in sick!" She rolls her eyes, clearly frustrated with me, which just makes me more determined.

"I'm sorry, I can't. I can't call in sick." I'm glaring at her and I feel really embarrassed to be fighting like this in front of Connor.

"Well, I'm not going home, Alex. So just take these, take the car."

She's dangling her car keys in front of me and I can't believe she's doing this, but I just swipe them out of her hand and say, "Well what about you, how are you getting home?"

"Don't you worry about me, I'll find a way." She gives me a smug look and I'm so mad I just stare out the window for the rest of the ride.

When we get back to Trevor's, Connor gets out of the Hummer and M climbs into the front seat and slams the door between us. She waves at me as they drive away, and I cannot believe she's ditching me like this.

"Are you going to be okay?" Connor asks "I know it's a long drive."

I give him a smile I don't really own and say, "Yeah, I'll be fine. I'll just listen to some music."

Then he kisses me good-bye and he tastes like pancakes and maple syrup and it's really hard to stop.

Chapter 11

O n Monday morning I pull into the student lot and look around for M's car, partly because we usually park next to each other and partly because I'm wondering if she's here yet since I haven't talked to her since she ditched me on Saturday night.

I tried calling her yesterday after I got home from work but her mom answered the phone. I could hear her go, "Hello? Hello?" and then "Who is this?" and that's when I hung up. I know that's a terrible thing to do, but I didn't feel like talking to her and I couldn't figure out why she was in M's room answering her private line. I spent the rest of the night hoping she wouldn't star sixty-nine me.

But since M wasn't in French or Calculus, or even at our lunch tree, I'm starting to worry that maybe something happened to her, like maybe she didn't get home safely, and that makes me feel guilty about being mad at her.

I switch books at my locker and run to my English class because I don't want to be late and attract any unnecessary attention. When I get to the door, I look around for M but she's not here either, so I just sort of slink to my desk and hope for the best.

Mr. Sommers walks in, glances at us briefly, then goes over to his desk where he starts flipping through some papers and rubbing his scraggly beard in a distracted way. And I'm thinking, well today must be the day. The day when he finally hands back those *Anna K* papers, the one I still haven't started. He'll look at me when the papers have all been handed out and then he'll say in front of the entire class, "Alex, I need to speak to you later." And then everyone will turn around and snicker at the former-homecoming-princess-now-big-loser sitting in the next-to-last row.

I watch him get up from his desk clutching some paper in one hand and still fingering his beard with the other. He's standing in front of us and he's looking right at me with these dark eyes that look like they've seen things he's not going to tell you about in this AP English class. And as much as I want to look away I can't, because part of me is just like all the others. Part of me wants to watch this train wreck that is surely headed my way.

He clears his throat like he always does at the beginning of class and I sink a little lower in my seat, preparing for a verbal caning, when he says, "I'd like to read you a story written by one of my students that really impressed me."

So I relax. I'm relieved that it's not about me and I wonder why I've become so paranoid. Then he starts reading "Holly Would," that short story I turned in instead of the Tolstoy paper. I sit frozen at my desk. I can't even believe it.

When he's finished reading someone goes, "Who wrote that? Whose was that? That was really good."

And then Mr. Sommers looks at me and waits and in an unsure voice I say, "I wrote it?"

And then everyone turns around and stares at me in disbelief. And then someone who I used to dismiss, someone who once felt like a total loser because of me, someone who is now well aware of my social decline, says, "No way. No way, she wrote that."

And now everyone is staring at me to see how I'll respond.

But I don't say anything because I remember how I once treated this person and how it always comes back to you.

Mr. Sommers sits on the edge of his desk and says, "Alex did indeed write it and it got me thinking. For your next assignment I'd like you to write a short story, fifteen-hundred words, due Monday."

I sit up straighter, feeling good about myself in a classroom for the first time in two years. No homework for me! I've got plenty more where that came from, a whole drawer full of stories that I've written, and they're not all about Richard Branson either. But it's just a little hobby of mine. I mean, it's not serious or anything.

Christine the Collector raises her hand and asks, "Mr. Sommers what should the story be about?"

And he goes, "This is a creative exercise. It can be about anything you want. Just use your imagination."

She pushes her headband back an invisible inch then looks at Mr. Sommers and goes, "I was wondering if it's possible to get an alternate assignment?"

Now the whole class is staring at her and her eyes are all red, and she looks like she's gonna cry or something.

He gives her a concerned look and says, "Christine, relax. Just try to have fun with it. Get creative."

And then, get this, she says, "But I don't know how to be creative."

And I just look at her and give her the smirk I've been holding in for the last two years because that's the most pathetic statement I've ever heard.

Mr. Sommers just shrugs and says, "Do your best." Then he hands me my story, and gives everyone else their graded Tolstoy papers.

And right there, in red ink, in the upper-left-hand corner, is an A. I just stare at it for the longest time. I haven't received a letter from that far north in the alphabet in like two years. He also wrote a note at the bottom saying something like, even if I didn't write what was assigned, he's glad that I chose to write, and to write well.

And even though that makes me feel really good for a change, it also makes me feel guilty. Like now I seriously have to write that *Anna K* paper.

Chapter 12

On my way home from school I decide to stop in at my dad's office. I mean, he's really left me with no choice since he refuses to return my calls. Besides, I'm feeling pretty good about the A I just got, and since good moments in my life tend to be pretty fleeting, I figure I better strike while I'm hot, right?

I pull into the lot and park right next to a brand new, shiny, black Porsche that I know belongs to my father since he would never allow another mortal to park in his reserved space. And I consider this a good sign because if he can afford a Porsche he can certainly pay my way through college.

I stare at my reflection in the rearview mirror and try to muster the courage to face him. The last time I came here was over a year ago when I had to beg for my child-support check, and I left empty-handed. I try to summon one good memory, just one decent moment we might have shared when I was a kid, just a little something to get me through this meeting. But the truth is he really wasn't around much and the few times he was, well, it's not worth remembering.

I run my hands through my hair, recheck my lip gloss, and climb out of my car. I may be quaking with fear inside, but I walk with intent and purpose just in case someone is watching from a

Faking 19 69

distant window. And when I push through the double glass doors with the words Sky Investments etched on them, I wonder why he's always so reluctant to invest in me.

I stand in front of the modern, steel reception desk waiting to see who it will be this time. Every time I come to his office there's a new secretary. I mean, he changes them almost as often as he changes girlfriends.

"Can I help you?" A skinny, Clairol blonde, with an abundant chest walks down the hallway and slides around the other side of the desk. She's wearing an outfit that would normally be paired with a thick, black bar across the eyes and the word, DON'T! in red capital letters and extreme punctuation overhead.

"I'm here to see my dad." I look directly at her and fight the urge to fidget.

She looks me over, then in a condescending tone asks, "And who might that be?"

I narrow my eyes and say, "My dad is Brad Sky, the President of Sky Investments. Your boss. Can I see him now?"

Her expression instantly changes to one of curiosity and caution. "Oh. Okay. And your name please?"

"Alex."

I watch her pick up the phone, push a button, and in an intimate tone that tells me they've slept together says, "There's an Alex here? She says she's your daughter? I didn't know you had a daughter. Oh, all right." Then she looks at me and gestures, "Go right in."

When I open the door he's waiting on the other side. "Alex!" He says, "What a wonderful surprise!"

He's acting all happy to see me and tries to give me a big hug. I let him grab hold of me for about half a second, then I duck out of it and settle into the cracked, brown-leather club chair across from his desk.

"What brings you here?" he asks, his face clad in his deal-closing smile and a pair of trendy titanium glasses that are resting on the bridge of his nose.

I watch him ease into his executive chair on the other side of the desk, then I look around the office walls, at the framed degrees and certificates, and that stupid Nagel print he bought in the eighties and refuses to take down. College degrees, schlock art, but not one picture of my sister or me. It's like we've ceased to exist in this new, postdivorce world he created for himself.

I face him and say, "You haven't returned my calls so I decided to visit."

"What? I didn't know you called." He runs his hand through his salt-and-pepper Richard Gere–style hair and gestures toward the general vicinity of the reception desk, "Cheri must have forgotten to give me the message."

"I called you at home dad." I look right at him. "Did you say her name was Cherry?" I ask incredulously.

"So what can I do for you?" he asks, ignoring my question.

I take a deep breath and clasp my hands in my lap so I won't fidget, then I look directly at him and just say it. "I need your help."

He looks at me with controlled panic, adjusts his pastel, silk tie that color coordinates with his light pink shirt, and charcoal gray pin-striped suit, and nods. "Okay, what kind of help?"

"Financial help." I glance down at my lap and see that I'm squeezing my hands together so tightly that my knuckles are white.

"Okay, okay." He's bobbing his head up and down like he does when he's thinking up a good exit strategy. "What do you need it for? A new prom dress?"

"A prom dress?" I shake my head. Is he kidding? "What? You think I drove here because of a prom dress? I'm not living in Dawson's fucking Creek Dad."

"Watch your language!" he shouts.

I roll my eyes and shake my head. I know I shouldn't have used the *f* word, but I can't believe him. He doesn't even know me! I try to center myself, and calm down, because getting mad never works with him. So I take a deep breath and start over. "Dad, no, I'm not going to the prom, okay? My life isn't really like that anymore. I need money for my future, you know? So I can have one?"

He locks eyes with me for a second, then reaches into his desk drawer for his checkbook, and his big, important, Montblanc pen. Then he writes out a check for five hundred dollars. "Will this help?" he asks, holding it up so I can see it.

I look at the money he's offering and I can't believe it. That barely covers one month's child support. I lean back in my chair and say, "Are you joking?"

He drops the check on the desk between us and says, "Well, how much are we talking here Alex?"

"I need to know if you're going to pay for college." I wipe my sweaty palms onto my jeans.

"Have you applied?"

"Yes." I look directly at him and hold his gaze.

"And were you accepted?"

"Yes. Into one." He doesn't need to know it was on a contingent basis.

I watch him rock back in his chair and regard me from over the top of his trendy glasses. "Have you asked your mother for help?"

"Are you kidding? She works like a dog just to pay the mortgage you stuck her with!"

He takes on a smug expression and says, "She should have sold while the market was hot. I told her."

Five years later and he's still judging her. I just can't take it anymore. "And you should have paid your alimony and child support like the judge ordered!" I shout. "Look, she won't go after you, and this is not easy for me either, but I really need your help. Please. I'm not kidding. This is my life. It's not a joke." I look across the desk at him and I can't believe it's come to this. I can't believe I'm begging.

He looks at me completely unaffected and says, "Now is not a good time."

"What?" I say. "Not a good time? I saw your new Porsche outside! That's four years at a state school just sitting in your parking space!"

He shakes his head and gestures to a stack of papers on his desk, "It's not like you think. You see this? All bills. The Porsche? It's leased. I just can't help you right now."

I look at the check lying on the desk between us and then I lock eyes with him. When he's the first to look away, I stand up. I grab the door handle then turn back and look at his stupid pink shirt, his crappy art, and his greedy face. I don't know why I expected anything different.

When I open the door Cheri is standing right there but I don't start crying until I'm safely inside my car.

Chapter 13

hen I get home my mom has set the table for two, which is kind of surprising since we rarely eat together and I'm guessing this must be because of the conference at school the other day. I look at her tentatively since I don't know what to expect. I mean, I know she hasn't been too pleased with me lately.

"Hi," she says, pouring a big pot full of pasta into one of those draining bowls with all the holes. "I'm glad you're home, I made spaghetti."

I walk over to where she stands and check out the steaming noodles. "You made spaghetti? Really?" I throw my stuff on the counter and sit at the table and let her serve me a plate full of pasta. "What's the occasion?" I ask.

"I just thought maybe we could spend some time together. We haven't had a chance to really talk since our meeting with Mrs. Gross. So how've you been?" She passes me the grated Parmesan cheese and looks at me expectantly.

"Fine," I lie. She doesn't need to know about my dad.

She nods her head then says, "I saw M's mother in the grocery store the other day."

"M's mom goes to the grocery store?" I ask, taking a bite of my pasta.

My mom covers her mouth and says, "No, I don't think she does. She made it clear she was just on her way home from yoga and needed a bottle of water."

"Did you tell her that you were just on your way home from work and needed a week's worth of groceries?"

She just shrugs. "We didn't talk long." And then she looks at me and her eyes grow darker when she asks, "So how's school going Alex? Do you need any help? Anything you want to talk about?"

"No, I'm doing better," I say, and I'm surprised to realize that it's actually true, well for today anyway. "My English teacher liked a short story I wrote and he read it out loud to the class."

"Really?"

"Yeah, and he gave me an A too." I break off a piece of garlic bread and drag it along the top of my pasta, caking it with red sauce.

"I used to do a little writing," she says. "But one day your father made fun of one of my stories so I stopped."

She cuts a meatball in half with her fork and looks at me closely, and all I can think is, *Here-we-go.* I take a drink of my water and look down at my plate, waiting for the retelling of her favorite story, the one about how he wrecked her life.

But instead she says, "So you're studying creative writing?"

I look at her surprised, but I just say, "Not really, We just finished reading *Anna Karenina.* Have you read it?"

She nods. "Years ago, when I was your age. She gets hit by a train or something, right?"

"Yeah, something like that."

"Do you have to write a paper on it?"

She's looking right at me and I hate lying to her so I just go, "Um, yeah, I do." And then the phone rings and I practically jump through a hoop of fire to get it.

It's my sister calling from New York. She moved there right after she graduated college, and she has this totally cool job as an editor with a major fashion magazine. They don't pay as much as you'd think and New York is like a totally expensive place to live, but I really do admire her. Her whole life just seems really glamorous. She has a studio apartment in a place called SoHo which stands for something I can't remember, but it's supposed to be really hip. And she has this boyfriend that she showed me a picture of once and he looked really cute. His eyes were sort of squinted closed, but she said that's because it was taken in the sun at the beach in the Hamptons. That's supposed to be some chichi place in the East.

"Hey, Alex, how are you?" she asks.

"Okay, how's New York?"

"Bad weather, very crowded, terribly exciting. I still love it here."

"Yeah, I still love it here too."

"I'll bet." She laughs. "So what's new?"

And even though I promised myself I wouldn't tell anyone what happened today, I just can't keep it in, so I go, "Dad just leased a new Porsche, has a girlfriend named Cherry, and he's not paying for me to go to college."

"What?" she asks, all the way from Manhattan. "Are you serious?"

I look at my mother who is staring at me, straining to hear both sides of the conversation, and suddenly I feel bad about mentioning his stupid girlfriend. I didn't mean to make my mom feel bad. I turn and face the wall and even though she can still hear me I say, "Well, he wouldn't return my calls so I ambushed him at his office. He says he's broke and can't do it. But I don't believe him."

"I don't believe him either. Oh Alex, I'm sorry."

"It's not your fault," I say.

"Can I help in any way?"

"No, but I'll let you know how it all turns out." I look at my mom. She's practically falling out of her chair. "I think Mom wants to talk to you."

I hand the phone to my mother and start clearing my plate. I wished I hadn't said anything, and just kept it to myself because my mom is going to ask me all the details now and I don't feel like talking about it anymore. It is what it is and there's nothing I can do about it. I mean, I can't force him to care about me.

Sure enough, she hangs up the phone and says, "What was that I heard about you going to your father's office today?"

I pour some dish soap onto a damp sponge and say, "Nothing. Don't worry about it."

She turns in her chair until she's facing me and says, "Well I am worried about it because it obviously upset you and I'd like to know what happened."

"Really?" I look at her. The wet, soapy plate I'm holding is dripping onto the floor. "Do you really want to know about it because it upset me? Or because you just want to know about him?" It's a terrible thing to say, especially when I saw her eyes right after I said it. But it's out there now and I can't take it back.

"What is that supposed to mean?"

I finish rinsing the plate and say, "Plenty of things upset me, Mom, but you never want to know about them unless it involves Dad."

"That's not true!"

"It is true. You never ask me how I am."

"How can you say that? I even went to your school!"

"You showed up only because Mrs. Gross called you at work and guilted you into it. And then you kept looking at your watch, the whole time. You have no idea what it's like for me, and you never bother to ask." I shake my head and reach for a dish towel.

"Well maybe you have no idea what it's like for me."

"How could I *not* know?" I'm yelling now, but I just don't care. "You remind me every chance you get! It's been five solid years of living in the past. He's *gone* Mom, and you've still got a drawer full of his stuff in your bedroom. He doesn't pay alimony, he doesn't pay child support, but you don't do a damn thing about it because you'd rather just sit back and suffer and talk about how it's all his fault."

"He let me down!" She looks a little shaky when she says it and I know I've really upset her, but I'm a little upset too.

"Yeah, well, he let me down too! He was my only shot at college but he won't pay for it, so now I can't go. He left both of us, Mom, not just you." I throw the dish towel on the counter and face her.

She gives me a long look and I know I've gone too far, so I turn around and busy myself at the sink. I've got my back to her when I hear her say, "I had dreams too you know."

"Whatever." I roll my eyes and shake my head and put the dry plate in the cupboard overhead.

"If I had it to do over again—"

There's no way I'm going to listen to the rest of that. What, so I can hear her say she wouldn't have had me if she had it to do over again? No thanks. Being ditched by one parent is enough for today. So I turn around and face her and put my hand in the air and say, "Just stop. I don't want to hear anymore."

She looks at me and shakes her head and says, "I don't know why you thought you could count on him. I don't know what gave you that idea."

I grab my backpack and sling it over my shoulder and look at her and say, "I guess I just wanted to believe that he really did care about me. But don't worry. Now I know better." Then I leave the kitchen before she can say anything else.

Chapter 14

The next day at school I see M walking across the quad talking on her cell phone. When she sees me she runs over and goes, "Say hi to Trevor!"

I grab the phone she's thrusting in my face and go, "Hi Trevor," then I hand it back and walk toward my locker.

I'm standing in front of it, trying to remember the combination, when M comes over and goes, "Oh my god! Did you see Tiffany's sling? What a faker! Did you see it?"

"I didn't even notice."

"How could you miss it? It's freakin' furry zebra striped!"

"Yeah?" I finally get my locker open. I grab a handful of textbooks I have no intention of reading and put them in my backpack.

M's still going on about Tiffany but I'm not listening. Finally she looks at me and goes, "Are you okay?"

I slam my locker shut, look right at her, and go, "No. I guess I'm not."

"Well what's wrong?"

"In case you didn't notice, you totally ditched me at that party."

"I didn't ditch you. You had to go home and I wasn't ready, so I gave you the keys. What's the damage?"

"I just didn't think it was cool."

"Are you serious?" She looks at me in shock and it makes me wonder if I'm overreacting. "I'm sorry, really. I guess I got a little caught up."

I just shrug and start walking toward class and she follows me. "What happened to you yesterday?" I look over at her. "How come you weren't at school?"

"I was home sick." She looks away.

"What'd you have?"

She stops in front of the door and whispers, "A massive hangover. I didn't get in until Sunday night and like, my mom was already home. It was a serious close call."

"You were at Trevor's that whole time?"

"We went *everywhere*. It's like he knows every cool person, and every cool place in LA. You wouldn't even believe the stuff we did." She shakes her head and looks around the campus. "God, this place is such a dump. It totally sucks being stuck here after a weekend like that."

"Did you sleep with him?" I ask, figuring she did, but still wanting to know.

"Yeah, and it was completely amazing. I think I'm in love."

She gives me a searching look but I don't say anything. I'm starting to feel like I'm falling further and further behind in the maturity race, and soon I won't be able to catch up.

"Anyway, by the time I got home I looked pretty bad, and I didn't expect my mom to be home. I thought they were at some doctor's conference, but apparently she decided not to go 'cause she's leaving for some spa or something instead. So, I hope you don't mind but I told her I was at your house."

"Whatever," I say.

"I'm sorry if you felt like I ditched you, really. I just thought it was a good solution. I didn't mean to hurt your feelings."

She's giving me this sad look and I decide to just let it go. "Okay, forget it. You know I tried calling you but your mom answered."

"She did? Shit!"

"Yeah, it was weird."

"What did you say? Did you talk to her?" M looks panicked.

"I didn't say anything. I hung up."

"No way!"

"Way. But I felt bad about it afterwards."

"I wonder what the hell she was doing in my room?"

"Who knows," I say. "I've got bigger issues right now anyway."

"Like what?"

I look at her and shake my head. I feel like I'm on the verge of tears but I hold it back with all my might. "I had it out with my dad last night. I went to his office. He's not paying for college, end of story." I move away from the door so some of my classmates can get in, and then I wipe my nose with the back of my hand and continue. "Lets face it, my grades are crap, I can't swing a scholarship, and the only school that did accept me did so on a contingent basis, only if I could get my grades up, but now even if I do, I still can't afford it. So I guess it's just not gonna happen for me."

"Well, you could always get a loan or something."

"Yeah, whatever." She's looking at me with pity and I just can't take it. "Listen," I push past her, "I have to go to the bathroom. I'll see you in class," I say. But as soon as I'm around the corner I beeline for the parking lot and get in my car.

I check my wallet. I just got paid so I've got three crumbled twenties, a fresh ten, a stained five, and two crisp ones. And since I filled up recently I should have enough gas to get me to LA and back.

Only my car won't start. I turn the key in the ignition, nothing. I turn the key and bang on the steering wheel, nothing. I turn the key and bang on the steering wheel and scream every bad word I know, and still, nothing.

Well, that's just great. The bell rang like five minutes ago and if I go to class now I'll get in trouble for being tardy. And if I'm gonna get in trouble then I may as well go all the way and get in trouble for truancy. So I sit in my turquoise blue Karmann Ghia and start crying. And after a few minutes of that, I wipe my nose on my sleeve and look in the rearview mirror and I look even worse than I imagined. So I grab a faded, red bandanna from the glove compartment, spit on it, and wipe the supposedly waterproof mascara from my cheeks. I know it sounds gross, but what was I supposed to do?

So then, just to be a glass-half-full kinda girl, I turn the key again, and the engine starts. So now that I look like crap, with makeup and saliva smeared across my face, my car decides to take me to LA. That's the kind of karma I have.

I've never been to LA by myself, and it feels a little weird to be navigating the freeways alone. But the sun is shining hot and bright and I roll both windows down so I can feel the wind rushing around me, almost like in M's convertible. And even though my car is an old clunker, it's got a really great stereo system that I saved up for. So I insert that Nelly Furtado CD that I love, the one that has that song about being like a bird and flying away, and since I know all the words to all the songs I sing along at the top of my lungs, all the way to LA. And it feels really good to be young and free like this. It's almost like with each spin of my wheels, I get farther and farther from my troubles. Like I can just drive straight into my future and leave all the bad stuff behind.

I go to the sandwich shack. I'm not even hungry but it's what we always do. When the cute guy behind the counter sees me, he gets all happy and looks immediately to my right, then left, then over my shoulder, frantically searching for M.

"It's just me today." I shrug, and he definitely looks disappointed. "Um, can I get a bottle of water?"

"Yeah. Hey, how's your friend?" He's trying to act nonchalant, but just asking about her has got him all lit up.

"She's fine. She's perfect." I give him a dollar fifty, then I go find a place to sit.

The same old cast of characters is out today, the hippie girl who sells colorful, blown-glass bongs, the creepy magician with the extra-long sleeves, and those fake henna tattoo people. I did that once like a year ago. The actual tattoo faded in a day, but the tribal band lived on in the form of a nasty rash for about a month.

I sit on the concrete bench and close my eyes and enjoy the warmth of the sun beating down on me.

I'm in Marrakech. The desert heat is unrelenting, but I'm dressed for it in a breezy, sheer, caftan, and those little pointy slippers that are made here in Morocco. My hair is pulled back into a complicated twist, and my eyes are shielded by my celebrity-size, shiny, black, Chanel sunglasses. I rise from my luxurious divan and walk out into the courtyard. I remove my caftan and let it fall to the ground, revealing my perfect nakedness. Some of the houseboys stop working and stare, but I ignore them, as I walk to the edge of the pool and dive in a perfect arc. I glide underwater to the other side, where Connor is waiting . . .

When I open my eyes that crazy iguana man is standing right in front of me, blocking my rays. Jeez, he's like the cruelest reality check imaginable.

"Wanna pet the iguana?" He smiles at me, but his pupils look crazy.

"Um, no thanks." I try to scoot back without being too obvious about it. He has a weird smell.

"It's just two dollars," he says.

"What's just two dollars?"

"To pet the iguana!" He's practically yelling at me now.

"Um, yeah, well, no thanks. I really don't want to pet him." I take a sip of my water and look around nervously.

"Suit yourself," he gives me a look like I'm missing out on a huge opportunity and turns to walk away.

And even though he creeps me out, now that he's leaving I'm reluctant to let him go, so I say, "Can I ask you a question?"

"Maybe." He looks at me expectantly.

"What do you do?"

"What?" He squints at me and his eyes contain so much red I can't tell what color they're supposed to be.

"I mean, I see you here all the time and I'm wondering what it is that you do. Do you work here?"

"Yeah, yeah, I work here." He raises his eyebrows and smiles.

"Well, where do you work?" I ask. I really am curious.

He starts pointing and twirling, "Where do I work?" he says. "Right here, and over there, and down there, and back there. I distribute happiness."

"You what?" I give him a skeptical look.

"I *distribute happiness!*" he says it slowly like I'm the moron, not him.

"You mean, by letting people pet your lizard?"

"That's one way." He nods, seemingly pleased that I'm catching on.

"Are *you* happy?" I don't know why, but I feel like I have to know.

"Happier than you," he says.

"How would you know?"

"Because you're lost, and I'm not." He says this with such certainty, that it really pisses me off.

"Yeah well, you never leave the boardwalk, so how could you get lost?" I give him an ugly look.

He shakes his head. "You've got to find your way, before it's too late."

"Oh yeah, like you did? I mean, where do you live?" I look down at his disgusting, bare feet. "And where are your shoes?" I don't know why but he's making me feel really defensive.

He looks down at his thick, nasty, yellow toenails and laughs. "Life is a journey. This is mine."

He's standing there laughing but I can tell he pities me. The iguana man feels sorry for *me!* I finish my water and stand up carefully, because I don't want him to see how much he's upsetting me. "Okay, well, nice meeting you," I say, waving my hand in the air.

And as I'm walking away I hear him yell, "We're not so different you know. You and me, we're the same!"

When I get to my car I lock the door and grip the steering wheel and try to calm down. I scan my side- and rearview mirrors watching him wandering aimlessly, up and down the boardwalk. He walks the same walk every day, the miles just adding up but he's always here. He's putting all his effort into going nowhere. And I wonder if he's right. If we really are the same. Like, maybe that will be me someday, some big, weirdo, lizard chick, wearing a fake Versace suit and stilettos, with some funky reptile shitting all over my shoulder. It's so hard for me to imagine my future that it seems like a real possibility.

I shake my head and refuse to think like this any longer. Then I dig my cell phone out of my purse and call Connor. The moment he answers I panic and nearly hang up.

"Hello?"

"Hey, Connor? It's Alex."

"Alex, hey. What's going on?"

"Um, nothing. Um, well, it's just that I'm in LA and I thought I'd call and say hey." Oh god, I sound like a total retard.

"You're in LA? Are you with M?"

"No, it's just me."

"Brilliant! Why don't you come by?"

"Now?"

"Well, no. Not now. I'm wrapping up a little business. How 'bout in a couple hours, say around six?"

"Okay."

"Listen, even better. Meet me at Harry's. Do you know where it is?"

"Yes," I lie. I think it's in Santa Monica but I'm really not sure, and I don't want him to know that I don't know, 'cause Harry's is one of those places where you're just supposed to know where it is.

"Great, we can grab some dinner then go see this band I might sign."

"Okay, Harry's at six." I look at my watch. I've got three hours to figure out where it is.

I put my car in reverse and glance at myself in the rearview mirror. I really need to find a makeup counter.

So I go to the LA location of the store where I work 'cause all I have to do is show my employee ID card and I can get a 20 percent discount. When I walk in I go right past the girls in those creepy white lab coats, past the ones caked in overpriced French makeup, and straight for those club kids working behind the cool counter.

I plop myself onto some tall awkward stool, smile at the Marilyn Manson wannabe wielding a powder brush and say, "Help!"

"Hmmmm." He holds my face up to the most unforgiving light and asks, "So what are your makeup goals?"

Goals? Is he kidding? I don't even have life goals, much less cosmetic ones. "Well," I begin, "I need to look nineteen, and I need to look way better than I do right now. Maybe a little like Gisele Bundchen? Is that possible?"

He purses his lips and shakes his head. "Gisele? Negative. I'm thinking for you a combination Betty Paige meets Liv Tyler."

"Have at it!" I say facing the light again.

One hour and several layers of makeup later, the only thing Betty, Liv, and I have in common is dark hair and a smoky eye pencil he swore he once sold to Liv's dad. But I scraped all my money together anyway and bought the pencil, the lipstick, and some powder, and now I have just enough left over for some new underwear.

I need the new underwear because I've decided I'm going to sleep with Connor. I figure if I'm gonna be a bad girl and ditch school, then I may as well be a really bad girl and lose my virginity. I mean, I think I'm finally ready. I pretty much know what to expect.

One day, back in like, fifth grade, I was peeking around my house, looking for some lost earring. I was really tearing the place apart, looking under beds, inside cupboards, everything. Well, under my parent's bed I found some creepy sex book. You know, the illustrated, how-to kind with captions and hairy armpits? I read that thing from cover to cover, trying to ignore how ugly the participants were drawn. I mean, I committed that book to memory, and it's a good thing too, because once, after the divorce, I went looking for it and it was gone. Either my dad took it with him, covertly stashing it under his arm, or my mom threw it out, vowing to never, ever, have that sort of illustrated sex again.

So I end up with a black lacy thong, which is a far cry from my usual pastel florals that my mom buys for me in three-packs. In the trunk of my car is a strapless black dress and some high-heeled sling backs that belong to M. So I go back to the parking lot, grab my stuff and take it into the department store bathroom and change. When I walk out of the stall I swear I don't look anything like the virginal, truant, high school senior that I am. Then I dial four-one-one on my cell phone and get the address to this Harry's place.

Chapter 15

W ell, it's not in Santa Monica like I thought so I'm really glad that I didn't mention that to Connor. It's in Century City, which is a part of town that I'm not too familiar with because it's mostly all corporate and stuff so there's really no reason for me to ever go there.

So I'm driving down Century Boulevard and I'm wondering how long it will be before the school sends a cut card to my house, and if I'll be able to retrieve it before my mom can get her hands on it. And then I wonder why I even care if she sees it since there's not much she can do about it anyway. I mean, I can't see how it really matters since I can't go to college now because of my grades and my dad and all.

But you know what? Screw college! I mean, maybe I really, like deep down inside, maybe I don't really want to go. Maybe that's why I've been carrying on like this, you know, so like, there'd be no choice to make. And who says I have to go anyway? Who made that rule? Plenty of people have skipped out on college and have done really well. For instance, look at Richard Branson! He didn't even make it out of high school and look what he's done! He's worth billions of dollars and has even been knighted by the Queen of England (which means people *have* to call him

Sir). And now that I'm hanging out with Connor and stuff, I'm gonna get all the real-life connections and experience that you can't get from some stupid college dorm room or textbook. I mean, think of all the big-time people Connor probably knows from being in the music industry on two different continents. And who knows where that will lead? The chances of ending up somewhere really great are almost guaranteed, and I'll probably even get there faster than all those losers who waste four good years and more going to school.

When I see the sign for Harry's I pull over and park on the street because I don't have much cash on me and I don't want to waste whatever's left on valet parking.

I walk into a room that's so dim it takes a minute for my eyes to adjust. The bar looks just like it did in the picture I saw in a "Hip Hangouts" article in *Instyle* magazine, all dark wood and big mirrors. I don't see Connor anywhere, but I grab an empty stool and squint at the multicolored chalkboard drink menu. They have like fifty different kinds of beer but I don't want to order that because it makes me bloated, and naked and bloated is not a good combination. I don't know enough about wine to even attempt that, so I think about playing it safe and just ordering a club soda with lime, but then I catch a glimpse of myself in the large mirror on the wall in front of me, and I don't know if it's the dim lighting or what, but I decide on a cosmopolitan. I've never actually had one before, but if it's good enough for the cast of *Sex and the City* it's good enough for me. I mean, I'm wearing new makeup and a thong, surely I can pull this off.

So when the bartender says in an English accent, "Can I help you?"

I go, "I'll have a cosmopolitan, please."

Then he looks at me closely and says, "I'll need to see your ID."

And I break out in an immediate sweat. I guess there's a big difference between faking nineteen and faking twenty-one. He's giving me this all-knowing stare as I unzip my Hello Kitty purse, which right now looks not at all hip but entirely juvenile. As I'm fishing around for my matching Hello Kitty wallet my hands are shaking and I'm contemplating whether I should really go through with this, or just ditch this plan and order a Shirley Temple, when Connor walks up and goes, "Alex! You look brilliant!" And then he hugs me and kisses me and says, "I see you've met Simon." And then he slaps hands with the bartender and says, "Bring me a beer, and get Alex anything she wants." Then he puts his arm around me and goes, "I've got us a booth in the corner."

I don't relax until I'm safely seated in the booth with a menu on my plate and a cosmopolitan on the table in front of me. Then I make a mental note to trash this cartoon purse first thing tomorrow.

"So what brings you to the neighborhood?" Connor leans on the table and takes a sip of his beer.

I'm prepared for this question, so I say, "Well, I was up here for a meeting. Um, you know, with a professor. From my college." Shit, that did not sound convincing.

"And how was your meeting?" He looks at me and waits.

"It went very well." I nod my head and smile and try to look directly at him without blinking so I'll appear more honest. "What about you? How was your day?" It's better if he talks since I'm just not pulling this off like I thought I could.

"My day was brilliant. Everything is coming together. But I can't go into all the details just yet, it's early still, and I don't want to jinx it." He winks at me.

"Oh." I nod my head and smile and take another sip of my drink. It's sweeter than I imagined, and I'm not sure if I like it, but I feel like I should finish it after all I went through to get it.

So when the waitress brings our fish and chips I look down at my plate and I'm disappointed to see that everything is beige. And I'm not even sure if I like fish and chips, but it's what you're supposed to get at Harry's so that's what we ordered. I watch Connor reach for some weird liquid stuff with a familiar scent and sprinkle it all over his food.

"What's that?" I ask, hoping this question won't make me look like a dork.

"Malt Vinegar, want some?"

He's offering the bottle and I can't imagine why you'd put vinegar on anything, but since he's English I figure he knows what he's doing when it comes to fish and chips so I grab the bottle and start sprinkling. When I take my first bite, I'm surprised that I like it.

"So," he says, covering his mouth while he chews and talks simultaneously, "I may have to go back across the pond sooner than I expected."

"What?" I nearly choke on a chip.

"Well, I'm not sure yet, but we have some contract issues that I might have to take care of back home."

"You mean, back in London?" Oh god, duh, of course he means London.

"Yeah, maybe as soon as next week."

He wipes his mouth and takes a sip of his beer, then rakes his hand through his Hugh Grant hair and looks at me. "You see, we signed this band about six months ago and . . ."

And he's off, going on and on about business. I'm kind of listening, don't get me wrong, and I'm definitely trying to act interested and happy for him, but the last thing I want to talk about is his leaving. Shit! I mean, where does that leave me? Not to mention the plans that I've made with him that he doesn't know about yet. It's like everybody has somewhere to go, and I'm the only one without a plan. M's going to Princeton, Blake's going to New York, and Connor has the record company and London. It's like everyone has a map and a destination and I'm just wandering way off the trail.

Thinking about this stuff just makes it really clear that tonight is just tonight, it's completely temporary. A moment ago I was feeling so happy; just being in this cool place that was featured in a magazine, with an awesome guy that's a younger, cuter, version of Richard Branson, it felt like enough. But by tomorrow morning my crappy life will still be there, patiently waiting for me. This whole night is starting to feel as borrowed as the dress I'm wearing.

Connor looks at me with concern and says, "I'm sorry, am I boring you?"

"No, of course not," I say. I give him a smile and mask my thoughts, and when he reaches across the table to squeeze my hand, I squeeze back even harder.

Chapter 16

We're driving down Sunset looking for this club, and I'm thinking with the amount of time M and I spend down here, you'd think I would know where it is. But with Connor, it's a whole new scene.

So his hand is on my knee and it feels warm and nice, so I place my hand on top of his and notice how small mine is in comparison. I've made a pact with myself to not think about how he's leaving for London soon because I'm sure he goes back and forth a lot on business, which means he'll definitely be back. And then the next time I'll probably be going with him and my life will really start.

"It should be coming up on the right. Give a shout if you see it," he says.

"What's the name of it again?" I ask, fingering the hem of my dress and squinting out the window.

"B Bar."

"I think you just missed it." I look in my side-view mirror, watching the neon sign shrink as we drive past it.

"No worries," Connor says, and I clutch the edge of my seat as he makes an illegal U-turn and pulls into the tiny parking lot.

He's holding my hand when we walk inside, and I'm praying

that I won't get carded. But like Harry's, he knows everyone so it's not even an issue.

We sit at a small table near the stage, and Connor leans in and goes, "So the band I want to see is the opening act. I just need to hear a few songs then we can leave if you want. I don't know if you'll like them, they're a little mainstream, and personally I'd rather listen to blues, but there's just more money to be made in pop." He shrugs and smiles and I'm wondering if that's what Richard Branson thought when he signed the Sex Pistols.

So right when they dim the lights and some guy walks on stage to do a mike check, that Sam chick walks right up to our table, leans down, and gives Connor a shot of some major cleavage along with a transatlantic kiss, you know, like one on each cheek. I just sit there and watch them and my stomach feels weird and I'm not sure what to do. When she finally looks at me, I smile and say, "Hey."

"Hey," she says, but I can tell she doesn't mean it.

Connor looks at her then and says, "You remember Alex?"

And Sam just squints at me briefly then looks at Connor and says, "Not really. Should I?"

I just sit there and I don't say anything, even though I can think of like, a million snotty answers to that.

Then Connor goes, "Trevor's party?"

But Sam just gives this innocent shrug, like she's so sorry but she just meets too many important people to remember someone like me, then she grabs the chair next to Connor's and slides it just slightly too close to his. She looks over at me then and gives me a big fake smile and even though I don't smile back, I've got to admit, I'm feeling like I'm in a little over my head right now.

I watch her turn to Connor and start talking in a voice so low it's hard for me to hear, so I just sit there awkwardly and sip my water because I feel like I should do something but I don't really know what.

When the band comes on she finally stops talking and Connor reaches for my hand and gives me a kiss on the side of my neck. I can totally feel her watching us but when I look at her she just looks away.

He's right about the band. I mean, they're not all choreo-graphed and bland in that Backstreet Boys kind of way, but they're definitely too top-ten list for me. But the lead singer is cute enough for MTV and that usually guarantees major record sales and *People* magazine covers.

Halfway through the fourth song Connor puts his mouth to my ear and whispers, "Wanna go?"

I turn and kiss him in a way that means yes and I hope that Sam is watching.

When we stand up to leave he says, "Sam we're taking off, I'll see you at the office tomorrow."

She looks surprised and says, "Where are you guys going? Maybe I'll join you."

Connor shakes his head and says, "We're going home. Calling it a night." Then he grabs my hand and pulls me away from the table and when I look back she's still watching us and it makes me feel really uncomfortable.

When we get to Connor's house I tell him I have to use the bathroom. Then like the second after he shows me where it is, I lock the door, turn on the faucet (so it will muffle the noise), then I practically ransack the place. I mean, I'm going at it like a jealous wife. Looking in his mirrored cabinet, his trash can, behind the plastic shower curtain, under the rug. I even look in the toilet tank because I saw that once on an old *Law and Order* episode.

And the truth is, I don't even know what the hell it is I'm looking for, but I just can't stop. I mean, maybe there will be a stray tube of lipstick lying around, something a blonde would wear. But I don't find anything, so then of course I feel totally ashamed.

I guess I could have saved myself the trouble of making this mess and then having to clean it up, by just coming right out and asking Connor what their deal is. But the truth is, he's not my boyfriend (yet), so it's really none of my business (so far).

Connor is in the living room sitting on the couch in front of a gas log fire. The room is all white walls with no art, no plants, just an overstuffed couch and an old carved door propped up on cinder blocks, and now serving as a coffee table covered in piles of papers, magazines, and CDs. There's some great-sounding blues coming from the speakers and I stand in front of him and ask, "Who is this?"

"Jonny Lang." He grabs my hand and pulls me down next to him.

"He's really good, who is he?" I take a sip from the glass of red wine he hands me and try to calm my nerves.

"He's just a kid. Well, actually he's maybe twenty now, but he was only seventeen when he made this. That's him on guitar and vocals."

I sit on Connor's couch and listen to the sound of yet another teenage overachiever, fully aware of Connor referring to a seventeen year old as "just a kid."

When he puts his arm around me and kisses me, I banish all thoughts of Sam, my crazy jealousy, and Jonny Lang's age, and just try to live in the now.

So, we're on the couch making out and, well, I'll spare some of the details, even though that's the stuff people usually want to know about. Anyway, he unzips my dress and pulls it all the way off and tosses it on the floor. I'm lying there, naked except for my new thong, but now he's pulling that off too, and even though he didn't compliment me on my choice of underwear I'm still glad I bought it because cotton panties would have been embarrassing.

He kisses me everywhere and I even let him continue where we left off last time in the cabana. It's nice, but I'm not sure how long I'm supposed to lie there like that, so I push him off, and start helping him undress. And when we're both lying naked on this beige, slip-covered couch I slide down and do to him what he just did to me. I don't know if that's too gross to mention, but the

fact is, I know how to give a blow job. Anyone who remains a virgin as long as I have pretty much has that covered.

So then he pulls me back up so we're face to face and then he
reaches his hand down to the ground and fumbles around until
he finds his jeans. His weight is sort of shifting on me and it's
kind of getting uncomfortable but when he comes back up with a
condom I breathe a sigh of relief since I really didn't know how to
bring that up. Then all of a sudden he's inside me and we're doing
it. And then we do it again. And then we go into his bedroom and
fall asleep. And it didn't hurt, and I didn't bleed, so go figure.

Chapter 17

When I wake up the next morning, Connor has his arms wrapped tightly around me and I can feel his warm breath on the back of my neck, and I close my eyes and think about how glad I am that I held out so that he was my first. Because I've never, in my entire life, felt as happy, warm, and safe as I do right now. I finally know what it feels like to be in love.

Then he whispers in my ear, "Are you awake?"

And when I nod my head yes, he moves on top of me, and I just lay there kind of still because I'm still not exactly sure just how much I'm supposed to move around. And it's not long until he grips me tightly, and mumbles my name, then he kisses me all over my face (but not on the mouth since neither one of us has brushed our teeth yet), then he rolls off me and says, "I'll be right back."

I lay on my side watching his butt as he walks across the room, and I think about what M said, how losing your virginity is no big deal. But I totally disagree because it really kind of is. I mean, even though I'm still the same person, my relationship with Connor is totally different now. I just feel so much closer to him.

I roll over and look at the clock next to the bed and totally panic when I see that it's already seven-thirty. Shit! There's just no way I'm gonna be able to shower and make it to school in time for first period.

I jump out of bed and run into the living room and start frantically gathering all my clothes together. As I'm struggling with my shoes Connor walks into the room and goes, "What are you doing?"

"Getting dressed," I say as I balance on one heel and adjust the strap.

"Why?" He rubs his eyes, and squints at me.

"Because I'm late."

"Late for what?" He comes over and kisses me. "Come on, take the morning off, we'll have breakfast."

I lean my body into his for a moment and he feels so nice and warm, but then I push him away and get down on my knees and look under the old door/coffee table for my purse. "I can't," I tell him as I reach around on the floor. "I ditched school yesterday and I'm in enough trouble already."

Then I stand up and brush the creases out of my dress and when I look at him I realize I just outed myself. I stand there frozen, holding my stupid kitty purse, knowing that I can't undo this.

"Alex? What did you say?"

Connor is looking at me with a face full of suspicion, and I know I have to come clean so I take a deep breath and say, "Okay. Okay. I know you thought I was in college, but I'm not. I'm only seventeen, well, seventeen and a half actually, almost eighteen! And I'm a senior in high school." I gulp for air like an asthmatic.

Silence.

I take a step toward him and reach for his hand. It lacks emotion and lies limp in mine. "I'm sorry I lied. I guess I just figured you wouldn't want to hang out with me if you knew the truth. But, I'm still the same person, really! That's the only lie, I swear." I look at him desperately and continue to squeeze his nonresponsive fingers.

He's staring at me, and he doesn't look very happy. He shakes his head walks over to the couch, sits down and goes, "Listen, maybe you're right, maybe I wouldn't be hanging out with you if you'd told me you were still in high school. Shit! I'm twenty-three! I'm six years older than you!"

"Five and a half!"

"Alex, please. This is crazy! High school! God, I hesitated when you told me you were nineteen. And we had sex! And you're underage!" He looks really upset and it's all my fault.

"Well, it's not like I'm gonna call the cops! I mean, look, I'm sorry, really, I am." I sit next to him on the couch and try to control my panic.

Then he sighs and says, "Listen, the point is, you do seem a little young sometimes, but it never occurred to me that you were that young."

"I'm sorry," I say. It's all I can say.

I'm facing Connor but he won't look at me, he just sits there staring at the wall. After awhile he turns and says, "Look. You're nice and I've enjoyed hanging out with you. But I don't know about this. This is a little weird."

So then I get up from the couch and rifle through my purse for my keys and by the time I look up I've got my emotions under control just enough to say good-bye.

I'm walking toward the door, when I remember. My car is still parked on the street at Harry's and I don't know how I'm going to get it. I turn and look at Connor still sitting on the couch, but he's so unhappy with me, that I just can't ask him. So I say, "I'm sorry. I'm sorry that I disappointed you, I'm sorry I lied. But I had a nice time last night. Thank you."

I wait for him to say something more but he doesn't.

Chapter 18

I walk hurriedly to the corner and pull my cardigan tight around me. The morning is cold and bright and I wish I had my sunglasses with me, partly because of the sun and partly because my eyes and my dress look like last night and it's kind of embarrassing to be walking around like this.

When I get to the corner I stop and fish my wallet out of my purse to see how much cash I have left. I count only seven dollars and eighty-seven cents, since I spent most of it at the makeup counter and the lingerie department and you see what a good investment in my future that turned out to be.

I have no idea what to do, or how the hell I'm supposed to get to Century City from wherever it is I am. I mean, *I don't even know where I am!* All I know is that it's kind of far because I remember being in the car for awhile on the drive from Harry's and then B Bar. So I just sit on the curb and I put my head in my hands and try to suppress the panic that is building inside me. And I wonder if my life will ever stabilize. It's like at seven-fifteen Connor and I were making love and it felt like we were in love, and then just half an hour later I am *literally* on the curb.

I blow my nose into a slightly used tissue I find in my purse, then I crumble it up and stick it back in there. I'm sorry, if that's gross, but I'm totally opposed to littering. And then I grab my cell phone and call M.

"Hello?"

"M, it's me."

"Hey, where are you? What happened to you yesterday?"

"I'm in LA," I tell her.

"Are you with Connor?" she asks.

"Um, no. Listen, I'm kind of stuck and I need to get my car; it's parked in Century City. Can you come get me?"

"What? Are you kidding? First period starts in like three seconds," she says.

"I know, but I just thought," I bite down on my lower lip. I shouldn't have called her. God, I'm such a loser.

"I'm sorry, but I already missed Monday, I can't skip out today. But you know what you should do? You should call Connor, he'll totally help you," she says.

"Um, yeah, okay," I say, knowing there's no way I'm doing that, but I'm just not ready to tell her yet.

"See you in a few?"

"Yeah, definitely," I say, hanging up and wondering what to do next.

I stand up and brush the wrinkles out of my dress and head for this coffee shop that's just up the block. It looks pretty busy and I figure there's gotta be someone in there that can give me a little direction, or at least tell me where I am.

The place is packed with people who look like they spend most of their days sitting at a desk, in a cubicle, under bad fluorescent lighting. I mean, no one looks very friendly or helpful, so I just grab a place in line and hope that someone behind the counter can help me. When it's my turn I go, "Can you tell me what city this is?"

The girl behind the register just gives me this lousy look and says, "What? You don't know where you are?" Then she starts looking around like she's gonna call for backup or something.

"No, no," I say quickly. "No, of course I know where I am.

What I meant was can you tell me how to get to Century City from here?"

She drums her fingers on the register and goes, "Are you driving?"

"No, um, my car's there. I need to go get it."

"So why don't you take a cab or something?"

"Oh, okay," I say. "Do you know how much that will cost?"

"I don't know," she shrugs. "Ten, fifteen dollars?"

"Oh, that much?" I clutch my purse tighter, knowing that my wallet's close to empty.

She just looks at me, and I can tell she's quickly losing her patience.

"Um, do you have the number for a cab company?" I ask.

"Yeah, four-one-one. Listen, are you gonna get a coffee or what?" She shakes her head and rolls her eyes, and I can feel the people behind me getting impatient so I look at the board and search for the cheapest thing I can order, something that won't cut into my budget. And I go, "Yeah, um, I'll have a cup of the daily brew, oh, a small one please."

I hand over a dollar fifty and she gives me fifteen cents worth of coffee in return and I take it over to a crowded bar with a vacant seat. I put my purse on the counter in front of me and take a sip. It's way too hot, so I blow on it before I take the next one.

The guy on my right has a bad tie, razor burn, and a serious case of male pattern baldness. He's reading the *Wall Street Journal* and I'm guessing he won't want to help me. So I decide to ask the lady on my left, even though she looks only slightly friendlier.

"Hi," I say, interrupting her staring session with the wall. "Um, I was wondering if you could tell me how to get to Century City."

She looks at me and her eyes are etched with deep crow's feet and her nose is covered in these tiny red veins that look like they're exploding, and she doesn't seem as kind as I hoped she might be. "I don't know," she says. "Why don't you call a cab?"

"It's too expensive. I'm running out of money," I tell her.

She looks me over carefully then says, "Why don't you take the bus then? There's a stop on the next block. Why don't you go read the sign?"

I look at her and say, "Okay, thanks." But she doesn't hear me since she's already back to looking at the wall.

I look at my watch and it's eight-fifteen and I can't believe that my day already sucks this much. I mean, I have no idea how to take the bus. The only bus I've ever been on is the school bus. I consider walking back to Connor's and asking him for a ride to my car, but I can't do that. He's just not an option anymore. So I grab my coffee and my purse and head for the bus stop.

The driver is this old guy with a really stern face and I'm kind of afraid to talk to him so I let everyone go ahead and when there's no one left but me he goes, "If you want a ride you better get on now." I climb the two steps and reach for something to grab on to as he pulls away from the curb.

"Um, I was wondering if you could help me?" I ask.

He glances at me briefly and says, "Get behind the white line."

I look down at the floor and sure enough there's a line and I'm apparently on the wrong side of it. So I take a step back and now that I'm standing in the right spot I wonder if I should continue. He seems kind of mean.

He stops at the next light and turns and looks at me, and still stern but a little friendlier, he says, "What do you need?"

"I need to get to Century City and I'm not even sure if this is the right bus."

"This is the right bus," he says, changing gears with the changing light. "But it's only one of them."

"What?" I ask. I feel like we're speaking different languages. Like bus riding is a culture that I'm not a part of.

He shakes his head and goes, "You need to stay on this bus to Santa Monica Boulevard. From there you need to catch the number four to Century Park East. And from there you need to take the twenty-eight to Olympic."

He turns and looks at me and I'm just staring at him. I'll never remember all that. "But that's three different buses!" I say. "How much is that going to cost me?"

"A dollar twenty-five."

"Each?" I ask. Frantically doing the math in my head and hoping I'll have enough.

"Total. It's seventy-five cents plus twenty-five cents for each transfer."

"Where do I get those?" I ask. Digging through my wallet for change.

"You get one from me, and the other on the next bus," he says, handing me a strip of paper. "Now take a seat."

He brakes at the next stop and the bus lurches forward and back and I grab the first available seat because I'm lousy at keeping my balance in a moving vehicle. Then I just sit there and stare out the window at a string of run-down minimalls and try to remember the exact moment when I decided to give up.

By the time I'm at my third bus stop, I realize this is gonna take a lot longer than I thought and that the second-period bell rang a long time ago, and I never called my mom last night to tell her where I was. And even though all that stuff is true, I gotta tell you that part of me feels pretty damn good at having figured this out and getting this far on my own. I mean, most people would have just called a cab. But I didn't have that option so I took a more difficult route and made it all the same.

I dig my cell phone out of my purse and call my mom at work. She's away from her desk so I leave a message and say that I spent the night at M's, and I'm sorry I forgot to call, and that I'll see her tonight. Then I pray that she doesn't decide to follow up on any of that.

When I finally get to my car after a two-and-a-half-hour mass transit tour of LA, I find a piece of pink paper stuck under my windshield wiper. I reach for it excitedly, knowing it's from Connor, and I can't wait to read his apology. But when I turn it over I see that it's only a parking ticket, a love note from the LAPD. I fold it in half and toss it in my glove compartment and head to school.

Chapter 19

'm walking through the quad looking at my watch trying to figure out what class I should be heading to when M runs up and goes, "Is that my dress?"

I look down at the clothes I wore last night and just shrug and say, "Yeah, I guess it is."

"Are you okay?" she asks. " 'Cause you don't look so great."

"Thanks," I say and head for my locker.

"So, what happened?"

She's walking alongside me, giving me a concerned look. I think about the Iguana Man, and Connor dumping me, and the bus ride, and the fact that I'm still a little pissed at her for ditching me, but I just say, "I cut." Then I focus on spinning the lock, trying to remember my combination.

She doesn't say anything but I can hear the disapproval in her breath. Then she goes, "Remember when you told me how my mom was in my room Sunday night, you know, answering my phone and stuff?"

"Yeah." I close my locker and I start walking toward class. It's eleven o'clock, time for Economics, which I think I already had a real-life lesson in this morning.

"Well, shit, I think she found my stash."

"Your what?" I turn and look at her.

"My stash. You know some blunts and stuff that I had hidden in there."

I don't even know what to say to her. I can't believe she's doing drugs. I mean, sometimes I feel like I don't even know her.

"*Hello?* Did you hear me? Anyway, I'm kind of freakin' here. I don't know what to do."

"Are they your drugs?" I stop in the middle of the hall and stare at her.

"Yeah, it's all mine. And shit, I'm totally screwed."

"What kind of drugs did you have?" I ask.

"Shhh!" She looks around nervously then whispers, "Just pot and some X that Trevor and I were gonna do this weekend."

"Jeez, M, what are you doing with that stuff?"

"God, what is this? What are you, a cop?"

I don't say anything. I can't believe she's that far gone.

"Hel-lo?"

"Whatever." I start walking toward class.

"Okay, look. I told you, I'm freaking out."

"Well, what makes you think she found them?"

"Well, this morning I went to wear those JP Todd driving mocs? You know the ones I wear with my jeans and stuff? Well anyway, they're gone. I think my mom borrowed them. She booked herself in at some spa for the week and apparently she took those shoes with her, and unfortunately they're the ones I had my stash in."

"You hide your stash in your shoes?"

"I have immaculate feet."

"Why would you put it there? You know your mom's always taking your stuff."

"Because I didn't think she'd want to wear those. Shit!"

"Well, don't you think if she'd found it she'd cancel her plans and stay home to ask you about it?"

"My mom? Let a little parental responsibility get in the way of a massage and a Botox injection? I don't think so." She shakes her head.

"Well, when is she coming back?" I ask.

"Not until Sunday."

"So, at least you've got the rest of the week to figure a way out of it."

"Yeah, I guess. Hey, so did you call Connor?"

I open the classroom door. I'm not ready to talk about Connor. "M," I say, "you're gonna be late for your psych class. I'll see you at lunch okay?" She gives me a strange look but I close the door on her anyway.

So I buy a salad and a bottle of water and carry it over to our lunch tree, where M is waiting with M&Ms and a Diet Coke. She rips the bag open and starts separating them by color, then she hands me all of the brown ones and lies back on the grass. "Hey, do you have to work today after school?" she asks.

"Yeah, but I'm thinking about calling in sick." God, I'm just losing interest in everything these days.

"Good. Let's go to LA. But, by ourselves, let's not call the guys. Let's just do our own thing."

I'm just about to tell her that my day started in LA and that calling the guys is no longer an option for me, when Tiffany and Amber approach us. Tiffany's wearing a sparkly sling in our school colors and they're standing in front of us, and they look all happy to be hanging out together so I guess that whole Dylan/flirting/vomiting fiasco is over. They look at us and go, "Hey M, hey Alex."

We just look at them and go, "Hey."

Then Tiffany looks me over and goes, "Nice dress."

I say, "Thanks," but I wonder if that was actually sarcasm I heard in her voice.

"So who are you guys going to THE PROM with?" That's how she says it, in capital letters.

I look at her and go, "When is it?"

And now Amber looks at Tiffany and rolls her eyes and shakes her head and Tiffany says, "Hel-*lo*? It's like totally coming up. There's signs all over campus. You still go here right?"

Wow. That was pretty bitchy for someone who recently vomited orange right in front of me. But I just sit there in front of them and shrug and say, "Well, I guess I'm not going then."

"What? Why?" They're both scrutinizing me now, and I know they think I'm hiding something. That deep down inside I must be feeling really sad to not be taking part in this most sacred of high school rituals. They've spent the better half of senior year preparing for this, you know bagging the right date and buying the right dress. It's like almost as important as their SATs. I mean, it's sick how seriously they take all this stuff.

So then Tiffany goes, "Well don't you have a boyfriend or something? I thought I heard M say that you're dating someone."

I look over at M wondering why she would be talking about me to Tiffany but she just shrugs. Then I look back at Tiffany and Amber, standing there, judging me. And I hate to admit it, but part of me cares about what they think. Part of me wants to have something important. So I tell them all about Connor, even though he doesn't really exist for me anymore.

"Well," I say, "actually, I am dating someone. His name is Connor and he's from London, England, but he lives in Los Angeles right now and he owns his own record company. So if the prom is on a Saturday night, then we'll probably be at a club or something so we wont be able to make it." Then I sit back and watch them chew on *that*.

Amber looks at me and raises her eyebrows but doesn't say anything. And Tiffany nods her head and goes, "Cool." And I actually think I detect a little envy.

Then they look at M and ask her if she's going and M nods her head and goes, "Totally."

And I look at her waiting to hear more, but that's all the information she's giving.

And then Tiffany goes, "Well, we're working on the yearbook, as you know, and we're going to have a sort of 'Senior Inspiration' page in it."

I look at them and say, "You guys have been watching way too much *Oprah.*"

M cracks up but they don't think it's funny. So then they go, "What we're doing is going around and asking certain seniors what their biggest achievement has been in their lives so far."

And I'm thinking "certain seniors" means just the popular people. Unpopular people are lucky just to get their class picture published. God, I totally hate this stuff.

So they're looking at M waiting for an answer and she's really deep in thought, obviously taking this question very seriously. Then she goes, "My biggest achievement thus far is being named in the *Who's Who Among American High School Students.*"

I look at her in shock. I didn't even know there was such a thing. They write it down and then look at me waiting for my answer. But I just look at them and shrug and go, "Um, I guess my biggest achievement so far is growing my bangs out." They look at me to see if I'm joking, but I'm not. So they write it down and walk away and I'm thinking I can't wait to see that in print.

The bell rings; man I hate how lunch hour really isn't an hour. I pick up my trash and head to the class I dread the most, AP History. I know it's shallow, but I'm so stuck in the now that it's hard for me to care about things that happened, like, a hundred years ago.

Chapter 20

S o I'm sitting at my desk in AP History, and I'm surrounded by the same people from most of my other classes. All us AP people stick together, we just change rooms that's all. On my desk, lying face down is my test paper from last week. And I really don't want to flip it over because I already know that I choked, and I don't need to see it. I mean, I didn't even read the questions, I just made a perfect zigzag by shading in the *a, b, c, d,* and *e,* circles accordingly, and then I turned it in.

Everyone is eagerly flipping them over and shouting out their results, but I just sit there. I've got a major headache, I'm nauseous and I'm totally sweating. I mean, I'm a wreck. I feel like bolting out of class but I don't want to attract that kind of attention. I know that my life is really getting out of control, that I'm just totally blowing it for myself, but I just can't seem to stop it. I raise my hand and ask my teacher if I can get a hall pass for the restroom. He gives me the pass and a disapproving look.

I grab my test paper, and stash it in my purse and run out of the room. I barely make it to the stall when I start vomiting. The salad I just ate is history. I drag myself over to the mirror and stare intently at my reflection. I look like a girl who didn't go home last night. I look like a girl that normal girls back away from. I splash cold water on my face, swish it around in my mouth and spit it back into the sink. Then I brush my hair, and fix my makeup, and swallow a mint that I found unwrapped at the bottom of my purse.

I look better now, but I still feel awful and I know that it's not at all physical but completely emotional. I pull my test paper out of my purse, and rip it into tiny shreds. I drop the pieces slowly into the trash, watching them fall, but never once looking at my score. I'm not even curious.

I'm tempted to stay in the bathroom until the bell rings. I'm tempted to stay in here until graduation. But then this girl walks in, leans against the wall, gives me a sullen look, and lights a cigarette. We just sort of look at each other then she says, "Hey, what class are you ditching?"

"AP History," I say. "But I'm not ditching. I just had to use the bathroom."

She takes a drag on her cigarette. "AP? Really?" She squints at me through the smoke.

"Yeah really. Why?" I ask, somewhat defensively.

She shrugs, "I just didn't picture you as the type."

I just look at her for a moment and I wonder what she means by that. "What year are you?" I ask.

"Sophomore."

Well that explains it. She doesn't know my history. She didn't know me in my glory days. "I used to be involved," I tell her. "I used to win contests, and elections. I used to care about things. I wasn't always like this," I say.

"Whatever." She rolls her eyes and takes another drag.

And I'm left standing there feeling like a loser for going on like that. Because the truth is, it doesn't really matter who I used to be. It's all about who I've become.

"Well anyway," I say, turning to leave.

"Hey do you have a breath mint so I won't reek when I go to my next class?" she asks.

"No," I tell her, shaking my head. "You're on your own."

———

When I walk back in the classroom my teacher totally ignores me. I mean, his lecture doesn't miss a beat, and I'm wondering if I'm invisible to people now. Like I'm so pathetic that people just refuse to see me. I sit at my desk and realize I have no idea what this lecture is about, or even what we are supposed to be studying. A couple of students raise their hands to ask questions, and I am amazed at their powers of concentration. I wonder if they really care about the answers or if they've just figured out that he likes it when you show interest.

After thirty minutes of doodling on a piece of notebook paper, pretending I'm taking notes, the bell finally rings and I gather my things and get up to leave when my teacher asks me if I could stay a minute. I don't really want to but I realize it's what you call a rhetorical question. I slowly sink back into my chair and try to ignore the smirks of my fellow AP students as they leave the room. When the last one is gone, he gets up and shuts the door and takes a seat at the desk next to mine. I'm sweating big time and don't care for the proximity, but I remain silent, I mean, I just sit there.

"Are you aware that you're failing this class?" he says.

I nod.

"Well, I'm wondering what we are going to do about it."

I'm thinking, "*We?*" but I just shrug.

"I'm wondering why I can't seem to reach you." He leans toward me and it's creeping me out. "I take it somewhat personally when a bright student like you fails. It makes me feel as though I'm also failing, by not being able to reach you, by not being able to inspire you."

And then I get it. What he really wants is for me to confirm what a great teacher he is. For me to take full responsibility for my sorry performance. To let him off the hook. I'm more than willing to do this. If it means cutting this short, I'll say just about anything. So I clear my throat and say, "I've been having a rough year at home. I have to work. I mean, I'm working a lot, and sometimes I have trouble concentrating, but it's absolutely, entirely, one hundred percent my fault. You are a wonderful teacher, really inspiring, it's just me, it's all me, the problem is mine." This seems to satisfy him. Adults are no different from us. They're all ego and insecurity.

I bolt out of class, I mean, I really run. I don't stop until I get to the parking lot and see M waiting in her car. I jump in without opening the door, and M goes, "Wow, that's what Brandon used to do on *90210*." I throw my books on the floor and crank the volume on her car stereo. I put on my sunglasses and sit back and decide to just let go of it all, to just be in the moment. To locate my Zen spot. Some students wave at us as we pull out of the parking lot, but we just totally ignore them. We get on the freeway and head to LA.

"Where should we go?" M asks.

That's kind of a weird question because we always just do the same old stuff. Veggie rolls, shopping, coffee, drinking, meeting people, then singing to some CD all the way home. I just look at her and shrug, "I don't know, the usual I guess." And then I go, "No, you know what? Let's do something different. I'm really up for something new, aren't you?" And I think I am. I mean, the last person I want to run into is the Iguana Man. Well, the Iguana Man and Connor.

Chapter 21

We decide to go to Griffith Park Observatory and check out the telescopes. I haven't been there since a class trip in sixth grade when we briefly studied the solar system, and all the planets and stuff, and I dreamed, (for a short time) about being an astronomer.

I had the biggest crush ever on the second cutest boy in the class. His name was Bobby and M had a crush on the first cutest boy in the class, Bobby's best friend Wes.

So that day we were all nervous about who we were going to sit with on the bus and who we were going to sit with in *the dark* during the laser show. I remember some notes being exchanged and some whispering going on for days beforehand and even though we didn't sit next to them on the bus, we definitely sat next to them during the show. And since it was dark and the teachers and chaperones were all in another row, Bobby reached over and held my hand. And at one point, while the laser lights were all dancing to that Rolling Stones song, "Angie," he kissed me on the lips. It was the kind of kiss we used to call a "romantic kiss," which meant it wasn't from a relative, it lasted more than ten seconds, and it involved two tongues. I remember feeling so great about it, and being so happy. And to this day I cannot listen to that song without thinking of Bobby holding my hand and kissing me.

We're driving up the long, winding road that leads to the Observatory when M blurts out, "My dad is having an affair." The statement just sort of hangs in the air, taking shape. And I'm really surprised, though I'm not sure why. I guess I just always thought M would be protected from all that.

Not knowing what else to say, I ask, "Are you sure?"

"Oh, yeah. I'm sure." She turns to look at me briefly. "I saw him with another woman. Remember that medical conference he was supposed to be at? Well he wasn't. He was in LA shacking up with his girlfriend at the Hotel Bel Air. Trevor and I went there for lunch on Sunday and I saw them at the bar. They were holding hands but they may as well have been fucking."

I just sit there, looking at her.

Then she shakes her head and says, "And do you know what the worst part is, the really fucking sick part? My mom knows. I know she knows. I can tell. She's known all along. And it's not like she's taking some liberal, European view of these things. Oh no. She just looks the other way because she's enjoying the cars, and vacations, and credit cards so damn much. Just can't bear to give all that up. She has no intention of going to work, or even setting a goddamn alarm clock for that matter. It's probably been going on for years. But she'd rather be well dressed and in denial, than grab hold of her life and not be two-timed like that. You should have seen them together, they looked really happy."

"Did he see you?" I ask.

She sighs, "No, and that's the good thing because I wasn't where I said I would be, but then again, neither was he."

"So what happens now? Do you think they'll get divorced?"

She looks in her rearview mirror and changes lanes. "Not a chance. My mom would never allow it, and my dad's got the best of both worlds, why would he mess with that? God, the least she could do is screw the pool boy, I might have more respect for her if she did that."

M says that, but I know she doesn't mean it.

"Do you realize how important it is to be independent? To be able to take care of yourself? To not rely on someone else for your most basic needs? And to not get so damn attached to stuff that you'd rather demean yourself than live without it?" She grips the steering wheel and looks at me and I tell her I'm pretty well versed in all of that.

She parks the car and we walk toward the building. Night is falling quickly and I run over to the nearest telescope, insert a quarter, and look at all the big houses until the sun disappears. Then we go inside and walk around reading the exhibits and looking at the people. There's a pretty big crowd here for the laser show, and they're not all stoners either.

M buys me a ticket and we grab two seats and wait for the show to start. I feel sorry for M, I really do. I've been where she is. I know what it's like to have your parents play Russian Roulette with your future.

The lights go out and I lay my head back on the padded neck rest. I watch the ceiling light up in a riot of color and sound as the squiggly stars and lights dance to seventies glam rock, David Bowie, Lou Reed, Iggy Pop. I love all that old music. I look over at M and see that she's crying so I look away, giving her some privacy.

Chapter 22

After the show we end up at this little sushi joint that unfortunately is not far from Connor's house. And I'm sitting here feeling really nervous, and wishing I was somewhere else, because I don't want to see him. But I couldn't tell M that, because she's so upset about her dad, and she really wanted sushi, and it's almost like if I don't talk about it, then I can pretend it didn't really happen. Which is probably a sign of mental instability, but I can't help it, I'm just not ready to face it.

M orders two big hot sakes and nearly one of everything on the menu. But I just stick with the California rolls. I like my fish cooked. I'm making a humiliating attempt to eat with my chopsticks when she goes, "So what really happened to you yesterday and this morning?"

I look at her and I know I should tell the truth, that my lying is really getting out of control, but I don't want to talk about the bad stuff so I go, "I hung out with Connor." Then I look down at my plate, determined to secure my California roll between those stupid chopsticks.

"Really?" she asks.

"Really," I tell her. Then I plop the roll into my mouth and when I'm done chewing I go, "And we slept together."

"No way!"

"Way." I look at her and nod my head affirmatively.

"And? Come on, you have to tell me," she pleads.

"And . . . it was . . . good," I say, suddenly wishing I hadn't mentioned it.

But she nods her head eagerly, waiting for something more, so I lean in and go, "We did it like, three times."

"Really?" she says.

Her eyes are wide and she's looking right at me, and I hate to lie but so far, technically, everything I said is true. "Really . . . it was really . . . nice," I say.

"Wow. Are you guys like, in love now?"

I look down at my plate and shrug.

"Come on, give it up. I can tell you're totally into him."

I just shrug, and when I look at her I try to smile but it feels false on my face.

"You know Alex, I can't believe how lucky we are right now. I mean, I have Trevor, you have Connor, and it's like, so big time, you know?"

"Yeah," I say, and then I look over at the door and freeze.

M sees me looking and goes, "Oh my god! Isn't that Connor?"

I look down at my plate because I don't want him to see me looking at him. "Who's he with?" I whisper.

She squints toward the door. "Some strange-looking guy I don't know and some blond chick."

"Does she look like Madonna?" I hold my breath.

"No, more like Heather Graham."

"That's what I mean," I say. "Ray of Light Madonna." And then I look up again, just in time to see Connor, James, and that girl Sam leaving the restaurant.

"They're leaving! Aren't you gonna say hi?" M looks at me in disbelief.

"No." I shake my head, but my eyes are glued to the door.

"You're such a chicken!"

She starts to get up from the table to do it for me, when I go, "M, no!"

But she ignores me and stands up and goes, "Connor! Hey!"

And while she's waving her arms around, I'm sinking lower in my chair. I see Sam look back at me and roll her eyes. But James doesn't see me because he's already out the door. Then Connor stops and turns and looks right at me and I feel my stomach go all weird, and I'm hoping that he'll smile and come over and tell me he's sorry, and he misses me, and he wants me back. But instead he just hesitates at the door, gives me a sort of half wave, and then follows his friends outside.

M stares after him and goes, "What was that about? Why did he leave?"

I just shake my head and go, "There's something I didn't tell you." And I feel like a total loser for having to say what I'm about to.

And then I tell her everything.

When I'm finished she just looks at me and goes, "You kept this in all day? Until now?"

I nod.

"Why? Why didn't you tell me?"

"I couldn't." I look down at my chopsticks and tap them against the side of my plate.

"Oh man. I don't even know what to say."

"Well that's a first." I try to laugh but it feels like the end of the world.

"God, I'm so sorry. Connor's a jerk. I can't believe he just walked out like that, without saying anything. What an ass."

I shake my head. "No, he's not. He's just a guy. And I lied to him." I bite down on my lower lip and try to keep from crying.

"Oh my god, do you think he's doing it with that Sam chick?" M asks, her eyes wide.

"I can't even think about that," I say.

She looks at me for a long time then she goes, "I'm really sorry."

I just shrug.

"Well, at least you're not a virgin anymore."

"What's that supposed to mean?" I ask.

"Well, it's just that it's out of the way now. You can just move on. It's like, now it won't be such a big deal to you."

I run my finger along the rim of my empty sake cup and say, "Well, I don't know about that. I mean, it kind of is a big deal and I can't imagine it ever not being a big deal." I shake my head. "Do you remember that time we got really tanked on vodka, and watched your dad's porno tapes?"

M starts laughing, "Yeah, we were sophomores, right?"

"Yeah. Well, when we were watching those, I remember thinking that there was no way that all that suntanned, silicone, video stuff really represented the real thing. I just couldn't believe it could be that detached when you let some other person inside your body. Do you remember how in that one movie, the star, right in the middle of some heavy thrusting, checked out the time on her watch?"

M laughs. "Yeah, I guess they missed that in the editing room."

"Well, when I first woke up I felt so happy and special. You know, like I had something really good in my life. But later, when it was over and I was out on the street, I felt like the girl with the watch. I felt disposable."

"Don't say that." M looks at me, alarmed.

"It's true. That's how I feel. And I'll probably never see him again, since it's pretty clear he doesn't want to see me." I push my sake cup away and fold my napkin.

M looks at me and grabs my hand from across the table. "You know what?" she says. "Most of the time it doesn't work out. That's just the way it is."

Then she pays the bill with her dad's credit card and we go home.

Chapter 23

When I walked in the door I found my mom sitting at the kitchen table, apparently waiting up for me. Something about the look on her face told me I was in big trouble.

"Alexandra, where have you been?" she asks.

Okay, she hasn't done this to me, like, ever. And it's making me nervous but I just go, "At school, and then I went shopping with M."

"And yesterday?"

And I go, "Yeah, and yesterday too." Because it's not really a lie if you think about it. I mean, I did start my day at school and I did go shopping.

"That's not what the school says."

"What do you mean?" I nervously shift my purse to my other shoulder and wait.

"They called me at work to say that you had an unexcused absence yesterday, and that you missed your first three classes this morning. They say you weren't there, you say you were. Who's right?"

She's not fooling around and I know I can't lie anymore. I mean, all these lies are just making everything worse. So I take a deep breath and go, "Um, they are?"

She nods her head and drums her fingers on the table. After a moment she asks, "And where were you if you weren't at school?"

I rub the toe of my shoe against the linoleum floor and say, "With a friend." And I feel like the world's biggest loser.

"Which friend? M?"

I take a deep breath, "No."

My mom just looks at me and shakes her head and says, "I don't know what to do with you anymore. But you cannot go on like this. Not under my roof. You've completely abused the freedom I gave you so now I'm going to take it away. You're grounded."

"What?"

"Until further notice."

"You can't ground me!" I say.

"I just did. I want you in school every day, and on the nights you're not working I want you home doing your homework."

"Like it matters," I mumble under my breath and start to leave the room.

"What did you say to me?"

"I said, what does it matter?" I turn around and face her and I'm screaming but I don't care. "I told you the truth, but you punish me anyway! It's like I can't win no matter what I do!"

"Has it ever occurred to you that maybe you won't let yourself win?"

I stand in front of her and roll my eyes, but I don't say anything.

"Alex, you have to apply yourself to something! You cannot continue like this."

"In case you don't get it mom, I'm not going to college! I messed up my grades so bad that I can't get a scholarship, and Dad won't help me because he sunk all of his money into his midlife-crisis kit with his bachelor pad, his Porsche, and his girlfriend's new boobs! And you certainly can't help me. So why bother with high school? Why try?"

My mom just looks at me and shakes her head and says, "Because at seventeen your mistakes are not permanent. There's no reason you can't turn your life around." She looks more frustrated than mad.

"Whatever," I roll my eyes and shake my head.

"You are the only one who can make your dreams happen." She says it quietly and emphatically and it really pisses me off.

"What're you quoting Hallmark now?" I give her an angry look.

"I'm serious. If you want to make something of yourself, it's going to be up to you. Don't expect other people to help you."

"Nobody gets it," I scream.

"Maybe you're the one that doesn't get it." She gives me a hard look and I grab my stuff and I run out of the kitchen. And when I get to my room I slam the door as hard as I can and throw my stuff against the wall and watch it fall to the ground. Then I pick up that stupid *Anna K* book and rip the cover off and crumple it up and toss it in the trash. Then I throw myself on my bed, and wonder if this is what "rock bottom" feels like.

Chapter 24

The next day at school I'm walking to our lunch tree and I can't help but notice all the sparkly prom signs hanging all over campus. It's like Tiffany and her prom crew went a little crazy with the silver glitter, and exclamation points. Apparently this year's theme is "My Heart Will Go On" and since I'm trying to be more honest I'm just gonna come right out and say how much I despise that song, and don't even get me started on the person who sings it.

Yet part of me also feels bad about not being able to care about this stuff. It's like the whole damn school is so into this. I mean, the girls that aren't going think about it just as much as the girls that are going. And I wish I could be on either one of those teams. Either the excited ones that're busy buying their stupid celebrity-knock-off prom dresses, or the reject ones who will sit in their rooms on prom night listening to that stupid prom song over and over again and wishing they were important, and popular like Tiffany, or Amber, or maybe even M. And I wish this because if I belonged to either one of these groups that would mean that I care about something that matters to other people. That would make me someone who belongs to something. But like this, I'm totally on my own. I mean, if what they say is true, if these are truly the best years of my life, then I'm totally screwed.

M is waiting for me under the tree, with a big fruit salad her maid packed for her this morning, and just as I figured, she's totally panicked about snagging a prom date. And there's no way she's asking Trevor. I mean, she might kind of like showing him off, but she's also pretty hesitant about involving him in the more juvenile side of her life. So now she's in a total state of emergency since she pretty much spent the better part of our junior and senior years blowing off every guy in our school that had the slightest interest in her. So now she's gonna have to find someone from another school. Only she doesn't really know anyone from any other school.

"Shit, what am I gonna do?" she asks.

"I thought you didn't care about going to the prom?" I say, stealing a strawberry.

She looks at me and rolls her eyes and goes, "You know I have to go. I'm a cheerleader for god's sake, how will it look if I don't show up?"

"And what will you tell your grandchildren?" I reach for a piece of pineapple.

The warning bell rings but we just continue to sit there. "So what's going on this weekend?" she asks. "Are we hanging in LA or what?"

"Maybe you are but, technically, I'm grounded," I tell her.

"What?"

"You heard me."

"I heard you but I can't believe what I heard. Aren't we a little too old for that?"

"That's what I thought, but my mom has other ideas." I take another strawberry and hand her the lid to the plastic container.

"You're not going along with it are you?" M looks at me like I'm crazy.

"Well, actually, I'm thinking that if I'm good today and tomorrow then maybe I'll get time off for good behavior this weekend."

"That's just weird," M shakes her head.

"Tell me."

"Have you heard from Connor?"

"No. Thanks for asking though." I shake my head.

"I didn't mean anything by it. I'm kind of surprised really. You know he told Trevor that we were underage."

"And?"

"Trevor didn't seem to care, he thought it was kind of funny. He likes the idea of corrupting a minor. Pervert."

I just roll my eyes. "Hey, did anything ever come of that missing stash?"

M starts gathering her things and stands up. "Yeah, my mom found it when she went to wear those shoes," she says without looking at me.

"And you didn't mention that until just now? What happened?"

M just shrugs, "It's really no big deal. I'm not in trouble if that's what you're worried about."

"You mean she didn't care?" I ask.

"Well, we talked about it last night on the phone, but I convinced her that I don't have a problem and they're not mine."

I notice that she still won't look at me. "What? Did you blame it on the maid?" I stand there staring at her; she's acting really strange.

She starts walking away, then turns around and says, "No, I just said I was holding it for someone. Listen, I need to get to class. You do too. We'll talk later okay?"

I just stand there and watch her walk away and wonder what is going on with her.

Chapter 25

So, my mom did not give me the weekend off for good behavior. Apparently she is taking this whole discipline thing very seriously. And even though I think it's a little late in the game to start all this, the pathetic truth is that other than going to work, I don't have anything else to do anyway.

So Sunday morning I'm sitting at my desk, working on my Tolstoy paper, if you can believe it. I even woke up early to get started on it since I spent last night in front of the TV, and everyone knows that Saturday night network TV is nothing but bad sitcoms, and bad made-for-TV movies starring former stars of bad sitcoms. I mean, you can just picture those overpaid network executives sitting around some big table, drinking mineral water and saying things like, "Just put on any old piece of shit from seven to midnight since only losers watch on the weekends."

Well, my mom knocks on my door, and when I get up to open it she's standing there with a strange look on her face. Then she says, "M's here."

I open the door wide and find M standing behind my mom and now I know what the weird look was all about. I pull M into my room and quickly close the door on my mom's curiosity.

I watch her plop herself onto my bed and I go, "So what's

going on with you? You look, tired," I say. Even though everyone knows that "tired" really means "awful."

"Thanks a lot," she says rolling her eyes. "Do you have something I can change into?"

I open a drawer and toss her a pair of sweatpants and a tank top. She strips off a tiny black dress I've never seen before and a pair of Jimmy Choo sandals that belong to her mother, puts on the sweats, then grabs a tissue from a box on my dresser and starts wiping off last night's makeup.

"So you want to hear it?" She looks at me through the mirror.

"Whenever you're ready," I tell her.

"Okay." She sits on my bed with one eye still made up and goes, "Trevor and I had a little argument this morning. We broke up."

"Oh my god, what happened?" I ask.

She gets up from the bed and walks toward the mirror. She stands in front of it looking at herself and then grabs a tissue and goes to work on the other eye. "You won't even believe it," she says.

"Tell me."

"Start to finish? Or just the good stuff?"

"Whatever."

"Okay, well, we were out last night having fun at this club, hanging out in the VIP room, which by the way, is so awesome, I don't know if I can ever not be in a VIP room. Anyway, Trevor goes to the bathroom and some friend of his asks me if I want to dance. So I'm like, 'Okay,' so we start dancing. Then Trevor comes back and when he sees me he comes over and taps me on the shoulder and says he wants to go home."

"Why did he want to go home?"

" 'Cause he's an ass that's why." She's finished with her eye and now she's using my hairbrush. "So anyway, I'm having a good time and I really don't feel like leaving, but I'm not gonna argue about it either, so I wave good-bye to his friend and follow Trevor outside. So we're in the car driving home and he asks me if I had a good time dancing with Jake. So I go, 'Who's Jake?' And he goes, 'Jake is the guy you were dancing with.' And I go, 'I'm a little lost here, where are you going with this?' And he goes, 'I'm going nowhere, we're going nowhere.' And I go, 'Whatever.' "

"What was that all about?" I ask. "That doesn't sound like Trevor."

"It sounds like all of them if you think about it, competitive, territorial, caveman! So then we get back to the house and do a little X."

"You did ecstasy?"

She rolls her eyes.

"Jeez, I still can't believe you're doing X."

"Don't get all preachy on me. It's practically easier to do X than to not do X these days. You're like some, I don't know, DEA wannabe." She makes a face at me and pulls her long blonde hair back into a ponytail.

"Whatever." I grab a magazine and start flipping through it.

"Okay, I'm sorry. Listen, I just wanted to try it. I mean, what's the big deal? It just makes you feel really really happy. *You* should try it."

"I'm already really, really happy," I tell her.

"Alex, I don't want to argue with you. I've had a long night."

I roll my eyes.

"Okay, so where was I? Oh yeah, we take the pills and we crank some music and get a little wild. You know, just running around, dancing and stuff. At some point we pass out. Then when we wake up this morning we're rolling around under the sheets when my hand gets caught in something. So I pull my hand out from under the blanket to see what it is and hanging off of my wrist is a pair of little, pink, thong panties. I hold my hand up to the light and just look at them for a minute. Then I put my hand right up in Trevor's face, really close you know, and I say, 'You bastard!' He looks like a deer caught in headlights and he's trying to say that they're mine."

"But you hate pink," I say.

"Exactly. So then I go, 'You fucking bastard! You didn't even change the fucking sheets!' Then I throw the panties at him and they land on his head!" She starts laughing then. "You should have seen it. He looked like that picture of Monica Lewinsky that they always show! You know the one where she's wearing the beret? So then I get up, grab my clothes, and go into the bathroom. Asshole is banging on the door all the while trying to get me to come out. He's got a really good explanation he says. And all I can think of is last night when he blasts me for very innocently dancing with Jake, or whatever his name is. That is sooo typical. It's always the guilty one who convicts!" She uses what's left of my Dior Addict sample, dabbing it on each wrist, and lies down on my bed.

"When I finally vacate the bathroom I find him sleeping in the hall next to the door. So just as I'm trying to step over him he grabs my ankle and begs me to just please listen to him. I tell him to let go of my ankle. And he goes, 'Just please listen to me,' and I go, 'Let go of my ankle or I'm gonna kick you.' And he goes, 'C'mon M.' And then I kick him and I go, 'See I told you I was gonna kick you. I'm not the liar here.' And then I left." She looks at me and shakes her head.

"Wow."

"Tell me about it."

"All of that happened last night?" I ask.

"Can you believe it?" She sits up and reaches in her purse for a cigarette.

"Don't smoke that, my mom will freak."

"Oh, sorry." I watch her toss it back in her purse.

"So whose panties were they?"

"I don't care." She shrugs.

"Are you sure? Because it kind of seems like you do."

"What am I supposed to do? Take them in for DNA testing?"

I just shrug. "So what are you gonna do?"

"Ignore him and act like I don't care."

"So you do care."

"Of course I care! We were having such a good time together! My god, first my dad, and now Trevor. Chain of pain, it never ends."

"I'm sorry."

"Yeah, me too. Hey, I'm really tired," she says. "Do you mind if I sleep here for a little while? I don't feel like going home."

"Why? Are your parents there?" I ask.

She shakes her head. "No, I've barely seen them all month. I just don't feel like being alone right now."

"Feel free," I say.

She lies down and pulls the comforter up over her head and dozes off immediately. I sit in my chair and watch her sleep and think how weird it is that she doesn't want to go home. I always thought M was really lucky that her parents were never around. I mean, she just has so much freedom. I guess I never realized that she might not see it as such a great thing.

It's weird because M's parents are still married but it's like she's divorced from them, and my parents are divorced but I still have my mom. I mean, even though she put me on restriction and stuff, at least I know that she cares about me.

I turn back to my desk and crack open my Tolstoy novel (with the cover still slightly crumpled but taped back on), and get back to work.

Chapter 26

After like, a week and a half of being grounded (which translates to nine days of me being on my best behavior), Friday morning finally arrived and I was praying for an early release from my mother's sudden and inexplicable totalitarian rule. I was up, dressed, and in the kitchen grabbing a Pop-Tart to take to school when my mom walked in and said, "About this weekend."

"Yeah?" I look up at her all nervous, positive she's going to extend my punishment."

"Would you be all right if I left you here alone?"

Is she kidding? "Sure," I answer as nonchalant as possible. "Why? Are you going somewhere?"

"Your aunt Sandy invited me down to San Diego for the weekend. I'm leaving after work and I won't be home until Sunday."

"Okay," I say, trying to contain my excitement.

She looks at me very seriously. "You've acted very mature this last week, so I'm going to end your restriction now. I hope that I can trust you while I'm gone?"

"Of course you can," I say.

"Good." She looks at me steadily. "Have a good day at school. I'll see you on Sunday." She goes into her bedroom to get dressed for work, and I can barely wait to tell M the good news.

But I don't see her until history class since all the cheerleaders were away on some kind of school spirit field trip. So I just walk in and wave at her on the other side of the room and go to my desk. After roll call, my teacher walks up to the chalkboard and starts writing down all these random dates. And with each new one he shouts, "What happened on this date?"

And then everyone gets all competitive to see who can yell out the answer first. I'm just sitting there, staring at the chalkboard, and none of it looks familiar. I mean, the only date I've memorized is the one on my fake ID.

I try to look interested and involved, and I even flip through my textbook trying to find an answer, but the truth is, I don't even know what chapter we're on. So after awhile I just give up and put my head on my desk and I stay like that until the bell rings and my teacher doesn't say a word about it. He gives us an assignment right before he releases us but I don't waste my time writing it down since I know I won't be doing it anyway.

I wait for M outside the door and we walk toward the student parking lot. "What's going on this weekend?" she asks.

"I don't know. I don't have any plans, but my mom's out of town, and I'm off restriction."

"Really?"

"Yeah, really," I say.

"Wanna go to LA?" She opens her car door and throws her books in the back.

"And do what?" I ask.

"Do whatever," she says, starting her car.

Something about the way she said that makes me suspicious, but I'm tired of being under house arrest. So against my better judgment, I throw my stuff into the back and climb in.

We're in this boutique on Robertson when M goes, "I've got a plan. I'm going to nonstop shop. I'm going to swipe this credit card until it bleeds. And when the bill comes in, and my dad tries to confront me with it, well I'm just gonna inform him that I saw him with a certain redhead at the Hotel Bel Air and ask him just what he plans to do about that."

"Uh, that's called blackmail," I say.

"I don't care."

She's loading up on all kinds of stuff and trying to convince me to do the same. And while I may be tempted, I just don't feel right about being part of that plan.

My job in the fitting room is to make stacks of yes's and no's as she rapidly works through the piles of clothes. She just sort of throws stuff on the floor when she's done with it, kicking the piles with her foot. And it bugs me to watch her do that since I work in retail and I'm the one that has to go in later to clean it up, just like I'm doing now.

She tries on a pair of dark denim jeans and they really rock. "Here, try these on, they'll look good on you," she says as she takes them off and tosses them at me.

So I squeeze them over my hips and zip 'em up. God, they fit perfect, low and tight, these are seriously the coolest, but when I look at the price tag, it's more than I make in two weeks, and there's just no way I can afford it. So I hand them back to M and think about how much it sucks living in Southern California when you're impoverished. It's such a celebrity stuffed, look-at-me place, and if you're gonna live here you've got to try to keep up. I mean, sometimes I wish I didn't care about having stuff, but I just can't help it. I'm a resident.

I help her carry all the bags to her car and then she hands me the one with the cool jeans, and goes, "Here, they look better on you anyway."

I hold the bag in my hand and go, "I can't take these from you."

"But they're not from me. They're from my father. Enjoy."

"But what if he finds out?"

"God, you're such a Girl Scout. Relax, he won't find out. Besides, he does not want to mess with me right now. He just doesn't." She slams the door, and starts the car and pulls into traffic.

So we're driving around, trying to figure out what to do next when we see the Java Daze sign and decide to go in. It's this really cool, independent coffee bar and last time we went there we saw Brad and Jen wearing tank tops and cargo pants and drinking chai teas.

M orders her coffee first and I hate to admit it but she's a totally typical California coffee drinker. You know what I mean? It's like, "I'll have a café latte please, but with skim milk not two percent, and with nonfat whipped cream, and I'll put my own sprinkles on so if you could just give them to me in a little cup on the side please." By the time she's finished it's like the next day already. When it's my turn I just order, "One latte, fat and bitter." My god it's just coffee, you know?

So we're sitting at this table and I'm just playing with the foam on my latte while M is sitting there counting her sprinkles. I know she's looking for just the right number and then she'll add them into her coffee. It has something to do with calories, or numerology, or feng-shui. I forget. I mean, it's just one of her quirks.

I notice these two guys at another table and they're really cute and I can tell they're looking at us, but they're trying to be all cool about it, you know like, Okay maybe I'm looking at you but if you don't look back it's okay because I'm secure and girls like me. That kind of thing.

So I look away and start drinking my coffee because if they want to talk they know where to find us. And then like two minutes later I hear someone go, "Hi, my name's Guy."

And I look up and one of them is standing right next to me with his hand extended, waiting to be shaken.

So I shake his hand and go, "I'm Alex, this is M."

Then M looks over at the other table and goes, "Well, what about your friend over there?"

Guy starts laughing and waves his friend over and we start rearranging the table and chairs so there's room for everyone.

"So, what's your story?" M asks Guy's friend Mark, when we're all settled in.

He just kind of shrugs and goes, "Well, we were just out . . ."

"No, no, not that stuff. I mean like what do you do?"

So Mark looks at Guy then he goes, "Oh, well, we're both in grad school."

"Really?" M asks as though she's truly fascinated. "What are you studying?"

"We're both studying economics. And then I'm going on to law school." He smiles at her.

"Hmm," says M. "Well then maybe you should give me your card, I have a feeling I'm going to need a good lawyer someday." She leans in and smiles and Mark has the look of a grand-prize winner.

"So what's your story?" he asks, leaning in closer to her.

M looks at me briefly then goes, "Well, Alex and I are both finishing up our undergrad and planning a big trip to celebrate."

"A trip?"

"Yeah. We're planning a trip to Europe. We're leaving in three weeks!"

"Where are you guys going?" Guy looks at me. But I have no idea where we're going on this fantasy trip so I just look at M.

"Oh, we're just traveling around. We're doing the whole Eurailpass thing. We'll probably end up in Greece or something. We'll be gone for the whole summer, maybe longer."

"Wow, that sounds great," he says.

I look at Guy smiling at me and I feel really bad about lying, but now that it's out there I have to play along. So I smile back and nod my head and say, "Doesn't it? Doesn't it sound great? I really can't wait."

We're finishing up our coffees when Guy goes, "Hey, I know it's short notice and all but there's a party tonight in Brentwood, if you guys want to go. Or if you're busy now, I can just give you the address and stuff and maybe we can meet up later. There's supposed to be a band, so it should go on pretty late."

I kind of want to go, I mean, I think it could be fun, and he's really cute. But then M goes, "Oh, that sounds great, but we already have plans. Maybe some other time?"

So we exchange numbers and say good-bye and when we're back inside the car I go, "What are these other plans we supposedly have?"

M looks at me and says, "Don't tell me you wanted to go to that stupid party in Brentwood?"

"How do you know it was stupid?" I ask.

"Oh, please. It's probably some retard frat party with a bunch of drunken college boys trying to get to third base."

"I thought they were nice, and really cute too," I say, defending them.

"Yeah? I thought they were dweebs. I've got something much better lined up for you anyway."

"What?" I ask, staring at her.

But she just looks at me and smiles.

Shit. I knew she was up to something back in the school parking lot when she was trying to act all spontaneous about coming up here. I mean, let's face it, M's always got a plan. And now, like it or not, I'm part of it.

Chapter 27

I'm just looking out the window, listening to some CD, and not talking to M since I've now asked her three times where we're going and she just keeps saying, "You'll see."

And when we pull into the driveway, I can't say I'm surprised but I'm definitely pissed. "Why are we here?" I ask.

She just looks at me and goes, "He invited us."

"Why? I thought you guys broke up?"

"We made up." She shrugs.

"What? When?" I ask.

"The other night, on the phone. And don't be so judgmental. I really like him."

"But what about the panties and stuff?"

She rolls her eyes and pulls the key from the ignition. "There is no 'and stuff,' it was just those stupid panties, and he explained it to me and it made sense. I was clearly overreacting."

"Are you kidding me?" I look at her like she's crazy. "What could he have possibly said that could make you think you were overreacting?"

M gives me an impatient look and says, "They have maids, and a lot of house guests. This is his parents' house you know."

"So?"

"So, the maid makes the bed. It's not like Trevor does that. She washes the sheets too, so the underwear got tangled in the sheets in the wash and ended up in the bed like that. That's why I didn't find them until the next morning, they came loose in the night."

She looks at me and smiles and I can't believe that she's willing to believe a story like that. I shake my head and look at the house I refuse to go inside of.

She opens the car door and gets out, then stops and stares at me 'cause I'm still just sitting there. "Are you coming?" she asks.

I turn and look at her standing there all excited to see Trevor and totally annoyed with me, and I'm not at all happy about this. I mean, what if Connor's here? So I just look at her and shake my head and say, "No, I'm not coming! And I can't believe you're doing this to me. I mean, what if Connor's inside?"

"Connor is inside." She looks right at me.

"What? Oh my god! How could you do this to me?"

I watch her lean on the door and say, "He knows we're coming. He wants to see you. And I know you want to see him. And you know you want to see him."

"He wants to see me?" I ask, looking at her suspiciously.

"Yes."

"How do you know?"

M just shrugs. "Trevor told me."

"If he wants to see me so bad, why hasn't he called?"

M looks totally annoyed when she says, "I don't know, but now's your chance to ask him."

I stare at her for a minute then look in the rearview mirror and check my makeup. "You should have warned me," I tell her.

"You wouldn't have come if I told you. Come on," she motions with her hand. "It's gonna be great. Trust me."

Then she turns and walks toward the house and after watching her for a moment I get out of the car and follow.

Trevor opens the door and hugs M and looks at me and goes, "Connor ran out to the store. He'll be back soon."

And now I feel like a total loser because I know he ran out because he doesn't want to see me. I bet he was totally suckered into this too.

Trevor goes into the kitchen to get us something to drink and M and I go into that huge room with the pool table and I plop myself onto that same old velvet beanbag chair while M sorts through Trevor's CDs, making piles of which ones suck and which ones rock.

"Are his parents here?" I whisper.

"No. And why are you whispering?" she asks, waving an Oasis CD in the air, not sure which pile to put it in.

"I was whispering because I wasn't sure if they were here."

"Oh, well they're not," she says placing it in the suck pile. "They're like my parent's, totally absentee."

"Maybe you have the same parents," I say. "Do you realize you guys kind of look alike?"

"'Cause we're both blonde?" She rolls her eyes at me. "Get real."

Trevor walks into the room carrying a six-pack of beer and M puts on some vintage Hendrix CD that she's decided does not suck. There's still no sign of Connor, and I'm beginning to feel anxious and totally annoyed with M, so I get up, grab a beer, and go for a walk down the hall.

As I'm leaving the room I hear Trevor say, "What's her problem?" And instead of sticking up for me, M just goes, "Who knows?"

I go outside and lay on a lounge chair by the pool. It's quiet and peaceful, and I close my eyes and remember the dream I had last night. I dreamed that I dove into a pool without checking the depth, and my body was sleek, and fast, and careening through the water. All around me it was clear, but right in my path, right in front of me, it was all murky and I couldn't see. I knew I could smash into the bottom at any second and that the only way to save myself was to start climbing for the surface, but I was reluctant to do that because part of me wanted to see the really deep parts. Part of me was curious to see just how bad the crash would be. When I woke up I had this feeling that soon nothing would be the same.

So then someone who smells like soap and fresh air, walks up, casting a shadow over me and blocking what little remains of the sun. "Alex, wake up," he says. And I open my eyes to find Connor standing over me, and my stomach goes all weird, because he's still as gorgeous as ever. "Where's M and Trevor?" he asks.

I look into his eyes, but only for a second, because looking into his eyes can be dangerous, and make me feel things I don't want to. "In that room with the pool table, listening to Hendrix," I tell him.

"I looked in there, I didn't see them."

I shrug. "Then I don't know. Maybe they went upstairs?"

"Mind if I join you?" He sits on the lounge chair next to mine and looks out at the sunset. "Nice colors," he says, motioning toward the sky.

I look at the streaks of pink and orange and purple, colors I wouldn't normally put together, and think how weird it is that even though I slept with him I feel really nervous now. I guess talking is always the hard part.

He turns toward me and says, "I feel bad about the other morning."

I just shrug, but I don't look at him. I focus on the horizon.

"I remembered later that you left your car at Harry's. How'd you get there? Cab?"

I shake my head. "I took the bus." I look right at him.

"You're kidding?" he says, looking surprised.

"I'm not kidding," I tell him. "But it wasn't that bad."

"I'm sorry."

"Are you?" I search his face, trying to find out if it's true.

"Yeah, really." He runs his hand through his hair and he looks pretty uncomfortable.

"You could have told me that at the sushi restaurant," I say.

"I know." He shrugs.

I hold his gaze for a moment, then shake my head. "You know what? Forget it, okay? It really doesn't matter anymore." I look out at the sunset again, and try to get a grip on myself.

"So what have you been doing?" he asks after awhile.

I take a deep breath and decide to be honest for a change. "Nothing, just school and work," I say.

"Where do you work?"

"At a department store. I've worked there for almost two years now."

"Do you like it?" he asks.

I shrug. "It's okay for now. You know, for being a minor and all." I look over at him and he gives me a worried look, but I just laugh.

"When do you graduate?" he asks.

"Soon. A few weeks." I look at him and smile.

"What are you going to do next?"

I look out at the sinking sun and think how funny it is we're having this kind of conversation after all that's happened. "Honestly?" I say, "I really don't know."

"Aren't you going to college?" he asks.

"I messed up. I don't think it's gonna happen for me."

"You could go to, what do you call it? Community college?"

I shake my head and look at him. "God, you sound like my counselor, Mrs. Gross."

"A wise woman." He smiles.

"She wears polyester pants and sensible shoes."

"A fashion-challenged wise woman."

"Maybe." I sit up and put my arms around my knees.

"What do you want to do tonight?" He looks at me.

"I don't know." I shrug, and look away.

"Do you want to get out of here?"

"And go where?" I ask cautiously.

"I don't know, dinner, a club, a movie, somewhere."

"But what about M and Trevor?"

"I've got a feeling they might not surface for awhile," he says.

"Yeah, you're probably right." I roll my eyes. God, I can't believe M. And then I look at Connor and say, "I have to tell you, I was tricked into coming here. And now I'm kind of stuck and have no way to get home."

"I'll take you home if you want," he says, giving me a concerned look.

I shake my head. "It's pretty far. Besides, I'm a pro at the whole bus thing now."

"You're not riding the bus again."

Connor leans toward me and reaches for my hand. I'm not sure I want this to happen, but I fold my fingers around his anyway, because even though I spent a week and a half trying to get over him, it doesn't mean that I did.

His face is close to mine when he says, "I'm glad you're here. I knew you were coming, but I didn't know you were tricked into it. I get the feeling you don't want to hang out with me."

He squeezes my hand and I can feel my entire nervous system running amok. But then I remember how he made me feel disposable and I can't just undo that, so I look him right in the eyes and force myself to say, "Well, I'm not sure that I do."

He looks surprised and shakes his head and goes, "Well at least you're honest."

And I go, "Yeah, for a change." But it's not the truth. It's a big fat lie. Because the real truth is that I want to be with him more than anything.

We go inside the house and while Connor gets a beer, I go searching for the bathroom, only I don't know where the downstairs ones are and this house is so big it's confusing. So I go upstairs to one that I used before.

I stand in front of the mirror and stare at my reflection and wonder what to do. I can't deny the way I feel about Connor, even though I know those feelings are risky. I mean, it took me like, nine days to stop obsessing over him, and now he just appears in front of me and it's like all the bad stuff never happened.

But what if he really is sorry? What if after being without me, he decided that he misses me and really wants me back? I know he didn't exactly say that, but he did say that he knew I was coming over and that he was glad about it.

I reach into my bag, find my lip gloss, and reapply. The best thing to do is just fight the overwhelming urge to jump on top of him and insist on hanging out here at the house in a mellow, platonic way. M and Trevor have got to come up for air eventually and it will be a lot safer for me, emotionally, to not be alone with him. That's it. I'll just hang out and be strong. I look at myself in the mirror one final time, and head out the door.

Halfway down the hall I can hear music coming from one of the rooms, and I'm thinking everyone must be in there. So I push the door open and start to walk in when I see Trevor lying on the couch. He looks up at me and then over at M who doesn't see me because she's busy leaning over a desk, half naked, snorting a line of coke. I just stand there watching her, and I'm totally in shock. When the mirror is clean she looks at Trevor and goes, "Is there any more?" And then she looks over and sees me and goes, "Oh my god, Alex!"

I run down the hall, down the stairs, and into the den where I find Connor sitting on the couch, finishing up his beer. I stand in front of him, short of breath, and go, "Let's go. Let's just go somewhere."

He gives me a concerned look. "Are you okay?"

"Yeah, but let's get out of here."

"Okay." He sets down his beer and stands up. "Where do you want to go?"

"Anywhere."

Chapter 28

We go to a movie and then afterward we grab a pizza and a six-pack of beer and we take it back to Connor's. We're eating it in the living room because there's no table in the dining room, and so we're sitting on the floor, and our knees are touching, and it's really nice and comfortable and platonic.

He puts on some demo CD that he wants me to hear and after two songs he looks at me and asks, "What do you think?"

I cover my mouth because I'm chewing on a piece of pizza and I say, "They're really good. Who are they?"

Then he goes, "Some garage band from Liverpool."

"Oh, you mean like the Beatles?" I ask.

"That would be nice." He takes a sip of his beer and wipes the corner of his mouth with the side of his hand. "You know, I haven't heard anything that fresh and original in a long time."

So I go, "Yeah, they're really good."

"They're brilliant." He nods. "I'm really hoping we can sign them."

He takes another sip of his beer and looks at me in that sexy way that he has and now my stomach is going all weird again and

I'm not sure what to do. I mean, I promised myself I would keep it casual, but it's not so easy when he looks at me like that.

So he moves closer, and puts his arm around me and says, "I'm sorry that things got sort of messed up." Then he kisses me on my hair, right above my ear.

I nod and half smile and say, "Yeah, well, I'm sorry too." And then I look at him and I just have to know, and now's my chance, and I have nothing to lose, so I go, "What about Sam?"

He looks at me intently and goes, "What about her?"

And I go, "Well, are you guys going out?"

"Why would you ask that?" He leans back and looks at me strangely.

And I realize that I can't explain the subtle looks and weird frequency that happens between girls that guys can't tune into, and I guess I never really saw anything concrete anyway, so I just go, "I don't know, I guess I thought . . ."

"We're not dating. She works for me. That's it." He shakes his head and gives me a serious look.

"Okay," I say. But I'm not sure if I believe him.

And then he leans in again and this time he kisses me on the lips. Softly at first and then it grows into something more. And it feels so good, to feel his arms wrapped tight around me, and I find myself pushing into this kiss, pushing into his whole body. And then his hands are on my breasts, and I'm melting into him once again, just like I did the last time. Only this time I know it will be different, because there are no lies between us.

The next morning I wake up alone. I'm still half asleep as I reach over to Connor's side of the bed wanting to snuggle with him, but he's not there and the sheet feels cold, like he hasn't been there for awhile.

I climb out of bed and grab his shirt off the floor, put it on, and holding the front part closed I go looking for him.

I find him in the living room with the phone cradled in his neck putting something into a duffle bag that's sitting on the coffee table.

"Hey," I say standing there.

He turns and smiles and waves and points at the phone and then puts his index finger up in the "just a minute" signal.

So I go into the kitchen and as I'm pouring myself a cup of coffee I freeze when I hear him say, "Okay Sam, six o'clock, don't be late."

He said "Sam." Why would he be talking to Sam? I lean my head toward the doorway trying to hear more, but he already hung up. So I force the whole thing out of my mind because he told me last night that nothing was going on between them. I mean, I'm sure it's just business. And if we're going to be together now, I have to learn to trust him, just like I want him to trust me after all of my lies.

He comes up behind me and says, "Good morning," and then he wraps his arms around me and kisses the back of my neck, and I lean back into him, and he smells so nice and feels so good. And right when I'm thinking how lucky I am that my mom is out of town, and it's only Saturday, and I still have until Sunday night to hang out with him, and how I wouldn't mind crawling back into bed for the rest of the day, he goes, "So why don't you shower, while I make you a big American breakfast, and then I'll drive you home."

Chapter 29

So after a British version of an "American" breakfast consisting of bacon, eggs, toast, fruit, juice, coffee, and a choice of cereals (I mean all the Americans I know just eat Pop-Tarts), we took the long, scenic route home, all the way down the coast to Newport Beach where we stopped for frozen yogurt, and took a walk to the end of the Pier. We talked about things we never talked about before, and I felt so close to him, and so lucky, and I couldn't help thinking how much better my life was now that Connor was definitely back in it.

When he pulls into my high school parking lot, mine is the only car sitting there.

"That's your car I'm assuming," he says as he pulls up next to it.

"Yeah," I say grabbing my purse from the backseat, wondering what to do next.

"I like Karmann Ghias. I think they're really cool."

"It's okay." I shrug.

"So, this is your school?" He cranes his neck around, but all you can really see from the student lot is the tennis courts and the stupid mascot that's painted on the gym.

"This is it," I say, staring at his profile.

And then he leans across and hugs me and I can feel his warm breath in my hair and smell his skin and feel his heart beat under his sweater and it's right next to mine. He holds me like that for a moment then he pulls back and looks at his watch and says, "I should go. Our flight leaves early."

And I go, "What?" And I'm staring at him, trying to make sense of what he just said because I don't remember him mentioning anything about a flight, and the way he just said "our flight" makes me wonder if it's like a surprise for me or something. Like maybe he really is going to take me away somewhere and we can be together and I can just forget about school and all the other things that are dragging me down.

But he looks really uncomfortable when he goes, "I'm going back to London tomorrow."

I sit there stunned, and I feel like I just got the wind knocked out of me, and I don't even know what to say, so I don't say anything.

"Please don't look at me like that. I told you I was leaving," he says.

"You did?" I search his face, trying to remember when he might possibly have said that.

"Yeah. I was supposed to leave a week ago, but it got postponed."

And then I remember. He mentioned something that night at Harry's, but for some reason back then it didn't seem like a big threat, but now it kind of does. And I still want to know what he meant by "our flight" but part of me is afraid to ask because I don't think he meant "our" like "us." But I really have to know so I go, "Who are you going with?"

And he totally avoids looking at me when he says, "Uh, Sam is on my flight."

And I can't believe he said that. And I can't believe that he said it *like that,* like it's just some random coincidence. "You're going to London with Sam?" I ask.

"Yeah, but it's not like you think. She works for me. She's my assistant. She has to come."

He looks at me and smiles and nods, but I just bite down on my lower lip and look away. I mean, I really wish I could believe that story, but I'm not a total idiot.

"Hey," he pulls me back toward him, and touches my cheek softly. "Last night was really great." And then he kisses me, and I let him, but I don't kiss back, and when it's over he says, "I'll write you as soon as I get settled."

And I look at him and go, "You're going to write me?"

"Well, yeah, if that's okay?" He looks confused.

"But why would you write me? I mean, Connor how long are you going for?"

He looks at me closely and goes, "I'm moving back to London. I'll be gone for quite awhile."

"But what about all of your business here?" I ask, even though what I really mean is *what about me?*

He takes a strand of my hair and tucks it behind my ear and goes, "I'm sorry. I thought you knew."

"How could I know?" I'm starting to sound unstable but I don't care. "How could I know if you never told me?"

"But I did tell you I was leaving."

"But not like that! Not like you were moving there! You made it sound like some casual business trip."

"Alex, I'm sorry if you misunderstood, but I'm English, London is home."

I sink down lower in my seat and stare out the window and try to gain control over my emotions because there's no way I'm gonna cry in front of him. "I just wish you were more clear about it. I just wish you had told me before," I say, avoiding his eyes.

"Before what?" he asks.

"Before last night!" I shake my head. God, I never learn, I'm so pathetic.

"Would it have made a difference?"

I look at him and say, "It would have made a big difference, Connor."

He looks at me for a long moment. "I'm sorry," he says.

And he says it quietly, like he really means it. But I just shrug and think how we've said that an awful lot for two people who aren't really boyfriend and girlfriend.

So I grab my purse and reach for the door handle and right when I open it he says, "Alex."

And I look over and he kisses me again and it's nice, but after a moment I break away, and push the door all the way open and say, "Have a safe flight." I resist the urge to finish that by saying *"with Sam!"* even though it's screaming inside me, wanting to get out.

So I climb out of his car and into mine, and after I start my engine I wave from my window, so he'll know that everything is okay. And when I see him pull out of the parking lot and onto the road, I scream at the top of my lungs for the longest time. And I know I should stop, but I can't. It just keeps coming out. But I don't cry. I won't let myself cry.

Chapter 30

T he next afternoon when my mom returned from visiting my aunt in San Diego I met her out on the driveway and helped her bring her things in. I smiled, and made small talk, and thanked her for the "San Diego!" T-shirt she bought me, even though I don't wear things like that. And I did all this even though I felt like I was in the final stages of death because I promised myself I would keep the whole Connor mess to myself, and just get through it alone.

I go back into my room where I was working on the tenth page of my *Anna K* paper but I decide I need a break. So I pick up the phone and call M just to see what's up, since the last time I saw her she was cracked out on coke. And even though I'm mad at her for tricking me into going to Trevor's and all the other shitty things she's done to me lately, I'm also kind of worried about her.

When she picks up on the fourth ring, I hear her yell, "I got it, Mom! Shit. Hello?"

I go, "M?"

"Hang on," she whispers. And then, "Mom, it's just Tiffany, all right?"

I go, "M, it's Alex."

"I know."

"Well, why did you tell your mom I was Tiffany?"

"Okay. Listen. I didn't know how to tell you this but I guess I have to and I hope you'll understand."

I just listen.

"Remember when my mom found that stash?"

"Yeah, I remember."

"Well, she confronted me and wanted to know what I was doing with it. She was really mad, and I was scared, and so I said it wasn't mine."

"You didn't tell her it was mine did you?"

"Not exactly."

"What the hell does that mean?" I yell.

"Alex, please. Don't be mad. I didn't actually say it was yours. She just sort of assumed."

"Why would she assume that? I've never done drugs!"

"I know, I know. Look I guess she just thought . . ."

"What?" I demand.

"I guess she just thought, well, you know, because your parents are divorced and your mom has to work, and you're not doing that well in school, well I guess that made her think that they were yours."

"All of those things are supposed to make me a drug user?" I scream. "You didn't even stand up for me? I can't fucking believe this!"

"Alex! Listen! I tried to tell her that it wasn't you I was holding them for but she didn't believe me. It's like she convinced herself that I was trying to protect you or something. Anyway, what's the real harm here? It's not like we hang out with my parents. As long as you don't call here or come over when they're home, we can still totally see each other at school and hang out in LA on the weekends. It's really not that big a deal."

"Not that big a deal? Fuck you M."

"But Alex!"

I slam down the phone. And then I pick it up and slam it down again. And then I do that one more time. And when it starts ringing I'm amazed to see that it's not broken. But I don't answer it because I know it's M and I don't want to talk to her.

My mom must have heard me screaming because she comes in my room a few minutes later and when I see her I start sobbing uncontrollably. Then she comes over and hugs me and I feel like I'm six years old again.

"What's wrong?" she asks, her voice full of concern.

"Everything," I say. "I hate my life."

"Don't say that. Tell me what happened."

I wipe my face on the hem of my tank top and go sit on the edge of my bed. My mom comes over and sits next to me and puts her arm around me and waits for me to start. So I tell her all about M and her drug use, and how she told her mom they were mine. And instead of getting mad, instead of saying what I thought she would, my mom goes, "Poor M."

"Poor M!" I practically shout. "What about me?"

She looks right at me and says, "What about you? You and I both know the truth. I know those drugs aren't yours. But look what M's reduced to. Lying about her behavior and blaming you." She shakes her head, "There's something very sad about that girl."

"About M?" I say incredulously.

My mom looks at me and nods, "Yes, I feel sorry for her. She always seems like she needs a hot meal and a hug."

"M? That I've known forever? That M? Like, what could be sad about her? She has *everything* and she always has! She's going to Princeton, she's beautiful, and smart, and popular, and rich."

"Yes, and you're all those things too, minus the lying and the drug use."

I shake my head, "That's just delusional," I say.

"Maybe we're not rich like M's family, but you're beautiful, and smart, and you used to be involved with a lot of different friends, you used to be on the honor roll, you used to be college bound too. Somewhere along the way, you just seemed to give up on all that. But that was a choice you made, it wasn't something that just happened to you."

I sit there with my head in my hands going over what she just said. I mean, I guess I always knew that I was the one blowing it, but I've also been acting like it's not my fault. "I'm such a loser," I say. "And I'm a liar too." I take my hands off my face and look at my mom. "I told a really big lie to someone I cared about, someone I thought I loved, and he dumped me because of it. And then I lied and pretended he didn't dump me, and then I got caught in that too. And then I saw him last night, and part of me hoped all the bad stuff would go away and we'd be together. And everything was so great, and it felt so right, but today he went back to London, and he went with someone else."

"Who is this boy?" she asks.

I shrug. "Just some guy I met. His name is Connor. He's from London. He was here on business."

"On business?" she says, somewhat alarmed. "How old is he?"

"Twenty-three," I say.

"Don't you think that's too old for you?"

I just look at her and go, "I don't even know anymore. I mean, before I didn't think so, but after everything that's happened, I just don't know."

And then I can't help it, I just start crying again, and she hugs me for the longest time and I just cry until I'm empty.

Chapter 31

t's weird at school not hanging out with M at lunch and trying to pretend like I don't see her in class. The first day in French she kept trying to get my attention but by AP History she had totally given up. I guess it's a good thing that we never did sit next to each other.

Tiffany came over to my locker recently and asked what's going on with M and me. I pretended I didn't know what she was talking about.

She said, "For your information, there are two freshmen sitting at the tree that you guys have been eating lunch at since ninth grade. And I never see you guys together anymore."

I knew she was just looking for a juicy story and that really annoyed me so I said, "God, it's not like we were dating you know."

"Well, M said . . ."

I didn't stand there long enough to hear the rest of that. While I have no idea where M is eating lunch, I'm sure she's not answering Tiffany's questions. I mean, she can't be feeling very proud of what she did.

So I'm actually going to all of my classes, getting there early, and paying attention. I have to admit I feel a little lost in most of them; it's kind of like sitting down in the theater just half an hour before the movie ends and trying to figure out what you missed.

About a week after Connor left I got a postcard from him with a picture of the Queen on it, and then a few days later he left a message on my machine. I admit that I listened to the message more than twice, but when I was done, I erased it, even though I had the option to save it for thirty days. And then I sent him a postcard too; it had a picture of Richard Nixon and Elvis; it's called "The President and the King."

Even Guy (remember him, from Java Daze?) called and left a voice mail message, but I'm not sure if I'm gonna call him back. I mean, I thought he was really cute and nice. Not a dweeb like M said. But I lied to him too and pretended I was in college and stuff. Well, technically it was M's lie, but it's not like I tried to stop it. And I'm just not sure I'm willing to start something that's based on lies again.

I went out with Blake the other night after work. Nothing special, we just went to that little coffee place by the store. I didn't plan on telling him, but when he asked, "How's M?" The whole story just came spilling out.

When I was finished, he whistled and said, "Wow, that's ugly."

I go, "Tell me about it."

"Does she know that Connor left?" He breaks his biscotto in half and offers me a piece.

"I have no idea," I say, taking it and swirling the Italian cookie in my cappuccino.

"Well, you know M's always been a little bit of a princess and all, but you guys were best friends."

"Since we were eight," I tell him.

"Listen, you've got to think of a way to work it out. Has she tried to apologize?"

"Several times." I take a bite of my now soggy cookie.

"But you're not accepting apologies right now?" he asks.

"Nope, not right now." I look at him and shake my head. "Look, I'm really mad, and hurt, and offended. She totally lied! She totally betrayed me! I mean, M's mom can think whatever she wants. I don't care about her. But the fact is M didn't even try to stand up for me. She just saw an easy way out and went for it. She threw me overboard and saved herself, and I think that's messed up. Jeez, Blake, if nothing else she could have said they were Tiffany's."

He gives me a horrified look and says, "Don't even say the name. Is she still around?"

"She's still around. Anyway, let's talk about you." I take a sip of my coffee.

"Finally." He smiles.

"When are you leaving?"

"Middle of June."

"I'm gonna miss you." I reach across the table and squeeze his hand.

"Of course you are. But wouldn't you know it, right when I have everything in order, I meet the man of my dreams." He finishes his biscotto and wipes the crumbs from his mouth.

"Are you serious?" I ask.

"Very."

"Blake, you've said that before," I remind him.

"I mean it this time. His name is Ken, and he's gorgeous, and smart, and he cooks." He uses his fingers to list those attributes.

"Wow, I'd settle for just smart. So what are you gonna do?" I ask.

"By June he'll be so in love with me he'll follow me anywhere, right?"

"Totally." I nod my head in agreement and drink the last of my coffee.

"The question is, what are you gonna do?" He looks right at me.

I put my head in my hands.

"How many times do I have to tell you that you can do whatever you want? You're smart and talented. You're setting your own limits you know. You don't need your dad, or Connor, or anybody else. But you've got to get it together." He reaches across the table and says, "High School is almost over, and you're wasting your life if you stay here."

When I got home I was still thinking about what Blake said. The idea of being stuck here for another year after everyone else has moved on is too horrible to imagine. I mean, everyone keeps asking me what I want to do and I realize that I'm no closer to an answer. So I grab a piece of paper and make a list of the five things that I like to do. Kind of a modified version of the aptitude test they made us take sophomore year.

At the top of the list I put READ/WRITE. Which I know sounds totally hypocritical considering my grades and all, but I'm not talking about textbooks and essays. I mean, I really like to read and write fiction, but even though Mr. Sommers liked that one story, I'm not sure if it's like, a realistic goal.

Next I put CLOTHES. But it's not like you can make a living buying clothes for yourself (unless you're M's mom). So that means you have to shop for other people and I kind of already do that right now. So I definitely know that I don't want to do it forever.

Third is MUSIC. But I can't sing or play an instrument so I'm not gonna get too far with that. And I don't know how to run a record company like Connor. And I'm no longer delusional about running a record company *with* Connor.

At number four I put HANGING OUT. But the only people

who can make a career out of that are the Hilton sisters. And I don't think I need to explain at this point how I'm not exactly related.

And number five was blank. Oh well, it's not like it's a *real* aptitude test.

Chapter 32

So after days and days of secretly obsessing about it more than I care to admit, Mr. Sommers finally starts passing out our graded short stories. When he gets to Christine the Collector's seat, I admit, I'm practically standing on top of my desk to get a glimpse of her grade. On the upper-right-hand corner of her paper is a large, red, unmistakable C. Wow, I bet she's never received one of those before. Underneath it is a short note, also in red ink, that unfortunately I'm unable to read from such a distance. She looks at her grade and quickly turns her paper over, and when we make eye contact she looks like she's about to cry. And I gotta tell you, I enjoy every minute of it.

So he hands out all the short stories in his stack and walks to the front of the room. But my desktop is still empty and when I look around I notice that everyone has their paper except me. And now I'm in a total panic thinking that maybe he somehow lost mine. I mean, that would be just my luck, to actually complete an assignment only to have the teacher lose it and assume I didn't do it.

But then he goes, "I'd like to read you a story that I thought was very good."

And then he reads my story, just like last time.

When he's done reading it, someone goes, "Did Alex write that one too?"

And when he answers, "Yes," everyone turns to gawk at me and I know that they're shocked that it wasn't just a fluke the first time.

When Mr. Sommers returns it to me, there's a big red A in the upper-right-hand corner, no note, just a single letter.

Christine the Collector glances at my paper and asks, "Mr. Sommers, is this going to count toward our final grade?"

When he says yes, she drops her head on her desk and sits like that even after he dismisses us. And this may sound crazy, but part of me actually feels a little sorry for her.

When I walk out the door M is standing there waiting for me. But I'm feeling so good about Mr. Sommers reading my story out loud, and giving me an A, that I just can't be mad right now. I look at her briefly and say, "Hey," then head to my locker.

She's right behind me when she says, "Alex, that was a really great story."

So I stop. And I turn, and I look at her and say, "Thanks." Because even though I haven't talked to her in quite a while, the stories I write are really important to me, and it makes me feel good when people say that.

"I never knew you were such a good writer," she says, following me.

And I can't help it. I'm a sucker for a compliment. So I smile and thank her again, and open my locker and switch my books.

"Your characters are like, so real," she says. "It's really amazing how you do that."

I've got my backpack balanced on my knee, trying to get my books inside, when she goes, "Trevor told me that Connor went back to London. I'm really sorry. I'm really sorry about everything that's happened."

I just look at her and go, "Okay, I hear you. I hear your apology, okay?" Because now I know that all those compliments on my story were just a way for her to get my attention so I would forgive her.

"But you won't accept it?"

I shake my head and reach into my locker and grab those jeans she gave me that day we were shopping on Robertson. They still have the tag on them, because I never wore them.

"What's this?" she says, holding up the jeans trying to figure out where they came from.

"You gave them to me that day you tricked me into going to Trevor's. They've never been worn. So you can keep them, or return them. I really don't care."

"But I gave them to you. I don't want them back," she says, holding them down at her side so that one of the legs is dragging on the floor.

"Yeah?" I slam my locker shut. "Well, I don't want them either. You can't buy me stuff then treat me like shit. You can't bribe me into being your friend. I may be poor, but I'm not desperate."

"I wasn't bribing you! I never said you were desperate!"

I just look at her and go, "I don't even know who you are anymore." Then I turn and walk away. I just can't be her friend right now.

When I got home from school I asked my mom if she wanted to rent a movie or something and do you know what she said?

"I'm sorry, but I can't. I have a date."

Wow. I would be big-time lying if I told you that didn't make me feel totally pathetic. I mean, I'm happy for my mom don't get me wrong, but it's pretty weird when she's getting all dressed up for dinner when the most I can hope for is a "very special episode" of Seventh Heaven.

So around seven-thirty, her date comes to the door and I answer it because she's still in her room putting on the finishing touches.

He's tall and dressed all business casual, and he goes, "You must be Alex."

I go, "That's me."

And he goes, "I'm Chris."

We shake hands and I invite him in and tell him to have a seat on the couch while I go get my mom. While he's walking toward the living room I totally check him out and I've got to say he's pretty handsome for an old guy in his forties.

So I go down the hall and knock on my mom's door and when she opens it, I go, "Mom, your date's here."

And she asks, "Are these shoes okay?"

And when I look at her I can't believe how pretty she is. I mean, I knew she was pretty but this is different. This is the glamorous kind. I tell her, "Those shoes look great. You look beautiful."

She looks really happy and gives me a quick hug and kiss and when I look in her mirror I can see a faint lipstick mark on my cheek but I just leave it there. "So, Mom, how long have you and Chris been dating?" I ask.

"Are you checking up on me?" She looks at me and smiles.

"Yeah. Unfortunately I have nothing better to do." I sit on her bed and watch her fix her hair.

"We've been dating for about a month I guess."

"Well, he's really handsome. Is he nice?"

"So far." She looks at me through the mirror and shrugs.

"Where did you meet him?" I ask.

"He's actually a friend of your Uncle Terry."

"Do they work together?"

"Yes," she says. Then she asks, "Have you talked to your father lately?"

I lie down on the comforter and look at the ceiling. I can't believe she's going to quiz me about my dad while she's getting ready to go on a date. "No," I say. And I'm thinking I should probably get up and leave now before this goes any further.

"He hasn't tried to call you?" she asks.

I'm sitting on the edge of the bed and I am not about to have this conversation with her, so I go, "No, he hasn't tried to call, because he doesn't give a shit about me, okay? We've already been through this."

My mom just looks at me for a moment with her eyebrows raised and I don't know if it's because I used the *s* word, or because of what I said about him not caring.

"Alex, between your argument with M and your relationship with your father I'm worried about the amount of energy you spend on being angry."

I roll my eyes and go, "What's that supposed to mean?"

She comes over and sits next to me and puts her hand on mine. "I want to share something with you that might help you put things in perspective, and I probably should have told you this a long time ago."

I'm still sitting on the edge of the bed, ready to bolt at any minute because she looks like she's going to say something really serious and the truth is I just don't know if I'm up for it. But she still has her hand on mine and she's looking at me all intense so I don't bolt, I just sit there.

"When I was growing up," she begins, "my father, your grandfather, was an alcoholic and a bum. And I was angry. Angry at my father for not being able to control his sickness, angry with him for constantly embarrassing our family. But I was also angry at my mother, for putting up with him, for being dependent on him, for not protecting us from him."

She gets this faraway look in her eyes and then she bites down on her lower lip just like I always do. And I sit there stunned because I never knew that about Grandpa, but then she never really talked about him before now.

"And when he died, I felt guilty. Guilty because I had secretly wished for it every night that he came home late, smelling of alcohol and starting fights." She shakes her head and looks at me. "And my mother, your grandmother, who never seemed happy when he was around, completely fell apart without him. And so I became responsible for raising your aunt Sandy and taking care of the family. And I was angry again. Because that was her job. I was supposed to be a kid, out running around having fun, not stuck at home making dinner for my helpless mother and my baby sister."

She gets up from the bed and walks over to the mirror where she rechecks her makeup and runs her index finger gently under each eye. "I swore that as soon as I could I was getting out of that house no matter what. Then I met your father, and we married, and we were both far too young." She turns and looks at me. "He came from a similar background, and we just sort of glommed on to each other. Well I know that we both had bad examples of marriage and problem solving, but still, when your father left I found myself very angry all over again. I was angry at being saddled with kids to raise on my own. I was angry with him for walking out on his responsibilities. And I was angry at the way I had let my life turn out."

She comes over and sits down next to me again. "I know I haven't been there for you much, and I worry about the bad example we've given you, because I see you making similar mistakes and I don't want you to repeat my patterns. I want so much more for you." She reaches up and touches me briefly on the cheek. "I know your father abandoned you, and M betrayed you, and I know how much that hurt. But you cannot control other people's actions. You can only control your response to them. And you have to pick your battles wisely, because it just takes so much energy to be angry. Energy that you can put to better use. Your father has limitations that have nothing to do with you. And I'm sure that someday he will have a lot of regrets. But it's time you held yourself accountable for what happens next. And not to use your past as an excuse for not getting where you want to go."

She looks at me for a long time and I just nod. It's a lot to process.

Then she pats me on the leg and asks, "Do you think Chris fell asleep out there waiting for me?" She gets up and grabs her purse and when she opens the door she looks back at me and goes, "What are you going to do tonight?"

I look at her and smile. "Believe it or not, schoolwork."

I sit on her bed until well after I hear them leave, and I think about everything she just told me. I guess I never saw my parents like that before. As real people still struggling to cope with their pasts and the shit their parents dealt them, just like I'm trying to deal with their bad decisions.

And I guess my mom is right. I've spent a lot of time and energy being angry with my dad and blaming him for everything bad in my life. And even though I can't help but hope that he'll have some big-time regrets someday, that's really between him and his conscience.

I'm glad my mom's dating again but it feels kind of weird to witness. I wonder if this means she's finished being angry with my dad?

Chapter 33

The next Friday after school I'm walking to the parking lot when I run into my guidance counselor. I had successfully avoided her since that last meeting, but it looked like my luck had just run out.

"Alex, how are you?" she asks, approaching me.

Shit. I can't just keep walking and ignore her so I go, "Um, okay. You?"

"Fine. Do you have a minute?"

Damn! I look at her and jangle my keys and say, "Well, I was really on my way home. I mean, the bell just rang and all."

"This will only take a minute." I just stand there hesitating and then she goes, "Don't you have a minute to talk about your future?"

I should have run. But instead I just follow her into her office, like a big retard, and sit in that same old chair in front of her desk and look around. Everything is just like last time, except the plant is missing. I bet she killed it.

She sits at her desk, folds her hands together, and leans toward me. I'm trying not to squirm but she's already making me really nervous. "You haven't held up to your end of the deal," she says.

"What deal?" I fidget with my silver hoop earring. I have no idea what she's talking about.

"The deal where you got your grades together. Early reports on your semester grades are very troubling." She looks right at me.

I look over at the filing cabinet. "Don't you want to pull my file?" I ask. "You know, just to make sure?"

"I don't need to see your file to know that you're failing."

I look at her hair that's permed poodle tight, but just for a second, and then I focus on her outfit. She's wearing a light blue crisply ironed cotton blouse, a belt with flowers painted on it, and pleated white cotton twill pants. And I'd bet you anything she's wearing high-rise, full coverage, cotton crotch, underwear.

"I thought after our meeting you had a firm understanding of what you needed to do to get into a decent school. But you've let your grades suffer to the point where the best we can hope for is community college, and that's only if you graduate."

There's that "we" again. They act like this is a team effort or something. "So, what's so bad about community college?" I ask.

"Nothing, provided you're motivated enough to even go there." She looks frustrated and reaches her hands toward me, palms up. "You are a very bright girl, and it's such a tragedy to watch you waste your potential like this. You are capable of so much more. But I'm afraid if you don't apply yourself this very minute, and if you don't do extremely well on your finals, you will not be graduating with your class. Your future is in jeopardy Alex."

She's looking straight at me and she's trying to get to me, trying to reach me, but I can't stand it so I sink lower in my chair and stare at the floor. We just sit there quiet like that for the longest time. I mean, I don't owe this woman anything. And I don't remember making a deal with her. She railroaded me into all of this and she wouldn't listen when I told her I couldn't do it anymore. If I want to mess it all up, well, that's my business. She can just go back home to her photogenic family and forget this ever happened.

We just continue to sit like that and I can feel her staring at me and I don't know what to do, so finally, I reach into my backpack and pull out the paper I'd been carrying around all week. It's my latest short story, the one with the big red A on it. I look at it for a moment and then hand it to her and go, "I'm trying, okay? I really am. I'm going to all of my classes, and everything." And then I start crying. What a total dork.

She doesn't come around the desk and try to hug me, thank god. She just reaches across her desk, grabs a tissue, and quietly hands it to me. After awhile she says, "I didn't know you liked to write."

I twist the tissue around and around and go, "It's just something I do sometimes. I'm not all that serious about it."

"Why not?"

I just look at her, "What do you mean?"

"Well, you enjoy doing it so much you even do it in your free time. Your English teacher seemed to be impressed and from reading the first paragraph I am too."

"I've got others," I say.

"Okay, now we're getting somewhere." She sets my story on her desk and looks at me. "You don't have to love History and Economics, but you have to get through them to get to the good stuff, the stuff you do like. I know your grades in French are okay and English too, but it's not enough. You can't graduate on that alone."

"But even if I do start applying myself, or whatever, I still won't get into a good school for next year. I mean, I've totally blown it, and my dad told me he won't pay for it anyway," I tell her.

She looks at me steadily and says, "You're young, and very bright. You can still go to a good school and get a scholarship. Maybe not next fall, but there's still the year after that. But you can't just put it off until then. You have to start trying now. You have to graduate."

I look at her for a moment, and it's clear that she really does care. She's not just trying to shame me. Then I look at the picture on her desk of her kids and husband and I wonder if she means well with them too.

"There's a statewide, library-sponsored, teen fiction writers contest." She stops and shuffles around inside her desk until she finds the papers she's looking for. Then she picks one up and reads from the back. "The winner will receive a two thousand dollar scholarship, and the chance to compete in the nationwide finals for additional scholarship money, a trip to New York, and publication in *Sixteen* magazine." She sets it down and looks at me. "I'd like to enter your story, if it's not too late. What do you think?"

"No." I shake my head emphatically.

She gives me a disappointed look and it makes me feel bad, but I'm not budging. "Why not?" she asks.

"I don't compete anymore," I tell her.

"Competition is healthy."

"Only for the winners," I tell her. "Not for the losers."

"It inspires people to do better, to be better."

"I'm sorry. I can't," I say, avoiding the look in her eyes.

She sits there for a moment and then without saying anything she gets up from her desk and leaves the office. But I'm not sure if she's done trying to convince me yet, or if I should stay seated for round two. So I just sit there for a while staring at the floor, and then I grow a little bored, so I pick up one of those papers about the contest and start reading it. But then I hear her coming back and I don't want her to see me reading that, so I fold it up and stick it in my bag real quick.

"I'm sorry," she says, rushing back into the room. "I have to pick up my daughter from school now. But I do hope you'll take me seriously about your grades, and I do hope you'll reconsider this contest."

I just nod as though I'm already considering all of that, and then I grab my backpack and head for the parking lot.

When I get home I grab a container of strawberry yogurt and a spoon and sit in front of the TV and try to find something interesting to watch. But as I flip through the channels I keep thinking about what Mrs. Gross said about graduating, and how close I am to not doing it. And the thought of having to go to summer school, or even worse, returning to that dreadful place next year is unbearable. So I turn off the TV and go into my room, determined to open my textbooks and get my act together.

I change into some sweats and sit at my desk, and just to boost my confidence, I prop my latest short story with the A on it against a stack of books so I can steal a glance at it every now and then when I start to get a little bored (which is inevitable since I'm going to devote one hour to each subject that I'm failing, and that's pretty much all of them).

When I'm well into economics, my second study subject, my phone starts ringing. I stop reading and stare at it, and I hate to admit it but that might be the first time it's done that since Connor left and I stopped hanging out with M.

I watch it ring until it goes into voice mail and then I go back to my book and focus on reading because I promised myself I would get through this without distractions.

But not five minutes later my purse starts ringing so I close my book and walk across the room to get it. I mean, just because I'm not going to answer it doesn't mean I can't look at the display and see who's calling. But I get there too late and now it just says "missed call."

So I turn my cell phone off and start to toss it back into my purse when I see that paper I took from Mrs. Gross's office all crumpled up inside. I smooth it out against the hard wood of my desk and read through it quickly, and I'm surprised at how simple it is. I mean, it's basically an application that just needs to be filled out, attached to a story, and then mailed in. I don't know why but for some reason I thought it would be more complicated. I thought it would be a bigger deal.

So I grab a pen and start filling in the boxes in all capital letters. (I'm not sure why I use all caps. I guess I just think it looks more official). And then I sign my full name at the bottom with a little more care than usual.

But that was the easy part. Because when I pick up my story and read through it, I start to feel panicked at the idea of some professional editors reading it and judging it. I mean, I know it's a contest with judges, but I mean *judging it* like, "that story sucks," kind of judging it.

I can't do this. There's just no way. I throw the application on the floor and stare at it lying there on my ugly, outdated, shag carpet, and I wonder when I got so used to losing. Just two years ago losing didn't even occur to me, but now, it's like I expect it.

But I don't want to be like this anymore and maybe the only way out is to start trying again. I mean, maybe if I send it in secretly, without telling anyone, then I'm the only one who will know if I fail. And it won't be that big of a deal since I'm used to it anyway.

I pick up the application, prop it up next to my story, and stare at the big, red A on the title page for a long time.

If I don't try I won't lose, but then I won't win either.

Chapter 34

So on the night of the prom, do you know what I'm doing? I'm going on a date with Guy. I guess I started feeling a little sad and lonely, and I had no other prospects. My mom was going out with Chris again, Blake was nervously meeting Ken's parents, and I heard Tiffany announce in a very loud voice in the girls bathroom that M was going to the dance with her mother's tennis buddy's son. Can you believe it? I mean, there was just no way I was gonna sit at home by myself. So I decided to return Guy's call.

He seemed pretty happy that I called him back and as we were talking I decided to come clean. I just couldn't stand the idea of another lie out there. So when he asked me about the weekend I mentioned that it was prom but I wasn't going. That way he could be the one to sort of drag it out of me.

So of course he goes, "What? The prom? I thought you were in college?"

So I take a deep breath and I go, "I know."

He sounds confused when he says, "What?"

"Well I guess I just didn't want to admit that I'm still in high school. It's like, you guys are in grad school and stuff, and well, it just seems so juvenile." God, I sound like a dork.

So then he does the strangest thing. He starts cracking up. So I just sit there, holding the phone, not really knowing what to do, when he goes, "Well, I guess if you're gonna come clean then I'll come clean too, we're not really grad students, we're freshmen at UCLA."

I totally can't believe this, but I talk myself out of being upset, because that would be hypocritical. So I go, "Why did you lie?"

And he goes, "I guess for the same reason you did."

"Wow."

"Does that mean there's no trip to Europe either?" he asks.

"Only in my dreams," I tell him.

So then he goes, "Hey, if you don't have a prom date, I'd be honored to take you."

I swear that's just how he says it, kind of old-fashioned but I like it.

"You know what, Guy," I tell him, "I have no interest in the prom. Why don't we just go to dinner or something instead?"

"Done. I'll pick you up Saturday at seven."

So Guy knocks on my door at seven sharp and when I peek at him through the peephole I see a very cute, kind of preppy, Paul Ruddish–looking guy, which was pretty much how I remembered him.

When I open the door he goes, "Wow, you look great."

I'm just wearing my favorite low-cut, boot-cut jeans, a white baby-T, a little black blazer I bought in the boys' department at work (I like the way it's kind of shrunken looking), my favorite black, super-high-heeled Steve Madden, platform sandals (which kill to walk in but I love them), and my hair is wavy, loose, and long.

I smile and say thanks and start to close the door behind me when he goes, "Are your parents home?" Like he's all prepared to make a good impression on them or something.

I just laugh and say, "No, my parents haven't been in the same house since I was twelve. They're divorced. My mom's on a date."

"Isn't that the weirdest?" he says as he opens the car door for me. "My parents are split too, and it's so bizarre when they start dating about the same time you do."

He gets into the driver's seat of his very cool, black Jeep Wrangler and starts the engine.

"I like your jeep," I say as he pulls out of my driveway.

He looks at me and smiles. "It's not the most comfortable ride, but I like to mountain bike and hike and stuff so it comes in handy."

I nod and smile and say, "The closest I've been to the great outdoors would be the boardwalk in Venice Beach."

"No, that can't be true?" He looks at me briefly and I nod my head that it is indeed true.

"Well, we'll have to change that. I know some great spots for hiking and horseback riding, right here in Orange County. I grew up here."

"You did?" I'm not sure why, but I'm surprised to hear that.

"Yeah. Well not here, but in Laguna Beach."

"Oh," I say. "Well that may be part of Orange County, but it's way cooler than here."

"True." He looks at me and laughs.

"Did you have a horse?" I ask.

"Yeah, I still do. I have two. I keep them at my mom's house."

"I used to have a horse," I tell him as I look out the window. "A long time ago."

When we get to the restaurant he goes, "I hope you like Indian food."

Now normally, in the past, I would just lie and say I love it, and try to fake my way through it. But I'm not lying anymore, unless I absolutely have to. So I say, "Well, I've never had it before."

He smiles and says, "Then you're at the right place because the food here is great, so if you don't like this, then you'll know you don't like Indian food."

He helps me translate the menu into food groups I'm familiar with, then we just order a bunch of different plates so we can share. And I have to say that even though some of it is surprisingly spicy, I think it's absolutely awesome.

We enjoy a really nice dinner together. I mean there are a few awkward moments of silence, but for the most part he keeps it going pretty well and he's interesting and easy to talk to. And I've only compared him to Connor a few times and even then I've tried to stop myself because that's just not fair, it's like apples and Oreos really.

So after he pays the check he goes, "Hey, let's do something fun, something different. Are you up for it?"

"I'm always up for fun and different," I say.

"Good, then let's go bowling!"

"What?" There's just no way I heard him right.

"Yeah, bowling." He's laughing and looking at me expectantly. "They have this late-night thing called 'rock 'n' bowl' and it's really fun. They turn the lights down low and they use these black lights that make the pins glow fluorescent. And the music is great. C'mon, Alex. What? Do you think you're gonna lose?"

"Yes, of course I'll lose. I haven't bowled since grade school," I tell him.

"That's why it will be fun. Listen we can do the whole bar, club thing if you want, but that scene gets so old after awhile."

And hearing him say that, I've got to agree. Suddenly I don't feel like hanging out in some smoky scene, drinking and trying to act like I belong. I don't know if bowling is the answer but it's worth a try. "Do you know where there's a bowling alley around here?" I ask.

"As a matter of fact I do."

So we go bowling. I take off my cute sandals and replace them with some ugly red-and-green flats, and some socks Guy purchased from a vending machine. Then I grab some weird, shiny, bright pink ball I can barely lift, stick three fingers in it, and give up all hope of looking cool while I hurl it toward the fluorescent pins. I mean, if you're going to bowl well, you have to be willing to look like a dork.

I start off good, getting a few strikes and spares, but my game quickly falls apart and turns into a series of gutter balls. But it doesn't really matter 'cause it's not like we're playing competitively or really keeping score, which is good for me since Guy just happens to be a great bowler.

We are having so much fun that we want to keep playing but they're getting ready to close up, so Guy looks at me and says, "So, what's next?"

I look at my watch and I'm amazed to see that it's almost one o'clock. It's not like I have a curfew but I've been having so much fun, I'm sad to know that it's almost over.

"Um, I don't know," I say. "It's kind of late."

"You want to get a coffee?" he asks.

And even though I'm glad to see that he's reluctant to end it too, I shake my head and go, "We're in Orange County, remember? Everything closes early. But I have coffee at my house if you want."

"Should we head there?"

I look at him and smile and nod, and I hope that he doesn't think I'm trying to seduce him by inviting him back to my place.

Chapter 35

When Guy pulls into my driveway I'm praying that my mom and her date won't be here because it would be way too weird to hang out on the couch, making small talk with them. But all the lights are off, and I don't see Chris's car anywhere, so I'm hoping that means the coast is clear.

We walk in the door and Guy is right behind me with his hand on the small of my back and I'm getting kind of nervous and I'm wondering if this is still about coffee. I mean, he's totally cute, and really nice, but I'm just not ready to fling myself on the couch and start making out with him, so I go straight to Mr. Coffee and start filling up the glass carafe and locating two clean mugs that don't have anything embarrassing printed on them.

"Nice house!" Guy shouts, competing with the sound of grinding beans.

"It's okay." I look at him and smile and shrug.

"Is this you?" he asks, picking up a silver frame that holds a picture of a naked, bald, fat, drooling, eight-month-old, which unfortunately is me.

"Uh, yeah." I cringe. "Hey, why don't you go put on a CD in the living room?" I say, hoping he won't see the picture of me in my Girl Scout uniform that my mom insists on displaying.

I put two mugs full of coffee, a little porcelain cow filled with cream, and a couple cubes of natural sugar on a tray and carry it into the living room where Guy is hanging on the couch humming along to that Jonny Lang CD I bought right after Connor dumped me the first time.

"Oh, you like Jonny Lang?" I ask, trying to hide my dismay as I set the tray on the table.

"Yeah, he's awesome. I saw him perform a couple years ago, he was amazing."

I smile at him and add some cream to my coffee, stirring it slowly and watching the colors blend then change, and I'm wondering how I can ask him to choose a different CD without seeming weird. It's like, I feel really nervous being alone on the couch with him because I know he's probably going to try to kiss me soon and I think I want him to, but I wonder if it will be creepy if he does it with that CD playing in the background. I know it sounds kind of stupid, because I'm sure that plenty of people own it, but I think of that as my own personal soundtrack for when I lost my virginity.

So we're just sitting next to each other, drinking our coffees, when Guy sets his down, looks at me, and goes, "I'm glad I met you. I had a lot of fun tonight."

"Me too," I say, and I'm wondering if he's getting ready to leave or something, because that's the kind of thing you usually say right before "good-bye." But then he leans in and kisses me and it's so unbelievably good, that I suddenly couldn't care less who is singing in the background because now it's all about Guy and me and nobody else exists.

His arms are around me and his hand is buried in my hair and I'm clutching the fabric of his shirt, pulling him closer, and kissing him deeper, when I hear someone say, "Uh, you left the door unlocked."

We spring apart. Practically to opposite sides of the couch, and I'm wiping my mouth, and shifting my top around, and I'm not even looking up because I have no idea how I'm going to explain this to my mom, but then I hear Guy go, "M?"

And I look up and see her standing right in front of me, wearing her prom dress. "What the hell?" I say, and it comes out sounding really angry because I am really angry, but I'm not sure if I should be angry in front of Guy.

"Sorry," she shrugs. "Am I interrupting?"

"Uh, yeah," I say rolling my eyes and trying to tone down the anger, even though the sarcasm is loud and clear. "What, you don't knock?"

"I did knock, but you didn't answer so I tried the door and it was open." She sits down on the lumpy ottoman, and runs her hands over the front of her dress and I can't believe she's actually making herself comfortable, because there's no way I'm letting her stay.

"I should go," Guy says, looking at M and then me.

"No," I say. "Don't go. M won't be long." I give her a menacing look, but she doesn't notice because she's busy rummaging through her tiny prom purse.

"M, what are you doing here? Why aren't you at the prom?" I ask, sliding back toward Guy, and reaching for his hand.

"Prom sucked," she says, setting down her purse and reaching for a sugar cube that she plops into her mouth. "Fucking Tiffany won Prom Queen." She shakes her head.

"Of course she did. What, did you wanna win it?" I ask incredulously.

"No, I didn't. It's just, this night is just totally annoying. And I miss you. I just wanted to go out and do something fun like we used to. Come on, what more can I say? I'm so incredibly sorry, I mean it. And I really need to talk to you."

"What happened to your date?" I ask, glancing briefly at Guy. I really don't want him to know about our argument.

"My date? I went to the prom with Harry Potter. I'm not kidding. He was four feet tall, wore thick glasses, and I think he was ten years old. I made a total fool of myself and then I sent him home. I thanked him, and told him he could keep the boutonniere, and I sent him on his way."

Guy laughs out loud, but all I can think is that's karma for you.

Then she looks at Guy and goes, "Hey, Guy, I'm sorry for crashing your date."

He just shrugs and squeezes my hand.

"Is there any coffee left?" she asks.

I glare at her and I can't believe she refuses to get the hint and pack it up. But I just go, "Yeah, I'll get you some. You look like you could use some coffee."

"Thanks," she says. And I can't tell whether she means it or whether she's being sarcastic, but I don't really care either.

When I walk back into the living room I hand M a cup of coffee in an unfortunate mug that has, That's my girl! printed over a picture of a little kid in an orange baseball hat. But it's a picture of my sister this time, not me. She takes a sip of the coffee and looks at Guy and goes, "So what's your friend doing tonight?" She sits up straighter and smiles hopefully, like we're gonna fix her up on a date at one-thirty in the morning.

"Mark? I don't know, I think he's on a date."

"Figures," she says, slumping down again. "Story of my life."

She nods her head and picks at the tacky corsage she's still wearing and I wonder what she could possibly mean by that. From my vantage point it always seems like guys jump through hoops for her.

"Hey, M, there's something I've been wondering?" Guy asks, taking a sip of his coffee.

"Yeah?" she looks at him warily.

"Well, you don't have to tell me if you don't want, but, what's your real name?"

She looks at me and we both start laughing.

"I'll tell ya but it's gonna cost," she says.

"How much," he asks, reaching for his wallet.

"How much is it worth to you?"

"Ten bucks?"

"Never!" She shakes her head and gives him an offended look.

"Twenty?"

She narrows her eyes at him and goes, "Okay, but no checks, no credit cards, just cash."

Guy tosses a twenty on the coffee table and M swiftly picks it up and stuffs it in the top of her prom dress.

I sit next to Guy and wait for her to say it. She heaves a big dramatic sigh and says, "Madison. My name is Madison."

Guy gives her a disappointed look. "I want my money back! I thought it was going to be something awful, like Matilda, or something. Why do you go by M?"

She looks at me and I answer for her, "Because since her first day of kindergarten all the way until junior high, at least one article of her clothing was always monogrammed. I mean, sometimes it was her T-shirt, or sweater, or even her socks, but there was always at least one big blue M. After awhile people just started calling her that and it stuck."

Guy looks at her and shakes his head, "I would have never pictured you as the preppy, monogrammed type."

"That was back when my mom still picked out my clothes," she says.

So we're drinking our coffees and it's kind of weird because I really want M to leave so I can hang out with Guy and kiss him some more, but she just keeps sitting there in no apparent hurry to be anywhere else and it's really pissing me off but I don't want to have it out with her in front of him so I'm acting all normal like this is fun, but it's not.

So finally Guy looks at his watch and goes, "I gotta go."

And I look over at M but she just sits there, and I know I won't be able to get rid of her without a lot of drama, so I just surrender to the situation and look at Guy and go, "Okay. I'll walk you out."

We're standing next to his Jeep when he says, "Is your friend gonna be alright? She seems upset."

And I think it's weird that he said that because if anyone is upset it's me. But I just say, "Sorry about all that."

Then he leans in and kisses me and it's really nice and completely amazing and when he pulls away he goes, "Next time, let's go horseback riding."

And I smile and say, "Okay."

When I go back in the house M has abandoned the ottoman for the couch. And she's sprawled out on it, and her shoes are off and her feet are propped on the coffee table. So I go over to the CD player and turn off Jonny Lang since it's now my soundtrack for making out with Guy, and I put on a Tori Amos CD because it doesn't remind me of anyone. And then I look back at M and I'm so pissed at her for just showing up like that, and barging in, and I'm just about to tell her, but something about the way she looks, lying there like that, makes me go, "Are you okay?"

She sighs heavily and scrunches her face into the palms of her hands like she's trying not to cry. She sits like that for awhile then she says, "Shit, Alex, I'm so sorry. I've been such an ass."

I sit on the ottoman and face her, but I don't say anything because I totally agree.

She wipes her face with the hem of her prom dress and looks at me and goes, "Trevor and I broke up."

I just sit there and stare at her, and I know I'm supposed to say something, but to be honest, that really doesn't make such a big impact anymore. I mean, not after the last time.

"What happened?" I ask.

"Prom sucked. The whole night was a disaster. So I left early and I kept trying to call Trevor on his cell but he wouldn't answer. So I drove all the way up to LA, and long story short, I caught him with another girl."

"I'm sorry," I tell her.

"It's my own fault," she says, shaking her head. "I should have dumped him the last time. I can't believe the lies I let him feed me, just so I could keep hanging out in that whole, stupid, shallow scene." She shakes her head and looks at me.

"He kept trying to act like I'm just as bad, you know. Like it's my fault he was out with another girl, since I was out with another guy at the prom. And I'm like, 'Trevor, you didn't want to go to the prom, remember? You told me to go and have fun.'" I watch her reach over and pick a tiny rose off her corsage and hold it up to her nose.

"He knows damn well that the only reason I went to the prom is because it's supposed to be some kind of big deal, and that for the last few months, I haven't dated anyone else. And because of that, I didn't have anyone to go with, so as everyone knows I was set up on a date with a fucking Hogwarts reject. I had a terrible time, the whole night sucked! All I wanted was to find Trevor and be with him. It never even occurred to me that he was totally taking advantage of the situation. Asshole!" She shakes her head and throws the rose across the room, watching it land on a hanging plant.

"M, did you find out who she is?" I ask.

"Oh yeah, that's the really brilliant part. It's his fucking ex-girlfriend that he's told me all about. Can you believe that? So I go, 'Hey Trevor, the definition of ex means prior not current. It means past not present. It means then not now.' Then I told him that he's a fucking loser for jumping back into a pool that he already peed in. Then I told him to *fuck off!*"

She covers her face with her hands and she sits like that for awhile. And in the background I hear Tori Amos sing, "Never was a cornflake girl, thought that was a good solution."

After awhile she sits up and looks at me and goes, "I know you think I'm totally spoiled and that my life is one long easy ride. And maybe in some ways, it's true. But that doesn't mean my life is perfect. Far from it." She reaches into her purse and pulls out a tissue and presses it against her nose for a minute.

"You know, sometimes I feel like I've been dumped in the middle of the ocean without a life vest, but everyone just expects me to be able to swim to shore, and break the speed record, and get a gold medal for doing it. It's like, everyone has these huge expectations of who I should be, you know, 'M's a cheerleader, M gets good grades, M's going to Princeton. Mommy and Daddy's perfect little M.' "

She shakes her head and rolls the tissue up into a tiny ball. "I'm so fucking perfect that they don't even have to pay attention to me. I'm so fucking perfect that they wouldn't even consider that those drugs were mine. Do you know how much that hurt? That my mom was so unconcerned about me that she just pawned the whole thing off on you? And do you know why she did that? Because that made it easier for her."

She looks at me for a moment, then she puts her head in her hands and starts sobbing these giant, shoulder-shaking tears. I just sit there and watch her cry, and think about what she just said, and I can't believe how alike we really are. It's like, we've both been really busy sabotaging ourselves. Just messing up anyway we could, hoping someone would pay attention. But the people we want to notice just don't care as much as we wish they would and there's nothing we can do about it.

She wipes her face on the hem of her dress and says, "I'm sorry about messing up your date, really."

I just look at her and shrug. "Don't worry about it. We're going on another one."

Chapter 36

Graduation is just two weeks away and I'm definitely earning my diploma. It's like, on the nights I'm not at work I've stuck to my new routine of turning off my phone, TV, and stereo (anything that might distract me), and spending an hour on each of my subjects. It's kind of like being on restriction again, only this time it's self-imposed.

When I finished my *Anna Karenina* essay I actually held on to it for two full days before turning it in. I just didn't know how to go about it. I mean, I didn't want to walk up to Mr. Sommers's desk and give it to him in front of the whole class, and I really didn't want to stay late and give it to him when no one was there. So one day when he got called out of class for a few minutes and everybody started acting all wild, I went up to his desk and slid it under some other papers and hoped that he'd find it, but not until after the bell rang.

And even though I feel like I'm making some progress, it still seems like I'm the only person in this whole damn school that doesn't have the slightest clue of what I'm going to do this summer. Practically everyone is either going on some great vacation, or on a major nonstop shopping spree for their new college wardrobe, and of course M is doing both. Her family is cruising the Greek Isles, and then stopping in Paris for a few days on the way home so she can load up on cool stuff to wear at Princeton. I'll probably just put in more time at the store and wait for something to happen.

I talked to Guy a few times, but I've only seen him once since that night with M 'cause we've both been pretty busy studying for finals.

So I'm just sitting in my room, taking a break from my French workbook, and reading my numerology in the new *Elle,* when the phone rings. I'm assuming it's M so I pick it up on the first ring.

Someone with a British accent goes, "Alex!"

And I go, "Connor?"

And the connection is kind of strange so I know he's still in England. And he says, "What's up?"

And I want to pretend that tons of things are up, you know. But the truth is this magazine I'm reading has pretty much been the zenith of my day. So as part of my new honesty campaign I say, "Nothing."

So then he goes, "How's school?"

And I say, "Great!" Which isn't as big of a lie as it would normally be. "How's the band, did you sign them?"

"We did, and I think it's going to be really big. I'll send you some studio tracks later. Hey, I heard Trevor and M broke up," he says.

"Yeah." I close the magazine and put my feet up on my desk.

"Wow, that's too bad."

"I guess."

"So when are you coming to London?" he asks.

"What?" I say. I mean, is he joking?

He laughs and goes, "When are you going to visit me?"

So of course I give a nervous laugh, and go, "Um, I don't know."

"Well, think about it. It could be fun."

So then we chat for maybe a minute more and hang up. And I sit at my desk wondering what that was all about. It wasn't long ago that I dreamed about going to London with Connor. I thought that would solve all my problems, and change my life. But now,

I'm not so sure. And like, what would happen once I got there? Would I be his girlfriend? And more important, do I even want to be his girlfriend?

I guess after all that happened it never occurred to me that I would ever go there. But then I never really thought I would hear from Connor again and this is the second time he's called.

But maybe I could go there. I mean, I have nothing else planned, and I've even managed to save a little money from working at the store.

So on my way to work I stop at a bookstore and pick up a travel guide to England. You know, just to skim through it and see what it's really like there.

About an hour before closing Blake calls me from the Men's Department.

"Alex," he whispers, "I just gave Ronette my two weeks' notice."

"No way," I say. "How'd she take it? What'd she say?"

"She wished me luck and great success. She was so nice about it I didn't get to say anything nasty to her. And then she hugged me."

"Gross."

"Yeah, it was kind of. What are you doing?" he asks. "Because it's dead over here."

"It's dead here too," I tell him. "I've had two customers all night. But I don't care 'cause I got this book on London and it's pretty much taking up all of my time." I close the book and run my hand over the picture of Big Ben on the cover.

"Don't you think you're maybe taking your Richard Branson fantasy a little too far?" he says.

I just laugh and say, "No, it's not about that. Connor called and he invited me to visit."

"Are you going?" he asks cautiously.

"I don't know." I twist the phone cord around my wrist and turn to look at myself in the mirror.

"Did I tell you that Ken's moving to New York with me?"

"Are you serious?"

"Yeah, his company has an office there. He's putting in for a transfer and there's a really good chance he'll get it. You know it would be really great if you came to New York this summer too. Between me and your sister, you've got plenty of places to stay."

"You don't think I should visit London?" I ask him.

"It's not London I don't think you should visit."

"Oh, you mean Connor."

"Well, I'm just worried about you."

"What do you mean?"

"I don't want you to get hurt," he says.

"Well, what about giving someone a second chance?" I ask.

"Alex, the only one you should be giving a second chance is you."

Chapter 37

After work I go to M's house. Her parents are out for the night at some charity dinner, and we're just taking our time getting ready to go out. And I feel kind of guilty because I'm sort of halfhearted about being here. I mean I'd really rather be home studying for next week's finals, because our friendship just isn't what it used to be, and I'm kind of over the whole going-out scene. But she kept going on and on about how it was our last big night out before summer and college and all that stuff, and I figured that one more night out on the town wasn't gonna kill me. But just to be safe, I made her promise that no matter what, we wouldn't end up at a club. I know it sounds crazy to be jaded at seventeen and a half, but I just can't help it.

So M's painting her toenails in a color called Tangerine Dream with her right hand and drinking a glass of her parents' champagne with the other. While I'm rifling through her closet looking for something cool to wear.

I'm only halfway through one of the dress racks when I go, "Are you really gonna take all this stuff to college with you? I mean, you're gonna fill up the entire dorm room just with your clothes."

M looks at her overflowing closet and shrugs. "After my mom's done pilfering, you can have whatever I don't take."

"Really?" I ask.

"Yeah, why not?"

I pull out a suede halter-top I've coveted all year, and slip it over my head. Then I pull on some suede pants I found folded on a shelf. I walk over to the full-length mirror and gaze at my reflection. Then I turn to M and go, "Pocahontas?"

She looks at me and laughs. "Totally."

So I take it all off and start over.

Then M goes, "Did I tell you that my dad cornered me about the 'extravagant,' as he puts it, balance on the credit card?"

"Oh my god, no. What happened?" I grab a black silk skirt off a hanger.

"Nothing happened. I just explained that if he wanted to really experience an *'extravagant balance'* he could just wait and see what the divorce was gonna cost him when I tell my mom about his mistress."

"No way!"

"Way."

"But I thought your mom already knows and isn't doing anything about it."

"Yeah, she knows. But he doesn't know that I know that she knows. He was so floored by me knowing that he just sat there all red in the face and then he started yelling at me about some totally unrelated situation. So I stood up and told him that as much as I enjoyed our little chat, I had other places to be."

"What'd he do?"

"Nothing. Bastard." She rolls her eyes. "Hey, have you talked to your dad since that big argument?"

"No." I just look at her and shrug.

M nods and goes, "God, I hope when the time comes we can pick 'em a little better than our moms did." Then she pours more champagne into her glass, takes a sip and goes, "What are you gonna do?"

"What do you mean?" I ask. "After graduation? I have no idea. Why? What are you gonna do?" I pull a lacy, silk camisole over my head and search her shoe racks for something I can walk in.

"Apparently I'm going Greek Island hopping and then on to Princeton."

I reach down for a pair of kitten-heeled sandals and sit on the edge of the bed while I slide them onto my feet. "What do you mean 'apparently'?"

M takes a sip of her champagne and goes, "I don't know. Sometimes, it just doesn't feel like it's my decision. Sometimes, I just wish I could cut my hair short, dye it blue, and say 'fuck you' to my mom and dad. You know, in a note, on the fridge. It's not like they're ever around so I could say it to their face." She looks at me and laughs.

"That's just nerves," I tell her and reach for one of her little denim jackets.

"What if it's not?" she says, and she really looks panicked.

"You're gonna be fine. I promise."

She goes over to the mirror and runs her fingers through her long blond hair, and gazes at her perfect reflection. "Yeah, you're right." And then she turns and looks at me and goes, "Do you realize you haven't mentioned Richard Branson lately?"

I look at her and roll my eyes. "Yeah, I guess I'm getting a life, huh?"

I'm searching in my bag for some lip gloss when she goes, "Heads up!" Then she tosses a robin's-egg-blue box at me.

"What the—?" I catch it before it hits the floor and stare at it in my hand.

"Just open it," she says.

So I pull off the white ribbon, and remove the top, and inside I find this really cool, silver, Tiffany charm bracelet just like the one she wears that I've always admired. She even had my initials engraved on it. I hold it up in front of me and ask, "What's this for? I mean, it's not my birthday or anything."

"I don't know. I guess it's for graduation." She shrugs.

"But I don't have anything for you!" I say.

"Okay, then it's not for graduation. Listen, I guess it's just sort of a thank-you present for being such a good friend." She takes a sip of her champagne and looks at me. "I mean it, even after what I did to you, you were still there for me. I totally crashed your date with Guy but you still helped me that night and I don't know what I would have done if you hadn't been there. I was in worse shape than you realized."

I hold the bracelet in my hand and I feel weird about accepting it because sometimes M's gifts turn into bribes. But then I glance at her and she looks so happy and excited and it makes me feel guilty for thinking that. I mean, we've been friends forever and if she says it's a thank-you gift, then it's a thank-you gift. And I shouldn't be so suspicious. And it's not like I don't deserve it. So I put it on, and I admire the way it hangs on my wrist, next to my watch.

So we end up at a club. When we pull into the valet I look right at her and say, "I can't believe you!"

"What?" she asks innocently.

"We agreed. *No clubs,* remember?"

She hands the valet her keys and says, "Relax, it's not a club. It's a bar."

"It has valet parking, a big line, and a cover charge, M. It's a *club.*"

"Sorry, Alex, you're wrong. It's called, Bar None. See," she says, pointing to the neon sign over the door. "It's a *bar.*"

And I stand there in front of the door and then I look down at the shiny, silver bracelet on my wrist, and I know that, once again, I've been bribed.

Chapter 38

She just happens to know the bouncer from her Trevor days so we don't have to stand in line and we go right upstairs to the VIP room.

I'm not really into the VIP scene like M is. It just seems so pretentious to me. I mean, it's really not so different from the downstairs room except that everyone up here is busy patting themselves on the back for being hip enough to be up here. I really can't stand that self-congratulatory stuff.

So we're sitting in this tiny booth and M is flirting big time with some guy in the corner who just sent over two glasses of champagne from the big bottle that's sitting on his table. And I'm just looking around the room at all these fakers and posers who are acting like this is so important. At the beginning of the year I would have been thinking I was so cool to be sitting here too, but now I just feel tired.

I look over at M and watch her reach into her purse and pull out a joint and a silver lighter.

I just sit there looking at her, thinking there's no way she's gonna smoke that here, in a public place, where it's against the law to even smoke cigarettes.

When she starts to light it up, I get all panicky and go, "M, you're not gonna smoke that are you?"

She gives me this annoyed look and says, "Would you just chill out? I just want to relax a little. You know, maybe you need to relax a little too. It's like, you're so judgmental and you've never even tried it."

I look around the club to see if anyone is watching. A few people are looking at us, but no one seems to care. I watch M inhale and hold it, then go into a major coughing fit as she exhales. And her face is all red, and she certainly doesn't look any more relaxed to me, but what do I know? I mean, maybe she's right. I am kind of judgmental about doing drugs, especially for someone who's never tried any. So I look at her, and go, "Do you think I should try it?"

She looks at me all surprised and says, "Yeah, have at it."

So I take the tiny smoldering blunt from between her fingers and hold it up to my mouth. And I can't believe I'm gonna do this because I made a promise to myself that I wouldn't do things like this. I know it sounds lame, and it's just pot, which is natural, and the Indians did it and stuff, and it's really no big deal, but a while back I made this list of things I wouldn't do and dorky as it seems smoking pot was number three.

But maybe I outgrew that stupid list. Because to be honest I wrote it back in like, ninth grade when I was all into getting straight A's, and being the class president, and all those other activities that I've since abandoned. I mean, I'm just not any of those things anymore, so maybe this is what I am now, a person that smokes pot in the VIP room of a trendy new club.

So I hold it up to my mouth and just as I'm about to inhale I look at M and she's got this huge smile on her face, and she's all excited, and it really bugs me that my doing something that goes against my personal value system would bring her so much joy. So I take the joint and drop it into my champagne glass and watch it float briefly with the bubbles and then submerge."

"What the fuck, Alex?" she yells.

"I changed my mind," I say.

"Yeah? Well you didn't have to drown it! Shit! You wrecked the champagne *and* the pot!" She rolls her eyes and looks at the ceiling. "You're so fucking holy. God, I was just trying to relax a little. Everything is such a big fucking deal with you."

She's glaring at me and I just can't stand it anymore. I can't stand this stupid club, and I can't stand her. But I don't say anything, I just give her a nasty look, grab my purse, and leave.

I go into the bathroom.

There's a crowd of girls at the mirror, putting on lipstick and saying mean things about some girls they know that aren't in the restroom. So I push into an empty stall, grab my cell phone, and check my messages. There are two. The first one is from Connor. He's talking the usual telephone talk, you know "How are you? Blah blah blah." Then he asks me if I've decided about London, because he's reserved a first-class ticket for me on Virgin! I stop and play the message again so I can hear him tell me that a second time, then I push two to save. Then I listen to my next message. It's my dad. So right as I have my index finger poised over three to erase, he tells me he got married last weekend. I feel sick. I don't hit three. I press one to listen to it again and it's for real. It's weird how he doesn't mention who he married. But I have to assume it was Cheri.

Oh my god. Am I supposed to be happy for him? Because I feel totally nauseous. It's the same sick feeling I had that day when I vomited in the bathroom at school. I lean against the door and try to piece it all together.

Let's see, Connor gave me a first-class invitation to London, and my dad gave me a stepmom that's younger than my sister, and named after a fruit. I wrap my arms tightly around myself and try to keep from crying. And I don't even know why I'm so upset. Because the truth is, I was replaced long ago. And I've wasted a lot of time trying to pretend otherwise.

I make my way back to the table, hoping I can convince M to go home, but she's no longer sitting there because she is now at the corner table sitting on top of that Big Muscular Blond Guy with the free champagne.

When she sees me she waves and shouts, "Hey Alex, come over and hang out with us."

So I go and sit with M and her new friends because I don't really know what else to do. I just sit there watching her down like, her fifth drink and at one point when her friend gets up to go somewhere she leans over and says, "Jeez, is he like hot, or what?"

I just look at her and shrug.

And she goes, "What's wrong with you?"

But she doesn't say it like she's concerned. She says it like she's annoyed. So I don't tell her about my dad's message, and the decision I have to make about Connor. Instead I just shrug and go, "You wanna go soon?"

Then she rolls her eyes and says, "Would you please just relax. This is our last big night out! Why are you trying to wreck it? We'll probably never get to do this again, since I'm leaving for college and stuff!"

And right when I'm about to tell her that I don't consider this quality time, her friend comes back and she totally ignores me again.

Eventually we all end up at someone's house and I'm sitting on the couch next to some guy. I have no idea where M is, and I don't even know this guy's name. But he's totally getting on my nerves, because it's all too obvious that he's just looking to get laid. And you know what? I'm just not into it. I'm not saying I'll never have sex again, or that I have to fall in love first. I'm just saying that I want to belong to me for awhile, and not share myself with anyone else.

So I get up from the couch and say, "Excuse me."

And what's-his-name goes, "Where are you going?"

So I stand in front of him and say, "Listen, no offense, I just want to be alone right now."

He gives me an odd look and shrugs. He'll get over it.

I wander around the house looking for M, because I'm not having fun and I'm determined to go, but I can't find her anywhere. So I go outside in the backyard and I see her in the Jacuzzi with her new friend, and they look just like a commercial for some sleazy, new, Reality TV show.

They're both naked and totally making out, but I walk up to them anyway because it's nothing I haven't seen before and I'm serious about going home. I clear my throat so they'll know I'm standing there and M breaks away and sees me and goes, "Hey, what's going on?" and she gives me that same annoyed look that she's given me a lot tonight.

But the truth is, I don't care about looks like that from her anymore, so I just say, "I want to go home."

"What? Now? Uh, I'm a little busy here." And she nods her head toward her friend who is rolling his eyes at me.

"I'm serious," I say. "I want to go."

Then she looks right at me and says, "Well, I'm not leaving, so I don't know what to tell you."

I'm standing in front of her and I'm on the verge of tears. But I also know that this is the very last time that she gets to treat me like this.

I shake my head and say, "Okay then, I'll see you later." And I turn to walk away.

"Yeah, right," she says. "Like where are you going?"

I stop and turn to look at her. I look at her until she starts to get uncomfortable. And then I say, "I don't know where I'm going M, but I'm going somewhere."

Chapter 39

The sun is making its slow ascent, lighting up the sky, but not yet burning off the morning chill, so I wrap my arms tightly around my waist and start walking. And I'm hoping I don't get mugged, or kidnapped, or raped because I'm all alone, and I have no idea where I am, where I'm going, or even how I'll get there. I guess I'm starting to feel a little panicked. I mean, now that I've made my point with M by storming out like that, part of me wants to just duck back in, wait it out, and get a ride home in her comfortable, warm, safe BMW.

The parked cars lining the street are coated in a thick, silvery layer of morning dew, and other than the faint bleeping of a distant car alarm the neighborhood is quiet. I turn the corner on to what seems like a busier, less residential street and I immediately regret it when I see these two guys walking right toward me. They're wearing baggy jeans and similar sweatshirts with the hoods pulled up over their heads, but I can't tell if that's because it's cold out, or if it's so I won't be able to identify them when they're done torturing me.

I glance longingly at the other side of the street and wonder if I should cross before they reach me, but I hesitate too long and now they're coming right at me. So I just look straight ahead and start walking faster and right as they pass me they nod and say, "Hey," and I exhale the breath I'd been holding without realizing it, and I wonder if I'm crazy to be wandering around, by myself, somewhere in LA, when it's still kind of dark out.

I cross the street and walk another block, passing storefronts that will remain locked for at least another three hours, and then I turn another corner for no apparent reason and suddenly I know exactly where I am.

So I head over to this little coffee place that's just opening for business and I get in line behind two of those *Pacific Blue* cops. They turn around and really look me over, but there's no law against getting a latte after a long night, so I just totally ignore them. I mean, it's hard to take a cop in bicycle shorts seriously.

I'm just leaning against the wall, waiting for my order when these two women walk in. They're speaking Spanish, and I watch them point at the donuts in the glass case, and listen to the soft sounds of their language. And it's so nice and musical that I wish I could understand and be a part of it. Then one of them starts laughing at something the other one said, and you can hear that high tinny sound bounce off the ugly tiled walls, and the counter covered in fingerprints, and even the old man behind the register looks up and smiles. I mean, it's really a beautiful thing to hear at six in the morning when you've been up all night, and you've lost your best friend.

I grab my large latte and an oversize glazed donut and carry it out to my usual spot on Venice Beach. I've never been here in the morning like this and it's really nice, serene and peaceful, which are not words you would normally use to describe this place.

Most of the homeless and junkies are waking up or going to sleep, and some of the vendors are slowly starting to arrive. And as I tear a piece off my donut, I think about second chances and how I've been giving them to all the wrong people. And how maybe Blake is right, maybe I'm the one that deserves one.

I mean, it's time I face my future and accept the fact that M isn't really such a good friend to me, and hasn't been for awhile now. My dad doesn't care about me, and now that he's remarried, the sick fact is he'll probably give himself a second chance and have a few more kids. So if I was holding onto any smidgen of hope that he'd come around, well, I'd better just let it go right now.

My grades suck, especially in History and Economics, and there's just no getting around the fact that it's completely my fault. I totally blew my junior and senior years. I just buried the whole thing in a big pile of apathy.

And even though I've been doing better about going to class and stuff, it's still too late for a scholarship and it won't get me into a good school. But that doesn't mean I can't fix it. I mean, maybe it's time I write the story of my own happy ending.

I dig around in my purse looking for a pen and a scrap of paper. I've got to make a list. I've got to have a plan. Because I refuse to be running around like this the same time next year. I want to have something of value.

So at the top of the page I write ME in capital letters, then I underline it. Then next to the number one I put SCHOOL. School is very important. Duh. Okay, I may be a little late in figuring that out but better late than never, right? So what if I have to go to community college for awhile. If I work during the day and go at night, maybe it won't be so bad. And if I really buckle down and get serious then I can wipe out the last two pathetic years, get my A.A., and apply for a scholarship for a better school in a year or two.

At number two I put WORK. The truth is I'd like to be a writer. But until that happens, I could probably do more with the job I have now. I can probably switch to full time after graduation and even inquire about that assistant buyer position that I heard is opening up soon.

Next to three, I put FAMILY. Then I write DEAL WITH IT.

Next to four, I put LONDON. But I'm not going. I mean, it was nice of Connor to invite me, and to offer me a first-class ticket, but I've been sidetracked by too many people for too long. I've wasted a lot of time waiting for other people to start my life for me, and I'm just not willing to put my dreams on hold for some guy. Connor is not my future. And I'm not gonna make the same mistakes my mom made.

I guess I got a little ahead of myself when I numbered the page to five because I really can't think of a fifth. It just always seems that every list should include at least five items. But Rome wasn't built in a day, was it? At least I think that's what they said in AP History.

Then at the very bottom of the page I write, CHANGE IS CONSTANT. 'Cause that pretty much sums it all up for me. Then I carefully fold up my list and put it in my purse and I just lean back and watch the people and try to make my coffee last.

And right when I'm thinking I should probably get up and head home, I see him, the Iguana Man. He's dressed in a pair of dirty old cutoffs and the same old Grateful Dead T-shirt with the same old iguana sitting right there on his shoulder, like it's permanently attached or something. I'm just watching him walk aimlessly down the boardwalk when all of a sudden he stops and looks up. We stare at each other for a moment and now he's cutting across the sand, quickly heading toward me. I look around nervously, hoping I'm mistaken, hoping that there's someone else he's fixated on. But I'm the only one sitting here.

I know I should get up and get out of here, but it's like I've grown roots deep into the earth and I'm unable to move. So I just sit and hold my breath, and pray that he won't recognize me, that he won't speak to me.

As he approaches I can hear the song he always hums under his breath, and smell his strange odor, and my body tenses up in a primal preparation for fight or flight. But when he's right, exactly in front of me, I start to relax. Because the truth is, he no longer scares me. I've got a plan now, a direction, and there's just no way I'm gonna end up like that.

He passes by, as though we'd never met, and goes straight for a big, metal trash can and starts rummaging through it. I watch him retrieve an old, empty beer bottle, and as he's walking away I realize there's something I want to do.

I grab my purse and go after him and when I'm right behind him I say, "Hey, Iguana Man! Stop! I have something for you."

He stops and turns and looks at me and his eyes are still red like last time but I can tell they don't recognize me. I remove the Tiffany bracelet that M gave me and I hold it out to him in offering and say, "Here. This is for you. I want you to have it."

He holds it up and squints at it, then peers at me closely. "Why?" he asks.

I just shrug and say, "I helped someone once and she gave it to me. You helped me, so I want to give it to you."

He looks at me for a moment as though he's trying to place me, and then he just nods his head and puts it in his pocket. And as I watch him wander away I wonder if it ever occurs to him to try another beach, another city, another zip code. Or if he got tired long ago and just gave up. I vow to just keep moving forward, no matter what, because there's just no way it stops here for me.

When I can no longer see him I tell myself I'm ready to move on. And this time I really mean it.

Chapter 40

The last days of school are total chaos, but somehow I manage to keep up with it all. I took the week off work, doubled up on my study time, and even offered to do some last-ditch extra credit for History and Economics. I guess I forgot how much work it is to be a good student, but if they give me a diploma, then it will all be worth it.

I haven't seen much of M. She's missed some days of school and I guess her mom is keeping a pretty tight rein on her now. A few days after I left her in LA, she knocked on my door and apologized while her mom waited outside in the car. She told me that she spent the entire weekend getting high with those guys and when she finally made it home she was pretty messed up. But she just walked right into the kitchen where her parents were having breakfast, stood next to the table until they looked up from their newspapers, then she said, "I have something to tell you."

She told them all about the drugs, and the drinking, and how it had nothing to do with me, that it was all her. I guess her dad started yelling at her but her mom told him to shut up. Then her mom came around the table and put her arm around her daughter for the first time in years and walked her down the hall to her bedroom where they could talk in private.

M's mom made her see a psychiatrist, but after one or two sessions the doctor insisted that her parents go too, and that's when M finally confronted her dad about his mistress. So now her parents have their own weekly sessions, and the trip to Greece and France has been delayed indefinitely, but M seems pretty okay with it. She said it's kind of a pain having them all involved in her life again, and that she can't wait to get out of Orange County, go to Princeton, and get a fresh start in a new place. I have no doubt that she'll totally excel there too.

My sister called on Tuesday and said, "Hey Alex, I bought a ticket to visit you and Mom. And while I'm there I was hoping I'd get to see you in a cap and gown?"

I started laughing. "I think it's gonna happen. I've been study- ing really hard."

"Congratulations!" she said. "I'm really proud of you."

"So I guess you heard about Dad?" I asked, twisting the phone cord around my arm.

"Yeah, Cheri sent me an announcement. He didn't even call. Can you believe it?"

"Yeah, I can believe it," I said.

"Does Mom know yet?"

"Well," I said. "I was really nervous about telling her, you know? But it didn't go too badly. She just shrugged and said, 'Bet- ter her than me.'"

By Thursday, I'd taken all of my finals and although there's no doubt that I could have done better, I didn't choke near as much as I could have. And the good news is they're going to let me grad- uate.

M waited for me after AP History and asked me if I'd sign her yearbook. She seemed nervous about asking, and even though we're not best friends anymore it still made me feel bad. So she gave me hers and I gave her mine and we took them home over night so that we could write something really meaningful.

But when I got home, I sat in my room and stared at the empty page she reserved for me and I tried to come up with something good, but my mind just kind of went blank. It's like, I've known her forever, and we've had some crazy good times and more recently, some crazy bad times, but I didn't feel like recapping them, and I've never been very good at the mushy stuff, and I definitely wasn't writing "don't ever change," because change is what it's all about. So I borrowed a line from a Sheryl Crow song and wrote, "Regret reminds you you're alive." Because I guess we've both had a few things to regret lately. And then I borrowed a line from some famous French lady and wrote, *"Non, je ne regrette rien."* Because you just can't regret the things you learned from.

The last day of school I'm sitting at my desk in French listening to the morning announcements drone on and on, stuff about a final bake sale at noon, and last-minute grad night info. And then this, "Congratulations goes out to graduating senior Alexandra Sky for winning first place in the statewide Teen Fiction Writers Contest. Alexandra will be receiving a two-thousand-dollar scholarship award, and will go on to compete in the Nationals for a trip to New York City, an additional five-thousand-dollar scholarship, and publication in *Sixteen* magazine."

I sit at my desk stunned at hearing my name over the loudspeaker. After I secretly submitted my story that day, I just put it out of my mind. I mean, I was so convinced I didn't stand a chance that I didn't mention it to anyone.

Everyone in my French class just stares at me, but then M starts clapping and whistling and they all join in. And I just sit there and smile because *I got a scholarship!* and I never thought that would happen.

When Mr. Sommers sees me at my locker he comes over and says, "Alex, it's been a pleasure knowing you the last few years."

I'm shocked that he'd say that and I look at him and go, "It has?"

He laughs and says, "I'm aware of your attendance record and I'm flattered that you managed to make it to my class more than any other." I just look at him and then he goes, "And congratulations on the Fiction contest. I think you're very talented."

I go, "Really?"

And he goes, "Really. And thanks for the Tolstoy essay."

He smiles at me then and wishes me the best of luck in my future. Six months ago I never could have imagined that happening.

M's parents have invited us to dinner after the ceremony. I guess they're trying to make amends or something. But even though I'm not angry about the whole drug mess anymore, I'm not going. I'm not going to grad night either. Instead I made plans to have dinner with my mom and my sister, and afterward I'm meeting up with Guy for a late-night horseback ride.

My dad never did call or send a card, but I'm okay with that, really I am. I guess he's just busy honeymooning with his virgin bride. Okay, maybe that was a little sarcastic, indicating that I'm not entirely over it, but you know what? I will be. I'm working on it. After all it's number three on my list.

And speaking of my list, I carry it around all the time. Even sitting in the hot sun with this graduation gown sticking to the dress that Blake designed and made for me. In one pocket I'm carrying my list, and in the other is the scholarship check that Mrs. Gross presented to me after school.

It was the first time in the last two years that I was called into her office for something positive. When she handed me the check she came around her desk and hugged me and said, "I knew you could do it."

You probably think it's foolish to carry the check around in my pocket. Like, I may end up losing it or something. But no way is that gonna happen. I've finally got a good firm grip on the future.

I look out into the stands and search the crowd and see my mom and my sister. I wave at them and they see me and wave back. And then I see M's parents, the size two and the doctor, but they don't see me, they're too busy looking at all the other parents. Then I look over at M and she rolls her eyes at me and I stick out my tongue at her, and we both crack up.

One

They say there are five stages of grief:

1. Denial
2. Anger
3. Bargaining
4. Depression
5. Acceptance

Up until last year I didn't know there were lists like that. I had no idea people actually kept track of these things. But still, even if I had known, I never would've guessed that just a few days before my fourteenth birthday I'd be stuck in stage one.

But then you never think that kind of bad news will knock on your door. Because those kinds of stories, the kind that involve a stone-faced newscaster interrupting your favorite TV show to report a crucial piece of "late breaking news," are always about someone else's unfortunate family. They're never supposed to be about yours.

But what made it even worse is that I was the first to know.

Well, after the cops.

And, of course, Zoë.

Not to mention the freak who was responsible for the whole mess in the first place.

And even though they didn't exactly say anything other than "May we please speak to your parents?" It was the regret on those two detectives' faces, the defeat in their weary eyes, that pretty much gave it all away.

It was after school and I was home alone, trying to keep to my standard cookie-eating, TV-watching, homework-avoiding routine, even though I really couldn't concentrate on any of it. I mean, normally at 4:10 P.M. both my parents would still be at work, my sister, Zoë, would be out with her boyfriend, and I would be sitting cross-legged on the floor, wedged between the couch and the coffee table, dunking Oreos into a tall glass of cold milk until my teeth were all black, the milk was all sopped up, and my stomach was all swollen and queasy.

So I guess in a way I was just trying to emulate all of that, go through the motions, and pretend everything was normal. That my parents weren't really out searching for Zoë, and that I wasn't already in denial long before I had good reason to be.

But now, almost a year later, I can honestly say that I'm able to check off stages one through three, and am settling into stage five. Though sometimes, in the early morning hours, when the house is quiet and my parents are still asleep, I find myself regressing toward four. Especially now that September's here, putting us just days away from the one-year anniversary of the last time Zoë shimmied up the big oak tree, climbed onto my balcony, and came in through my unlocked french doors.

I remember rolling over and squinting against the morning light, watching as she pressed her index finger to her smiling lips, her short red nail like the bottom of an upside-down exclamation point, as she performed her exaggerated, cartoonish, stealth tiptoe through my room, out my door, and down the hall.

Sometimes now, when I think back on that day, I add a whole new scene. One where, instead of turning over and falling back to sleep, I say something important, something meaningful, something that would've let her know, beyond all doubt, just how much I loved and admired her.

But the truth is, I didn't say anything.

I mean, how was I supposed to know that was the last time I'd ever see her?

Two

When the woman at the funeral home, the one in the long floral dress, with the frizzy french braid, asked for a picture of Zoë, my mom dropped her head in her hands and sobbed so hysterically that my dad pulled her close, clenched his jaw, and nodded firmly, as though he was already working on it.

I stared at the toe of my black Converse sneaker, noticing how the fabric was wearing thin, and wondering what that lady could possibly need a picture for. I guess it seemed like a weird request, considering how pretty much everywhere you looked in our town you'd see a picture of Zoë. And since my sister was always so elusive and hard to pin down in life, it seemed like I actually saw more of her after her disappearance than I had when she lived down the hall.

First there were the two "missing person" flyers taped to just about every available surface. One a stiff, grainy, black-and-white grabbed in a panic and copied from last year's yearbook.

The other, one of Zoë's more recent headshots, depicting her as beautiful, loose, and happy, more like the sister I knew, that also included a generous reward for anyone with any information, no questions asked.

And then, as the days ticked by, her face started appearing just about everywhere—in newspapers, magazines, and nationally televised news reports. Even the makeshift memorial, built by well-wishers and propped up in front of our house, contained so many candles, poems, stuffed animals, angels, and photos of Zoë that it threatened to take over the entire street until my dad enlisted a neighbor's help and hauled it all away.

The funny thing was, Zoë had always dreamed of being a model, an actress, someone famous and admired by all. She longed for the day when she could escape our small, boring town, and go somewhere glamorous, like L.A., or New York, just someplace exciting and far from here. And so, while we were out searching, while we were busy smothering our doubt with hope, I played this kind of game in my head where I pretended that all of this was great exposure for Zoë and her future as a famous person. Like it was the ultimate casting call. And I spent those long, empty, thankless moments imagining how excited she'd be when she finally came home and saw her face plastered all across the nation.

But then later, in the mortuary, as I watched my parents make the world's most depressing arrangements, encouraged into credit card debt by the man in the stark black suit who guided them toward the most luxurious casket, the most abundant flowers, and the whitest doves—sparing no expense at her memory—I sat wide-eyed, realizing the lucrative business of loss, while wondering if my mom got the irony behind Zoë's ambition and the woman's request, and if that's why she was crying so hard.

But then, I guess there were millions of reasons to cry that day. So it's not like I had to go searching for The One.

I didn't know why that woman wanted a photo, but I doubted my dad, grief stricken and distracted, would ever remember to give her one. So after they'd signed away their savings and were headed out the door, I reached into my old blue nylon wallet, the one with the surf brand sticker still partially stuck to the front, its edges frayed and curled all around, and retrieved the photo Zoë had given me just a few weeks before, the one that showcased her large dark eyes, generous smile, high cheekbones, and long wavy, dark hair. The one she'd planned to send to the big New York and L.A. agencies.

"Here," I said, pressing it into the woman's soft, round hand, watching as she did the quick intake of breath I was so used to seeing when confronted with an image of Zoë for the very first time.

She looked at me and smiled, the fine lines around her blue eyes merging together until almost joining as one. "I'll be doing her makeup, and I want to get it just right. So, thank you—" She left that last part dangling, looking embarrassed that she knew all about my loss, but didn't know my name.

"Echo." I smiled. "My name is Echo. And you can keep the picture. Zoë would've liked that." Then I ran outside to catch up with my parents.

Three

Zoë and Echo are Greek names, even though we're not at all Greek. Zoë means life, and Echo, well, I know you know what it means, so I'll just say that it's also a nymph who pined away for some guy named Narcissus until nothing was left but her voice. Which is something, by the way, that I would never do. You know, fade away over some guy. I mean, not even Chess Williams, the cutest guy in my class since fourth grade, is worth crumbling for. Anyway, it's basically a Greek mythology thing, and I guess that's why we got names like that. Nothing to do with nationality, and everything to do with academics.

My parents are big on academics. Which I guess is why they're both professors. And, knowing I'll risk looking like a total brainiac nerd, I'll just go ahead and admit, right now and for the record, that I'm pretty big on academics too. But Zoë? Zoë hated all that. She was beautiful, and wild, and too busy getting into trouble and sneaking out of the house to ever slow down long enough to actually finish a book. Yet she was so sweet about it, and had such uncontained enthusiasm (for everything but homework), that no one ever held a grudge or judged her too harshly.

"Life is too exhilarating to read about! You gotta get out there and live it!" she'd say, just moments before sneaking onto my balcony and down the old oak tree, as I lay in bed reading one of my numerous library-issued novels.

But I'm nothing like Zoë. I'm average, not beautiful. I mean, my hair is medium brown and kind of limp, not rich and wavy like hers. And where she had amazing dark eyes with extra-thick long lashes, mine are light hazel, which may sound nice on paper, but believe me, they're far more functional than special. And my body, well, I'm really, really hoping that the years between fourteen and sixteen will be as kind and generous to me as they were to her (though so far, I'm a couple weeks shy of fifteen and there's nothing to report). And I've definitely never been in any kind of trouble. Well, at least not the serious kind. I mean, so far my biggest offense is returning a library book two weeks late because I liked it so much I decided to read it again.

But Zoë? Well, let's just say that had she actually made it home that day, she would've been in for it big time.

"Echo?" my mom calls from the bottom of the stairs. "I'm leaving. Are you sure you don't need a ride?"

"Nope. Have a good day." I peek around my bedroom door, catching a quick glimpse of her as she heads outside before locking all three dead bolts, even though I'll be leaving in less than two minutes.

But that's how we live now, overly cautious, verging on completely paranoid. And it took a solid fifty-five minutes of carefully argued debate, during last night's meatloaf, steamed asparagus, and garlic mashed potatoes dinner to get both of my parents to let me walk to school, as opposed to getting door-to-door service from one of them.

And it's not like I'm going it alone or anything, since all I have to do is go halfway down the block to my best friend Abby's, before we both stop on the corner to pick up our other best friend, Jenay.

Though I guess it's pretty much a miracle my mom decided to go back to teaching in the first place. I mean, right after everything happened she took a sabbatical so she could stay home and "look after me." I guess my parents blamed themselves for what happened. Thinking that their busy, working lives didn't allow for the kind of constant vigilance required to protect us.

But really, how much can you actually protect someone before it turns into imprisonment? Because just a few months into it, that's exactly how I started to feel, like a prisoner in my own home. I mean, at first I thought it would be nice to spend more time with my mom, especially after what we'd all just been through, but it didn't take long before she started acting more like a warden. And all she required of me was to go to school, come straight home, not to talk too much, and never to venture past the front door without:

> A valid reason and detailed explanation containing
> all of the whos, hows, whys, and wheres
> &
> an approximately exact ETA and ETD.

But none of that would've been so bad if I hadn't been so lonely. I mean, Abby and Jenay didn't come over nearly as much as you'd think. Mostly because their parents wouldn't let them, always mumbling some excuse about our family "needing our space during our difficult time." But I knew that wasn't the reason.

It's like when something really horrible and tragic happens, pretty much everyone starts giving you these sad, regretful looks as they slowly back away. Like our tragedy was contagious. Like our once warm and inviting home was now a place of darkness and doom, where extreme caution was clearly warranted.

So basically, all last year, when I wasn't at school, I was pretty much alone. I mean, my mom mostly stayed curled up on the couch, clad in her old blue terry cloth robe, staring blankly at the TV, tears pouring down her cheeks, while my dad lingered at work, staying later and later, and only rarely making it home before my bedtime.

And the weekends? Well, that's when they argued. Hurling accusations back and forth like blows in a boxing match, never tiring of their need to prove, once and for all, just who was more responsible for what happened to Zoë.

I used to think that tragedy brought people closer. But now, from everything I've experienced, I know it pretty much tears them apart.

Then again, all of that happened before my mom started taking her "happy pills," which enabled her to get off the couch, out of her robe, and back to work. The fighting stopped too. Only to be replaced with a flood of formality and excessive politeness, like we're all just strangers on a cruise ship, forced to eat our meals together, and act like we're interested.

And even though on the surface we seem to be doing better, the truth is my dad still "works" late, and my mom's eyes are more vacant than ever.

And as much as I miss Zoë, as much as my heart aches, as much as I'd do anything in the world just to get her back, there are times when I actually hate her too. Because this is what she's done to me. This is what she's left me with. Two broken, deeply suspicious, hollowed-out shells for parents, and the morbid curiosity of everyone I encounter.

Tucking my hair behind my ears, I grab my backpack, run down the stairs, lock all three locks, and head toward Abby's. But before I'm even halfway there, I see her heading toward me.

"Hey," she says, her long black ponytail swinging from side to side as her face breaks into a smile, exposing the blue metal braces she can't wait to get off, as her brown eyes squint against the sun.

"Am I late?" I ask, glancing at my watch, then back at her.

"I'm early. Aaron's driving me crazy, so I bailed," she says, shaking her head and rolling her eyes as we head toward the corner where we'll pick up Jenay. Abby's brother Aaron is two years younger and pretty much the bane of her otherwise extremely orderly existence.

"What's up with Aaron?" I ask.

"What *isn't* up with Aaron?" She shakes her head again. "He bugs me so bad, sometimes I wish he'd just disappear, never to return. Then I'd have some peace. I mean, just this morning—" Suddenly she stops walking, stops talking, and just stands there, gaping at me, her mouth hanging open, her brown eyes full of sorry and regret. "Oh God, I didn't mean—"

"It's okay," I say quickly, forcing my face to smile. "Seriously. So you were eating breakfast *and . . .*" I loop my arm through hers, leading her toward the corner, and hopefully away from her guilt. Everyone is always apologizing to me now, and sometimes I wonder if it will ever stop.

"*And* there's Jenay," she says, deftly changing the subject. "Omigod, are those—? Oh man, she is *so* lucky! How did she talk her stepmom into buying those jeans? *How?*"

"Hey, you guys," Jenay says, leaning in to give each of us a hug.

But Abby's strictly business, determined to gather the facts. "I need details," she says. "*How* did you get those? *What* did you do? And will it work on my mom too?" she asks, slowly circling Jenay, her eyes coming to rest on those telltale designer back pockets, the ones with the gold embroidery that makes the whole $220 price tag seem worth it.

"Well, if you promise to get straight As, babysit my little brother every Saturday night for the rest of your life, and remain a virgin until you're old and gray, then maybe she'll get you a pair too." Jenay laughs.

"Call me when you've got that whole potty training thing handled. The last thing I need is another squirt in the eye," Abby says, maneuvering herself into the center, looping her arms through ours, and leading us toward school.

Since Abby, Jenay, and I don't share any classes, this is the last time we'll see each other until the ten-minute break between second and third periods. Which, even though technically it's only two hours away, I have to admit that right now it feels like forever.

"Okay, so everyone remembers where to go, right?" Abby asks, having deemed herself our group leader sometime back in early elementary school, when Jenay and I were too oblivious to argue or engage in any kind of power struggle.

I nod and gaze nervously around campus, as Jenay laughs. "Yes, Mom." She smiles.

"Okay, and remember, you can totally text me if you need anything. Because I'm leaving my cell on vibrate," Abby adds.

And even though I'm gazing across campus at Marc—who up until last week I hadn't seen for nearly a year—I'm fully aware of Abby's stare and how that last part was meant for me.

If you were going to categorize us, and let's face it, most people just naturally do, you could say that Jenay is the clumsy, funny, pretty one (even though most of the time she doesn't know it), Abby's the super-organized, bossy one (and yeah, most of the time she does know it), and I'm the completely tragic one. Though before last year, most people probably would've said that I'm the cynical, brainy one. But that doesn't mean that Jenay's not smart, or that Abby's not pretty, or that I can't be hopeful. Those are just the things that people usually notice first. But since Abby and Jenay have been my best friends for as long as I can remember, I guess I don't really see them that way. When I look at them I just see two people who are always there for me, who can always make me laugh, and who can sometimes even help me forget.

Clutching my schedule, I recheck my room number, even though it's practically tattooed on my brain, ever since the "dry run" Abby subjected us to a little over a week ago, so we wouldn't look like "your typical clueless freshmen" (even though we were) on our very first day.

"They're here. The schedules. Check your mailbox and meet me on the corner in five," she'd said, as I slipped on some flip-flops and fled out the door, thankful that my mom was out running errands, which spared me the usual detailed explanations.

When I got to the corner, Jenay was already waiting, her long blond hair flowing loose around her shoulders, as her fingers picked at the hems of her layered blue and white tank tops.

"Hey," she said, gazing up and smiling, her blue eyes squinting against the sun. "Abby forgot her cell so she ran back to get it."

"Why?" I asked.

But Jenay just shrugged. "You know Abby," she said, reaching for my schedule. "Damn. Once again, no classes together. Well that's what you get for being so smart." She laughed, returning the yellow slip of paper and getting back to her double frayed hems.

I just stood there, not saying a word, since I never really know what to say when she gets all self-effacing like that. But then Abby ran up, waving her phone, as evidence of her mission accomplished, and led us on the three-and-a-half-block trek to our future home away from home for the next four years—Bella Vista High. Go Bobcats.

Having grown up in this town, it's not like I hadn't already been there like a zillion times before, not to mention how it's the same school Zoë went to right up until the first month of her junior year. But still, every time I approached that concrete slab of a campus I couldn't help but wonder just exactly what those founders were thinking when they named it Bella Vista. Because as far as beautiful views went, well, there weren't any.

We navigated our way around, located our lockers (which thankfully weren't all that far apart), and decided where we'd meet on our ten-minute break (Abby's locker), and then again at lunch (Abby's locker—until we secured a more solid place). And after we'd memorized all of our room numbers and their corresponding locations, we headed back home, with Jenay doing an impersonation of Ashlee Simpson that had me bent over laughing the entire way.

Well, until I saw Marc.

I stopped midstride, just stood there and stared. Noticing how his shoulders slumped low, how his dark eyes stayed guarded, and how each drag of his cigarette seemed filled with intent, like he was meant to be sitting on the hood of his car, just outside the Circle K, at precisely that moment. But just as he lifted his head and his eyes fixed on mine, Abby and Jenay each grabbed an arm, pulling me away from him and closer to the safety of home.

But now, having just seen him again, I realize this will probably become like a daily occurrence. And I can't believe I didn't grasp that before. I mean, even though I don't share the same opinion of him as most people in this town, having to go to the same school with him just totally sucks. Because now it's like there's no safe place, nowhere I can just be me without the constant shadow of Zoë. No place where I can start fresh and try to move on.

Four

Even though it probably seems like Abby would've been the one to secure the good lunch table, it was Jenay who succeeded. Because in the world of cafeteria real estate, long blond hair, big blue eyes, a great smile, and a nicely filled out snug white T-shirt trumps the best laid plans of a future life coach every single time.

"It must be the jeans. They're magic, that's why they cost so damn much," Abby says, sliding in next to Jenay and gawking at Chess Williams and the almost equally cute Parker Hendricks, who are sitting just mere inches away.

But Jenay just shakes her head and laughs. "Don't forget that they've just been demoted to lowly freshmen in a sea of hot seniors. So technically, they're lucky to be sitting by *us*," she whispers, smiling triumphantly.

I slide onto the end of the bench and unzip my lunch pack, curious to see what's inside, and hoping it's not the dreaded leftover meatloaf sandwich that only my mom could view as a logical choice. I mean, for someone with an I.Q. ranked firmly among genius, who makes her living as an academic (aka professional smart person), she just can't seem to grasp the fact that some leftovers were never meant for cafeteria consumption or any other lunchtime scenario that doesn't entail complete privacy, a bib, and the luxury of eating over a sink. But as I unzip the top and peek inside, I'm relieved to see the unmistakable tubelike shape of my favorite deli wrap sandwich and not a white bread monstrosity dripping with meat juice on my very first day.

I tear open my chips and fish one out, pretending not to notice how just about every single Bella Vista student sitting within a two-mile radius is totally staring at me. I mean, if I thought things were a little rough this morning in Honors English, American History, Geometry, and French, well, most of my fellow classmates went to school with me last year too, which means they've pretty much gotten an eyeful ever since it all began. But now, being surrounded by all of these people who used to know Zoë, who were friends with Zoë, or who, now that she's gone, like to pretend they were friends with Zoë, makes me feel completely naked and exposed. Like a regretful "life art" model being stared at and scrutinized as everyone takes it all in, draws it all down, and interprets everything they see in their own biased way.

And even though I kind of expected this, that doesn't mean I can actually handle it. And there's just no way I can finish my lunch with everyone whispering, pointing, and gawking.

So just as Jenay starts talking to Chess, so casually and easily you'd think she'd been at it for years, and Abby scoots even closer to Parker—who she's secretly crushed on forever—I rise from the table and move for the door, hoping I can make it safely inside the bathroom before I start hurling.

It's weird how you can hire a bodyguard to protect you from physical harm, yet there's no one who can keep you from emotional harm. And as great as my friends have been, doing their best to shield me from everything they can, there's just no way they can defend me from all of the prying eyes, pointed fingers, and loudly whispered, *"Omigod! That's her! You know, the little sister,"* that follows me wherever I go.

I push into the empty bathroom, dump the contents of my lunch pack into the big green trash can against the far wall, then run cold water over my hands until the nausea passes. Then I smooth my hair, straighten my shirt, and head right back outside, and straight into Marc.

"Echo," he says, his dark brown eyes peering into mine, as his pale slim hands clasp nervously at his sides. Up close, he seems thinner, and his hair looks darker, hanging long and loose around his angular face. But he's still amazing, only different. Less contrived, more authentic, yet also kind of lost.

I just stand there, smelling the nicotine wafting off of him, remembering how it was Zoë who got him started.

And just as he opens his mouth to speak, Abby runs up and grabs hold of my shirt. "Echo! Hey! Let's go," she says, tugging on my sleeve and pulling me away.

Five

Every day gets a little easier. But not because the whispering stops, or the staring ceases, or the teachers stop giving me that "Oh, you poor sad thing" look. Nope, all of that remains as blatant as ever. The reason things are getting easier is because every day I get a little better at ignoring it. It's like, if no one else is willing to change, then I'll be the one who does. So, I've simply stopped reacting. I mean, now, when people whisper as I pass in the hall, I refuse to hear it. And when my English teacher gives me *that look,* I avert my eyes. And when I walk through the cafeteria and everyone stops eating and talking so they can point and stare, I absolutely refuse to care. I just focus on eating my sandwich, drinking my Snapple, and watching Jenay flirt with Chess.

"Omigod, do you think he'll ask you to homecoming?" Abby asks, just seconds after the lunch bell rings and Chess and Parker head for class.

But Jenay just gazes down at the ground, blushing and shrugging like she hasn't even considered it.

"Homecoming? Jeez, I haven't even thought about going," I say, walking alongside them and gazing at Jenay, knowing that in a race between the three of us, she's definitely the best bet. I mean, the odds are pretty much against a trifecta, at least with me in the race, and since Abby's also like me, and has no idea how to flirt, I'm placing my wager on Jenay, for win, place, and show.

"He likes you, anyone can tell," Abby says, smiling when she sees her blush.

But Jenay just shrugs. "Well, I guess we'll just see what happens next weekend then, won't we?" she says, waving over her shoulder and heading toward class.

"What's going on next weekend?" I ask, searching Abby's face, wondering what they could possibly be keeping from me.

But she just shrugs. "You know Jenay." She laughs, bringing her finger to her temple and making the universal sign for looney toons. "See you after school?"

"Not today," I say, watching her go and wondering if she heard me.

After school I have an appointment with a shrink. Though I guess when most people are seeing someone like that they usually say "my shrink." As in, "after school I have an appointment with MY shrink." But I don't like to think of him like that. I mean, I can barely stand the guy, so I certainly don't want to think of him as *mine*.

Besides, it's not like I see him all that often anymore. And it's not like he actually ever helped me when I did. I mean, okay, so this completely horrible thing happened to my family. I still can't see how sitting in his office and sobbing my eyes out to the tune of $150 for a fifty-minute hour is ever going to benefit anyone other than *him.*

But my parents, being intellectually minded, called on their most sought-after colleague, who, according to my mom, actually gets away with charging twice that amount, and who "out of kindness, compassion, and as a huge favor to our family has decided to give us a deeply discounted rate."

So because of all that, I was pretty much forced to spend every Tuesday after school, for almost my entire eighth grade year, sitting on that brown leather couch, with a beige floral Kleenex box placed squarely before me, as the Dr. Phil wannabe tried to trick me into saying the *actual words,* to *verbalize* and not *euphemize* what really happened to Zoë.

But even though I like to read and write, and even though I really do believe that words do hold the power to harm or heal, this was just one of those cases where words didn't seem all that important. And no way was I giving in, just so he could feel all smug and accomplished and like he just might actually know what he's doing.

But since I haven't been to see him since the beginning of last summer, today is supposed to serve as some sort of checkup or progress report or something. I guess since it also happens to be the one-year anniversary of Zoë's disappearance, my parents figured it was a good idea to have me stop by and pay the good doctor a little fifty-minute visit.

"Echo, come in. How've you been?" he asks, as I slide onto the familiar brown couch, eyeing the strategically placed tissues.

"I'm okay." I shrug, gazing around the room, noticing how some of the artwork has changed but knowing better than to mention it. I mean, these people analyze everything you do, from the moment you arrive to the moment you leave, so extreme caution is advised.

"How's school?" he asks, gazing at me through the upper

part of his glasses, like he thinks wearing them down around the tip of his nose makes him look smarter or something.

"Fine." I cross my legs and fold my hands in my lap, but then I immediately undo it since I don't want him to think I'm feeling anything other than totally relaxed, happy-go-lucky, and free.

"How are your classes, your teachers?"

"Good, and good," I say, cracking a smile so he'll know just how light and breezy I'm feeling today.

"And your friends? Still hanging around with those two girls?"

"Yup, pretty much since the beginning of time," I tell him, gazing at his bald head and pathetic goatee, and wondering why he can't see the oh so obvious symbolism in *that*.

"Any boyfriends?" He smiles gently.

But I refuse to answer. He's always pushing me to talk about boys and sex and stuff. But instead, I just give him a baleful look.

"Zoë always had lots of friends and boyfriends." He says that like he used to hang out with her or something. Like he knew her really well, better than me.

"Yeah? Well, I'm not Zoë, am I?" I fold my arms across my chest, even though I know full well that he's only trying to bait me. "And even though she may have had a lot of friends, she only had *one* boyfriend," I say, wondering just how crazy you have to be to pay three hundred dollars for fifty minutes of *this*.

"Are you still angry with Zoë?" He leans back in his chair and crosses his legs, causing me to catch an unfortunate glimpse of his brown argyle socks and flaky white shin that is almost as bald as his head.

"Why would I be angry with Zoë? She was my *friend*, and my *sister*, and I *loved* her." I roll my eyes, shake my head, and focus hard on my watch.

He sits there, watching me carefully, not saying a word. But I'm not buying it. This is just another one of his traps. I mean, I watch enough TV crime dramas, and I've read enough thrillers to know that cops, journalists, shrinks—they all rely on the same lame tricks. They all worship the power of the long penetrating stare and lingering silence that practically never fails in getting their suspect to divulge all of the personal, private information they never intended to spill.

But unlike most people, I'm not afraid of silence. And I couldn't care less about being stared at. In fact, I've grown so used to it that it doesn't even faze me.

So we sit. Him staring at me. Me staring at my watch. Seeing the second hand go round and round, knowing that each silent minute is costing my parents another three bucks.

And when our time is finally up, he looks at me and says, "Echo, are you ready to talk about Zoë?"

But I just grab my backpack and head out the door. "Zoë's gone," I tell him, closing it firmly behind me.

Six

My friends are acting weird. And if I didn't know better, if I was the more paranoid type, I would probably start to wonder if they still wanted to be my friends. But since we walk to school together every day, meet at break, sit together at lunch, and then walk all the way home again, it's not like they're trying to ditch me. It's more like they're trying to keep a secret from me. One that Jenay almost keeps giving away, which causes Abby to glare at her with narrowed eyes and a shaking head. I mean, I don't know what they're up to, but it definitely has something to do with this weekend.

"So, any b-day plans?" Abby asks, slipping her arm through the strap on her bag and hoisting it onto her shoulder.

I gaze at the ground, retracing the steps toward home, while remembering my last birthday, which, having fallen right in the middle of all the Zoë stuff, was hardly worth celebrating. And I seriously doubt this year will be any better. I mean, from here on out, every time I make it to another year, it will only remind me of how Zoë *didn't*. And tell me, where's the "Happy" in that?

But I don't want to share that with my friends and drag them down too, so instead I just go, "I don't know. We'll probably go to dinner or something." I shrug. "Though my mom did promise to bake my favorite cake, so if you guys wanna come over after, it's probably okay."

"Pineapple upside-down?" Jenay asks, her eyes lighting up as she smiles.

"No, that's *your* favorite. Mine's red velvet." I adjust my backpack, redistributing the weight so I won't end up all lopsided and bent when I'm old.

"I *love* red velvet. Just give me a time and I'm there." Abby smiles.

"I don't know, eight, eight thirty?" I say, glancing up just in time to catch them exchanging a secret look.

The second I slip my key in the door, my cell phone rings. And I freeze, trying to decide which is more important, turning the key and beginning the long process of getting inside, or answering my phone. Because with two more dead bolts and a knob lock to go, there's just no way I can accomplish both.

I heave a loud sigh, drop my bag, and ransack through the books and papers as I search for my cell. And by the time I find it, it's almost too late, so instead of checking ID I head straight for hello.

"Echo?" The voice is definitely male but decidedly unfamiliar. I mean, the only male that ever calls is my dad.

"Yeah?" I mumble, curious who it could be.

"It's me. Marc."

"Oh." I just stand there, clutching the phone, wondering what he wants. I mean, after that first day at school, I've definitely seen him a few more times, but it's not like we stop and talk. But then, nobody talks to Marc anymore. And even though that makes me feel pretty sad on his behalf, that doesn't mean I want to talk to him either.

"I know this is weird, but I was kind of hoping I could see you," he says.

I gaze at the driveway and the long crack that runs down the center, as I search for a way out. "Oh, I don't know. I mean, I'm kind of busy and all," I finally say, cringing at how false that sounds.

"Listen, I know it's awkward. And I know how your parents don't want me around. But I also know that tomorrow's your birthday, and I have something for you, something I think you're gonna like. So, how 'bout it? Will you meet me?"

I hesitate, gripping the phone and weighing my options. Then I hoist my bag onto my shoulder, slide my key out of the lock, and go, "Where should we meet?"

There's this lake in a park not far from my house that I always used to go to as a kid. Even though it's not the kind of lake you'd ever want to swim in, since the water is murky and polluted and full of Big Gulp cups and beer cans floating along the top like they have every right to be there. I mean, someone would pretty much have to hate you to actually throw you in. But still, every weekend, people show up by the dozens, toting picnic baskets and spreading out towels, eager to spend the day lazing around, gazing at the scenery, and pretending they're somewhere better. And even though I used to like to do that too, heading there now reminds me of just how long it's been.

I see him sitting by the water's edge just before he sees me. And even though I hate to admit it, my first instinct is to bolt. To just take off running, as fast and far as I can, as though my very life depends on it. But since I'm pretty sure he doesn't deserve that, I force myself to keep putting one foot in front of the other until I'm standing directly before him.

"You made it," he says, his smile like a question mark, his eyes more unsure than I ever could've imagined.

I stand there and shrug. Then drop my bag and sit down beside him.

"Zoë and I used to come here all the time," he says, dipping his hand into a bag full of Wonder bread, tossing fat handfuls to a flock of greedy ducks. "She used to feed them so much, I teased her about making them obese, and inflicting them with type two diabetes. But she'd just laugh and say she was trying to build trust, so that someday they'd come waddling up and eat the crumbs right out of her hand."

I glance at him briefly, wondering if his eyes will fill with tears. But when he turns to me and smiles, I know he's beyond all that, having moved his way through the grief list, and is now settled in some other place.

"How are you?" he asks, searching my face.

"Okay." I avert my eyes toward the ducks, but nod so he'll believe it. I know he has something to give me, something to tell me, but my heart is pounding so hard and my palms are growing so sweaty, I'm pretty sure I no longer want it.

We sit like that for a while, him feeding the ducks, me nervous and freaked. Then he shakes his head, turns to me, and says, "Thanks for coming. I know it's probably weird for you, but it really is important. So, well, here." He reaches into the old khaki schoolbag, the one he's always lugging around, then hands me a small leather-bound book, the cover bearing a cobalt so rich and blue, I immediately think of Zoë.

"What's this?" I ask, rubbing my fingers over the smooth soft leather, the same shade of blue as her walls.

"Her diary." He looks right at me, his dark eyes intense and no longer blinking. "It was in her backpack. The one she left with me that day, the day she—" He stops and shakes his head. "Anyway, it's hers and it's personal, and I didn't want the cops to get their hands on it because there's nothing in there that would've helped them, nothing they didn't already know. Not to mention how it's none of their business. And I didn't want your parents to see it since there's stuff in there that she never wanted them to see. So I kept it. I've had it this whole time. But now I want you to have it." He sees the look on my face and raises his right hand, like he's on a witness stand. "I gave them everything else, though, I swear."

I hold the book with both hands, too shaky and scared to peek. "Why me?" I ask, still gazing at the cover. "I mean, why don't you just keep it?"

"I think you should know her," he says, his eyes fixed on mine.

"But I *did* know her! And I *do* know her!" I grab my backpack and stand up quickly, wanting nothing more than to get away.

"You didn't know her like that. You didn't know the whole person," he says, his face solid and set, like he's just so sure about everything he's saying.

"Did *you* read it?" I ask, my hands shaky, watching as he nods in answer.

I stand there, taking him in, the lean build, the longish hair, the black T-shirt, the faded jeans, the chiseled face with the most amazing dark eyes. "You're not supposed to read other people's diaries," I say, turning away and running toward home.

Seven

The second I hear "Surprise!" I feel like an idiot. I mean, thinking back on Jenay's inability to keep a secret, and Abby's oh-so-obvious attempts to cover, it's pretty clear I should've known from the start. But after last year's birthday, when the only candles I was asked to blow out were for Zoë's candlelight vigil, my expectations for any future celebrations were at an all-time low.

"Were you surprised?" Jenay and Abby ask, obviously delighted at being able to pull it off so successfully.

"Totally," I say, slipping out of my favorite navy blue peacoat and gazing at all the decorations: the purple, orange, and pink paper lanterns; the matching candles, floor pillows, and balloons; not to mention the big red velvet cake pierced in the center with fifteen pink candles that my mom must have dropped off when I was bogged down in homework.

"So I guess you don't really need this after all?" I say, smiling as I hold up the dog-eared copy of *Le Petit Prince,* which is not only required reading for French I, but also Jenay's excuse for luring me over.

But she just laughs as she leads me deeper into the room.

I'm surprised by how crowded it is. And even though I smile and wave and say hi to all of these people I recognize from school, if you tried to test me, pop quiz me on their names, the truth is I'd totally fail. I mean, just because they came doesn't mean I actually know them. And it feels like one of those episodes of *Friends,* where they throw a party and all of these extras show up. All of these supposed *other* good friends, lounging on that famous TV couch, talking and laughing and sharing the screen, like they've been there all along and you just hadn't noticed.

And even though I'd like to believe that all of these people are here to see me, the truth is I know it's because of Abby and Jenay. They're the ones who invited them. They're the ones who've gone out of their way to know them.

Abby runs off to get me a drink as I squeeze into a narrow space on the end of the couch, smiling awkwardly at the girl sitting beside me, who turns to me and says, "Omigod, you should've seen your face when you first walked in! You looked so surprised, like you'd just seen a ghost!"

Then I watch as her face freezes in horror, just seconds after realizing what she really just said.

But I just launch straight into my well-honed "damage control" routine. The one where I smile and nod and give a friendly look, one that hopefully conveys the message: *as far as I'm concerned you have nothing to feel bad about.* Then I get up off the couch and mumble something about needing to go help Abby.

And as I'm walking away I hear her friend say, "Omigod, I can't believe you just said that! Hello? Remember what happened to her sister?"

Eventually it's gotta stop, right? The way people look at

me. The way they treat me. The way everyone around me goes out of their way to avoid certain words in my presence. As though the mere sound of *missing, vanished, Internet predator, gone, lost,* or *disappeared* will somehow reduce me to tears.

I know she meant well. I know she was only trying to make conversation with me, a girl whose party she's at and yet barely knows. But how can I ever be friends with someone who can't see me as anything other than Tragedy Girl?

How can I hang with people who refuse to see that despite the whole thing with my sister, I'm really not so different from them?

How can I make new friends when everyone feels so uncomfortable and guarded around me all the time?

I mean, right after the whole thing with Zoë, I became hugely, insanely popular. All of these kids who'd barely spoken to me before started lining up in hopes of being my new best friend. But even though at first I kind of liked all of the attention, it didn't take long to figure out how most of them were just voyeurs. Just a bunch of tragedy whores who wanted to get close to me so they could report back to the others. As though their social standing would somehow elevate once they told the story of how they went for ice cream with the sister of the girl who got . . .

Anyway, I learned pretty quick how to spot those people a mile away. And Abby and Jenay wasted no time in forming a tight, secure shield, protecting me from any and all future fake friendship attempts.

But now that we're in high school, it's obvious they want to branch out, meet new people, expand their horizons, whatever. And it's not that I blame them, or would ever try to stop them. I'm actually more worried about holding them back.

Or even worse, attracting all the wrong people, like the sideshow circus freak that I am.

"Here's the birthday girl," Jenay says, acting all giddy,

even though I'm 100 percent certain the only thing occupying her cup is crushed ice and Sprite.

Abby hands me my drink and sits on the couch, as Parker scootches away from her so he can make room for me. "Have a seat," he says, smiling and patting the free space beside him.

I glance at Abby wondering if she minds, then squeeze in beside Parker, thinking how weird it feels to be doing that considering how long I've known him, and how that's the first time he's ever scooted anywhere for me. But then again, the only time he ever spoke to me before was to say, "Sorry" as he fetched a soccer ball he'd just accidentally kicked at my head.

But I guess that's because Parker always hangs with Chess, and Chess always hangs with the popular crowd. And even though our junior high was just as cliqued up as any other school, and even though Abby, Jenay, and I have never been part of that über-cool group, we somehow managed to get out of there pretty much unscathed, avoiding a big, dramatic, *Mean Girls* showdown, which left us with a clean slate and no grudges to carry over into high school.

But now, with Parker making room for me, I realize Jenay was right about them being demoted, as most of the girls from their old group have already moved on, setting their sights on all the hot sophomores, juniors, and seniors. Which pretty much leaves the pick of the freshman litter for the rest of us to browse.

"We should play spin the bottle," Chess says, his eyes darting among us, looking to see who, if any, will bite.

"Why not seven minutes in Heaven?" Parker says, laughing and high-fiving Chess.

"Um, when did my party become a Judy Blume book?" I ask, hoping and praying that they're not at all serious.

"I think it sounds kind of fun," Jenay says, looking at me with eyes that are practically begging me to lighten up. "You know, retro." She smiles.

Retro for who? I think, since neither she, I, nor Abby has ever played this game before. Remember what I said about not being cool? Well, that means we weren't invited to any of the cool parties either. But since it's obvious she just wants an excuse to kiss Chess, and since I don't want to be the one who gets in her way, I just shrug and act like I really don't care.

Then Teresa, the alpha girl who held the top junior high royalty position solidly through both seventh and eighth grades, and who's now decided to join our meager group (probably because her original group disbanded and she'd rather be a big fish in our tiny little pond than a guppy in an ocean of upperclassmen), rolls her eyes and says, "Please, those games are so juvenile."

"But I just saw Carrie play it on *Sex and the City*," Jenay says, her voice sounding as pouty as her face looks.

"Again, *over! Syndication!*" Teresa shakes her head as she digs through her purse, having positioned herself on the rug near our feet. "I mean, if you guys want to make out with someone then just make out. Get over it already, because nobody cares." She pulls a vodka mini from her bag and unscrews the cap. "Anybody?" she asks, holding it up in offering.

I glance at Jenay and it's clear that she's torn. Partly pissed that Teresa's taking over the party, yet partly wondering if she should maybe just relax and let her. I mean, the fact that Teresa deigned to show up probably feels like a major coup.

"None for me," Abby says, leaning back against the cushions and narrowing her eyes at this new, bossy intruder.

"Ditto," I say as a show of support, even though I do kind of want some, just to see what it's like.

And when I look over at Jenay, waiting for her to chime in, she just shrugs and holds up her cup, pushing it toward Teresa.

Apparently Teresa's dad is a frequent flyer, which basically means she's got a purse full of airplane minis. And with pretty much everyone drinking (except Abby and me), and the lights turned low, and the music turned up, Parker leans in and whispers, "Wanna take a walk?"

I glance over at Jenay and Chess, who are totally making out right in front of us, then I squint at Parker and go, "Where? I mean, Jenay's parents are upstairs so we really shouldn't leave the basement."

But he just smiles. "I know a place," he says, standing before me and offering his hand.

And even though it sounds totally fishy to me, I still get up and follow.

When I think of coat closets, I usually think of itchy wool and cloying mothballs. But that's only because I don't have three brothers. Because from the moment I stepped inside there's been a hockey stick wedged against my butt, and it's accompanied by the most gag-worthy smell of B.O. I've ever encountered. Though I'm sure it's not coming from Parker since I don't remember him ever smelling bad, not to mention how this entire time, both his hands have been wrapped loosely around my waist and haven't wandered anywhere near my butt.

"Have you ever done this before?" he whispers, pulling me close.

I squint into the dark space before me, trying to make out the blondishness of his hair, the bluishness of his eyes, and the overall cuteness of his face that's kept him solidly in the number two position, directly beneath Chess, on the "cutest boys in school" list we've been keeping since fourth grade. But all I can make out is the vague outline of his head, and I wonder if he's asking if I've ever been in this closet before, or if I've ever kissed a guy before. Because to be honest, that wasn't exactly clear. But still, I guess the answer to both of those questions is pretty much the same, no and no. So that's what I tell him.

"Are you sure you're okay with this?" he asks, his voice filled with so much sweetness and concern that I'm shocked. Because honestly, I thought he'd be in full grope mode by now. "I mean, you're so nice. And I like you. So I don't want to push or anything."

I'd give anything to see his face right now, because this is not at all the cocky, loud, overconfident Parker from the lunch table, the one I assumed I'd be wrestling with. And the truth is, whether he actually kisses me or not really doesn't matter. I mean, I feel pretty neutral about the whole thing. I'm more surprised by the fact of how he even *wants* to kiss me. And how he's being so nice. And how he just said he *likes me!*

And I know I probably shouldn't waste this opportunity since things like this never happen to me, and because of that, this could be my one and only shot at a normal adolescent experience. But still, I can't help but ask, "Did you just say you like me?" I know it's lame and insecure, but I need a little clarification, 'cause to be honest, this is pretty hard to believe.

"Yeah. I think you're really cute, and nice, and stuff. Always have. You just never seemed very interested," he says.

I know I should probably be satisfied with that, and just shut up and let him kiss me already, but I really need to get to the bottom of this. So I go, "Seriously?"

"Seriously." He laughs. "But it's like, you and Jenay and Abby were always so tight that I guess I was too shy to try to break in."

"You're shy?" I say, unable to keep my disbelief in check.

"Yeah, but I'm working on it," he says, pulling me even closer. "So, is it okay? Can I kiss you now?"

I kind of wish he hadn't asked, 'cause it makes me feel really awkward to give him permission. But still, I guess it's better than never being asked, and possibly never being kissed. So I just nod and go, "Um, okay."

So he does. He leans in and kisses me. First he does it with his mouth closed. Then with it slightly open. And at one point he even slips his tongue in for a little bit. Then he pulls away, and says, "Was that okay?"

I nod. But then I remember how dark it is, which means he probably couldn't see that, so I clear my throat and say, "Um, yeah, it was nice."

And that's when he does it again.

Eight

By the time I get home, the house is mostly dark. And as I tiptoe upstairs and peek into their room, I'm surprised to find my parents already asleep. I mean, normally, well, I guess *normally* I don't go to parties, but still, for the last year, every time I left the house unchaperoned, I always returned to blazing lights, a flickering TV, and at least one, if not both, of my parents staying up late, playing night sentinel.

But maybe this is a good sign. Maybe things are finally looking up. Maybe my parents' paranoid period is coming to an end. Or maybe, this is just the result of my mom's addiction to happy pills, and my dad's utter exhaustion.

I change out of my clothes and slip into my pink-and-white striped pajamas, then I pad into the bathroom to brush my teeth and wash my face of what little makeup I bothered to wear. And as I peer at my reflection, I lean closer to the mirror, noticing how my lips are all red and swollen, and my cheeks all flushed and tender, and I watch them grow even redder when I realize it's because of Parker.

I guess I just never imagined something like that would happen to me. I mean, don't get me wrong, it's not like I planned to join a nunnery, or take a vow of celibacy, or anything crazy like that. Heck, I even assumed I'd get married someday, giving birth to the requisite number of kids. But all of that seemed so distant and far away. Like it was just one more thing on life's big "To Do" list. Just stuff that grownups did, like subscribing to a newspaper or paying bills.

I guess I never thought about the whole *attracting* part of it. And how I might feel about someone. And how they might feel about me.

And it's not like I'm hideous or anything. I mean, I'm pretty much your basic, all-American, standard issue girl. But still, it's not like I'm fun and sparkly like Jenay. And I'm certainly not amazing like Zoë. So I guess that's why it's hard for me to make sense of that kiss. And how afterward, Parker stuck by me for the rest of the night.

When I wake up soaked in sweat at 3:06 A.M., feeling panicky, with my face all wet and my throat all tight and sore as though I've been sobbing in my sleep, I force myself to just lay there, slowly breathing in and out as I count, starting at one hundred and working my way down, just like that shrink suggested that time I accidentally told him about my dreams.

But even after counting, even after changing out of my damp pajamas and into clean dry ones, even after drinking a glass of water and assuring myself that there's absolutely no reason to panic, I still can't seem to relax enough to fall back to sleep. And then I make it even worse when I start thinking about my party, and how everything's changing so fast in a way I once anticipated, only now that it's happening, I'm no longer so sure.

I mean, my parents didn't wait up, and a boy actually *wanted* to kiss me. And even though at the beginning of the night those two things would've sounded amazingly cool, now at o dark thirty, they no longer do.

Because, let's face it, there's comfort in being cautious. And there's peace in the predictable.

But now, if everything's going to be different, if everything's going to be filled with possibility and opportunity, how will I know if I'm ready? How will I know how to deal?

And it's not like Zoë ever worried about these things. "Better to ask forgiveness than permission," she'd say. And God knows she doled out her fair share of apologies. But still, nothing ever fazed her. Nothing ever tripped her up. She just moved through life at lightning speed, expecting nothing but cooperation, approval, laughter, and fun.

Zoë was street smart and naïve.

She was thoughtful yet reckless.

She was sexy but innocent.

She was a walking dichotomy.

And I want to be just like her.

I climb out of bed, grab my backpack, and retrieve the cobalt blue book that Marc gave me. Then I switch on my reading light, slip back between the sheets, and with totally shaking hands, turn to the first page, shivering when I see her familiar, round, loopy scrawl, and read:

This is Zoë's diary. And you should NOT be reading it!

I knew she was right. But I also knew she had something to teach me. So I ignored the warning, and turned the page.

Nine

June 14 (finally!)

I don't know why they call it the last day of school, when really it's the first day of freedom. Cuz the second that minimum day bell rings at 12:20 P.M., there's not a teacher, principal, or school administrator w/in 50 miles that can touch me—and that includes YOU, Coach Warner, you disgusting old pig. You think I don't notice when you look down my top? Next year I'm gonna stick a tiny mirror down there so you can see your own ugly reflection staring back at you!!!

As usual, classes were a joke—everyone just ignoring the teachers, running around, signing yearbooks, and promising to hook up sometime during the hot days ahead. All I could do was nod and smile and go through the motions, because the whole entire time I was thinking about ditching Stephen so I can hook up with Marc.

I know he's into me.

I'm never wrong about these things.

June 15

Didn't make it downstairs 'til after 11, still feeling drunk from last night. Walked right into the edge of the kitchen table and had to grab the corner to steady myself. Thank G nobody noticed. Dad had his nose buried in a pile of papers (as usual), Mom was outside working in her overachiever garden wearing her big old hat, SPF 75, wrap-around sunglasses, gloves, and a long-sleeved shirt—like she's allergic to the sun or something. Only Echo sniffed the air as I passed, flashed me a knowing look, but didn't say a word as I headed for the coffeemaker. Didn't even get to the second sip before Carly called, wanting to bitch me out for ditching Stephen and trying to hook up with Marc behind his back.

So I reminded her that I'm her BFF, NOT Stephen. I'm the one who covered for her that time when she said she was at my house but was really out with H, not to mention the gazillion other favors I've done for her over the last 5 years. Not to mention that Marc was already gone by the time I finally made it outside, so no damage done, right?

But even after I reminded her of all that she still has the nerve to go, "Yeah, but still."

I mean, I love Carly, really I do. But this holier than thou crap has got to stop.

Maybe she should get together with Stephen if she cares so much about his stupid feelings.

June 16

I'm psychic! Just call me Claire Voyant. Because the very last line I wrote in my very last entry came true. That's right, Carly hooked up with Stephen. And I'm not even that mad about it. Really. I barely even care. Well, other than the fact that she went behind my back. But really, as far as I'm concerned she can have him because I am sooooo over him. I'm sick of how his life revolves around sports and those stupid instant replays he insists on watching over and over and over again. I'm sick of the way he eats with his mouth open, all those chucked up particles tossing from side to side as he laughs out loud at his own lame-ass jokes. But mostly I'm sick of the way he bicep peeks during sex. It's like he gets more excited watching the way they bulge out than by seeing me naked beneath him. And if I sound like some bitter old hausfrau who got married too young, and stayed married too long, well, then, whose fault is that? He stole a year of my life, robbed me of time I'll never get back.

Not to mention how it's been totally obvious from the start how Carly's been crushing on him, since day one. It's like she's been waiting this entire time for me to dump him. Even the six months she was with H, she was just passing time. So if she wants him that bad, she can have him. I hope they're very happy together, really I do.

I just think she could've waited 'til I'd actually broken up with him first. I just think she could've waited 'til things were official. Not to mention how she could have at least pretended to look guilty when I walked in on them.

But instead she just looked up and said, "Well you said you were gonna leave him."

Which, of course, made Stephen gawk at me in shock. But I just kept right on looking at her. Shaking my head as I used her words right back at her, saying, "Yeah, but still."

Then I went back downstairs and ended up smoking some really powerful shit with Kevin and Kristin who are so freaking in love they'll probably get married or something. I mean it's just so weird how they've been together *since eighth grade, and how they never ever think about what they could be missing.*

I'm always thinking about what I'm missing.

Even when I'm happy with what I have.

Anyway, we just hung in the backyard, looking at the stars 'til we were cold and hungry and misted with dew. And everything felt so vast, and unlimited, and extremely close to perfect.

But now I have to figure out a way to fill up the summer before my parents decide that for me. So, good luck to me!

I stifle a yawn, and close Zoë's diary, sliding it under my mattress for safekeeping. Not one thing I read surprised me. Seriously, not the drugs, not the sex, not even that whole big drama with Carly. Though I'd always been kind of curious why she stopped coming over so much. I guess I just assumed it had something to do with Marc. But then Zoë's life had always been dramatic, and mysterious, and far more adventurous than mine. And even though I like Carly, I know it had to be a pretty tough gig to be my sister's best friend. I mean, Zoë was just one of those people who the clouds always cleared for, the sun always shined on, and the stars came out for.

She's the reason they invented spotlights.

And she left anyone standing next to her feeling like a dull, spent bulb.

But what did surprise me was the way I felt as I was reading. So close to Zoë, like she was sitting right there beside me, whispering the words in my ear, and urging me to turn the page.

And it feels so good to finally have her back, that I switch off the light and close my eyes, saving Zoë for another day.

Saving Zoë

Ten

By Monday at school Jenay and Chess are officially a couple. Though that's really no surprise for those of us forced to watch them make out for the remainder of my party. And as I head for the lunch table that has gotten so crowded we've merged with the one beside it, I actually have to fight the urge to just turn around and bolt.

I mean, where would I go? Back to junior high? Because obviously, that's no longer an option. So instead I take a deep breath and smile at everyone, including Parker—who I've managed to avoid until now.

"Hey," I say, dropping my lunch on the table, and easing onto the long yellow bench.

Jenay smiles then goes right back to her story, and by the time she's finished everyone is laughing. Well, everyone but me. Since it's the one about how when she and Abby were watching her baby brother and he squirted them both in the face just as they were changing his diaper, which believe me, I've heard like a million times before.

So I just reach into my lunch pack and retrieve my sandwich, trying to ignore the fact that Parker is waving at me, trying to get my attention.

"Hey, wake up," he says, leaning toward me and smiling. "I called you last night but it went straight to voice mail. I got your number from Jenay. I hope that's okay?"

"Oh, sorry about that," I say, twisting the top off my Snapple and taking a sip. "My phone was off, and by the time I realized you'd called . . ." I just shrug, letting that trail off to nothing. Because the truth is, it's not like I was going to call him back anyway. And it's not because I don't like him, I mean, I'm not exactly sure how I feel about him. It's mostly because I'm so freaking lame I don't know what to say after "hello."

"Did you have a good weekend?" he asks.

I think about the book I read, the homework I finished, Zoë's diary, and shrug. "Yeah. You?"

He nods, still leaning toward me, still smiling, still gazing at me with those deep blue eyes.

But when I see him looking at me like that, ignoring everyone else just so he can concentrate solely on me, it makes me feel so freaked out, so nervous, and so totally inadequate, that I stand up and say, "Um, I'll be right back."

Then I abandon my lunch, abandon the table, and run out the door, desperate for fresh air and a temporary respite from the worst part of me—the pathetic, fearful, morbidly insecure part. The part that wonders why a guy as cute as Parker would ever like a girl as dorky as me, why anyone anywhere would ever like me.

I run past the burnout tree, the one where all the hard-core partiers hang, thinking how they're the only group in this whole entire school who never point, stare, or whisper as I pass.

But maybe that's because they're just too stoned to care. I mean the cheerleaders, the song leaders, the drill teamers, the mascots, the jocks, the drama freaks, the band geeks, the science nerds, the fashionistas, the club leaders, the council reps, the Goths, the Preps, the ROTC marchers, the girls who starve to be skinny, the girls who barf to be skinny, the scrawny guys, the wannabes, the techies, the sluts, the virgins, the cutters, the Future Farmers of America, the alterna artists, the rainbow kids—the one thing they all have in common is that they all stare at me. Every single one of them. But the major druggies? Not so much. So it feels pretty safe to pass by.

I head toward the bathroom, even though I don't really plan on going inside. But it's good to have as a decoy route in case Abby decides to come looking for me again. And then just as I turn down the hall where I'd planned to lean against the wall until the bell rings, I see Marc sitting not two feet away.

"Oh. Hey," I say, surprised to not only run into him again, but also to see that he's smoking, on campus, as though it's actually allowed or something.

He just looks at me and nods, squinting his eyes as he takes another drag.

"I was just on my way to—" I point straight ahead, feeling the need to explain my presence, yet feeling embarrassed by how fake I sound.

But he just drops his cigarette, smashes it with his thick, rubber-soled boot, looks up at me, and goes, "Did you read it?"

I gaze down at the ground, not wanting him to know.

Then he gets up from the bench and brushes right past me. "You will when you're ready," he says, walking away.

"Where the heck did you go? Parker thinks you hate him." Jenay merges her brows together and shakes her head. "He waited so long, he was late to class."

"Why would I hate him?" I ask, focusing my guilt-ridden gaze on the sidewalk, as we head toward home.

"Uh, because you ran off and never returned? I'm serious, Echo, you should've seen him. He just sat there with your lunch right in front of him, wondering if he should save it, eat it, toss it, or what."

She's staring at me, I can feel it. But since Abby's in the middle, that means I'll have to go through her if I want to confirm it. And I feel really uncomfortable talking about all of this, partly because it makes me feel weird, inept, and embarrassed, but also because I know Abby likes Parker too. She has for years. She just won't admit it.

But Abby's totally on to me, and she's not about to let me off easy. "Don't be going all AWOL on my account. So what if I think he's cute. I think a lot of guys are cute. And it's not like I was all attached or anything," she says, kicking a rock out of her path and shrugging like she really doesn't care. "So if you really like him, then just go for it, Echo. Don't hold back because of me."

"*Do* you like him?" Jenay asks, her eyes growing hopeful and wide as she waits for a definite answer.

Only the thing is, I don't have a definite answer. Because I'm not really sure how I feel. Though I do know there's a "right" answer, one that will make her happy, and hopefully put an end to all of this. So I take a deep breath and say, "Totally. I mean, why wouldn't I? He's cute, and sweet, and smart. And it's not like there's anything wrong with him, right?"

The second that's out, Abby starts cracking up. I mean full body bent over laughing, while Jenay just rolls her eyes and shakes her head and goes, "That's it? You like him because there's nothing *wrong* with him? You like him because he has no *obvious defects*? Jeez Echo, that's real romantic stuff. I mean, you're just head over heels then, aren't you?"

"No, I just . . ." I gaze back down at the ground, wondering who I'm trying to convince more, me or her. "I like him," I finally say. "Okay? Happy now? He's really nice, and a really good kisser too." I peek at both of them, feeling relieved when I see Jenay smile, hoping that means she believes me.

"Then it's settled. He can ask you to homecoming and you won't say no?" Jenay asks, her voice full of hope. "Cause it would be really fun if we could double date, don't you think?"

I nod at Jenay and then gaze at Abby. But she's no longer looking at me. She's busy staring straight ahead.

Eleven

Two days before the dance, I tell my mom I need a dress. Though of course Jenay had already bought hers, like the day after my party. And Parker, just naturally assuming I'd already gotten mine too, kept quizzing me about the color so his mom could order a matching corsage.

I didn't have the heart to tell him that I hadn't bothered to even think about a dress, much less go look for one. So I lied and said I was torn between a black one and a white one, so any old flowers should do.

"It would've been nice if you could've given me just a little more notice," my mom says, shaking her head as she trolls through the racks, trying to find something pretty and affordable that won't make me look like a slut.

I just stand there, amazed by the show of emotion. It's been so long since she's expressed sadness, annoyance, or anything stronger than zombie-like calm.

"Zoë and I always used to make a day of it. We'd buy the dress, have lunch, and then go looking for a bag, jewelry, and shoes. But this, this two days' notice." She shakes her head again, this time pursing her lips. "What if we need alterations? Did you ever consider that?" She looks at me, eyes clearly alarmed at the thought. Well, as alarmed as those happy pills allow.

But I just shrug. I mean, even though it's nice to see her thawing out of her usual, icy numbness, I really don't appreciate having to compete with Zoë. Especially when I'm so clearly the loser. I mean, I may be the good, obedient, straight-A daughter, but Zoë was the exciting one. Zoë was the fun one. Zoë was the glamorous one. Zoë was the kind of daughter you actually miss.

"Well, I guess if it's too long, I'll just get higher heels or something," I finally say, determined to ignore that last slight of hers and get through the rest of the day unscathed.

But she just ignores that, presses a handful of dresses into my arms, and goes, "Here. It's a start. Now where the heck is that salesgirl?"

If you were going to categorize my mom, you'd obviously choose words like "organized," "controlling," and "type-A personality." But that doesn't mean she can't be relaxed, compassionate, or fun. Though in the last year, it's like she's been riding an emotional roller coaster, and it's been kind of hard to adjust to all of the surprising twists and turns.

I mean, everything started off all fine and well. One of her papers finally got published and she was actually awarded tenure, which is like a really big deal. But then the whole Zoë thing happened, and she headed straight into this rapid descent, her tears and depression building at an alarming speed until one day, after an extended couch-sitting, food-avoiding, sleep-depriving crying jag, she reached for that bottle of doctor-prescribed happy pills, and ever since it's been miles of flat track, allowing for a safe but boring ride.

But that little show of annoyance back there in the store, when she compared me to Zoë and got all upset? Well, that's something she's never actually done before. And I wonder if it signals another drop ahead, one that I won't realize until it's too late.

"Well, under the conditions, I'd say that went much better than I anticipated," she says, carefully placing her linen napkin across the lap of her jeans, but not those high-rise, tapered-ankle, multipleated "mom jeans" (thank God), but still, dark blue and no-nonsense. "And you've got quite the figure, young lady. Who knew?" She raises her thin, arched eyebrows and cracks a brief smile.

"Yeah, quite the stick figure," I say, gazing down at my nearly concave chest, wondering if it will ever progress.

"Don't kid yourself. You've got your great-aunt Eleanor's figure." She nods, her short, brown, wash-and-wear hair barely moving. "And she was a model for Saks."

I think about Zoë, and how she always wanted to be a model, and I wonder if my mom ever said that to her.

"So tell me about this young man." She leans forward, taking a sip of iced tea.

I gaze down at my lap, knowing she's only trying to connect, and wishing I felt more comfortable talking about things like this. "Well, I've known him forever, but we never really hung out until now, and I don't know, his best friend asked Jenay, and so, he asked me." I shrug, using my straw to move the lemon wedge and block of ice that's impeding my progress to the good stuff below.

"Do you like him?" she asks, as though we always engage in these heart-to-heart girl talks, as though nothing's changed, like we're just picking up right where we left off. And it's been so long since she even tried, that it makes me want to give the right answer, the one that will keep it going, the one that will keep her feeling this way.

But I also don't want to lie. So instead, I just nod.

"Well, your father and I are looking forward to meeting him. And I'm so glad we went with that cobalt blue dress, aren't you? I was thinking maybe a silver purse and shoes? What are your thoughts?"

I reach for my menu and pretend to read it. "Um, I guess something cute and dressy, that I can actually walk in without falling over." I shrug.

"I know just the place." She nods.

The whole time Jenay's stepmom is taking our picture, all I can think about is Abby. And how she's missing. And how she should be standing right here beside us, overdressed, overexcited, and anxious to take part in her first limo, first dance, and first date too. But even though Jenay tried her best to set her up, Abby wouldn't have anything to do with it. Insisting she had a "family thing" that'd been planned for months, and that she'd "completely forgotten all about."

But I know better. I know Abby's just romantic enough to want a date who asked her for real, and stubborn enough to insist on that, or not go at all.

"Okay, everyone, just lean in, a little bit closer. Echo, move your hair out of your eyes so I can see your beautiful face," Jenay's stepmom says, the fingers on her free hand directing us toward the center, while she holds the tiny digital camera with the other. "Perfect. Hold it . . . great. One more. Okay, I'll e-mail copies to all of your parents." She leans against Jenay's dad and smiles. "Oops! There goes Landon! I knew it wouldn't last. Okay, have fun everyone, and girls, you look gorgeous!"

She hugs Jenay and me, careful not to mess up our hair,

then runs upstairs to the nursery in her bare feet, snug jeans, and tight pink T-shirt, with her stream of blond hair trailing behind her, making her look more like Jenay's hip older sister than her father's second wife.

"Okay, the limo's outside waiting. So everyone, be good, have fun, and stay out of trouble," her dad says, delivering the exact same speech my dad gave, just half an hour before.

One by one we crawl into the back of the limo, sliding across the long, leather seat. The second the door is closed and the driver pulls away from the curb, Jenay leans her head back, heaves a dramatic sigh, and goes, "Thank God that's over."

Chess grabs her hand and smiles. "What do you mean? Your mom's really nice, and your dad seems cool too." He shrugs.

"Well, she's actually my stepmom. My real mom died when I was little, and my dad didn't remarry until about four years ago. So yeah, she's nice and all, and it's good to have a mom again and not be the only girl in the house for a change. But still, parents, you know?" She smiles.

"Echo's parents are way cool," Parker says, obviously wanting to say something positive, even if it means he has to lie.

But Jenay and I just look at each other and burst out laughing. And even though it's really not all that funny, every time we look at each other we laugh that much harder. And I know it's kind of rude, and I know it excludes the guys, but still, being able to share a private joke like this makes me feel calmer, reminding me how whatever happens tonight, we're both in it together.

We go to this restaurant called the Blue Water Grill even though our town is completely landlocked and there's no blue water anywhere to be found (including the lake at the park where the water is polluted, murky, and brown). I mean, let's face it, a name like that can't help but conjure up images of vast ocean views and glamorous diners docking their yachts, before strolling inside for a nice sunset meal.

But here, instead of ocean views, you get a parking lot. And instead of a yacht, you get a smiling, plywood, cartoon pelican ushering you into the nautical-themed interior that's a lot closer to Moby Dick than luxury liner.

The hostess leads us to a table where Teresa and Sean, Lisa and Drew, and Kaitlin and Mike are already waiting, and I spend the entire time fiddling with my menu and napkin and pretty much doing whatever it takes to keep my hands busy and as far away from Parker's as possible.

I know I'm acting all weird and uptight and ridiculous, and it's not like I can even explain why. I mean, I used to love watching Zoë get ready for all her school dances, and I could hardly wait for the day when it would be my turn. I even used to dream about us going together, you know double-dating, just two cool sisters and their cute, hottie boyfriends, sharing a limo and acting all glamorous and sophisticated. And even after I learned how Zoë and her friends usually only stayed long enough to take the formal pictures before heading out to go party somewhere else, that still didn't change it for me.

I guess it just always seemed like Zoë was part of this mysterious, grown-up world, one that I couldn't wait to join. Only now that I'm being admitted, I no longer feel ready. And since everything Zoë did was always bigger, and brighter, and better than everyone else, I know that no matter how hard I try, I'll never be able to match her.

"Did I tell you how much I love your dress? That color is like, *so* amazing," Teresa says, leaning close to the bathroom mirror and applying a layer of pale pink lip gloss over the dark pink lipstick she just applied.

I gaze down the length of my dress, all the way to my

strappy sandals, amazed at how it all came together so much better than I ever would've guessed.

"You and Parker are so cute together," she says, dropping her lip gloss into her bag and moving on to her blond highlighted hair, which has been professionally twisted, curled, and pinned into the world's most complicated updo.

I force my face into a smile, watching as she fishes around in her green, oversized tote bag, which I have to admit looks incredibly odd with her pink shiny dress and gold shoes.

"Want some?" she asks, retrieving a water bottle filled with some kind of red homemade brew. "I brought enough for everyone. That's why this bag is so big, in case you were wondering." She laughs. "I'll probably pass them out in the limos. But let's just get a head start and take a little hit now, K?" She unscrews the lid and takes a long, hearty sip. Then she shoves it toward me, urging me on with her wide, blue eyes. "Go ahead." She nods. "It's awesome. So sweet you can barely taste the alcohol."

I hesitate, but only for a moment. Then I tilt the bottle back and take a gulp. A much bigger gulp than I'd planned. Then I close my eyes and realize she's right. It is sweet. And other than the sting, burning its way down my throat, I can hardly taste the vodka.

Twelve

The second the band starts playing a slow song, I try to bolt for the bathroom. But then Parker grabs my arm and says, "No way. Forget it. Step away from the vodka, and come with me."

I grip his hand tightly as I follow behind, hoping he'll understand that my sudden display of hand passion has more to do with the effects of drinking than any romantic or passionate connection, because if I've bonded with anyone tonight it would definitely be Teresa, the former Queen Bee of Parkview Junior High. The girl with the moonshine water bottles.

I mean Jenay, now free to make out with Chess whenever she chooses and no longer needing alcohol as an excuse, took only a sip or two, before giving her bottle away. And even though everyone else was pretty much drinking on the way to the dance, it was Teresa and I who kept at it long after we'd arrived. And it's not that I actually like it all that much, because to be honest, it really is a little too sweet. But with Jenay totally focused on Chess and ignoring me, there's no way I can *not* drink and still manage to have a good time.

It's like, I've barely finished my bottle, and already I'm feeling lighter, looser, and free. More like my sister, and a lot less like me.

"Are you having fun?" Parker asks, tightening his grip on my waist and pulling me closer.

"Um, yeah." I shrug, gazing around at all the sparkly silver decorations, the fake snow at the edge of the stage, and the hot, sweaty lead singer, his eyes shut tight as he wails into the microphone, singing a song about lost love.

At first it all seems so pretty and sparkly, but soon it turns blurry and bendy. And when Parker brings his hand to my cheek and says, "Look at me," I push him away and rush for the door, mumbling something about needing some air.

"Are you okay?" he asks, concern in his voice as he trails close behind.

I rock from foot to foot, hugging myself with both arms, not having considered the cold in my rush to be free. All I wanted was some time alone, so I could clear my head, settle my stomach, and stand in the dark, watching my breath escape my body and then disappear into the night.

What I didn't want was for Parker to tag along. Partly because I wasn't sure if I was going to be sick, and partly because I'm not sure I'm ready for Parker, and me, and all that we entail. But now that he's here, I don't want him to think I'm a freak. So I try to say something just to fill up the quiet.

"Which one do you think is ours?" I ask, motioning to the long line of black shiny limos, as Parker removes his jacket and places it over my narrow, pale, goose bump–covered shoulders.

He squints across the parking lot and smiles. "Third one," he says, nodding like he's sure.

"No way." I shake my head and gaze at the long line of generic cars. "I mean, how can you even tell? They all look alike."

"See the guy standing next to it? He's our driver." He nods. "I can tell by the hat."

"They all wear hats, its part of the uniform," I say, gazing at him and laughing in spite of myself.

"Trust me. I can tell. His hat is different." He looks at me, those gorgeous blue eyes that used to ignore me, now searching for mine.

And even though my head has cleared, my stomach still feels a little weird. But I know it's just nerves. I also know how to get through it. "Wanna bet?" I ask, suddenly feeling better, braver, using Zoë as my guide.

"Bet what?" He gives me a dubious yet interested look.

"That you're wrong. That you're totally, completely off base. Because there's no way you can tell from all the way over here if that guy's really our driver." I look him in the eye, my gaze steady and sure, my mouth curving into a smile.

"And if I'm right?" he asks, obviously interested in where this might lead.

"Then you win." I shrug.

"Yeah, but *what* do I win?" He smiles as he moves in closer, quickly adapting to the new me. "It's a bet. So there's got to be a prize, right?"

I look at him, gazing directly into his eyes for the first time tonight. "Oh, there's a prize all right. But you won't know what it is until it's too late and you've already lost." I laugh, grabbing hold of his hand and pulling him across the lot, all the way over to limo number three.

"Hey," Parker says, reaching out to slap hands with the chauffeur, who squeezes his cell phone between his shoulder and ear so he can slap back.

"You guys ready to leave?" He places his hand over the mouthpiece, and gazes from Parker to me.

"No, we're just——" Parker starts, but I cut him off.

"I just need to get something out of the back. It'll only take a sec." I smile, watching as he winks at Parker before walking away.

"So, about this prize," Parker says, closing the door and appearing by my side so fast and seamless it's like he has springs in his shoes, ones that activate at the first hint of sex.

I look into his eyes and wait, knowing that soon, he'll lean in to kiss me.

We kiss for a while. And while it's nice, and sweet, and way better than that time in the closet since there's no bad smells or hockey sticks shoved against my butt, I'm still not fully convinced that he actually wants to make out with me—boring, inept, plain Jane me.

So in my head, I imagine I'm Zoë—that I'm beautiful, wild, glamorous, and experienced—that there's nothing in the world that can scare me.

And as Parker wraps his arms around my waist, I slide my hands down the front of his shirt, making my way down to his pants, hesitating near the spot that I would never try to touch, but that Zoë wouldn't think twice about.

"I don't get you," he whispers, suddenly pulling away. "It's like, inside the dance you'd barely even look at me, but now?" He shakes his head and squints, obviously not complaining, but still, more than a little perplexed.

But I just smile, knowing I'm no longer me. I ditched that nervous loser and became someone better. "I lost the bet," I say, gazing at him with Zoë's eyes, touching him with Zoë's hands, and kissing him with Zoë's lips.

He kisses me on the neck, as I lean back against the seat, feeling so incredibly daring and free. Then he slips his finger under my blue silk strap, sliding it all the way down, as I turn my head and gaze toward the window, shocked to see my own dull reflection staring back at me.

"I can't do this," I say, pushing him away, frantically reaching for my strap.

Parker just looks at me, his face flushed and confused, his hands halted in panic. "But you seemed so—"

I turn back toward the window, hoping not to see me, feeling disappointed when I do.

"Echo, really, I didn't mean . . . please don't be mad," he says, his hands fumbling awkwardly as he reaches for me, trying to make me face him.

I move farther away, my heart beating frantically as I run my hands through my hair and over my dress, erasing all evidence of my little digression, knowing I need to act fast, to come up with some excuse that will explain my bizarre behavior, so everything will get back to normal and stop being so weird. "Jeez Parker, it was only a limo bet. I mean, just how big a prize did you think you were gonna get?" I ask, chasing it with a laugh so he'll think we're okay.

He laughs too, his eyes relaxing, his face clearly relieved. Then he opens the door and steps onto the curb, offering his hand as a guide. "Well, I probably should've told you this before, and I hope you're not too mad, but I have a confession to make," he says, slipping his arm through mine as we head back inside.

I gaze up at him, happy that we've moved on, but only mildly interested in what it might be.

"That wasn't really our limo." He smiles.

Thirteen

The next morning when I woke I didn't feel nearly as bad as I expected. Or at least not in a physical way. I mean, I didn't throw up, I didn't have a headache, and I didn't feel the slightest bit queasy. Which basically means that all of my parents' warnings about the "high price one always pays for a night of overindulgence," didn't come true for me.

But mentally? Mentally I felt like crap. And I don't remember anyone ever cautioning me about that.

I roll over and gaze out the window, noticing how the big oak tree has lost most of its leaves, making it look stark, alone, and defensive. Or maybe that's just me. Maybe I'm getting all Freudian and weird, projecting all of my innermost feelings onto a tree. I mean after last night, and that whole freaky limo episode, I found myself feeling pretty stark, alone, and defensive too.

Yet I was also aware of how I was quite possibly making a

snowstorm out of a snowflake. I mean, there are tons of girls who practically line up to "go wild" and who end up going a whole lot further than that. And it's not like you ever see any of them stopping to think twice, or mentally torturing themselves like me.

But clearly, I'm nothing like those girls. And I'm obviously nothing like Zoë. And even though I know my life would be way more fun if I was, the truth is, I have no idea how to act like that and not lose myself in the process.

"I can't believe you actually brought your books," Teresa says, eyeing my bulging backpack and laughing.

"You said we were gonna study," I say, cringing at how whiny I sound, while wondering what I missed. I mean, earlier, when we were on the phone, I specifically heard her use the word "study." So excuse me for taking that literally.

"Well, I also said we were going to the library, but you don't see me heading there now, do you? The only reason I said all that is 'cause my mom has ginormous elephant ears, and she was totally listening to our conversation that whole time."

"So where are we going?" I ask, walking alongside her, my way-too-heavy backpack digging a wedge deep into my shoulder.

"The park. I told some people we'd meet them."

"What people?" I look at her, noticing for the first time how she's dressed so differently from how I'm used to seeing her at school, way less preppy and a lot more sexy.

"Just some guys, no one you know." She smiles.

"Like, friends of Sean's?" I ask, wondering why she's acting so undercover and secretive.

But she just laughs. "Please. Sean is totally sweet, don't get me wrong, and he's good for school dances and stuff like that, but, well, I don't know. There's this other guy, and it's kind of hard to explain." She shrugs. "But you'll see what I mean when you meet him."

When we get to the park, instead of going right down to the lake like I usually do, Teresa leads me over to the old fountain, the one with all the angels and cherubs and overblown biblical images, all molded from a single slab of cement.

"Omigod! There he is, Jason. He is *so* hot! So just act cool, okay?" she whispers, shooting me a doubtful look, obviously not convinced I'll be able to pull it off. She fluffs her hair around her shoulders, then straightens her sweater and picks up the pace, heading straight for these two guys who are drinking, smoking, and just overall loitering on the fountain's tiled edge.

"Hey," she says, stopping before them and tilting her head toward me. "This is Echo."

I gaze at the two of them, wondering which one of these delinquents she could possibly think is hot.

"Echo? Who names their kid that? What're your parents, like, hippies?" This comes from a fat guy wearing a size too small I DO MY OWN NUDE SCENES T-shirt that I hope is meant to be ironic. And when he laughs his whole belly shakes, stretching and bulging against the overburdened cotton, just like jolly ol' St. Nick. Only a whole lot grosser.

I stand there, wondering how soon I can leave, when Teresa shakes her head, pushes him playfully on the shoulder, and says, "Tom, you asshole. Leave her alone. Echo's cool." But when she looks at me, her expression tells a whole other story, having already decided I'm not.

She pulls a pack of cigarettes from her purse and settles herself onto the ground, sitting Indian style at their feet. "Somebody give me a light," she says, offering the pack to me, as the other guy, the one I'm assuming is "Hot Jason," leans toward her with a burning match.

I shake my head as I watch her inhale, then release it back

through her nose and mouth like an angry cartoon bull. Making sure to shift just ever so slightly, so that the V of her low-cut sweater is aimed straight at Jason—who's aiming for slick but nailing seedy, and who's definitely old enough to know better.

It's weird how she acts like this around me, yet plays it so straight at school. Like last night, when she was drinking, only I saw how much. And I'm willing to bet I'm the only one who knows about the smoking, the cleavage flaunting, and how she's hoping to cheat on Sean with this loser.

"How's your little boyfriend? What's his name? Sam?" asks Tom, who's already been called an asshole, and now seems intent on proving it.

"His name is Sean, you moron. And he's not my boyfriend, we just hang sometimes." She glances quickly at Jason, with his slicked-back, longish blond hair, faded Levis, motorcycle boots, dark T-shirt, and black leather jacket. And I realize he seems really familiar, though I can't imagine why.

"You go there too?" Tom asks, kicking his foot in my general direction, as opposed to, oh, I don't know, gesturing politely or addressing me by name.

"Bella Vista? Um, yeah," I say, feeling pretty squeamish under his heavy, judgmental gaze, and wondering not for the first time, why I'm still here.

"That school sucks. Principal Hames is a fucking loser! L-O-S-E-R," he says, pumping his beer-gripping fist in the air, proving he can spell.

I just stand there, not agreeing, not denying, not saying a word. Just trying to avoid the secondhand smoke while plotting my escape.

"You leaving soon?" he asks, dragging on his cigarette and sipping his beer, going from beer to cigarette, from cigarette to beer, barely taking a break in between.

"Bella Vista? No, I just started," I say, looking at Teresa who's ignoring me now, since she's too busy flirting with Jason.

"No, I mean now. You're just standing there like you've got an appointment or something." He sips his beer and laughs. "At least drop your bag and relax. It's not like we're gonna hurt you. Unless you want us to." He narrows his eyes, giving me a long, leisurely once-over, starting at my Converse tennis shoes and working his way to the top of my head.

"Oh, no, I just . . ." I gaze at Teresa who's still ignoring me, then I turn back toward the way we came. I mean, not to be a prude, but I don't like this scene. And not to be a freak, but I'm getting a really bad vibe.

"You guys got any more beer?" Teresa asks, getting the attention back on her, which believe me, is where we both want it. "I need a little hair of the dog. I swear I have like the worst hangover, *ever*. Echo and I got totally wasted last night, and I need some relief." She stands, moving toward Jason and grabbing his beer, tilting her head back and swinging her long blond hair as she guzzles.

"Want some?" she says, turning to me, her eyes wide and shiny, her mouth wet and open.

But I just shake my head and look away, cringing as my overloaded backpack carves a long, deep groove into the top of my shoulder.

"Your friend's a real blast," Tom says, tossing his bottle toward the silver metal trash can, not bothering to get up and retrieve it when it ricochets off the side and rolls across the grass.

Then just as I'm about to tell him to go pound sand (or something much worse), Jason flicks his lit cigarette right at him and goes, "Shut the fuck up." Then his eyes move over to me, embarking on an unhurried cruise along my skinny, undeveloped body, until finally coming to rest upon mine. "I knew your sister," he says, reaching for another beer, flipping the top, and nodding. Smiling as he pulls Teresa close, pressing her hard against him, and sliding his hand down her back until he reaches her butt and squeezes. His eyes never once wavering from mine.

I watch as Teresa gazes up at him and giggles, then I turn and walk away. Feeling angry with her for dragging me here, but even angrier with myself for staying.

"Echo, wait! Shit. You guys, I'll be right back," Teresa says, running to catch up with me. "Where the hell are you going?" she whispers, tugging on my jacket, as I pick up the pace, doing my best to ignore her. "Echo, jeez, don't be mad."

I shake my head and walk even faster, 'til I'm just short of running. I hate when people do that. I hate when they put you in a really bad position and then tell you how you should feel about it.

"Seriously, slow down, please? Just give me a sec to explain," she pleads.

I swing around and face her, making no attempt to hide my anger.

"Listen, I know Tom's kind of an asshole, and I probably should've warned you. I'm sorry, okay?"

"*Kind of* an asshole?" I look at her and shake my head. "Oh my God, you weren't trying to set me up with him, were you?" My eyes go wide, having just now thought of that totally disgusting possibility.

But she just rolls her eyes and shakes her head. "Don't be ridiculous. I know you're all into Parker, and I would never try to mess with that. It's just that I really, really, really like Jason. I mean I *really* like him. Don't you think he's cute?" she asks, moving right past me and back to her. Going from apology to confession in zero to five seconds.

"Honestly? I think he's creepy. Not to mention *old*," I say, far too mad to even care what she thinks.

"But that's why I like him." She shrugs. "He's got a car,

money, and ten times the maturity of all the guys at school put together."

"Teresa, he's a *drug dealer,*" I say, not entirely sure of this, but still convinced that it's true. "He's bad news. Trust me, you *don't* want to get involved with him."

But she just sucks on her cigarette and squints at me, and it's clear she's chosen not to listen. "You don't even know him. You just met him like, ten minutes ago."

I watch as she shakes her head and rolls her eyes, even though everything she just said is wrong. I mean, even though I haven't actually "met" him until now, that doesn't mean I don't know *about* him. But it's not like I'm gonna explain that to her, since it's not like she'd even listen if I tried. The only thing I want to do is just get the heck out of here. Now.

"Listen," I finally say. "You're right. It probably is none of my business. But maybe you should ask yourself why some twenty-five-year-old guy is hanging out with and supplying beer and drugs to a fifteen-year-old girl. I mean, come *on,* Teresa." But when I look at her, her eyes are blazing. And instead of persuading her, I've just made her mad.

"Okay, first of all, he's twenty-four, *not* twenty-five. And second, you only saw him give me a light and a beer. *That's all.* So you better not go telling people anything other than that. In fact, you better not go telling them anything at all. You also shouldn't be so judgmental. I mean, he was friends with your sister."

I look at her, standing before me, feeling so righteous even though she couldn't be more wrong. "He *knew* my sister, but he was *never* her friend," I say, glaring at her. "Believe me, there's a difference."

But she just rolls her eyes and flicks her ash to the ground, the gray and black particles hovering briefly before clinging to her feet. "Listen," she says, grabbing my arm just as I start to walk away. "No need to mention any of this at school, okay? I mean, it's not like it's anybody's business, and I don't want Sean to get all upset and get the wrong idea. All right?" She looks at me, her face showing fear for the first time today.

But I just release myself from her grip and head toward home. "Don't worry," I say without looking back. "I won't say a word."

Fourteen

Monday at lunch Teresa's sitting next to Sean, acting all cuddly and cute, like yesterday never happened. I line up my food, spreading it out before me, gazing from my orange to my cookie to my sandwich, wondering which to eat first.

"I can't believe your mom still packs a lunch for you," Teresa says, eyeballing my pastrami on rye. "I think that is *so* sweet."

I decide to skip the healthy stuff and just start with the chocolate chip cookie, wondering if by "sweet" what she really means is "juvenile."

"My mom would never take the time to do that," she continues, popping a tiny powdered donut into her mouth before washing it down with a slug of Diet Coke.

I chew my cookie, trying to think of a good response. *I'm the baby so she likes to take care of me? No, too babyish. I'm all she has left? Jeez, way too morbid.* So finally I just say, "Yeah, well, that's just her." But then I remember how that was never really her, at least not until the happy pills moved in.

"Hey, what happened yesterday? Your cell was off, and your mom said you were out," Parker says, kissing the top of my head and squeezing in beside me.

"Oh, yeah, I—" I start to give an excuse, but then Teresa butts in, deciding to provide one for me.

"I needed a little help with my homework, and Echo totally saved my life. Did you know she's like a mathematical genius?" She gives me a quick warning glance, one that nobody notices but me, then she smiles and rubs her shoulder lightly against Sean's.

"Wow, cute, nice, and good at math too?" Parker says, winking as he steals the rest of my cookie.

I just gaze at Teresa and shrug. "So she says."

After school I meet Abby at her locker. Only this time, Jenay's not there.

"She had a pep club meeting," Abby says, slamming her locker a little harder than necessary and looking at me. "I mean, *pep club*! Can you even believe it?"

I shrug my shoulders and walk beside her as we make our way off campus. "So how was your weekend, you know, the whole family thing?" I ask, not wanting to talk about Jenay behind her back, yet feeling like I have to at least keep up the appearance of believing Abby's excuse for not going to the dance.

But she just peers at me from the corner of her eye and sighs. "Okay, I think we both know there was no family thing," she says, shaking her head and looking away. "So go ahead, tell me everything. Was it awesome?"

"It was okay," I say, nervously shifting my backpack, not

wanting to make her feel any worse by yammering on and on about it.

"Just okay?" She raises her eyebrows and waits.

"Yeah, I mean, it was fun." I nod, wishing we could move away from this subject too.

"Well, I gotta tell ya, Jenay makes it sound a lot more exciting than you. I mean, you did go to the same dance, right?" She laughs.

"Even shared a limo." I shrug.

"Well, you should hear her version. She dropped by yesterday, and went on and on and on. By the time she left, I felt like *I* was the one dating Chess. Seriously, I'm officially a Chess Williams expert now. I know everything about him, and I can even prove it. Like, did you know that his favorite sandwich is chicken salad? Fascinating, right? And how about this little known fact—he actually loves basketball more than baseball! Which is so highly unusual, wouldn't you agree?" She shakes her head and rolls her eyes. "I'm sorry, I know I sound awful, but it's like, all she can talk about! Chess this, Chess that." She sighs. "Anyway, what's up with you and Teresa?" she asks, looking at me all sideways again. "You guys dating?"

"What do you mean?" I gaze at the busy street, noticing how almost all of the cars are driven by Bella Vista seniors, taking the long way home.

"Well, Jenay said you guys practically spent more time with each other than your dates. And then yesterday we tried to call you to ask you to come over, but your phone was off. I guess that's because you were helping her study. Or at least that's what I overheard you say at lunch. Are you guys like, good friends now?"

She's staring straight ahead, acting like it's perfectly okay with her that Jenay's ditched us for pep club and Chess, and that I'm supposedly best friends with Teresa. But I can tell it's really bothering her. And part of me wants to tell her about yesterday so she'll know there's nothing to worry about, that she and Jenay are still my best friends, and they won't be replaced. But the other part just wants to forget it ever happened. And in the end, that's the part that wins. "She sucks at math, so I helped her." I shrug.

"And Parker? Are you guys like, a couple now?" she asks, finally looking directly at me, her face a mix of worry and hope.

"I guess," I say, shrugging and smiling weakly.

"It's okay." She nods. "Really. I'm happy for you guys," she says, nodding again, this time more firmly.

I walk alongside her, running my index finger over the top of a neighbor's white picket fence. Thinking back to a time when things were so simple and easy.

"It's just . . . everything's changing," she says, staring far away.

"Tell me."

My mom left a note on the fridge, telling me how she and my dad are going to some faculty dinner party, but to go ahead and warm up the leftover lasagna and make myself a salad in case I get hungry.

I climb the stairs to my room, remove the jeans and sweater I wore to school, and replace them with my old, worn-out navy blue sweatpants, and my READING IS SEXY T-shirt that I ordered off the Internet mere seconds after seeing it on Rory Gilmore. Then I plop down on my bed and think about how I should probably be starting my homework even though I'd really rather not.

It's not often I get the whole house to myself, so I like to make the most of it when I do. Which usually translates to me just loafing around, wasting time, and not doing much of anything, since that seems to make the time last even longer.

It's weird how Jenay and Abby always get freaked out and scared when they're left home alone. Before their parents' car has even left the driveway, they're already on the phone, dialing everyone they know, trolling for company.

But not me. I totally love it. And I can't ever remember getting the slightest bit anxious or scared. Usually it's more the exact opposite. It makes me feel happy, expansive, and free. But that's probably because all last year my parents were like the gestapo, never allowing me more than a half hour's peace. And it's only in the last few months that they've finally begun to retreat.

I'm just about to turn on my iPod when my cell phone rings. And when I see that it's Parker my first instinct is to let it go straight into voice mail, even though I know that I shouldn't.

"Hey," I say, wedging it between my shoulder and cheek, trying to sound all upbeat and happy, like a good girlfriend would.

"What're you doing?" he asks.

"Um, nothing. Just lying here," I say, lifting my feet in the air, checking out my chipped-up pedicure, and thinking how I should probably cover it with some socks.

"Really?" he asks, sounding surprised.

"Yup, really," I tell him, adding no further comment.

"Who's all there?"

"Just me."

"You want company?" He laughs, but I can tell that he means it.

I roll over and gaze out the window. "You mean, now?" I ask, knowing he does, wishing he didn't.

"Yeah, I need a little help with my math homework and I hear you're the go-to math wiz."

"Oh really?" I say, laughing like I'm someone else, hoping I'll be mistaken for flirtatious.

"No, I just want to come over and hang. Is that cool?"

I stare at the oak tree, tall, dark, and barren. Then I roll back over and sigh. "Give me an hour," I tell him, closing the phone and reaching under the bed.

Fifteen

June 20
Last night my parents sat me down for a game of ulti-
matum. Saying if I don't land a job by next Monday, then
I'll find myself gainfully employed at the one they found for
me. Some psych doc who needs a little help with filing and
appt scheduling for all the sick heads that visit his office.

So of course I acted all offended, like it was way too
beneath me to even consider. But the truth is, I'm thinking
it could really work. Because, let's face it, making appoint-
ments for the mildly insane definitely beats wearing a poly-
ester uniform and hanging over a deep fryer, encouraging a
nasty case of adolescent acne, or standing on my feet all
day building bunions at some stupid, small-town boutique.

So now I can just screw around for the whole rest of
the week, pretending I'm job hunting, and then Monday

morning I'll show up fresh and eager and ready to report for duty at Dr. Freud's.

O yeah, Carly called last night, wanted to talk about what happened. I told her there's nothing to talk about, and wished her well. Then right before we hung up I just might have mentioned something about Stephen's annoying bicep-gazing-during-sex habit, and how she might want to look away when he eats since it's truly disgusting. And then I think she may have hung up on me. But, whatever.

Marc is as elusive and hard to reach as ever—which just makes me lust him even more! But I happen to know that he knows about Paula's party, so I'm wearing my cobalt blue halter top and white jeans in hopes that he shows.

June 23

Jeez—where to begin? Was it Lennon who said something about life being what happens when you're busy making other plans? Anyway, it's just so freaking true! I left the house around noon, dressed all conservative so everyone would think I was really going job hunting, when really I went straight to Paula's where I changed into my bikini and we spent all day reading magazines by the pool.

Then Kevin and Kristin stopped by (always together, together forever!), and by the time they finally split, Paula and I were so stoned we could barely move. Maybe that's the secret to their long-term romance, they're just way too messed up and unmotivated to go looking for someone else???

Anyway, before we even realized it, it was already getting dark, and all these people just started walking through the door, and we were still on our lounge chairs by the pool! And since it was Paula's party, and since she was all oiled up and still in her bikini, everyone just assumed it was supposed to be a moonlight pool party or something. So they just started stripping off their clothes and jumping in.

Including Paula who technically didn't have to get naked since she was already in a bikini, though I'm not really sure she realized that at the time. Anyway, I just lay there, making my way through a bag of chips, while my eyes searched for Marc, trying not to be too bummed out by the fact that I didn't see him anywhere, and trying not to care that everyone around me was all happy and hooked up, well, everyone but me.

So finally I decided to go into the house and look for something to change into, and I could not freaking believe it when I go past the den and see Marc sitting there, all alone, in front of the TV. Only the TV was off, and his eyes were closed. So I just assumed he was probably sleeping, stoned, or meditating or something. And I just stood there staring at him, thinking how peaceful and beautiful he looked being all still and mellow like that, but also wishing he'd open his eyes and see me.

But when he finally did, it was like nothing registered. He just sat there all silent, and then after awhile (which felt like forever) he finally patted the cushion beside him and passed me his iPod. And we sat there for like the longest time, just listening to music, and passing the earpiece back and forth.

And even though it was cool, and calm and really pretty nice, after awhile I started to get a little annoyed at how there I was, sitting right next to him, in my bikini, and all he wanted to do was listen to music by bands I've never even heard of! I mean, not to be stuck up or anything, but most guys are willing to drop way more than their iPods when I'm half naked and ready to go.

So finally, I just got up and left, thinking for sure he'd follow. Only he didn't. And when I finally got over myself and went back in the den, he was gone. And after searching the entire house, I realized he really was gone.

And I thought—screw him! But mostly I was feeling re-jected. I mean, what's with this guy? What's with the whole mysterious Mr. Enigma act?

Anyway, I got changed, got myself together, and got myself home. And then later, just as I'm falling asleep, I see this flash in my window. Kind of like an SOS or something, even though I'm not really sure how that SOS flash signal really goes. But it seemed like a flashlight being turned off and on, slowly, with short spaces of darkness in between.

So, feeling kind of annoyed, and also kind of scared—I mean, was it aliens? Some psycho mass murderer? Because who does that? I got out of bed and headed for the window, moving the curtains just a tiny bit. And when I peeked through the narrow opening, I immediately grabbed my cell phone and started dialing 911. But then I looked again and I just couldn't freaking believe what I saw. It's like I seri-ously had to blink my eyes a whole bunch of times. I even rubbed them like you see in cartoons. But still, every time I opened them again, I saw the exact same thing.

So I creeped down the hall, and into Echo's room, being careful not to wake her. Then I went out to her balcony, and gestured in a what-the-hell-do-you-want kind of way. But he just stood there, motioning for me to come down.

And I thought—No effin way! This guy is totally whacked and he's probably planning to knock me out with his iPod Nano and drag me away, or something.

But then he kept waving, and then he smiled. So I grabbed hold of a branch, and made my way down the oak tree, just like I'd done a gazillion times before.

And when he met me at the bottom I asked, "What're you, crazy?" And I tried to look mad and not scared like I really felt. I mean, it just then occurred to me how the front door was locked and how I'd never be able to get back up the tree in time, you know, in case I was in danger or something.

But he just looked at me and goes, "I forgot to play you this one song."

And I just stood there, looking at him like he was completely looped. I mean, what the hell? It was like two o'clock in the morning. But still, I just stood there, listening to the song. It was jazz, and it was beautiful, though I'd definitely never heard it before. Then I gave him back his earpiece, praying to every god from every religion, begging to please just let me get back to my room safely and away from this music-loving head case who I mistakenly thought I liked.

And just as I started to climb back up the tree, he placed his hand on my shoulder, forcing me to face him. Well, my first instinct was to scream, but I didn't want to wake everyone and risk facing a world of hurt and a severely stunted summer, so I just turned around calmly, hoping I could talk him out of whatever sick act he was planning to perform.

And that's when he leaned in and kissed me!

It was only once. And it was really brief. But still, it was the most amazing thing that ever happened to me.

And then he smiled.

And then he left.

And I just stood there on the lawn, shivering in my bare feet, cotton cami, and boxers. Watching as he sprinted across the wet grass, leaving dark footprints in his wake, until I could no longer see him.

June 24

Today, when Echo walked in the door, holding the mail, she had the weirdest expression on her face.

"So bizarre," she said.

And I go, "What's bizarre?" And then I barely even looked up because I was busy eating strawberry yogurt while pretending to search through the want ads.

And she goes, "This. It was sitting in the mailbox."

And she tosses this packet on the table in front of me and it makes this kind of rattling sound as it lands and skids.

So I pick it up to see what the heck it is, and I go, "Huh, weird. It's some kind of seeds."

And she goes, "What kind of seeds?"

So I turn it over and see a picture of a tree on front. And it looks a lot like our oak tree does in the middle of spring, when its branches are all filled in with leaves. And then I see in the bottom of the left hand corner, in very small writing, the hand-scrawled words—Lush Life. And I remember the song from last night. The one Marc shared with me at two in the morning.

And Echo goes, "Who would put seeds in the mailbox?"

And I looked at her and smiled and said, "These are for me."

I close the diary and close my eyes, my mind drifting back to the day I found the packet of seeds in the mailbox, and how strange it all seemed at the time. And how Zoë's reaction made it seem even stranger, the way she smiled so secretly, like it actually meant something to her. Something she intended to keep from me.

I guess having been born just two years apart allowed me to take her for granted. Assuming she'd always be there, that nothing could take her away. I mean, right from the beginning she was always there to cheer me on and teach me everything she'd learned during her two-year head start.

It was Zoë who taught me how to keep my balance on my bike the day they took away my training wheels. And it was she who showed me how to build the perfect Barbie biodome subdivision using some old cardboard shoeboxes and a striped flannel sheet.

But now, thinking back on all that, I also remember how

when she moved away from all of those childhood things, she also moved away from me.

And it's weird how reading her diary is kind of like getting a second chance, like one last shot at knowing the sister who'd been so loving yet elusive, especially during those last few months.

I prop my pillows against my headboard, until it's comfortable enough to lean against. Then I reach for Zoë's diary and flip through the pages, picking up where I left off.

June 27
At first I thought I'd take those seeds and plant them right underneath my window. You know, as an act of charity for some future generation, some yet-to-be-born teenage girl who won't have to sneak down the hall, looking for escape, like me. But now that three days have passed and Marc hasn't even bothered to call, I think I'll probably just dump them in the trash, and try to forget the whole sick thing ever happened.
I mean, why hasn't he called??
Maybe he really is crazy.
Maybe I should just hang up on him when (if) he does.

June 28
Hung by the pool with Paula all day, just working on my tan. All she could talk about was her crush on Keith, determined to get to the bottom of who he looks like more—Russell Crowe or Ben McKenzie? Boring! I just pretended to be asleep.
I know I'm being a bad friend, but what can I say? Marc still hasn't called, and because of that I've decided to take a vow of mental celibacy. That's right. No more thinking about, dreaming about, or even talking about guys.
Any guys.

Because they're all the same.
They all suck.

June 30
Still celibate.
Still hate guys (with the exception of Dad—well, most of the time).
Extremely tan though.

July 2
Omigod. Where to begin? OK, started my job at the head shrinker today—way way better than I thought, though it's not like I'll be confessing that anytime soon. As far as my parents are concerned he's a fair yet firm employer, who has exceedingly high expectations that I will struggle to meet, and that's the story I'm sticking to.

When the truth is he spends most of the day behind a closed door, listening to all those messed-up whiners drone on and on about their lonely, miserable, fucked-up lives.

Which means my day is filled with long, leisurely fifty-minute breaks where I can nap, talk on my cell, surf the Net, whatever, just as long as the filing gets done and the phone answered within the first three rings. Not bad for a summer job.

But today I mostly napped. Because I was sooooo tired from last night. And here's why—

I was in my room, watching TV with the volume down low, when I heard someone calling my name. Not like yelling it out or anything, more like a loud—okay, really loud—whisper. So I immediately jumped up, ran to the mirror, combed my fingers through my hair, dabbed on some lip gloss, and sprayed some perfume, the whole time my heart beating so fast I thought it would break through my chest.

And then right as I started to run to my window, I stopped and thought—*What the hell? He doesn't call for over a week, and now he shows up at one in the morning expecting me to do the whole Rapunzel thing again? Well, screw him.*

So I plopped right back down on my bed and lifted the remote, ready to turn up the volume and tune him out. But then he called my name again and I started to worry that he was gonna wake the whole house, so I opened my window and faced him.

"Shhh!" I said, pressing my finger against my lips and shaking my head so he'd know that I meant it.

But he just raised his arm, the one holding the bouquet of flowers.

So I slipped down the stairs and out the front door, running all the way across the lawn to meet him.

"Here," he said, handing me the flowers he probably clipped from my next-door neighbor's yard. And when I brought them to my nose their smell was so sweet, it was hard to stay mad.

"What's going on?" he said, all casual, like everything was totally normal and not at all weird.

I just looked at him, as gorgeous and sexy as ever, but seemingly unaware of the fact that it was the middle of the night! "Um, what's going on?" I said. "Well let's see. It's after midnight, I haven't heard from you all week, and now you decide to just drop by and yell out my name 'til you wake the whole house." I shook my head and looked at him, trying my best to appear really mad.

But he just shrugged. "I don't have your number," he said.

So I go, "OK, well, you could've asked somebody for my number, you know, like Paula, or someone?"

But he just goes, "I don't have Paula's number either."

Then, "Listen, I was up at the lake, at my grandmother's house, and I didn't get back until late."

I just looked at him. He didn't seem like the kind of guy to hang with his grandma. So I go, "Please, your grandmother's house?" Then I shook my head, rolling my eyes for emphasis. And then I realized that I really didn't have a good reason not to believe that, other than the fact that it just seemed like a lie. "OK so why are you here now?" I asked, holding the flowers tightly to my chest, my heart pounding like crazy.

"Because I wanted to do this," he whispered.

Then he leaned in and kissed me.

And when he pulled away he reached into his pocket and grabbed a pen. Then he pushed up his sleeve and held out his arm. "Here," he said. "Write down your number so I can call you. And write big so I can see it in the dark."

And when I was done, he flipped open his phone and walked away. And by the time I made it back to my room, mine was ringing. And we talked for so long, I had to plug it into my charger. And he told me so many things, and answered so many questions, I don't think I've ever known anyone as well as this. Seriously, he even told me about how . . .

Crap. I drop the diary and listen to the doorbell ring. One time, quickly followed by two. Gotta be Parker. And I hate to admit this, but I wish he'd just go away so I can finish reading about Zoë and Marc and how it all began. It's like, in the beginning they were so much in love, but then later, they were a lot less so. And I need to know what happened in that space between, learn exactly what it was that made everything change.

But then the bell rings again, and I push the diary back under my mattress, gazing at the tree outside, and wondering if I should try to rappel my way down and run across the lawn just like Zoë would've done. I mean, it definitely seems a lot more romantic than making my way downstairs, opening the front door, and letting him in the usual way.

But then again, I'm not Zoë.

Which means I don't even stop by the mirror to check my reflection before I go downstairs to greet him.

Sixteen

I've never cooked dinner for anyone before, much less a guy. Though to be honest, I guess I still haven't. I mean, my mom's the one who actually *made* the lasagna. All I did was reheat it.

"This is excellent," Parker says, taking another bite.

"Glad you like it." I nod, hating the way I sound so stiff and formal, and how it's practically impossible for me to ever relax and be normal around him.

"I had no idea you were such a good cook." He smiles. "Which makes me wonder what other talents you're hiding."

I reach for my glass and sip my water, even though it's really more about nerves than thirst. "Well actually, I didn't really make it. You know, the lasagna," I say, mentally rolling my eyes at my lame-brain self, wondering what the heck he's even doing here. I mean, is he desperate? Is this some kind of bet?

"Well, you've got the whole reheating gig down, and that's gotta count for something, right?" He smiles.

We mostly talk about school, classes, teachers, people we know. And every time there's a break, every time it gets silent, the scraping of his fork sounds so incredibly loud that I say just about anything to fill up the gap.

He helps me clear the table, then I lead him to the den. But just as I make a beeline for the couch he touches my arm and goes, "Where's your room?"

And I go, "Oh, um, it's upstairs." Then I point in that direction, like he doesn't know where *up* is. *Oh God.*

"Can I see it?"

I glance at the clock, then back at him, knowing my parents won't return for at least another hour. Which technically should make me want to say *yes,* even though I'm a lot closer to *no.*

"Come on. I just wanna see what it's like," he says, smiling in a way that's trying a little too hard to seem friendly and harmless, and like he has no ulterior motives.

If I was Zoë, I would've served the entire meal on my bed, sitting Indian style on my duvet, with plates and dishes spread all around, just lighting candles, cranking a CD, and not giving a shit if anything spilled. But even though I'm nothing like her, that doesn't mean I have to act like me. So I grab his hand and take a deep breath, promising myself it will all be okay.

He stands in the doorway, scoping it out. "Yup," he says, making his way across the room until he's standing before my bookshelf.

"Yup, what?" I ask, leaning against the wall and trying to see my room for the very first time, to see it like he sees it.

His eyes scan the titles of all of my books, as his fingers brush lightly over my softball trophies, second and third place, from fourth and fifth grade. "Just like I thought," he says, turning to smile.

I just stand there, wondering if I should feel more disappointed that I'm apparently so predictable and easy to read.

"Lots of books, a few CDs, but thank God no puppy posters or pictures of Aaron Carter." He laughs.

"Well, I got rid of all that on my fifteenth birthday. Dumped it right in the trash. I'm into older men now. You know, octogenarians. Know where I can find a good Harrison Ford centerfold?" I ask, going over to lean on the edge of my desk and smiling nervously.

He checks out my TV, my iPod dock, and my bulletin board full of cards and letters and photos, including the one of me, Jenay, and Abby, making faces and hamming it up for the camera, and the one right next to it of Zoë and me sitting at the kitchen table, heads close together, crossing our eyes and sticking our tongues out at my dad, who was taking the picture. Then he wanders over to my bed, and sits on the edge. "When're your parents coming back?" he asks, trying to sound casual, like he's only mildly interested in the answer.

"An hour, two at the most," I say, gazing down at my feet and my messed-up pedicure, and then curling my toes under so he won't see.

"Would they freak if they found me here?"

I shrug. I mean, I really don't know the answer to that since it's not like I've ever had the opportunity to risk that kind of trouble before.

"No worries," Parker says. "If they come home, I'll just jump off your balcony." He nods toward my open french doors. "Or scale down that tree." He smiles.

Then he pats the mattress like a silent invitation, and I take a deep breath and move toward him.

We're kissing. We're lying on my bed and kissing. And I can taste the lasagna lingering on his tongue, and smell the garlic mixed in with his breath. And even though it's not near as bad as it sounds, it's not what you'd call "amazing" either.

Still, I'm going through the motions, moving my lips against his and running my hands through his hair, even though all the while I can't help wishing it was just a little bit better, just a smidge more romantic than it actually is.

But maybe it will never be like that for me. Maybe I'm not the kind of girl who inspires guys to spontaneous midnight visits and secret-message gift giving. Maybe I'm just like all the other girls who pretend they're content with *this,* when really they're longing for something more.

So far Parker hasn't tried to do anything more than just kiss, which mostly makes me glad. And the only reason I say *mostly* is because I'm hoping he's just trying to be cautious and respectful, and *not* because he's turned off by my dowdy sweatpants and tee.

I know I should've brushed my hair. Or at the very least, smeared on some lip gloss. I mean, we've been dating for less than a month, and I've already let myself go.

I move in closer, kissing him harder, and shifting my body so I'm lying on top of his. Then I squeeze my eyes shut and dream of another place, one where he's not really him, and I'm no longer me.

I run my fingertips down the side of his face, imagining his long dark lashes resting against his high, chiseled cheekbones. And when I reach up to brush my hair out of the way, I pretend that it's smooth, wavy, and rich, not limp, lank, and dull.

"Echo," he says, rolling me off 'til we're facing each other, lying again on our sides.

"Hmmm," I mumble, my eyes still closed, feeling happy and dreamy and free.

"Open your eyes," he whispers.

So I do. Slowly lifting my lids, until I'm startled by the sight of his golden blond hair and blue eyes, so different from the familiar, dark stranger I held in my mind.

"Should I go?" he asks, gazing at me, before leaning in to kiss the side of my cheek.

I squint at him, wondering why he's asking.

"Your parents. They'll be back soon, and I don't want you to get in trouble. I was just joking about scaling down your tree, you know that, right?"

But of course you were, I think, feeling disappointed that we're back to being us, so different from who I really want to be. And just as I roll over, and start to get up, Zoë's diary slips from its hiding space, and lands hard at my feet.

"What's that?" he says, reaching down to retrieve it.

But luckily I'm closer, which makes me quicker as well. So I swoop it up and hold it tight to my chest, then I look at him and say, "I think you should leave."

Seventeen

All day at school I went through the motions—nodding, smiling, taking notes, acing pop quizzes, waving to friends, eating lunch, acting cute with Parker by sharing my brownie and laughing at all of his jokes. Yet the whole entire time, my eyes were searching for Marc. And I found myself lingering in the hall where he smokes, leaning against the wall where he eats, and stopping to tie my shoe in the area just outside the girl's bathroom where I ran into him that very first day.

And it's not like I was planning to actually talk to him or anything. I mean, I didn't even know what to say. It's more like I just wanted to see him, be near him, and share the same space with this person who I know so much about, but in such a strange, remote way.

And all the while, for the whole entire day, I was just waiting for the bell to ring, knowing that's when I could finally go home, lie on my bed, pick up Zoë's diary, and take up from where I left off.

Even last night after walking Parker to the door, I had every intention of bolting back up to my room and reading the diary. But then my parents drove up, and my dad, his face all flushed and happy from an evening of intellectual conversation and one too many glasses of wine, insisted we hang out in the den, watch a little TV, and get reacquainted during the three-minute commercial breaks.

And by the time I finally snuck out of there, it was late, I was tired, so I decided to call it a night.

"Are you guys going?" Jenay asks, shifting her books and stop-ping, having just reached the corner where we say good-bye and head our separate ways. "You know, to Teresa's party?" she adds, removing a piece of windblown blond hair from her lip gloss and tucking it back behind her ear.

I just shrug and look at Abby. I mean, it's not like Teresa actually invited me or anything. But then I guess it's not really that kind of a party. It's more the haphazard, last-minute kind. The kind that gets planned the moment someone's parents un-expectedly head out of town.

"I heard it's going to be couples only. So count me out," Abby says, staring off toward our street.

"Are you serious? Just couples? That's so elitist," I say, shaking my head and laughing, trying hard to appear like my normal, slightly sarcastic self, so my friends won't see just how much I'm changing, and how I no longer care about any of this, especially now that I prefer Zoë's world to my own.

"I think that's only to keep the head count in check, so it doesn't get all crazy and out of control. So no excuses, Ab. I mean, it's not like there's gonna be a velvet rope and a bouncer, so it's not like you'll get turned away at the door. At least think about it before you say no," Jenay says, nodding encouragingly. "Please? Besides, if you want a date, I have the perfect guy all lined up and ready to go. All you have to do is say the word."

"Forget it," Abby says, blushing furiously but standing her ground. "I don't accept donations, hand-me-downs, charity dates, or mercy hookups."

"But you haven't even met him! At least think it over, before you go all negative on me," Jenay says, rolling her eyes but still laughing. "Listen, this guy is perfect for you, and this isn't some crazy, random pairing because I've actually been thinking a lot about this. He's super nice, really funny, and he's incredibly smart too. And I mean like, majorly smart. He's in my history class and he's never once stumbled when he gets called on. Seriously, even when he's messing around, he still knows *all* the answers."

Abby puts her hand on her hip and shakes her head. "Did you even listen to your list? Nice, funny, smart, super smart even! Oh lucky day for me! But did you say hot? No. Gorgeous? *Niente.* Cute? Not so much. That's a really bad sign, Jenay. A really bad sign." She narrows her eyes.

But no way is Jenay giving up. "But that's the thing, he *is* cute. Seriously, I swear. And the only reason I didn't mention it first is because I know you're not at all shallow or superficial. I know for a fact that you would never, ever base your opinion on looks alone." She looks at each of us, smiling triumphantly, knowing there's no way for Abby to argue with that.

Abby just stands there, squinting at Jenay as she mulls it over. "What's his name?" she asks, as though that will somehow reveal which way to go.

"Jax. Jax Brannigan."

"Jacks? Like plural? Like there's two of him?" Abby says, her eyes going wide, as her head moves back and forth, indicating an immediate, "no way in hell" decision. "Jacks the nice, funny, super incredibly smart, *two-headed history buff?*"

"Jax with an *x*. And you can't hold his name against him since it's not like he named himself," Jenay says, rolling her eyes, clearly frustrated with all of the obstacles Abby insists on throwing onto the otherwise well-marked path of love.

"What would you name yourself?" I ask, suddenly interested in this conversation, but probably only because as far as weird names go, I'm the undisputed queen. "I mean, if you could have any name, what would you pick?"

Abby laughs. "Well, when I was seven I wanted to be named Candy. So my dad started calling me Junior Mint, and my mom started calling me Abba Zabba and Aaron started calling me Twizzler, until I begged them all to please just stop and call me Abby again."

Jenay smiles. "I always wanted a cute name. You know, one that ended in an I or E sound." She shrugs. "But as it turns out, Jenay's a family name. So I'll probably be expected to pass it down someday too. You?"

Abby and Jenay both look at me, obviously curious how you could possibly ever top a name like Echo. And even though the years from kindergarten through fifth grade were the worst, with all the boys chasing me around, going, "Echooooo! Echoooo!" I guess I never really thought about changing it, never once thought about being anyone else—until now. I look at Abby and Jenay and just shrug.

"Well, I gotta get home and babysit. Call me if you guys get bored and want to come over. And Abby, think about it. Please, I'm begging you. I promise you will not be disappointed," Jenay says, turning down her street as Abby and I head for ours.

"Are you and Parker going?" she asks, gazing at me briefly, then down at the ground.

"Where? The party?" I look at her. "I don't know, I guess."

"Do you think I should go?" She gazes at me, her face set and serious, like she wants me to be serious too.

"Sure, if that's what you want." I shrug.

"I mean with Jax?"

"Again, up to you," I say, not feeling nearly as gung ho on the possibility of love like the ever optimistic and happy Jenay.

"Listen," Abby says, stopping in front of my driveway and gazing at me. "I don't mean to sound strange or anything, so I hope you don't take it that way, but . . . what's it like having a boyfriend? I mean, is it weird?" She scrunches up her nose and looks at me.

"What do you mean?" I ask, gazing down at the hole in the toe of my black Converse sneaker, thinking how I need to either get a new pair or find a new look.

"Well, Jenay acts like it's so great, I mean, she even wrote 'Ms. Jenay Williams' on her notebook the other day. Seriously. And when she saw that I saw she turned bright red and scribbled over it. But like, while she always acts so love happy, you . . . well you're like the exact opposite. You're like some big-time reluctant girlfriend, who can't quite figure out how you got there." She laughs at the end of that, but only to soften the blow.

I take a deep breath and stare at the crack in my driveway, surprised to learn I wasn't putting on near as good a show as I thought. Though I guess it's hard to fool Abby. I mean, she knows me too well. "Truth?" I finally say, looking right at her. "Just between us?"

She nods, waiting.

"It *is* weird. And to be honest, I really *don't* know how I got here. It just kind of happened, and before I knew it, I was in." I shrug.

"But weird how?" she asks, narrowing her eyes, obviously wanting to follow and understand. "I mean, what's it *like*? Do you talk on the phone all night? Are you going to have sex?"

I think about Parker, how cute he is, how nice he is, and I shrug. Honestly, I have no idea what he sees in me, no idea what he's even doing with me. But one thing's for sure, he's not the one who makes it so weird. That blame lies entirely with me.

I look back at Abby, then quickly glance away. Then I take a deep breath and say, "Honestly? Sometimes when he calls I purposely let it go into voice mail, because I feel so awkward, and nervous, and stupid, and guilty. And up until now we've only kissed or made out or whatever. But nothing more. I'm just not ready for more, and it's not like he pushes it, either. And it's like, even though I'm fully aware of how practically everything about him is really amazing and great, and even though I keep reminding myself of how lucky I am that he likes me, it's almost as though my heart refuses to cooperate with my head, like it's blocked out all of that chatter and refuses to listen. Does that make any sense?" I ask, wondering if she thinks I'm a total freak now that I've confided all that.

But she just looks at me and shakes her head. "You know what the sad thing is?" she says, still looking at me. "I think I can relate to your version a whole lot better than Jenay's." She laughs.

I laugh too. Then I head up the driveway, following along the thin, jagged crack 'til I reach the front porch.

"You wanna study later?" Abby calls out.

I reach for my keys and unlock the door. "Sounds good," I say, before closing it firmly behind me.

The moment I'm inside I bolt for my room, drop to my knees, and shove my hand under the mattress, wanting nothing more than to lie on my bed and get between the pages of Zoë's diary.

Only it's not there.

So I push my hand farther, delving deeper into the tight space where my mattress meets my box spring. And when it's still not there, I dive headfirst into full-blown panic attack.

Grabbing the pillows, sheets, blanket, and duvet, and throwing them all to the ground, I lift the mattress all the way up 'til the side is pointing at the ceiling, the top is resting haphazardly against my nightstand, and the entire left side wobbles like it's gonna crash through the french doors or something, as my eyes scan the space quickly, but not finding a thing. So then I drag it off completely, pulling it to the floor and flipping it over, thinking maybe the cobalt book got stuck to the stitching, but again, nothing.

I sink to the ground, a sweaty, panting, heart-racing mess. And as I unravel the sheet from my leg, my mind is in turmoil, wondering where the hell it could be, and even worse, who could've found it.

And when I finally gaze down, I notice how the sheet wrapped around my leg is *not* the same one I woke up with this morning. Since I know for a fact that when I left for school, I left behind an unmade bed with pink striped sheets. And these are cream with blue stars.

And then I remember Mariska. Our cleaning lady. The one who comes on the fifteenth of every the month. The fifteenth, just like today.

So I pick myself up and head for my dresser, Mariska's drop spot for orphaned items. And wouldn't you know, right there, smack dab in the middle, is Zoë's diary, cover shiny and blue, pages seemingly undisturbed.

Then I fix my bed, change my clothes, and begin where I left off.

. . . *Seriously, he even told me about how he had to deal with his mom when his dad got shipped off to federal prison, how needy and weak she was, and how at just ten years old he was practically forced to grow up overnight.*

I'd always heard his family was mega, filthy rich, and supposedly had several more houses even bigger than the one he lives in now. And of course I'd heard all the crazy stories about his dad, but there were always so many rumors, so many insane legends—he killed a man, he robbed a bank, he embezzled a bunch of money, he was in the mob—that I just didn't know what to believe. So I didn't believe anything.

But I guess in the end, those stories were like a gazillion times more exciting than the true and boring fact of how his dad is just another greedy, rich bastard who wanted to be even richer.

Anyway, his mom ditched his dad, actually served him divorce papers during his first month in jail. Said there was no way she was living single for ten years minus time off for good behavior. So whenever Marc wanted to go see him, he had to get a ride with his uncle Mike (his dad's brother). And they'd both have to endure a full-body cavity search before they were allowed inside.

Only Marc didn't really say that part about the cavity search. He says that's how it is for hard-core criminals, not wealthy nonviolent types like his dad. Apparently all they had to do was sign in and go look for his dad—who, by the way, was allowed to wear clean pressed khakis instead of an orange jumpsuit. And then they all sat around at these plastic tables and chairs, eating vending-machine snacks and talking face to face (as opposed to being separated by a sheet of bulletproof glass and having to use a phone).

Whatever. My version's way better, way more dramatic. And I even told him he could show me a picture and I'd still choose to believe my story over his.

So he goes, "Oh yeah, and you're not allowed to take pictures either."

So I go, "See? In my version, they let you do that."

Anyway, I guess his mom became a major pill-popping heavy drinker, although she may have been one even before *all that. I mean, it's kind of unclear but it really sounds like it. And oh yeah, now she's apparently married to husband number three, and each one has been even more rich (and more messed up) than the one before.*

So I went, "Is that why you drive that old Camaro, cuz you hate money?"

But he just laughed and said, "I drive an old Camaro cuz I like old cars. What, would you like me better if I drove a Porsche?"

And then I—damn, I can't believe I said this (!) but then I go, "I can't imagine liking you any more than I already do"!!!! Seriously! I could die! And I thought I would! I mean it just slipped out before I could stop it.

But he just looked at me all serious and said, "I liked you from the very first moment I saw you."

Which is kind of like "you had me at hello" but better, because it's real, and spontaneous, and not from a movie. So then I laughed, because, please, the first time he saw me goes all the way back to fifth grade. Right before his mom started sending him away to all of those private schools.

But when I reminded him of that, he just said, "I know."

Sometimes when I'm reading Zoë's diary I need to take little breaks. I mean, part of me is anxious to move forward, and just burn through the pages as fast as I can. But the other part feels a little overwhelmed, like all of my senses are completely filled up, and I just really need to set it down, close my eyes, and try to regroup.

Though I guess I regrouped for too long, because the next thing I know, the sun is set, my room is dark, and Zoë's diary is gone.

"Who's there?" I sit up frantically, rubbing my eyes. "What

are you doing?" I ask, making an unsuccessful swipe for the book.

"What's this?" Abby asks, flipping through the pages, her eyes on the lookout for something good. "Are you holding out on me? Is this some kind of love journal, where you write down all of your heartfelt feelings for Parker?" She laughs, playing her version of keep-away.

I just look at her, forcing myself to take slow deep breaths, forcing myself to stay calm. "Abby, please. I'm serious. I really need that back," I say, struggling for patience as she scans the pages, though luckily without really reading. "Come on, Abby, please," I beg. "It used to be Zoë's."

I feel bad when it works. When I see her face go from gleeful to grave the second she hears my sister's name. But I had to get it back, and it's not like she left me with any other choice.

"I'm sorry," she says, shutting the book and handing it to me. "Honestly, I didn't know." She bites down on her bottom lip, her eyes wide and sad.

"It's okay," I say, sliding it back under my bed while giving her the "good sport" shrug. "Let's go study downstairs."

Eighteen

July 4
Fireworks! In the air, on the ground, vibrating all around
Exploding in a profusion of color and sound
We lay on the soft wet grass, staring up at a sky so lit
A moment so perfect—I closed my eyes to save it—
Then later, quiet, peaceful, just him and me
Two hearts reaching for infinity.

Carly was pissed I didn't go to her party—assumed it was because of her being all happy and hooked up with Stephen. Please, I could give a shit about all that. I mean, seriously. Whatever. I tried to tell her I'd already made plans, but it just made it worse. She got all hostile and hurt and accused me of ditching her for Marc!

"You've totally changed since you hooked up with him!

You've ditched everyone else just so you can be with him," she yelled.

I just held the phone and rolled my eyes, because no way was I getting sucked into her self-righteous not-so-mellow-drama.

So then she goes, "Everyone's talking about it, and I'm only telling you this because you're my best friend and I love you like a sister."

"Oh, is that why you stole my boyfriend?" I asked, which I know was stupid since it's not like I care. I guess I just couldn't stand to listen to her stupid, fake, best-friends-forever-and-ever-and-ever bullshit speech, especially since it's no longer true.

So she goes, "You were over Stephen and you know it. I can't believe you're acting like such a bitch, over a guy!"

But I didn't say anything. Seriously, I refused to get sucked in any further.

So then she goes, "Seriously, Zoë, I'm worried about you. Everyone's worried about you. I mean, how well do you even know him? 'Cause I've heard some pretty scary stories about his private school years. Why do you think he had to enroll in public again? It's because he had no choice, nobody else would take him. Honestly, I think that whole quiet and mysterious act is totally played. Because the truth is, he's just weird. And I know you know what everyone says about his family, right? I mean, they're bad news. It's like, he shows up at parties, but then barely even talks to anyone. He's got all that money but he drives that old, beater car. He's like some rich-ass grease monkey, and his mom is like a total pharm-hound boozaholic, not to mention she's been married like a zillion times, not to mention how his dad's supposed to get out of jail any-time now and Marc will probably go live with him—a convicted felon! A former prisoner! I mean, have you even thought about any of this?"

I know I shouldn't have let her get to me, I know I should've just ignored it, but I couldn't just let all that go. So I said, "You don't know what you're talking about. Everything you just said is all rumors and bullshit! None of it's true! And if you were my friend then you would believe me, not judge me, and stand by me no matter what!"

But she just goes, "Sorry Zoë, but I just can't do that."

So I go, "Then you know what, Carly? I guess you're not really my friend."

When I hung up I felt pretty bad, I mean, we really did used to be best friends. But then I used to think I had a lot of friends. I used to think everyone loved me and cared about me, and only wanted the best for me. So it feels pretty bad to know they're all talking shit about me instead.

But still, if I'm forced to choose, and apparently I am, then I choose Marc. And it's not like I owe Carly or anyone else an explanation for that.

Because if you're gonna make someone choose, then you shouldn't be surprised when they don't choose you.

July 7

Almost got caught taking a catnap at work today. Big time, serious close call. Normally I'm way more careful about stuff like that—I even set the alarm on the computer for ten minutes before the appt ends. But I guess I just didn't hear it go off, cuz the next thing I knew Doctor Freud was standing over me, fingers scraping against his graying old scraggle chin, going, "Zoë? Are you okay?"

Luckily, I was slumped so far down my face was practically in my lap, so without even flinching I just opened my eyes, reached down, and grabbed the pen that had fallen on the ground. Then I looked up at him and smiled and said, "Yeah, I was just looking for this." Then I held up that blue ballpoint, like it was solid evidence of a hard day's work. And even though I don't really think he bought it, he still just nodded, and then headed for the can. And by the time he got back his next appt was already there.

But the truth is, I was exhausted from Marc. And the fact that he spent the night last night! Seriously—the whole, entire, wonderful, glorious, outrageous, world-changing, life-altering night!

Since Echo left for her annual "Cerebral Campers" week or whatever they call that Camp Brainiac thing she goes to every year, Marc scaled the tree, came in through her room, crept down the hall, and spent the whole night with me until I heard both my parents making their way down the stairs in the morning.

It was the first time we'd actually slept together, first time we had sex together! And even though we've been dating for only two weeks—well two weeks ago since the first time he kissed me, then he left me hanging for a while but still, he's pretty much the one that made us both wait. He said he didn't want to rush it, that we should give it time to build.

I gotta admit, that worried me at first. I guess because I always figured he'd slept with a lot of girls. I mean he's so hot, and so cool, and so sexy, and so mega rich, and definitely has that mysterious bad-boy vibe going. So I figured there were tons of ritzy, ditzy, country-club sluts just lining up to be with him. But he said he was done with all that, after his last girlfriend a little over a year and a half ago, and now, I swear this is what he actually said—Now all he wants is ME!

I wanted to believe that, but I kind of had my doubts. Also, I felt like I had to test him, so I could see if he really *wanted me for me, or for the me that he wanted me to be. So I told him about all the guys I'd done it with, starting with the blow job I gave Bryan Boxer back when I was thirteen. And even though there really aren't all that many guys (I mean thirteen was just three years ago), and I was with Stephen for a full year and a half (minus the two times I cheated) but still, most guys freak out at that kind of information, which is why most girls lie. Isn't it funny how guys and girls always lie in opposite directions? Guys add, girls subtract.*

Anyway, Marc just lay there beside me, listening patiently, and when I was done, he just shrugged and said he didn't care. "Each step brings you closer to the next," he said. "And that's where we are now, the next step."

So then I asked him about the next step after me.

But he just kissed me on the forehead and said, "Shh. All we ever have is now."

How could I feel good about my life after reading that? Seriously. How could I possibly settle for my super nice, but ultimately boring (fine, there, I finally said it, okay?) boyfriend, and our low-to-no-passion makeout sessions, when I now know (albeit secondhand) just what it's like to have the real thing?

I mean, I know I should probably just set the diary down and back away slowly, go cold turkey and never peek at it again, since all it seems to do is feed my disappointment and make me yearn to be someone and to have something that was never meant to be mine.

But now that I'm so far in, I can't find my way out. And the truth is, with what I now know, I don't ever want to go back.

I have to break up with Parker. I mean, it's the right thing to do. Because staying with him, going through the motions, and pretending to be happy isn't fair to anyone, especially him. But I feel so inept, and inadequate, and meek, and stupid, that I'm just not sure how to do it.

Not to mention that I'm just not sure if I'm up for all the fallout. You know, all the wheres, whats, whys, and hows that'll ultimately follow. And what am I supposed to do at lunch? Do we still sit together, acting all amicable, while pretending it never happened? Or does one of us have to move? And if so, will it be me?

Nineteen

On the night of Teresa's party, Abby was no longer trying to play it cool. And after calling me like a ton of times trying to decide what to wear, she moved on to e-mailing me photos of her top three choices, all laid out and spread across her bed, with empty sweater arms waving hello, unfilled pant legs river dancing, vacant shoes pointing in every direction, while her most beloved childhood dolls and stuffed animals stood in for her head.

She'd decided to go with Jax. Ever since the day Jenay invited him to sit with us at lunch and he turned out to be not only nice, smart, and funny, but also pretty cute. And since technically this is Abby's first date, there's no way she's leaving anything to chance. Seriously, she has it all planned out. Even down to the conversations she expects to have.

I want to help her, really, I do. But my mind is totally stuck on Zoë's diary, as I skim through the pages and reread certain parts, reluctant to move ahead, not wanting it to end.

"Okay, so which is better?" Abby asks. "Winnie the Pooh wearing the white blouse, blue corduroy vest, and jeans? Or Lisa Simpson in the flowy blue skirt and sweater?"

"Neither. I'm liking the Bratz doll in the black sweater, black boots, and jeans," I say. "Although her head looks disproportionately small, and a bit lost inside that turtleneck. And that could make some of those well-scripted conversations more than a little bit awkward. Not to mention the kiss good night. So maybe you should switch to a V-necked sweater instead, you know, to even it out." I laugh.

But Abby's way too freaked to have a sense of humor. "Okay, that's it. I'm calling Jenay," she says, hanging up before I can even apologize.

I stare at the phone and think about Marc. Remembering how his number's still probably stored from that one time he called. And hating how I've been acting like such a wimp and determined to do something bold, I scroll down to his name and push *talk.* And before I can chicken out and hang up, he answers.

I sit on my bed, frozen, unable to speak. "Echo?" he says. "You okay?"

And I remember how the display works both ways.

"Um, yeah." I clear my throat while my fingers pick at a loose thread on my blanket.

"Where are you?" he asks, sounding calm, if not interested.

"Home," I mumble, wondering what to say next.

"So, how are you?" he asks, the background music growing softer as he turns it down.

"I miss her," I say, before I can stop.

He sighs. Then he says, "Wanna go for a ride?"

I would answer, but there's a speed bump in my throat, and it's stopping all my words.

But he doesn't need an answer. "I'll be right over," he says, before closing the phone.

I grab my purse and run downstairs, stopping by the kitchen just long enough to tell my mom that I'll be right back.

"Where are you going?" she asks, turning away from the sink just long enough to see what I'm wearing. For someone who was never much interested in fashion, she sure makes it a point to always take the time to check out my clothes now. But I guess that's just another lesson learned during the whole Zoë thing, and how the cops need that kind of information so they can fill in the "last seen wearing" box on the police report.

I pause long enough for her to get a good look, then I head for the door, yelling, "I have to run an errand, so I'll see you in a few." And before she can even respond, I'm out the door and sprinting toward the corner, hoping to meet up with Marc without anyone seeing.

And when he turns onto my street, and I see the shiny midnight blue of his restored Camaro glinting in the hard winter sun, I feel happier than I can ever possibly explain.

"Hey," he says, as he leans across the seat and props open the door.

I settle onto the black leather, noticing how the interior feels deeper and darker than my parents' cars, almost like a cave. And I remember how Zoë used to call it The Coffin, and how that used to be funny, but not anymore.

"Park okay?" he says, glancing at me before pulling away from the curb.

I just nod and gaze out the window, feeling excited for the first time in days.

We don't really talk along the way, we just listen to music by some band I've never heard. And when we get there, he parks the car and reaches behind my seat, the sleeve of his brown leather jacket brushing against mine. Then he tosses me a bag of breadcrumbs and we head for the lake, where the ducks are already gathering, waiting to be fed.

I settle onto the grass beside him and start tossing crumbs, wondering if the view looked better to Zoë, less polluted, more serene, like maybe being in love somehow improved it.

"I'm reading it," I finally say, knowing I owe him an explanation for pulling him away from his day. But my throat feels tight, and my eyes start to sting, and it's hard to say more, so I don't.

But he just looks at me. "I know."

I glance at him, wondering how.

"You called. And you're no longer angry." He shrugs.

"I was never angry," I say, pulling my hand away from an overly aggressive beak.

"Just give him the rest, so they'll all go away." He laughs.

I empty the bag and bite down on my lip, feeling this weird sense of comfort sitting so close to him, someone who I know so much about, and who knows that I know.

"How're your parents?" he asks.

I just shake my head and shrug.

"They still hate me?" He looks at me, eyes neither worried nor hopeful, just curious.

"Probably." I shrug. "You going to the trial?"

"Wouldn't miss it. I need to see that freak, I need to watch him pay. Couple more months though, right?"

"That's what they say." I watch the last duck, still pecking around near my feet, and I pull them in too so I won't lose a toe. "Thanks for bringing me here," I say, gazing up at him shyly. "I mean, I know this may sound weird and all, but being around you makes me feel close to her." I bite down on my lip, wondering how he'll take that.

But he just closes his eyes and lifts his face toward the fading sun. "Being here makes me feel close to her. That's why I come every day."

"Even when it rains?" I ask, trying to sound light and teasing, even though the moment is so clearly wrong for a joke. But that's what I do when I'm nervous, I make inappropriate, stupid jokes.

But he just sighs. "Every day feels like rain," he says, his eyes still closed, his long, thick lashes seeming almost fake the way they rest against his skin.

"Is your dad out?" I ask, wanting to change the subject, but suspecting this might not be the right way.

"Not yet." He shrugs.

"Will you live with him when he does get out?"

He shakes his head and looks at me. "I'm in the guest house now, it's like having my own place. So I plan to stay put until college."

"Where you going?" I ask, suddenly panicked at the thought of him leaving, especially now that I'm just getting to know him.

"Berkeley's my dream, Columbia would be cool, but my grades kind of suck, so probably right here."

"Don't say that," I tell him, even though part of me wants it to be true.

But he just shrugs. "Wanna grab a bite?" He looks at me.

I do. I really, really, really do. I want to go anywhere he wants to go. I'd follow him wherever, just to be with him. Only I can't. "I'm supposed to go to this party," I say, lifting my shoulders and rolling my eyes, trying to come off as grown up, world-weary, and jaded. But when he raises his eyebrows, I look away. Since it's obvious he still sees me as Zoë's little sister.

I wish he would notice how much I've changed, how the last year has shaped me, transformed me. But he doesn't. So I grab my purse and stand. "Can you drop me off? I need to go get ready," I say, my voice carrying an edge that's hard to miss.

He holds up his keys and they jangle together, then he stands and heads for the car.

And I walk alongside him, feeling small, silent, and frustrated. Wondering just what it will take to get his attention.

He comes around to my side, unlocking the door, and letting me in. And just as I start to move past him, my hip accidentally rubs against his, and his face is so close, and his eyes so deep, that I can't help but lift my fingers to his smooth, sculpted cheek. Then without even thinking, I close my eyes, lean in, and kiss him.

He hesitates at first, but only for a moment. Then he wraps his arms around me, pulling me tight against his chest, kissing me hard on the mouth, until he finally pulls away and whispers, "Echo, trust me, you don't want—"

But I do want. So I pull him back to me, leaving no room for questions, no room for doubt. Thinking this is exactly how a kiss should feel—glorious, heady, and intoxicating. Like those first three sips of vodka the night of the homecoming dance, only a gazillion trillion bazillion times better.

And even though I'm borrowing a moment from Zoë's life, one that will never truly be mine, at this moment I just don't care. I'm living for now.

"Echo," he whispers, pulling away, calling my name even though I'd rather be Zoë. "Echo, stop."

I open my eyes and smile, at first not noticing the dark cloudy look in his. But the moment I see it, I follow their trail.

And at the end stands Teresa.

Twenty

"Are you sure this is okay?" Abby whispers, for like the hundredth time since she and Jax arrived.

"Omigod, it's fine," Jenay says, rolling her eyes and laughing. "Seriously, you look amazing."

"Echo?" Abby looks at me. "Hello! Earth to Echo? Any comments on my outfit? Do these jeans make me look fat? C'mon, you can tell me, I can take it."

I look at her and force myself to smile. "Please, you couldn't look fat if you tried. Really. Now the Bratz doll? *She* looked fat. She just couldn't pull it off like you can."

Luckily Abby and Jenay both laugh, which means I'm pulling it off better than I thought. They have no idea how I'm not really here, that in my head, I'm back in the parking lot with Marc, just seconds after we both saw Teresa.

We didn't speak the whole way home, but when he stopped on my corner he turned to me and said, "Echo, I'm so sorry. I—"

"Don't." I stared straight ahead, listening to the steady hum of the engine, determined to be brave and say what I felt for a change, rather than chickening out and running away like usual. "Don't apologize," I said, turning toward him. "I wanted to see you. And I'm not at all sorry for what happened." I felt stronger after saying that, strong enough to actually look him in the eye.

"And Teresa?" He looked at me, his eyes filled with worry.

I took a deep breath, remembering the expression on her face, the wide eyes and gaping mouth so easy to translate, even from all the way across the parking lot. And how it turned into a slow curving smile as she watched us climb into the car and drive away. "I'll deal with Teresa," I said, having not the slightest idea how I'd actually do that. But it sounded convincing.

Then I grabbed my purse and crawled out of the car, shutting the door firmly between us. And just as I started to move toward my house, I turned back, leaned through the open window, and said, "Hey Marc, thanks. Thanks for today."

He smiled at me, holding my gaze for a moment. Then he turned up his stereo, shifted into gear, and drove away.

But now, with the three of us crowded into Teresa's guest bathroom for the sole purpose of talking Abby down from her self-induced, body-dysmorphic panic attack, I realize I still have no plan for how to handle Teresa.

But then again it's not like she doesn't have her own secrets to hide. And it's not like she was alone either.

"Listen, this is crazy. We've got to get out of here," Jenay says, having reached her limit as she reaches for the door handle.

"We're in here, the guys are out there, and there's something very wrong with this picture. Abby, you look great, you *are* great, and I can tell Jax is totally into you. But if you don't get out of this bathroom right this second and back to your date I'm going to scream."

Abby takes a deep breath and follows Jenay, while I linger behind the two of them, peering into the mirror as they head out the door, wondering how it's possible to still look like me, when I feel so different inside.

Okay, so normally on a Saturday night, when someone's parents are out of town and they decide to throw a party, you can pretty much expect to see the usual things—music blaring from somebody's docked iPod, a lamp and/or vase breaking into a million little pieces, a half-hearted fistfight that breaks up well before they can take it outside, sporadic alcohol-induced vomiting in the bushes, people sneaking upstairs to hook up—I mean, those are just some of your basic, all-purpose party ingredients, right? Not that I've been to that many parties, but still, I've watched a lot of TV and movies and read a lot of books, so I think I know what to expect.

But Teresa's party is nothing like that. Probably because she only invited her friends from school, which means she's acting more like her *lunch table* self—you know, cute, flirty, preppy, and fun, as opposed to her *off-campus* self—the slutty girl who smokes and drinks, wears low-cut sweaters, and has really bad taste in men. I mean, if "Hot Jason" and "Asshole Tom" were here, I doubt she'd be blasting the indie girl CD, serving snacks and appetizers from a carved, bamboo tray, and dispensing cocktails from her parents' sleek, well-stocked, mahogany bar.

It's like everything is so carefully coordinated—the plates match the cups match the napkins match the flowers—heck, even her outfit is in cahoots, with the belt, shoes, and earrings all coordinating with tonight's color scheme. And it's kind of bizarre to be hanging with a bunch of kids from school on a Saturday night, at a party that seems way more like a baby shower.

"I saw this same exact spread in *InStyle* magazine," Teresa says after Jenay compliments her on the tiny, matching, sky-blue bud vases she placed in an undulating pattern across the glass-topped coffee table. "It was for someone's baby shower, I can't remember who. Jennie Garth? Jennifer Garner?" She scrunches up her face. "No, someone else. Anyway, I clipped it because the second I saw it I knew I wanted my baby shower to be just like that, but then I thought, omigod, what am I waiting for? I mean, getting knocked up is like, at least a decade away. So I just made a few tweaks, and *voilà*!"

She says "*voilà!*" like "voy-la!" But I don't have the heart to correct her. I just stand there, sipping my drink and smiling, wondering if she has any immediate plans to out me.

I gaze over at Abby who's perched on the edge of the sofa, nodding at Jax's every word, and trying hard to look interested in whatever it is that he's saying. And then Parker walks up, slips his arm around my waist, and kisses me on the cheek.

And my eyes dart straight for Teresa, like the second he does that, wondering what she'll do. But she just smiles even wider and goes, "You guys are way too cute together." Then she winks at me and walks away.

"Come on, I wanna show you something," Parker says, tugging on my arm as he leads me upstairs. And when we end up in the guest room, well let's just say I'm not exactly surprised.

"Parker, I don't think—" I start, but then he puts his finger over my lips before quickly replacing it with his mouth.

So I let him kiss me. At least while we're still just standing by the door. But when he tries to pull me toward the bed, I shake my head and go, "No." Pulling away, attempting to free myself from his grip.

"Come on." He smiles. "No one's gonna walk in. It's just us."

But it's not about somebody walking in. It's about the fact that I just can't do this anymore. Not after having kissed Marc. Not after having tasted the real thing.

"I just want to go back downstairs and hang out with my friends," I say. "Come on, let's go. We can do this later."

"*I'm* your friend," he says in this syrupy voice that totally gets on my nerves. "And I'm right here."

"I mean my *other* friends. You know, like Jenay and Abby and everyone else." I shake my head and roll my eyes, making no attempt to hide it.

"What's your problem?" He squints at me, his face looking more hurt than angry. "You hardly answer your phone, you're always running off. It's like, if you don't want to be with me, Echo, then just say it."

I gaze down at the ground, then back at him, wishing I could be the right kind of girl. The kind who wouldn't just *know* that she's lucky to be with him, but actually *feel* it too. The kind of girl he deserves. But I've strayed so far from normal now, I'll never find my way back. And the truth is, I no longer want to.

"I don't think we should do this anymore," I finally whisper, still staring at the ground, yet feeling the weight of his stare upon me.

He stands there for a moment, not saying a word. Then he shakes his head and brushes right past me. "Whatever," he says, as he heads down the stairs.

By the time I make it back down, it's pretty clear that everyone knows. I can tell by the way they all look at me, eyes wide, lips parted, voices gone suddenly silent. Believe me, if anyone knows the signs of being the headline, the star of the big juicy story, it's me.

So I head straight for the door, knowing better than to stay. And just as I grab the handle, Jenay and Abby appear. "Where you going?" they ask, their voices careful, their faces concerned.

"It's a couples party," I remind them. "And since I'm no longer a couple . . ." I shrug, wanting to leave it at that, but knowing I can't. They're my best friends, which means they've earned the right to hear more. "Listen, don't worry. I'm fine. Just have fun and call me tomorrow. I'll explain it all then, okay?"

And before they can even respond, I'm already halfway down the drive. And just as I reach the end I hear Teresa call out, "Hey Echo, be careful out there, okay?"

And I don't know if she's referring to the walk home, or what she saw at the park. But either way, I just keep going.

Twenty-one

July 10

I've never felt like this before. It's like, I thought I knew what it was like to be in love—the first time with Bryan Boxer, back in seventh grade, for one crazy, completely awkward week, and then again freshman year, when I first hooked up with Stephen (when I was young and impressionable and didn't know any better). But now I know I was wrong.

Dead Smacking Wrong.

THIS is love.

Marc is Love.

Me + Marc = love.

I know it sounds crazy since I'm only sixteen, but I just can't help but believe that we were made to be together. I mean it. I love everything about him. There's nothing that annoys me or gets on my nerves (a total miracle, I know). And whenever we're apart for more than a few hours, I feel this major aching loss, like I'm weak and incomplete, until we're finally back together again.

Okay, I just reread that last part and totally cringed. And to be honest, I'm thinking I should probably just scribble it out and pretend I never wrote it. I mean, WEAK and INCOMPLETE? Get a freaking life already! I know. But still, I'm just gonna leave it there, cuz the truth is, it's how I really feel. And even though I can't imagine ever not feeling this way, I still want to write it all down—the good, the bad, and the completely embarrassing—so that I can read it again someday, when we're both old and gray, swinging in a hammock and listening to our iPods—or whatever old people will do in the future.

Anyway, Marc's been sneaking into my room practically every night for the last week, but now with Echo coming back soon, we're gonna have to find another way. I mean, she probably wouldn't care if he tiptoed past her bed, since she's a pretty deep sleeper and it's not like she's ever busted me before, but I'm still not one hundred percent positive I even want her to know. I just don't think it's such a good idea to involve her in this. So I guess I'll just have to think a little harder, and find another way.

Yesterday I snuck him into work, and stashed him under my desk. It's a HUGE wood desk, so trust me, he fit. And we totally made out during one of the fifty-minute sessions. And then right before our time was up he kissed me good-bye and said, "I better get out of here before the goateed wonder catches us."

And as I sat back in my chair, I readjusted my skirt and said, "You gonna go look at that Camaro? The one you told me about?"

And he just nodded and went for the door.

Then right before he walked out I went, "Hey, how'd

you know he has a goatee?" And when I looked at him, I noticed he had the weirdest expression on his face, but then just like that it was gone.

And he goes, "You told me."

And then he left.

But the thing is, I don't remember telling him that, since I never really talk about my job to anyone other than my parents who insist on a weekly report so they can make sure I'm working hard as opposed to humiliating them in front of a colleague.

But I guess I must've told him, because how else would he know?

July 11

Marc picked me up from work today in his same old Camaro, saying that in person, the one he was gonna buy was just not up to his standards. Whatever. I mean, to me it's just some old beater car that takes up most of his free time, and I just don't get the attraction. But as long as he's willing to drive me to work and back, I guess I can't really complain. Not to mention how it spares me from having to beg for my own car, since my parents are pretty much not cooperating and refusing to hear my pleas.

Speaking of parents, I have to say that it's kind of weird how I've never met his mom. Not to mention how I've never even been to his house! I mean he's here all the time, and even though my parents definitely don't know about him spending the night and stuff, at least I've introduced them! Though I did try to keep it all casual and act like he was just a friend.

I'm still not sure why I did that, and I could tell Marc was kind of hurt. Even though he didn't really say anything other than, "Why'd you call me your friend?"

But I just said, "Cuz you are my friend. And believe me, it's not like they need to know all the details."

So we just left it at that, but still, I could tell he was bothered.

I guess there's just so many crazy, mean rumors about his family that I didn't want my parents to get all freaked or anything. I mean, I LOVE HIM, I really, really do. But that doesn't mean they'll understand.

July 20

Echo's back. Which means I've barely had time to see Marc since I've been working all day, and I've yet to figure a way to get him into my room without getting caught. And because of that, we had our first fight.

And I know how most people keep journals specifically for moments like this, but it drags me down so bad, I don't feel like writing about it, much less thinking about it. I guess that's why I didn't write for a few days, but we're better now, so I'm back.

But if I'm gonna be honest (and if I can't be honest here, then where?) then I have to say that it's just not the same as it was before. Now it's different, altered. Like when you scrape your knee and you get a scar, but then the scar fades so much that no one can see it but you. But you know where it is. Cuz you remember what caused it. And no matter how hard you try, you can never forget how bad it hurt when it first happened.

Well, that's how it is with us. From the outside, everything looks the same, but on the inside, it's all different. And what makes it even worse is that it was all my fault to begin with.

It's just, sometimes Marc gets so detached and quiet that it makes me all needy. And then needy turns to whiny. And then, well, I started nagging him about not having enough time together (which is totally crazy, I know) but I was just hoping that would make him invite me over, even if his mom is half out of the bag all the time. I mean, he lives in a mansion, so it's not like she'll even notice.

But he didn't invite me. He didn't say anything. So then, of course, I started accusing him of not wanting to be with me (I know, pathetic, insecure, lame, etc). Until he goes, "Zoë, I'm 16. What do you want from me?"

And I went, "NOTHING!" Which obviously was a lie. So then I said, "Do you realize that not once have you invited me to your house?"

And he closed his eyes and shook his head, which only egged me on more.

So I go, "I'm serious. You've met my parents so why can't I meet yours?" Which I know is not exactly fair since that time when I first introduced them I didn't really cop to our relationship, instead I pretended we were study buddies.

But then he looked right at me and said, "Trust me, you so don't want to come to my house."

And I said, "You don't know what I want."

So then he shook his head and said, "Fine. But don't say I didn't warn you."

I lay in bed, with Zoë's journal facedown on my chest, watching the red message light on my cell phone flash on and off in my now darkened room. I know it's either Abby, Jenay, Parker, or Teresa. But it doesn't matter. My phone's been ringing off and on practically since I got home, but not once did I consider answering it.

I know my friends are probably just worried, and I know the least I can do is let them know I'm okay so I close the diary and pick up the phone, wondering just exactly where to start making amends.

But there's only one message, and when I hear it, I realize it's not really a message, just a bunch of music. And just as I'm about to delete it, thinking for sure it's a mistake, I remember the song from Marc's car, the one that was playing as he drove away.

And I lay there with the phone pressed tight to my ear, playing it over and over again, until I finally fall asleep.

Twenty-two

The next morning I'm listening to Abby's version of everything that happened, in sequential order, from the moment I left Teresa's party to the moment she left Teresa's party.

"So wait, Parker was flirting with who? I thought it was couples only," I said, phone clenched between my shoulder and ear as I paint my toenails a nice deep red. "Was he hitting on someone else's date?"

"Trust me, after you left, it all went to hell. And by ten o'clock word was out, and practically all of Bella Vista showed up."

"Seriously? What'd Teresa do? Whip out more cheese logs and little blue drink umbrellas?"

Abby laughs. "No. Always the perfect hostess, she just raided the liquor cabinet and the wine cellar. It got pretty crazy. I bet she's really gonna pay when her parents get home."

"I'm not so sure about that," I say, replacing the polish top and leaning down to blow on my toes. "I hear she's pretty spoiled, you know, only child, daddy's little princess, mommy's little protégée."

"Must be nice," Abby says. And then, "I mean, well, you know."

"Relax." I gaze out the window. "I may be the only child left, but I'm no princess. Anyway, back to you. You know you still haven't told me what I really want to hear. What happened with you and Jax? Disaster? Or love at second sight?"

Abby sighs loud and heavy, and for a moment she sounds much older than her years. "I don't know. He's cute, and nice, and all that, but when he walked me to the door and kissed me good night, well, there weren't really any sparks, you know? I mean, I know you can't always expect bottle rockets, but can't I at least get a sparkler?"

I think about the difference between Parker and Marc, and realize how funny it is that I, of all people, can now be considered some kind of expert. Well, at least where Abby's concerned. But then I remember how she doesn't actually know about Marc, at least not that I know of. "Did it seem kind of clinical?" I ask. "Or more like a relative? Like a frisky, drunken uncle?"

"That's disgusting, but no. It was more like two actors rehearsing a role, hoping they were getting it right. Like, the whole time my lips were moving my head was thinking, *That's it? You waited fifteen years for this?*"

"Yikes."

"Tell me," she says. "But here's the thing, do you think maybe it was just nerves? I mean, do you think I should try it again?"

And just as I'm about to answer, I get a new call. So I put Abby on hold, only to find Teresa on the other line.

"Hey," she says. "What're you doing?"

"Talking to Abby," I tell her, hoping that will speed it along.

"Dump her, I need to talk to you."

I roll my eyes. Apparently, now that she's got some dirt on me, she figures the usual pleasantries no longer apply. I guess she forgot how I saw her too. "She called first," I finally say.

"Fine. Listen, I was wondering if you wanted to come by and hang out. You know, so we can study." She laughs. "I hear you're really good at math."

I close my eyes and sigh. Teresa can really be a bitch, but apparently I'm the only one who knows it. "I'm busy," I say, anxious to get back to Abby.

"Yeah? Well, I think you might want to clear your calendar and try to stop by because Marc's coming over."

I just sit there, silent and still.

"In fact, he should be here within the hour."

Why is Marc going to Teresa's? I mean, they're not friends. At least not that I know of. And even though I could probably just ask and get it over with, I'm more than a little reluctant to give her the satisfaction. "We'll see," I finally say, trying to sound distracted and uninterested. "I've got a lot going on today."

"Door's open," she says, laughing in place of good-bye.

"What the hell? You were gone forever! I almost hung up," Abby says, not even trying to hide her annoyance.

For a second I think about telling her; it would be good to get a second opinion. But just as quickly, I'm over it. "Sorry," I say.

"Omigod, was it Parker?" she asks, her voice free of anger and now taking on a lower, more gossipy tone. "Is he begging you to come back?"

"Hardly," I say, my mind still reeling with thoughts of Teresa and Marc and what they could possibly have in common. "From what you said, it sounds like he's already moved on."

"So who was it? I waited for over an hour. I deserve to know."

"You're totally exaggerating, but it's not like it's a secret.

It was Teresa. She wants me to stop by," I say, heeding the number one rule about lying (well, maybe number two, after don't get caught) and how it's always safer not to stray too far from the truth.

"Don't do it!" Abby says, sounding completely ominous. "I'm totally serious, do *not* go over there."

"Why?" I ask, striving for blasé, but nailing panic.

"You should've seen the place when we left, I bet it's totally trashed by now. She probably wants you to help clean up. You know, payback for cutting out early."

I close my eyes and sigh in relief, glad that Abby's still unaware of at least some of my secrets. "Okay, listen, I should go," I tell her. "It's getting late, and I haven't even showered yet." I gaze into the mirror and scowl at my limp, boring hair.

"No, you can't go until you answer my question. Should I give Jax a second chance or not?"

I drop back onto my bed, grab two pillows, and prop them under my head. "I don't know, Ab. I mean, do you want to give him another shot?"

"That's why I called you, to help me sort that out."

"Well, what does Jenay say?"

"Jenay? Forget Jenay. I mean, I love her, we all love her, but between you and me, Jenay is now a pep club member. She also believes in pixie dust, pots of gold, unicorns, four-leaf clovers, guardian angels, and leprechauns. She thinks Mickey Mouse is a real person. That's why I called you. Because you're my only levelheaded friend."

I take a deep breath and close my eyes. "Then forget it," I tell her. "It's either there or it's not. And it shouldn't take GPS to locate it."

She sighs. "That's exactly what I was thinking." And then before she hangs up she goes, "Oh hey, what's that song you were humming under your breath?"

I sit up suddenly, my knuckles going white as my fingers grip the phone.

"You know, the one that's all da da dee, do da, da la la la? What is that? It's so haunting."

I listen to her rendition of the song I fell asleep to last night, totally unaware that I'd been humming it that whole time. "Um, I don't even know the name. I think I heard it somewhere on the radio, or maybe I dreamt it or something," I say, laughing nervously, hoping she'll believe me.

"Okay, well, gotta run," she says. "But I'm serious about avoiding Teresa's. If I were you I'd stay away."

Twenty-three

By the time I get to Teresa's, I know I'm too late. And it's not like it took me all that long to shower and dress, it was more the pacing, the hand wringing, and the pro-and-con-list making that ate up all my free time.

There's an old beat-up motorcycle leaning precariously on its kickstand, and one of those jacked-up, overaccessorized, overcompensating, fully loaded trucks parked right beside it. But no blue Camaro. And since neither of those vehicles looks remotely like anything Teresa or her parents would be willing to drive, I'm feeling more than a little anxious.

I hesitate at the door, thinking I should just forget about knocking, cut my losses, and head home. And just as I turn to do exactly that, the front door swings open as Teresa smiles and says, "I saw you from the living room window." Then she wiggles her fingers, motioning me inside.

She leads me past the formal dining room, which looks no

worse for the wear, and through the ultramodern kitchen that's shiny, clean, and pristine. And even though the house is showing absolutely no sings of a wild night of out-of-control teenage debauchery, Teresa's tight ripped jeans and tiny black tube top are giving off a whole other vibe.

So by the time we get to the den and I see those two over-age delinquents sprawled across the couch, let's just say I'm not the least bit surprised.

"You remember Tom and Jason?" she says, nodding at the losers I'd met that day in the park.

I just look at them, wondering why she lured me here, but determined not to show any fear.

"Beer?" she asks, raising a sweaty bottle in offering. Martha Stewart, look out.

But I just shake my head and drop onto an overstuffed chair, doing my best to ignore asshole Tom who, once again, seems dead set on staring at me.

"So, did you go to her little high school soiree?" Tom asks, tilting his head back as he guzzles his beer, his eyes still fixed on mine.

But before I can answer Teresa smiles and goes, "She stopped by, but she didn't stay long."

"Hot date?" he asks, lighting up a cigarette that Jason immediately grabs and breaks in half.

"No smoking in the palace, asshole," Jason says, taking the broken pieces and shoving them into his beer before chucking Tom hard on the back of his head.

I watch as Tom makes a face but still cowers away, and I feel like I'm in one of those weird art-school films. The kind filled with rain, symbolism, and dream sequences that you can't understand. I mean, on the surface, Teresa's probably one of the luckiest people I know. It's like she's living the teenage dream. She's got two parents who are still together, she lives in a beautiful, huge home, she has a walk in-closet that's jammed full of super-cute, designer-label clothes, she's pretty, she's popular, she gets good grades, and she's had the same boyfriend since the end of eighth grade who everyone unanimously agrees is totally hot. Heck, she even has real-deal Hollywood credentials, having starred in a baby-food commercial back when she was two, followed by some small, mostly nonspeaking roles over the last few years. Which also makes her one of the few people who can actually list on her Web page "model, singer, actress," and only the singer part is a lie.

So I don't get it. I mean, why would someone who has all of *that* want to hang out with a cheesy, creepy drug dealer and his mentally challenged sidekick? It just doesn't make any sense.

When I look up, Tom is still staring at me, which totally gives me the creeps, so I pretend I have to go to the bathroom, since it's the only place where I can be alone, clear my head, and hopefully figure out what to do next.

I'm standing in front of the sink, watching the water run down the drain, when Teresa barges in without even knocking. "He just got here," she says, standing in the doorway, looking at me. "I just let him in; I thought you should know. You know, so you don't stay in here all day, wasting water." She smiles, but it's not at all normal. In fact, it's not even kind.

"What's going on?" I ask. "Why'd you invite me here?"

"From what I saw in the park, it seems like you and Marc are really hitting it off," she says, looking right at me. "So I thought you might want to hang in a more private place, with people you can trust."

I just stand there, not saying a word. I mean, I can't exactly deny what she saw. But still, I know better than to trust her.

"I know what you're thinking," she says, nodding her head. "But you've got it all wrong. I'm actually a much better friend than you think. Like last night? After you left? Parker got all hammered and started hitting on someone's girlfriend. They almost got in a fight. But I just calmed everyone down, then I took him aside for a little chat. And you know what he asked? He wanted to know if you were into someone else. He said whenever you guys were alone together, it was like you were never really there."

I look at her, holding my breath.

"But I just told him to go home, sober up, and sleep it off." She shrugs. "So you see, we're not so different, you and me. We both look one way on the outside, but inside, we're something else. We've got secrets." She smiles.

"Why me?" I ask. "I mean, out of all the people you know, why do you share this stuff with me?"

"Because you're smart, and you're different, and you're one of the few people who get how nothing's ever what it seems."

We just stand there, looking at each other, and I wonder if it's really that simple, if even part of that is true. Then she grabs my hand and pulls me toward the door. "Let's go," she says. "Marc doesn't even know you're here."

I follow her out of the bathroom and into the den, where Marc is sitting on a chair, clutching a beer and looking uneasy.

"Look who's here," Teresa says, motioning to me like a game-show model presenting a shiny, new, energy-efficient appliance.

I slip onto a chair and try to act casual, like I hang out with drug dealers and dropouts all the time.

Marc glances at me then over at Jason. Then he sets down his beer and goes, "Listen, can we make this quick? I need to get out of here."

But Jason's taking it easy and refuses to be rushed. "Relax," he says. "Just chill and finish your drink."

I glance at Marc's bottle, seeing how it's still completely full, and remember how he rarely drinks, probably because of his mom's bad habit. "Sorry bro, but I really need to split," he says, like he's speaking a foreign language now, Jason's language.

But Jason just glares, his eyes becoming angry, narrow slits. "Apparently you didn't hear me. I'm. Finishing. My. Beer," he says, his voice firm and controlled, punctuating each separate word.

So we all just sit there. Avoiding each other's gaze while listening to Jason slurp and sip, until he finally finishes it off with one long, loud, disgusting belch. Then he sets his bottle hard on the table and says, "Me and my boy will be right back." He points at all of us, his index finger outstretched, his thumb arched up high, like a gun about to go off. When he pulls the trigger he laughs, as he ushers Marc out of the room.

It feels like forever. Seriously, from the time they leave 'til the moment they come back, it feels like my whole, entire life has passed.

And when Marc finally comes back into the den, he takes one look at me and goes, "Need a ride?"

And I grab my purse and head for the door, without once looking back.

Twenty-four

The second we get in the car, Marc shakes his head and says, "What the hell were you doing in there? Are those people your friends?"

"You know they're not my friends," I say, folding my arms across my chest and staring out the window. I mean, I don't like the tone of his voice. And I don't like the way he's acting. Like I'm some little baby that needs to be protected. Okay, yeah, maybe I didn't *love* being in there, and maybe I'm glad he's whisking me away now. But still, even if he hadn't shown, I totally would've made it out of there. Eventually.

"What were you even doing there in the first place?" he asks, his eyes shielded from me as he stares at the road.

"Teresa invited me." I shrug, deciding to leave it at that. I mean, the fact that I went there for him is clearly none of his business.

"Well, that's just great." He glances over at me and shakes

his head again. "Do you and Teresa even know who those guys are? Do you even know what you're getting yourselves into?"

"Well, you seem to be all filled in, so why don't you tell me?" I say, turning toward him.

But he just stares straight ahead, clenching his jaw as he drives. And when he stops at a light, he goes, "Look, I'm sorry. I'm not trying to sound like your dad or anything. It's just those guys are really bad news and you shouldn't be hanging around them. You shouldn't be anywhere near them."

"You were hanging around them."

"That's different," he mumbles, speeding again now that the light's turned green.

"Yeah? How? Exactly how is it different?"

He looks at me for a moment, then he shakes his head and stares back at the road. "It just is, okay?"

"Why?" I say, unwilling to let it go.

"Echo, Christ, just trust me on this one." He rolls his eyes and checks his side mirror.

I turn in my seat, my eyes traveling over him until coming to rest on his jacket. "I want to see what's in your pocket," I say.

"What?" He looks at me, his eyes wide.

"Show me what's in your pocket. And then I'll decide if I'll trust you."

He takes a deep breath and looks away, but his expression is worried.

"Before you left the room with Jason your pocket was flat and empty. And now it's not. Now it's all bulky like you've got something in it. And I want to know what it is."

"No."

I stare at him, my breath caught in my throat since I wasn't expecting to hear that. I mean, I admit at first I was partly just fooling around, but now that I know he's hiding something, I'm determined to know what it is. "Show me," I say, reaching toward him.

But he takes his hand off the wheel and holds me back against my seat, all the while refusing to look at me.

I stare at him in shock, wondering what he could possibly be hiding. "Then just take me home," I finally say, my voice sounding high pitched and fragile.

"Echo, please." He sighs.

"Now. Take me home right now!" I glare at him, my stomach jumping all around, doing the panic dance.

He looks at me and shakes his head, then he pulls an illegal U-turn and heads toward my home.

But by the time he gets to the end of my street I've changed my mind. I mean, maybe he is only trying to help me, and protect me, and save me in the way he couldn't with Zoë. And acting like this, so ridiculous and immature, only proves how much I need that. Besides, I think it's pretty obvious that there's no need for me to fear him. He's never done anything to hurt me, and he never hurt my sister, and whatever he's got in his pocket is clearly none of my business. "I'm sorry," I say, reaching toward him, hoping he won't push me away like before.

"Forget it," he says, smoothing his long fingers back and forth over the steering wheel while staring straight ahead.

"I guess I was just mad because—"

"No need to explain," he says, still not looking at me.

"I just, I don't like it when you treat me like that. Like I'm some stupid little girl. I mean, I'm all grown up now and you won't even see it." I peek at him, taking in the line of his nose, the strength of his chin, the sweep of his lashes, before looking away.

He takes a deep breath and turns. "Believe me, Echo, I've noticed," he says, his voice sounding thick and resigned.

And without even thinking, I grab his sleeve, pull him close, and kiss him. Softly at first, then harder, more urgent, trying to seal this moment in time, determined to leave an impression.

And after awhile, when he pulls away, he looks into my eyes, cradles my face between the palms of his hands, and says, "Promise me."

I nod, holding my breath, waiting.

"Promise me you'll stay away from Jason."

After dinner, and well after my parents have gone to sleep, I climb out of bed, creep down the hall, and sneak into Zoë's room.

I haven't been in here for over a year. Not since the day the cops showed up with empty hands and hopeless faces. But everything looks exactly the same as it did back then—her blue duvet is still haphazard, having been tossed aside in her usual, early morning rush, and there's a lone white sock still lying on the floor, right next to the rug, where she'd dropped it over a year before.

My mom's the only one who comes in here now, the only one who brushes away cobwebs and handpicks lint from the yellowing sheets. I guess because she couldn't save her daughter in the most important way, she's decided to save her like this. With this freeze-dried room, undisturbed, suspended in time. The perfect contrast to our lives now, which are so completely and irreversibly changed.

I go over to Zoë's dresser and lift her brush, my fingers gliding along the tangle of long dark hairs wrapped tightly around the bristles. Then I reach for her perfume, its cap long ago lost, and bring it to my nose, surprised to find still the faintest hint of scent.

This is where I'd waited while the cops sat downstairs. On the floor, in the middle of her room, right in the center of her crème-colored flokati rug. My eyes shut tight, my body rocking back and forth as my mind sped in reverse, remembering our lives before, refusing to believe how they were about to become.

But when my parents came home, and I heard my mother's long, painful cry, I picked myself up and headed downstairs, knowing it was time to stop pretending.

I move toward Zoë's bed, sit gently on her mattress, and run my hand along her soft, worn sheets. Then I spread my body across the top of her crumpled duvet, molding her soft abandoned pillow against my cheek as I close my eyes, yearning to tell her how much I miss her, wanting to explain about Marc and me. How living her life and sharing her experiences makes me feel closer, like she never really left.

I lay like this for a while, my eyes shut tight, calling her to me.

But when she doesn't come, I turn off the light and creep back to my room. Knowing I've stolen enough for one day.

Twenty-five

July 19

Okay, I'm totally short on time, but I just really need to write about how completely psyched I am that I'm going to Marc's tonight!! Yay! It's finally happening! In fact he's picking me up any second, and I really hope my outfit's okay. I mean, I've seen pictures of his mom and she always looks so polished and expensive. And I just really really want her to like me.

Anyway, it almost didn't happen since my parents were insisting that I stay home to watch Echo—which is so freaking ridiculous I can't even tell you. I mean, hello? Has anyone noticed she's 13 now? I mean, jeez, enough with the overprotective BS, she's a teenager now for G's sake!

But luckily Echo was pretty pissed too, so she told them they were making her feel like a needy little baby. Then after proving she knew how to dial 911 and perform *the Heimlich maneuver on herself in case she choked on an Oreo or something, they finally, reluctantly, gave in.*

Okay, Marc's here—gotta go!

Oh, never mind. It's just Abby and Jenay. Guess they're having a sleepover or something. Anyway, I'm wearing my favorite cobalt blue dress because I think it looks dressy—but not too dressy. You know, cuz I don't want to look like I'm trying too hard. Because according to Vogue magazine, trying too hard (or at least looking like you're trying too hard) is like fashion sin numero uno. And since his mom can actually afford to buy the clothes they show in Vogue, I figure she could spot a striver over a mile away.

Okay, this time it really is Marc, so I'm outta here! But first, let me just say—

No matter how bad Marc thinks tonight is going to be—I'm totally psyched to be going!!!!

Yay!

141

July 19
Should have known better. I always get way too excited for my own good. Too tired and sad to write, though, so more later.

July 21
Yesterday was the first time Marc and I went an entire day without speaking to each other. And what made it even worse is the fact that it was a Sunday, which is always our day to hang in the park and feed our adopted pet ducks, or whatever.

But I did try calling him. Only he didn't answer. And for once, I didn't leave a message. I mean, why should I? All he had to do is check the display to know that it was me. Besides, I really didn't know what to say.

He did warn me, though. I'll give him that.

But I guess I just got so excited about seeing the house and meeting his mom that I ignored all the rest. You'd think I would've known better, though. I mean, seriously.

Anyway, when we first got there his mom wasn't home, which made him happy and me disappointed. Not that I wanted to have a whole big thing with her, but still, I'd purposely sat all stiff and careful in the car so I wouldn't get all smudged up or wrinkled and so I'd look great when we got there. Since for the whole entire day I'd imagined the moment when she'd greet us at the door, welcoming me into her home with a big smile and a hug. Okay, so maybe I did kind of want a big thing. But it's not like it matters, since that's not how it turned out.

So Marc gave me a tour of the house and property, and it's so freaking big, I don't know how he finds his way around. Seriously, it's like one of those mansions you see in a magazine or on TV or something. Then afterward, he led me out to the guesthouse (which believe me, is pretty much the size of a normal house) and when I asked, "Who lives here?" he said, "No one. But senior year, it's mine. That's our deal."

"Seriously?" I asked, looking all around, trying to imagine having a sweet setup like that. To just be able to come and go as you please, without having to climb down a tree or creep down the hall, or something.

But he just shrugged like it was no big deal. But I guess rich, privileged people are just used to having sweet deals like that.

Anyway, so then of course he got all handsy and tried to get me to have sex. But no way was I going to get all messed up before I even had a chance to make a good impression on his mom. So after pushing him off like a gazillion times, we just sat on the couch, side by side, watching some dumb show on TV, while he kept groping at me, trying to get me to change my mind. Which I gotta admit, totally got on my nerves.

Then finally, after like the sixth time I thought I heard a car on the drive, there really was a car on the drive, and he looked at me and said, "Cruella's home."

And I go, "You call your mom Cruella?"

But he just laughed and led me back to the house.

"Mother," he said, leaning in for the air cheek kiss just like you see rich people do in movies. "This is Zoë."

She looked at me, her eyes starting at my shoes and working their way up to my forehead.

She's tall, thin, and blond, just like she appears in all those society-page pictures. Only in person, she's really blond. Like Texas blond, almost stripper blond. And when her eyes met mine they narrowed, and suddenly her face went from faded beauty to mean. And believe me, the artist who painted her portrait that hangs in the stairwell failed to capture that.

"Well aren't you a beauty," she said.

And even though that might sound like a compliment to those who weren't around to witness it, trust me, it wasn't. Her voice was hard, her eyes were slits, and her lips were pursed, which are pretty much all the signs for hate at first sight.

"Where'd you find this one?" she asked, glancing at Marc as her heavily ringed fingers sorted through the stack of mail.

I just stood there feeling small and stupid and wishing I'd just listened to Marc when he warned me, wishing I hadn't pushed him so much.

"We go to school together," he said.

"Is that right?" She looked at me again, up once, down once. Then her eyes flicked away, and I knew I'd just been discarded. "Has William returned?" she asked.

Marc said no.

"We'll start without him then. I'm going upstairs to change. Tell Celia to bring me my drink."

Dinner was a nightmare. Going from bad to worse with each passing drink. Things improved slightly when William (stepdad #3) came home, but only because that gave her a new target.

I feel sorry for Marc. I mean, before his mom got home, it all looked so amazing and glamorous. I mean, with the grand staircase, the marble floors, the guesthouse, and the infinity pool. I was actually feeling a little bit jealous, and also kind of judging him for not appreciating it more. But the second she came home, the whole picture changed. And by the time it was over, I just wanted to go home.

But the worst part is, it doesn't make me feel closer to Marc, like I want to help him get through it or anything.

It actually makes me want to run away.

July 29

Marc and I just went almost ten days without seeing each other, and I can still hardly believe it. I mean, it's not like we actually broke up or anything, since we talked on the phone and stuff. I guess it's more like things got so intense so fast that we both feel we need a little cool down. Or at least I do. I'm not really sure how he feels about it, since it's not like anything was ever actually said.

I mean, after that awful dinner, well, I guess I just started thinking about how I've ditched all my friends, and it made me feel bad. It's like, just because Marc likes being a loner doesn't mean I do too. So basically I just spent the last ten days working during the day and hanging with Carly and Paula at night.

At first they gave me a bunch of shit for ditching them like that. But then after, it was like we'd been hanging out the whole entire summer and I'd never really left. I didn't say anything about meeting Marc's mom though. I mean, of course they asked if I'd been to the house and stuff, cuz pretty much everyone always wants to know about that. And since I didn't want to lie I said yes. But then I pretty much left it at that, and any details I did give were totally vague.

Anyway, hanging with them just made me realize how much I missed them. It also made me realize how I'm way too young to keep getting so tied down all the time. I mean, don't get me wrong, I still totally and completely love Marc. But sometimes I just need to hang out and have a little fun with my friends.

August 5
All day yesterday I was at Carly's, setting up my very own page on this Web site where you post pictures of yourself, list all of your favorite things like bands, movies, etc., and try to collect as many friends as possible so you can feel all popular and famous or whatever. And since Carly's been on there for practically ever, she's been bugging me this whole entire time to get on there too, so I finally gave in.

At first it seemed kind of dumb since I can just call her on her cell if I need to leave a message or even send a picture. But then she goes, "What if my ringer's off?"

So I said, "Then I'll text you."

And she went, "Forget it. You have no idea how much better this is, because then everyone can see what you write and what you're doing and saying and stuff."

Which, to be honest, also sounded pretty lame. I mean, I know it's probably old fashioned to even write in a *journal when the rest of the world is blogging. But maybe I don't want all these strangers to know what I'm thinking, saying, and doing, you know?*

But then she said, "Uh, hello? What do you think it's gonna be like when you're famous? I mean, you think Jessica Simpson gets any privacy?"

She had a point.

Then she goes, "You always talk about how you want to be a model, or actress, or whatever, but if you're that attached to your privacy then maybe you should find a new dream."

So, long story short, I signed on, decorated my space, uploaded some photos, and even though it practically took all day, now I totally get it. Now I totally get what she's been talking about because it's so completely addicting! It's like, within seconds of uploading my first few photos I had like a hundred people asking to be my friend! Okay, maybe most of them were guys, but whatever. And the thing is, all I used are these three stupid little cell phone photos that Paula snapped of me one day when I was laying by her pool.

In one, I'm in my white bikini and I'm laying on the lounger, drinking a beer. In another I'm pretty much doing the same thing, only smiling. And in the third I'm standing up and smiling with my top off. (But only because I didn't want strap marks, and my hands are strategically placed so it's not like you can see anything.)

And I'm thinking, Jeez, if I get all this attention just from these cheesy little cell phone photos, who knows what could happen if I posted some really good, like really professional photos there. You know something sophisticated and classy but a little bit sexy, and yet still kind of innocent too. Since Carly says that all the big New York and L.A. agents are always trolling around on there, scoping for fresh, new faces.

I'm not sure how she actually knows all that, but still, it sounds very, very likely.

But then she also said that I probably shouldn't tell Marc because he'll definitely totally freak.

And even though I just rolled my eyes and refused to comment, I'm actually thinking she's right.

When I close Zoë's diary I feel a little sick. Though I know I have no one to blame but myself. I mean, it's not like I haven't already lived through all this. So I shouldn't be surprised where it leads.

I shove it back under my mattress, finished with it for now, not willing to claim it in any way.

But at least I know that Marc didn't lie. Not to my parents, and not to the police. He'd stuck by his story the entire time, never once wavering, even though his alibi has always been shaky.

He said he was waiting at the park, down by the lake, where they always used to sit. That he just hung out, doing his homework, and waiting 'til well after dark. But when she didn't come back, he tried calling her cell a bunch of times, only she never answered. And since her phone was never recovered, it took a few days for the cops to confirm that.

"Still," they said. "You could've stood right there, over the body, making those calls. You know, to cover. Because you panicked. Because you saw what you'd done to her, saw her lying there like that, and you freaked. Come on, you can tell us. We're here to help you. So the sooner you confess, the better."

Marc refused a lawyer, refused to change his story. He just handed over her backpack and said the only reason he even had it was because she'd left it with him as proof she'd return.

It's weird how the police uncovered her life a lot quicker than her body. How within just a few days they knew most all of her secrets—about the Web page, the photo shoot, and her increasingly volatile relationship with Marc. They even interviewed her friends—Carly, Paula, practically everyone she knew. And believe me, they were all too eager to spill the beans on some things, while completely clamming up on others. But the one thing they all had in common is that every one of them pointed the finger at Marc. Saying how they were always suspicious of his loner ways and his completely messed up family.

"He isolated Zoë."

"He kept her all to himself and totally freaked when she tried to pull away."

But none of it's true. None of it matches anything I've read.

And you'd think that Carly, of all people, would've been above that. Especially since she was Zoë's best friend. But the truth is, it took her awhile to finally give them the more important details, and I always wondered who she was trying to protect—Zoë or herself?

I mean, she's the one who pushed it. She's the one who encouraged her to go. Not that I think it's her fault or anything, because clearly it was Zoë's choice in the end. Though I guess it explains why she tries so hard to avoid me at school, and how she can barely manage to look me in the eye when we pass in the halls.

And yeah, so maybe Marc is kind of a loner. I mean, so what? That doesn't prove anything. That doesn't make him guilty of anything other than having the rare ability to be comfortable just being by himself. Not to mention that it's that *exact* quality, aside from his sexy good looks, that attracted Zoë to him in the first place. It's what made her want him even more.

Though I do know that he hated all of that modeling stuff, and Zoë's celebrity ambitions. He thought that whole world was sleazy and shallow and awful. That it took naïve hungry people and built them way up before spitting them right out again. So it's probably true that he would've freaked if he'd known about those pictures. But that's why Zoë kept it hidden. And by the time he found out, it was already too late.

It took six long months to catch the guy who did it. But only because he tried to do it again. He lured the victim to the exact same location using the exact same M.O. And just like with Zoë, instead of packing a camera, he brought a knife.

He left a six-inch scar across that poor girl's neck. But hey, at least she got to keep her head. My sister wasn't so lucky.

And it was *that,* they said, that finally took her.

And even though they caught him red-handed (trust me, no pun intended), not one thing changed for Marc. And those six months he spent as a suspect may as well have been a conviction. I mean, maybe he didn't go to prison for a crime he didn't commit. But then again, he didn't have to.

Our town became his jailer.

Twenty-six

At first I was worried how Parker would act. Would he be angry, dismissive, sad, happy, euphoric, grateful?

But then I decided not to care.

And it's not because I was the least bit proud of the way I'd handled things. To be honest, I wasn't proud of much of anything I'd done. It was more like now that it was over, I was over it too.

Though I was determined to deal with Teresa. I mean, I still had no idea what her motive might be, not to mention why she insisted on even hanging with me in the first place. And I needed her to know, once and for all, that she was wrong about me, that no matter what she thought, she and I were totally different, we had nothing in common, we were nothing alike. And that any secrets I may have had, I was now more than willing to blow right open.

So right before lunch I stand by her locker, just waiting for her to show. And when she sees me she waves and smiles and says, "Hey! Let me just dump these books and we'll head on over."

But I just look her right in the eye and recite the speech I'd been rehearsing all day in my head. "I'm not eating at the table," I say. "I'm hanging with Marc. And just so you know, I don't care who you tell, or what you say, because I'm all out of secrets. But don't forget, I still have yours." Then before she can even respond, I turn and walk away, heading over to where Marc sits, feeling the weight of her stare the entire way.

It feels good to have nothing to hide. To no longer care what everyone thinks. Because knowing the real truth makes nothing else matter. And the real truth is that the only thing Marc has ever been guilty of is loving my sister. Despite what these small-minded people still say.

Because the fact is, Zoë never told him! I read it for myself. And if he didn't know what she was up to, then how was he supposed to stop her? How could he possibly have done anything to save her?

And even though I feel pretty awful to admit it, I really need a break from Abby and Jenay. I mean, I love them, don't get me wrong. And the last thing I'd ever want is for them to feel hurt or abandoned by me. But all the stuff they're into now, everything they care about, is just so standard-issue teen—so normal and typical and boring and mundane, like they're living in a sitcom, instead of the real world like me.

And it's not that I don't wish I could live like that too, because I really truly do. But unfortunately, that's no longer an option. And no matter how much I might want for things to be different, there are some things I just can't change. I mean, they don't know what it's like to live under the shadow of a sister like Zoë. They don't know what it is to live with a vacant, numb, pill-popping mom and an absentee dad, and to have the whole town point and whisper whenever you go by. They'll never know the pain of hearing the exact same people who left angels and cards for my sister's memorial, gossiping behind her back, slandering her character, and acting like she somehow deserved it.

But I do know what it's like to live like that. And that's why I'll never be able to blend. I'll never be able to care about pep club or which jeans to wear to a party or who will ask me to a dance.

I'm a freak. There's just no getting around it. And even though it wasn't by choice, now that it's a fact I have to find a way to live with it. And hanging with Abby and Jenay and all of their "normalness" only emphasizes my "weirdness." So I need to find a place where I won't always feel so strange and obtrusive. I need to be with someone who's a lot more like me.

"Hey," I say, sliding onto the bench next to Marc and tapping him on the shoulder, since he's wearing earphones with his eyes closed, which means he can't hear or see me.

He opens his eyes and smiles, then scoots over to give me more space.

And when he removes his earpiece I say, "Is it okay if I sit here with you?" I tear into a bag of chips, then thrust it toward him, offering him first pick.

"What about your friends?" he asks, looking at me intently, his deep dark eyes traveling over my face.

But I just shrug. "I thought you were my friend."

He looks at me for a moment, then nods and inserts his earpiece.

And I eat my lunch while he listens to music. And even though it may look strange on the outside, on the inside, where it really counts, I'm finally at peace.

Abby and Jenay were so freaked about lunch, the whole way home it's pretty much all they talk about.

"I just don't get it," Abby says, while Jenay nods in agreement.

"There's nothing to get," I tell them, trying to maintain my calm, yet feeling completely annoyed at having to defend myself.

Abby shakes her head. "Um, actually there's plenty to get. Like your sister for instance? Not to mention what everyone's saying." They both look at me.

Before I respond, I take a deep breath, reminding myself not to get angry, that they're my best friends and they only want what's best for me.

But it doesn't work, so I shake my head and say, "I'm only going to say this once so I hope you both listen. Marc is in no way, shape, or form, the least bit responsible for what happened to Zoë." I look at them. "And if you guys think you or anyone else in this town knows more about it than I do, well, you're wrong. Because I'm the only one in this school, the only one in this whole entire *town*—outside of the cops and my parents—who knows *all* of the facts and details. And believe me, sometimes I wish I didn't, but I do, and there's nothing I can do about it. I'm also well aware of what all these small-minded idiots are saying, and how ninety-nine percent of it's lies." I shake my head and fold my arms across my chest. "But the worst part is knowing that half the people responsible for those lies used to be Zoë's friends. So I'm hoping you guys can do a little better. I'm hoping you can be a better friend to *me* than they were to *her*, and try not to judge me or second-guess me, because I just might know something you don't."

By the time I'm finished I'm totally shaking, and my friends just stand there, eyes wide, mouths open, not saying a word. And feeling kind of embarrassed for going off like that and not knowing how to recover, I just turn away and head toward home.

Later that night Teresa calls. But when I see her number on the display I completely ignore it. And then right before I've almost fallen asleep, it rings again. Only this time it's Marc.

"I'm outside. Wanna go for a ride?" he offers.

And after throwing on some jeans, boots, and my favorite sweater, I brush my hair, swipe on some lip gloss, spritz some perfume, open the french doors, shimmy down the tree, and run across the wet frosted grass toward his car.

As he navigates the dark quiet streets, I wonder if we're going to the park. But when he brakes at the top of old Water Tower Hill, all I can do is laugh.

"You're joking, right? The water tower?" I say, shaking my head. "I mean, if you've really got your own guesthouse all to yourself, then why are you bringing me here?"

During the day Water Tower Hill is known as the local eyesore. But at night, it's known as the local underage make out place—where teens from as far as three towns over come to park, drink, smoke, and hook up. It even has its own creepy legend that seems to attract more people than it scares away.

Rumor has it that a long time ago, like back in the seventies or something, some girl from the next town over came here to cheat on her boyfriend. But evidently he was on to her, because he followed her here, parked far away, then crept toward her car. When he peeked in through the window and saw her and her lover kissing, he freaked out so bad he reached for his gun, pressed the barrel against the glass, and pulled the trigger twice, one shot for each head.

Apparently the impact of the blast tore them apart, leaving one hanging half out the window, and the other slumped over the seat. And it wasn't until he opened the door and the lover fell out that he realized he was a she.

So now the story goes that the two slain lovers both haunt the place, protecting all the young innocent girls from men with bad intent.

And when I gaze at Marc I wonder about his intent, because I know I'm innocent, though maybe not for long.

Besides, it's not like I'd ever actually believe a story like that.

Because ghosts are only real if you don't really miss someone. When you do, they're just a cruel joke.

"It's beautiful up here. Just look at the lights," he says, the leather of his jacket squeaking as he rolls the window down just a crack.

"Yeah, the only time this town ever looks good is when you're looking down on it," I say, wondering if Zoë's looking down on us, and if so, what it is that she's thinking.

He kisses me then, as I knew he would. I mean, why even come here, if you're not gonna try?

My fingers are tangled in his hair, the pads of my thumbs smoothing those glorious, high cheekbones, as my mouth moves hungrily against his, wanting to capture this moment, willing it to never end.

"Zoë," he whispers, lifting my sweater as his hands search for my breasts.

I lean in, kissing him even harder, feeling his fingers fumbling with the clasp at my back. "Here, let me help you," I say, reaching behind.

But then he pushes me away, until I'm back in my seat, his face a horrified mask when he realizes what he just said.

But I don't mind. In fact, I prefer it. So I lean toward him again, my mouth seeking his, but settling for his cheek. "Don't worry," I say, my lips grazing against the coarse black stubble that grows along his jaw. "It's okay, really. I like being her."

But he shakes his head and pushes me off, dropping his head in his hands as he says, "Oh God, Echo. Oh my God, what have I done?" He hides his face in shame, as he trembles and shakes, mumbling a whole string of words I can't understand.

I just sit there, wanting to comfort him, desperately wanting to rewind and pick up right where we left off. But then he wipes his face with his sleeve, reaches for the key and turns it hard, startling the engine back to life. "I'm taking you home," he says, staring straight ahead, no longer willing to look at me.

But I just fold my arms across my chest and glare at him, refusing to be discarded, refusing to let go of the best thing that ever happened to me. "No," I say, my eyes narrowed, my mouth set.

He rubs his eyes and shakes his head, and suddenly he looks so much older and so incredibly tired. "I'm taking you home, Echo. We're leaving, now. So please fix your top, so we can get out of here."

I sit there, staring out the window, my lips trembling as though I might cry. Doesn't he realize how much I need to be here? Doesn't he realize how I'd much rather be Zoë than me?

But he just looks at me for the longest time, then he rubs his eyes again and says, "Don't you get it? I've done enough damage. I can't go hurting you too." His jaw is quivering, his eyes black and hard, and he looks like he's on the verge of something he can barely contain.

And when I realize his words I feel a chill down my spine. So I straighten my sweater, hug my knees to my chest, and stay like that the entire way.

Twenty-seven

When he stops at the corner, I throw the door open and hit the ground running. Sprinting across the frozen lawn with my shoes still in hand, my toes turning blue, my breath coming fast and quick, 'til I finally reach my room where I grab Zoë's diary and flop on the bed, desperate for answers, and knowing she's the only one who can provide them, the only one who can explain what Marc really meant when he said, "I can't go hurting you too."

August 7

Only three more days 'til Dr. Freud goes on vacation! Which means only three more days 'til I go on vacation too! But it's not like we're going together (gag). It's just that there's no work for me to do when he's gone.

Anyway, I can't freaking wait! I feel like I'm finally getting my summer back. And all I plan to do for those three blissful weeks is sleep, hang out with Paula during the day, and Marc every night.

We've been getting along so much better over the last few days, which makes me feel really bad about freaking out like that over his mom and stuff. I mean, it's not like he actually dragged me there, or even wanted me to go. It's more like I pushed and pushed 'til he finally gave up and gave in. And because of that, now I have to live with the consequences, along with the memory of her nasty little "Where'd you find this one?" comment. Like I'm just one more slut he dragged home.

Marc swears that's just her typical passive-aggressive game. So I looked that up in one of Dr. Freud's books, and it seems like the right diagnosis to me. He also said she's all freaked out about getting old, and about her fading looks and saggy chin (okay, he didn't really say that part about her chin, that was pure me!), so she pretty much hates anyone younger and prettier than her. Which is basically like half the population, but whatever.

So, Carly keeps begging me to go meet this guy she's been messaging back and forth on her Web page. But I'm like, "No freaking way. Forget it. Not to mention, hello, what about Stephen?"

And she goes, "I am so over Stephen! Why didn't you warn me about that bicep gazing bullshit?"

And I go, "Believe me, I did."

Anyway at first I said a definite no. But then, by the time I left I changed it to maybe. But I told her not to tell him I was coming too, because then he might get the wrong idea and try to bring a friend. And not only am I not going to cheat on Marc, but it will be a lot safer if it's two against one. I mean, just in case it comes to that.

So she goes, "What do you see in him anyway? I

mean, besides the gorgeous, hot, bad boy sexy stuff. Is it the money?"

But I just shrugged. Because even though she finally figured out the whole ugly truth about Stephen, that doesn't mean she can even begin to understand a guy like Marc. So I go, "He's just different from everyone else. He's not one size fits all."

And she just shook her head and looked at me and said, "I'll say."

August 8

Okay, so we're meeting Mr. Internet tonight at seven. And I've lied to just about everyone I know to pull it off. My parents think I'm going out with Carly (which I am, just not to where I said we were going), her parents think she's going out with me (ditto), but not a soul knows anything more. Not even Paula knows the truth, cuz I know she'd just totally freak. Actually, they'd all freak.

Though I do feel really bad about lying to Marc and telling him I'm staying home to hang out with Echo for a change. I mean, I know that's actually really really really seriously bad karma, since I've been meaning to spend more time with her, and now I supposedly am, only it's a lie.

But I swear, if this guy turns out to be totally cool and not some Dateline Special Internet predator freak, then I'll take the kid out for shopping and lunch. Really. Scout's honor.

August 9

Okay, so at first Carly and I were totally amazed that the guy turned out to look a lot like his picture, which was actually pretty cute. But what wasn't so amazing is that apparently the picture was taken like, over ten years ago. Because up close and in person he looks a lot more like thirty than twenty like he said on his page.

Anyway, you should've seen his face when he saw Carly and me walking toward him. His eyes went all wide and he got this big grin, like he just won the lottery or something. So we totally hung out and talked for a while, then Carly told him we wanted to party and asked him to go buy us some beer since we're underage and can't score it ourselves.

Well, it was pretty obvious that the whole "underage" bit got him major excited. So the second he returned and set the package down, Carly grabbed the bag and said, "Adios, loser!"

And then we totally took off!

Seriously, we just started walking away, but all casual, not like rushing or anything, which actually made him pretty mad, to say the least. So he yelled at us to come back, but I turned and went, "If you take one more step toward us I'm calling the cops and reporting you for the pervert you know that you are." And I held up my cell phone like I was just about to do it.

You should've seen his face! He just stood there, totally stunned. But still, he totally backed down. He just looked at us all sad and said, "Well, can I at least have the wine back? That's an expensive bottle."

But Carly goes, "No, because you're a pervert! Which means you don't deserve any wine."

Then we took our stash over to Paula's, where we hung in the Jacuzzi, and told her the story over and over, and each time it just got better.

August 10
Today was a short day since Dr. Freud had a flight to catch, so we said aloha then I waited outside for Marc.

Only he didn't show.

So then I called him and went, "Where are you?"

And he said, "Home."

"Well you're supposed to be here," I told him.

But he pretended he didn't know what I was talking about, which is totally ridiculous since I told him twice this morning and even left a message at lunch.

But he just goes, "Didn't get it."

"Well you're getting it now. So hurry up and come get me," I said, my patience running big-time thin.

And then, I still can't believe this, he goes, "I can't."

"What do you mean you can't? I thought you said you were home?" I was completely fuming and no longer trying to hide it. "I mean, it's like a hundred degrees out here and I'm melting," I tell him.

But he just gives me a bunch of bull about how busy he is, which is total crap since it's not like he has a job or chores or anything. And when I asked him just what exactly he was busy with he totally ignored me! He just went, "Sorry, I can't get you, but I'll definitely see you tonight though, okay?"

I felt like throwing my phone at the building I was so mad. But I didn't. Instead, I just sucked it up and went straight to Carly's. And by the time I got there I was still so pissed I ended up telling her the whole ugly story, which is something that I never, ever do. Mostly because once you tell your friends the bad stuff, that's all they seem to remember.

But still, it felt so much better just to get it off my chest. Not to mention how she was totally sympathetic and only a little bit judgmental. And then she grabbed her laptop and tried to find me a new boyfriend on the Internet, which I took as a joke, even though I think she was partly serious.

Then we clicked over to my page so I could upload some more pictures we took of us pretending to French-kiss each other. Then we made fun of all the perverts who messaged me, telling me how I looked totally cool and laid back and asking me if I wanted to maybe hang out and chill— please.

But I still hooked up later with Marc, and even though I was still pretty mad, I decided to just let it go because my vacation just started and I was determined to be happy and have fun. Plus, I hate to stay angry and carry grudges and stuff.

But still, every time I asked him where he was, he just changed the subject and moved on to something else.

I must have fallen asleep, because when I wake up my mom is standing over me and staring down at me. "Echo, are you feeling all right?" she asks, leaning toward me brushing her palm across my forehead, fever sweeping.

Physically, I'm fine. But emotionally, I'm a wreck. All I can think about is Marc, and the words he said right before driving me home. I mean, what exactly happened between my sister and him? And what was he hiding in his pocket that day? So far, I've yet to read a single thing in Zoë's diary that could even begin to explain.

Not to mention how there's no way I can face Abby and Jenay. Not after yesterday's emotional tirade.

So I decide to do something I haven't done since I was hell-bent on avoiding the presidential fitness test back in sixth grade—I fake sick.

"I'm feeling kinda lousy," I say, squinting at her as I conjure up images of hot furnaces, burning matches, the scorching desert heat, and the bowels of hell—method acting for raising my temperature.

"What's the matter?" she asks, sliding onto the edge of my bed and readjusting the covers in a way that brings her hand dangerously close to the partially exposed diary.

I shift my body, flopping the covers over it, trying to make it appear as though I'm sickly and distressed, when really I just need to keep that little blue book far out of her reach.

"I'm nauseous," I say, allowing myself a mental high five for the stroke of sudden genius. I mean, that's one that can never be disproved, since it's only felt by its host.

"Anything else?" she asks, her face growing worried and stained with concern.

Jeez, she wants more? What is this? "Um, yeah, I think I also feel a headache coming on, probably nothing major, but then again, it just started. I'm also a little weak, but that's probably just the fatigue," I mumble, rearranging my face to resemble someone who's fighting burgeoning, yet intolerable pain.

"Sounds like the flu. There's a bug going around," she says, smoothing her skirt as she stands. "I'll call the school and tell them you won't be there today."

"Do you think you can call Abby too? And tell her I won't be meeting them on the corner?" I ask, even though I doubt they're expecting me, not after my outburst.

"Of course," my mother says. "But I'm worried about leaving you here all alone, feeling this way."

"Oh, I'll be all right. Really," I say, hoping I haven't gone too far, praying she won't try to use this as an excuse to call in sick too.

Twenty-eight

Remember how I said I like having the house to myself? Well being home alone for the whole entire day is like Heaven. Seriously. And with my mom finally gone and fully convinced that I'm planning a day of bed rest (but that I won't hesitate to call her if necessary), I grab the diary and take it downstairs, where I make myself a nice, healthy (well, kind of) breakfast.

I pour some frosted cereal into a bowl then add more sugar and nonfat (that's the healthy part) milk, then I prop the diary before me and begin reading, trying to get the spoon from the bowl to my mouth without splattering the pages.

August 11
Today is the second official day of my vacation and I really thought it would be nice if I could spend it with my boyfriend but apparently he has other plans. Some big effin secret he refuses to tell me.

And to be honest, I'm really getting sick of it. I mean, it's not like I keep secrets from him, at least not about anything he actually needs to know about. But this is different, this is important. I can just tell.

But you know what? Screw him! I'm just gonna spend the whole day at Paula's, laying by the pool, and not even think about him or his stupid secret. I'm just gonna pretend that he and his little mystery don't even exist.

I know I probably sound like a brat, but it's just that lately, every single passing day is starting to feel exactly the same as the one before it. Like my life is just one long, continuous rerun, with no new episodes scheduled. And it's starting to make me feel really really restless, and more than a little anxious about the future. I mean, I know everything about my life probably seems pretty normal, and not all that bad compared to some, but the thing is, I never wanted to be normal, and I certainly never wanted to be just like everyone else. I've always dreamed of something bigger and better and brighter.

I've always wanted more.

Like, you know how when you watch those teen reality shows on MTV and stuff? And how everyone's always out shopping, or going to parties, or fashion shows, or clubs, or charity events, or whatever, and then how after their turn on the series is over they all get magazine covers, movie deals, recording contracts, product endorsements, and regular spots in the tabloids? When just one year before they were just another kid with a normal life, in a much-better-than-normal town? Well, that kind of stuff makes it so crystal clear just how slow and boring it is here. Not to mention how I'm missing out on some mega opportunities, all because my parents are determined to live in this wasteland—this stupid, boring, totally fucked-up zip code.

I mean, it's not like MTV would ever even consider coming here. So I think it's obvious that if I really want to make something of myself (of my life!), then I'm really left with no choice but to get the hell out of this dead-end town. Seriously. And even though my parents are already starting with the big expectations and college talk (well, as college professors they've actually been at it for years, only now it's more focused and serious), I have to find a way to tell them that their hopes and dreams have nothing in common with mine. And as far as college goes, well, it's just not gonna happen for me.

Because, let's face it, my grades are total sliders—good enough to pass class and not get yelled at too much, but nowhere near their Ivy League standards. And if they think I'm going local, then they're completely loco. I'd never go to the same lame school where my mom and dad teach.

It's like, let Echo go to Harvard, since she's the brainy one who cares about all that intellectual, deep stuff. Let her be the one who makes them proud. I mean, maybe I'm just not smart like that. Maybe I've got other (better) things to do. And going to college just to please them will only end up putting me four years behind.

So lately I've been thinking about graduating early. I figure I can either beef up my credits (not exactly sure how, but I plan to find out), or take my GED and say an early adios. I mean, I've always wanted to be a model/actress—seriously, ever since I was a really little kid that's all I've ever wanted to do. And I just read this article in one of my magazines about some 14-year-old girl who's storming the European runways! Seriously—the chick is only 14! And I'm already 16—and then next year I'll be 17—and it's just gonna keep on going like that! Which means I really can't afford to waste any more time messing around with my friends and waiting for my boyfriend to call.

I've got to start making a plan for escape. So I can ditch this town and go live my dream before it's too late!

I mean, if Carly and Paula want to lay around the pool all day, making dates with perverts in exchange for free beer, before moving on to junior college and husbands and babies and a bin full of smelly diapers and never once being interviewed on Access Hollywood, then that's fine. Whatever makes them happy.

But that kind of mundane life will never be enough for me. So with that in mind, I've decided to put my Web page to better use. I've decided to make it work for me. And no way am I mentioning it to Marc.

Because if he can have a secret, then I can too.

August 12

Went shopping for back-to-school clothes with Mom and Echo, and when Mom refused to buy me the jeans I wanted, I just pulled out a wad of cash and bought them myself. Hah! The power of employment! And seeing her face go all tight and twisted made it totally worth spending all of my hard-earned dough.

"You're the one who wanted me to work," I couldn't help but remind her. "You're the one who found me the high-paying job!"

I swear, I can't wait 'til I'm a model making a gazillion trillion dollars, driving a Mercedes, living in an awesome penthouse apartment chock full of Jimmy Choos and Prada bags, and sending my parents on vacations in exotic locales—just to get them out of my hair! Let's see who judges me then!

After shopping we went for lunch, and just as I stuck my fork in my salad Echo announced that she's already completed her summer reading list and is getting a head start on the books she heard she'll have to read during the school year.

Jeez! Sometimes I can't believe that we're actually sisters. Seriously. I mean, I love her, I really, really do, but sometimes it seems like she's from another planet. Or maybe it's me. Maybe I really am adopted like I used to dream about when I was younger. Because despite having my father's eyes and my mother's nose, there's no way in hell I'm even remotely DNA connected to these people.

Oh yeah, I also got these really awesome shoes, a couple new sweaters, and a really cute fall coat with a fake fur collar (since I would never wear real fur, I love animals too much, and I plan to make sure that's included in all of my modeling contracts).

But it's not like I can actually wear any of it right now since it's still so freaking hot out. But still, maybe I'll just pack it all up and drag it over to Carly's so she can take some photos of me in it. I need some new pictures for my page since I'm planning a complete overhaul. I'm totally gonna delete all the slutty, stupid, bullshit quotes, and any and all comments regarding drinking, sex, or partying. I'm even gonna switch the background wallpaper to something clean, and sleek, and modern. I'm gonna make it like my online portfolio. So it needs to look as professional as possible.

And even though I still haven't told Marc anything about it, last night when we were all at Kevin's, Paula totally let it slip.

"Omigod," she said. "Remember when we put that picture on your site, the one where you had your top off and then all those guys started instant messaging you?"

I just sat there, totally bugging, and thinking how I was going to kill her the second I could get her alone.

But then Carly goes, "That was my site, dummy. Zoë doesn't have a site, remember?"

And then Paula looks at me, and goes, "Oh yeah, duh! Somebody pass me another beer! Ha ha!"

And then everyone laughed, including me because I felt like I had to, to make it look real.

Marc was the only one who didn't laugh. Marc just stared.

August 16

One week down, two to go! Been hanging at Paula's every day, read the first two pages of one of the books from the eleventh-grade summer reading list—boring! Saw Marc every night except for one where he acted all mysterious so I acted like I didn't care.

Still working on the revamp of my new Web page, though I'm still not all that thrilled with the photos Carly took. I mean, right after I uploaded them, I waited for the usual comments to come pouring in, but mostly I just got stuff like:

Bikini pics way hotter!

Girl-on-girl action mo betta!

So I guess that means if I wanted to be a porn star I'd be set. But that's not gonna happen—I mean, disgusting! Not to mention how the only lingerie ads I'd ever be willing to do are for Victoria's Secret. I mean, if it's good enough for Giselle, then it's good enough for me, but otherwise, that kind of stuff is usually sleazy and cheesy.

Anyway, I think it's getting painfully obvious how I definitely need to get some professional pictures taken by a real photographer, in a real studio, as opposed to a bunch of cell phone digitals taken by my drunk, burnout friend in her poorly lit bathroom.

And then, wouldn't you know it, just when I was

actually considering returning those awesome two-hundred-dollar jeans (that I already wore) so I'll have more money to add to the professional photographer savings account I keep stashed under my mattress I get a message from a professional photographer!

Seriously! Apparently he stumbled across my page and saw my photos and thinks I have potential but the pictures are way too amateur! Duh. So he told me to check out his Web page to see some of his work, and to let him know if I'm interested.

So of course I clicked right over and checked out his pictures, which I gotta say are completely amazing! Seriously nice high fashion black-and-whites, along with some really great head shots, some of which feature models that I'm actually familiar with! And I was so majorly excited I was just about to e-mail him back, when Marc called. So instead I just bookmarked the page, figuring it's probably better to wait a few days and not look all desperate and overly eager.

But still—kismet, fate, destiny, providence, big-time amazing luck—call it what you want, it's finally starting to happen for me!

August 18

I'm totally freaked and don't know what to do. And the worst part is I can't tell anyone, at least not until I know what it means, because maybe it won't end up meaning anything. But at the moment, I just can't seem to figure it out. And believe me, I've tried.

Okay, so I was just out with my dad, on our way downtown, and just as we drove past the office where I work I saw Marc opening the door and going inside. And even though I immediately turned around in my seat and did a total double take just to make sure it was him, the whole thing happened so fast I just couldn't be positive.

But I still have to stress how it really, really, really looked like him. I mean, let me put it this way, how many guys in this town are that good looking and just happen to dress in all black and wear Doc Marten boots when it's one hundred and two in the shade?

Only one that I know of.

And it's not like it would be such a big deal, except for the fact of how he told me he was going to be home all day, doing some work on his car. So right after the sighting, I tried to reach him on his cell, but he must've turned it off cuz it went straight into voice mail. Which, okay, fine, maybe he doesn't want to have it on when he's working on his car, I mean, that makes sense, right?

But then here's the thing—the only people who occupy that office are two shrinks. My boss, who I know for a fact is away on vacation, and the other one who's this psychiatrist (which, I recently found out, means he went to school even longer so he can make even more money and prescribe drugs) who doesn't leave for vacation 'til my boss gets back.

And then I remember that comment Mark made that one day about my boss having a goatee, and how it got me all wondering how he would even know that since it's not like they'd ever met or had ever seen each other.

And even though I shrugged it off at the time, now I'm starting to wonder just how many secrets he's actually keeping from me.

Because to be honest, it seems like they're starting to multiply.

August 20

That photographer dude just sent me another message, which seems a little weird and desperate. But then Carly goes, "Well maybe he just wants to be the one who discovers you, because if you become famous, then it's like big-time kudos for him, right?"

And when you think about it, she really does have a point. Anyway, I didn't message him back yet, 'cause I'm meeting Carly soon and I need to concentrate on that right now. I mean, I finally broke down and told her all about how I saw Marc at the shrink's office and how weird things have been with us lately.

And then she was all, "What's that about?"

And I'm like, "Who knows?"

Then she says, "Well, don't you have a key?"

And I go, "Yeah, but it's only to the front door and his office. Not the other guy's place."

And she goes, "Well, it's a start."

August 21

Marc just called to make plans for our two-months-since-we-first-kissed anniversary and I don't even know what to say. I mean, just two days ago I would've thought that was extremely romantic, but now it's kind of creeping me out. I guess it's because of what I found out. Or more like what I kind of found out. Because sometimes having only a partial answer is worse than not knowing at all.

August 22

Finally called Marc back (I know, I know, bad girl-friend). Anyway, I told him dinner at Giorgio's tomorrow night sounds good, but that I wouldn't be able to see him 'til then.

But still, the more I think about it, the more I think it's probably nothing, since he's never done anything major to weird me out before (and you'd think I'd know by now if he had psycho tendencies or something). And I've definitely never seen him do anything remotely violent or destructive, and the only time he's ever playing with fire is when we're smoking, which doesn't really count as playing with fire, right? (Just playing with your health—ha ha!) Anyway, I'm actually starting to wonder if maybe I'm the one who's crazy!

I mean, I love him—I really, truly, totally do! And I can hardly believe the way I'm totally overreacting to something that in all likelihood is probably nothing! And I really have to stop acting like this because if I don't then I'm totally going to sabotage the only relationship I've ever had that's actually made me feel extremely happy.

Not to mention how I need to learn to give him some space and respect his privacy since it's really not necessary for two people to know absolutely everything about each other. In fact, it's better not to. At least that's what they say in Cosmo.

But still, I just can't stop wondering why Marc wouldn't tell me that he's seeing a shrink. Unless it's because I always make fun of my boss and the psychos who see him, in which case, I feel even worse.

August 23

Today I went shopping, thinking I'd buy something new and exciting to wear to my anniversary dinner tonight with Marc. But since everything that's out now is pretty much for fall, and with the daytime temperatures still in the triple digits—and the nighttime only slightly cooler than that—I decided to just save my money and wear something I already have. Besides, it's not like I'm all that excited about it anyway, not to mention how I need to start saving as much money as possible to invest in my photos, my future, and my one-way ticket out of this hell town.

And then just as I was about to leave, I remembered how Echo's b-day is totally coming up. And since I was *already out shopping, I figured I might as well get a head start and buy something early, as opposed to picking up something in a last-minute panic like I usually do.*

But since she's not all that into clothes yet, and since she barely wears any makeup or perfume, and since she doesn't seem to focus much on her hair, that pretty much ruled out all of my areas of expertise.

So I headed over to the bookstore, where she likes to spend all her free time, but even though it's not like it was the first time I'd ever gone in there (I mean, I'm not re-tarded, I just don't like to read), still, walking around and trying to choose a book for her was basically impossible. I mean, there's like so many titles, by so many writers, and that's just in the teen section! And knowing Echo, she's probably read every last one of them anyway. And not wanting to give her a repeat, I decided to bail.

Then just as I was on my way out the door, I spotted this display with like, all these book accessories and stuff, which I know probably sounds stupid since it's not like people actually dress up their books like you do a doll, I just mean stuff like fancy jeweled and beaded book-marks and little metal clip-on reading lights and stuff like that. And then just as I was thinking about getting her a bookmark/reading light combo gift set, I noticed this whole other shelf filled with diaries just like the one I'm writing in now!

And I thought, oh my God, that's it! I'll get her a di-ary. I mean, she's going into eighth grade, and that's pretty much when all the big drama starts, right? And it might be nice for her to have something private to record it all in, like when she gets her first crush, or first kiss, or starts fighting with Jenay and Abby, or reads a really exciting sentence in one of her books! (Just kidding about the last one because I know it sounds mean.) And since she's so into reading and writing and stuff, I figure she'll probably end up writing in her diary even more than I do mine.

So at first I reached for the cobalt blue one—I guess I'm just naturally drawn to that color—but then I thought how it's probably better if she doesn't have the exact same one as mine. I mean, for starters we're complete and total opposites which means we don't share the same taste in color either, and second, can you imagine if we had the exact same ones and then they somehow got switched!

And since that's the kind of risk I'm just not willing to take, I ended up buying her this really pretty turquoise one. Still blue, only different, calmer, like Echo. And since I still feel so guilty for never taking her to lunch (even after I promised I would if I survived that first Internet hookup meeting thing with Carly—which obviously I did), I bought some really pretty silver wrapping paper (instead of using old Xmas paper like I usually do), a pretty cobalt blue bow (so she'd know at first sight it's from me), and then this little vanilla-scented candle to go with it, so that she can close her door, light her candle, and write about all the amazing things that happen in eighth grade.

And then after I came back home and wrapped it all up, I hid it in the back of my closet, behind my big stack of shoe boxes so she won't find it. I just hope I don't forget that it's there—because you know how it goes, outta sight, outta mind and all that.

I drop the diary and bolt upstairs to Zoë's room, my hands shaking and my heart racing as I dive straight into her closet, pushing aside the tall stacks of shoe boxes, desecrating a space that's been preserved for well over a year.

And sure enough, just like she promised, there's a dark green shopping bag hidden in the back. So I take it over to her bed, where I sit on the edge, anxious to get inside.

But the moment that silver-wrapped box is on my lap, I'm suddenly reluctant to open it. Because this was meant to be unwrapped in a room full of laughter, family, and friends. It was never supposed to happen like this.

Though knowing Zoë, she'd want me to open it no matter what. And since so few of her plans had turned out as she'd hoped, I wasn't about to disappoint her now.

I remove the bow gently, smiling as I tuck it behind my ear, remembering how Zoë and I always used to do that on Christmas morning, posing together like two Tahitian goddesses, red and green ribbons woven through our hair, while our dad stood before us, taking our picture. Then I slip my finger under the tape, taking more care than usual not to rip the paper as I unfold the edges, lift the lid, and retrieve the diary.

When I open it, the first thing I see is Zoë's familiar loopy scrawl:

Happy 14th b-day Echo!

And then right below that:

May your days be filled with excitement and fun, and may you record it all here!

Then I unwrap the candle, bringing it to my nose and inhaling its still surprisingly warm scent. Then I replace all the shoe boxes, putting them back the way they were, before going to my room, depositing her gift on my bed, removing all of my clothes, and heading for the shower.

And just as I'm closing the door, my cell phone rings. But knowing it's either Abby or Jenay, or maybe even Marc, I just turn the taps up even higher, letting the spray beat hard and hot against my back as I sink down to the ground, bring my knees to my chest, shield my face from the deluge, and finally let myself cry.

I never cry. Even at Zoë's funeral, when everyone was falling all over each other, falling all over themselves, I wore dark sunglasses, a stiff upper lip, and refused to give in to any of that. I guess I've never been comfortable with public displays of emotion. Because those kinds of moments, where I let myself cave and totally lose control, are always saved for when I'm alone. I mean, they're really no one's business.

And with my parents being such absolute basket cases, I knew even then that someone had to stay strong. And since it obviously wasn't going to be them, I figured it had to be me. Besides, the last thing I needed was for a bunch of relatives, people who hadn't seen Zoë since she was a baby, hugging all over me, crying on my shoulder, and giving their heartfelt condolences for a loss they could never begin to imagine.

And even though I know that may sound awful, the truth is that no matter how sorry everyone may have been, there wasn't a single person on the planet who could ever understand how I felt about Zoë. How much I missed her. And the huge gaping hole she'd left in my heart.

But now, with everything veering so out of control, I know I can no longer go it alone. But wouldn't you know it, Marc, the one person I trusted enough to turn to, turns out to be one person I never should've gone near.

When the water starts to run cool, I turn off the taps, dry off with a towel, then slip on a pair of my favorite old sweats. Then I pull my wet hair back into a tight ponytail and head down the stairs to the couch in the den, tucking the afghan tightly under my feet and picking up the diary from where I left off.

Twenty-nine

August 24
Everything started off great. Marc picked me up and he looked so good in his blazer and jeans, and I wore my cool new jeans, some strappy sandals, and my favorite cobalt blue halter top, then we drove to the restaurant where we sat at a nice table in the corner of this tiny but romantic plant-filled patio. And after ordering some appetizers and a couple of Cokes, I leaned toward Marc and smiled and said, "Is there something going on that I should know about?"

And he just looked at me all innocent and went, "What do you mean?"

And I knew I had a choice. I could either act all coy and beat around the bush until one of us gave in, or I could just get right to it and tell him how I know he's been holding out on me. So I said, "I know you're hiding something from me and I want to know what it is."

And instead of getting mad or curious, he just said, "Okay." Then he took a sip of his Coke and gazed around the room.

And no way was I about to leave it at that and allow him to blow it off so easily. So I said, "Marc, really, I'm totally serious. The last couple times when you told me you were home, I know for a fact that you weren't. And there's this one time in particular when I called and called but you never once answered even though you said you were there."

Okay, the second it was out I cringed at how needy and overbearing that sounded. I even wondered why I couldn't have waited 'til after our dinner, or even 'til tomorrow or something. But since it was already out there, I figured I may as well continue, so I looked at him and said, "Well?" Then I kicked the tip of my sandal against the table leg as I waited for his reply.

But it never came, he just shrugged.

So I went, "But what I'm really talking about is this one time in particular, when you told me you were home, but then I actually saw you," and then I paused because the waitress had just brought our appetizers. I didn't want her to hear any of this and know that we're kind of arguing since when she first came to our table I told her all about how it was our anniversary. But then the second she left I leaned in and said, "But I know you weren't home. And I happen to know that, because I saw you somewhere else."

But he just went, "Yeah?" And then he shrugged and grabbed a shrimp by the tail, dunked it in that red cocktail sauce, and then popped it into his mouth.

And I started to get so worked up by his acting so blasé and unconcerned about lying to me that I shook my head, leaned in even more, and loud whispered, "I saw you at the office where I work. And since my boss is on vacation, that means you were there to see Dr. Kenner."

But he just said, "I think you're confusing me with someone else." Then he grabbed another shrimp, popped it in his mouth, and smiled at me with the tail all caught between his teeth, like that was actually funny or something.

But when I refused to laugh, he started to look worried. And I knew I better just go for it and get it over with, since I was clearly teetering on the edge of either a total confession, or a full-blown fight. So I said, "Marc, listen, don't even try to lie or cover it up, cuz I know for a fact it was you."

He just stared, then he set down his fork and said, "And how exactly do you know that, Zoë?"

And that's when I told him about reading his file. And how I know all about his juvenile arrest and violent background and the fires and stuff.

I can hear my cell phone ringing from all the way upstairs, but no way am I going to stop reading just so I can answer it. But when the house phone also starts to ring, like the second the other one stops, I know it's my mom, which means I've no choice but to pick up.

"Hey Mom," I say, trying to make my voice sound all thick and groggy and sick, yet not so sick that she'll rush home to save me.

But it's Marc who says, "Echo, it's me."

And my heart starts pounding hard in my chest, partly because I can't imagine why he'd risk calling me on this line, and partly because I can't imagine why he's calling me in the first place. I mean, not after last night. But still, I'm determined to sound cool, calm, and relaxed so he'll never guess just how spooked he's making me feel, so I clear my throat and say, "Oh hey, what's up?" Seemingly all normal, like it's just another day.

"Well, it's lunch, and since you're not here with me, and

since you're not at your old table with your friends, I figured you might be home. You feeling okay?" he asks in a voice that actually sounds concerned.

"Why are you calling me on this line?" I ask, choosing not to answer his question about whether or not I'm okay, since I'm really not sure of the answer myself.

"Because you didn't answer your cell," he says, sounding pretty matter-of-fact.

"But what if my parents answered? What would you do then?"

"I don't know. Hang up?" He laughs. "I guess I just assumed they were still at work, which means you're home alone, right?"

I'm not sure why, but I don't want him to know the answer to that. So I take a deep breath and say, "Maybe."

Which just makes him laugh even more. "Fine. Listen," he says. "I'm sorry about last night. And I'm totally willing to blow off the rest of my classes so I can come over and see you. I think it's time I explain a few things, I think it's the least I can do."

"There's really nothing to explain," I say, wanting to sound blasé, but coming off more like edgy, paranoid, and totally freaked. Knowing I need answers, but not willing to get them from him.

"Trust me, there's plenty to explain. But I need to do it in person. I need you to understand. So is it okay if I come over?" he asks.

I grip the phone tightly, partly because my hand is totally shaking and partly because practically all of me is shaking. Then I take a deep breath and say, "No."

Then I hang up the phone, and check all three dead bolts.

Thirty

Since I'm already up, I go into my room and grab my cell, scrolling through the missed calls and finding one from Marc and one from Teresa, but nothing from Abby or Jenay, which makes me feel even worse than I thought it would. Then I put on some old, thick socks, 'cause I can't stand it when my feet get cold, and bring my phone back to the den, where Zoë's diary is waiting.

"What do you mean you read my file?" His jaw was all clenched and his eyes blazed with so much anger he was actually starting to scare me.

And with everything out there in the big wide open, I knew it was time to explain. "Listen," I said. "Promise you won't get mad and think that I'm checking up on you or spying on you or something, okay? But the truth is you've been acting really weird lately, lying to me, keeping secrets, and don't even try to deny it 'cause we both know it's true. And then when I saw you going into the office that day, the same day you said you were home, well, it made me really suspicious."

The second I gazed up at him I knew it wasn't going so well. So I started talking even faster, just hoping to get through it before something really bad happened. "And then Carly said we should go to the office and get to the bottom of it, though it's not like I'm blaming Carly or anything, I mean, obviously, the choice was all mine. So, well anyway, we went and let ourselves in, and when I saw Dr. Kenner was there we almost fled, but when he saw me he was all, 'Oh Zoë, excellent. My assistant just called out sick for tomorrow, so would you mind filling in? I know you're on vacation, but I'll pay you double to just answer the phone and let people in, and it's only for half the day since my wife can take over in the afternoon, blah blah blah, what do you say?' So I said yes. But then as it turned out I only had to stay for like forty-five minutes, 'cause his wife got there way early, though it was still long enough for me to read the first few pages of your file."

I stopped, looked up at him, and held my breath.

"So you read my file," he said, more like a fact than a question, and his lips were all pressed together and his eyes looked grim. "Or excuse me, only part of my file. Only the first few pages," he added, his voice sounding sarcastic and mad.

And it's not like I didn't already feel pretty horrible about doing that, but hearing him say it out loud made me feel even worse.

"I can't believe this shit," he said. "I can't believe you!" Then he threw his napkin down, pushed his seat away, and acted like he was about to storm out or something.

"What're you doing?" I whispered, glancing around frantically, just as the waitress appeared with our meals.

"I'm outta here," he said, as she just stood there, gaping at us, and holding our plates, probably thinking, And a BIG happy anniversary to you too!

"You can just take that away and bring me the check," Marc said, speaking to her, even though his eyes were fixed on mine.

I watched the waitress leave, then looked at him and said, "Fine. Just let me call my dad then. I'm sure he'll be willing to come pick me up, especially when I explain to him why." My face felt all hot as my eyes clogged with tears, and I was hoping that if nothing else, that would make him feel bad.

Well it must've worked cuz he just sighed and said, "Leave your parents out of this. You know I'll take you home." Then he shook his head and flipped through the bills in his wallet, throwing down more than enough to cover our appetizers, Cokes, and uneaten meals.

Then we left the restaurant and got into the car, neither one of us speaking the entire way home. And with each passing street, I felt sicker and sicker, knowing full well that I'd gone way too far, but still hoping for some kind of answer.

But when he got to my house he just hit the brakes.

And as I opened the door I looked at him and said, "I just don't understand why you feel like you can't trust me enough to confide in me."

But he just shook his head and said, "I think you just proved it."

August 29

Well, I guess the fact that we haven't talked for days means we either broke up or that we're on a break, which, no matter how you slice it, is basically the same damn thing. And while part of me is totally bummed by the fact *that he ditched me, the other part, the smarter part, knows it's completely my fault.*

But still, with my vacation ending, summer ending, and only one final week left at my job, I guess maybe it's pretty much the end of a lot of things, including us. Even though I really hope that's not true.

But for now I'm just gonna try to work as much as I can, save as much as I can, try not to dwell on the whole mess with Marc, and finally get around to contacting that photographer guy so I can get his rates and see just how much my big lifelong dream is gonna cost me. But the one good thing is that with Marc out of the picture, all of those things just became that much easier.

I just wish I didn't miss him so much.

Sept 9

Okay, so I haven't written in awhile because a lot has been happening, and I've been way too busy to write it all down. For starters, my job recently ended, with a hand-shake, a glowing report for my parents, a good reference for my resume (like anyone in Hollywood is going to care), and a nice, fat bonus check—yay me!

And then school started, which, surprisingly, isn't nearly as bad as it sounds, except for the fact that I keep running into Marc practically everywhere I go, and since he still won't talk to me, it can get kind of awkward.

Also, I e-mailed that photographer guy and he got right back to me, and the good news is he's way more affordable than I thought he would be. And just as I was about to schedule an appt for next week, Carly goes, "Um, maybe you want to hold off for a while, you know, so you can work out a little first."

Which made me go, "Excuse me, are you calling me fat?"

But she just shook her head and said, "No, of course not! But what I am saying is that skinny means different things in different cities. Like thin in New York and L.A. is probably way totally different than thin here. You know, like a Saks Fifth Avenue versus Wal-Mart kind of thing."

And the more I thought about it, the more I realized she was probably right. So I decided to give myself ten to twelve days of laying off the chips and Cokes and pot smoking (since pot smoking makes me crave chips and Cokes), and start actually participating in PE (as opposed to my usual avoidance of all things physical), and start swimming laps in Carly's pool (as opposed to lazing around and eating chips and drinking Coke and smoking pot).

I'm also trying to lose a little bit of my tan. Not all of it mind you, but definitely some of it. Because as Carly pointed out, the models in Vogue are always way skinny and way pasty, yet in Hollywood the celebs are all way skinny (not counting the implants) and way tan. And since I'm basically interested in doing either if not both, I figure it's probably better if I strive for somewhere in between.

Anyway, I'm really excited about this upcoming shoot, and have even been playing around with some possible outfits and hairstyles so I can show different looks and different sides to my personality and stuff. But then Carly said I should strive for pretty, unadorned, and natural, like Kate Moss in the early days. She says they mostly want chameleons who can easily change from season to season, and even though I have no idea how she actually knows all this stuff, since it's not like she cares about being a model or a movie star, I still gotta admit it makes perfect sense.

And even though I kind of wish I could share all this with Marc, I know it's probably all for the best. I mean, especially since it's not even an option anymore. Especially now that I keep seeing him hanging with that Shauna chick. And I don't mean hanging like they're all casual and stuff, because, please, it's not like I'm some psychotic jealous person. It's more the way that they're hanging, they way they act when they're talking. Like him leaning toward her, and her all happy and smiling and stuff. Like there's no one else around. Like they're in their own little world.

Just like we used to be.

The first time I saw them together I just stood there gaping, my mouth hanging open, my chin on my knees. And when she reached out and touched him, placing her hand right there on his shoulder, I was consumed with this indescribable, jealous, flood of rage. But eventually it mostly passed.

I mean, clearly we're not together anymore, no longer a couple. And it's time I get used to it.

Sept 10

Good news! Carly has finally stopped with all those crazy Web page hookups and trolling for alcohol with all those perverted geezers she was meeting on the Internet, and I could not be more relieved. Though it's not like she stopped because she figured out that what she was doing was dangerous, stupid, and completely freaking lame.

Nope, it was mainly because she met someone better. Someone who she thinks is hot, sexy, and a total keeper. Someone who rarely makes her pay, and when he does it's at a deeply discounted rate. He also happens to live in our town, even graduated from our high school. Though to be honest, I'm really not so sure that he actually graduated, because he doesn't seem like the type to heed authority or wear a cap and gown, so he might've just stopped going.

Anyway, his name is Jason—don't know his last— and I guess if you were standing really far away, with no binoculars, and were also very drunk, you might think that he's hot. Or at least that's what I thought the first time I met him. He's definitely kind of snakelike with that slicked-back hair, lean muscled body that he crams into these fitted faded jeans, black leather jacket, and motorcycle boots he always wears. But I guess he's kind of starting to grow on me too, since there's just something about him, something kind of alluring and dangerous and sleazy but cool. Which I know probably sounds pretty weird and all, but I don't know how else to explain it. Not to mention how he pretty much knows everyone in this town, or at least all of the people who party, and so far he's been more than willing to hook Carly up with whatever it is that she wants.

Anyway, the other night Carly and I ended up over there, just hanging out and talking with a whole group of people, and pretty much everyone was drinking but me (since I don't need the extra calories, not to mention the puffiness before the big shoot), and I was just kicking back and sipping from my water bottle, when he said, "Here, try some of these, they'll help you lose weight."

And I immediately looked at Carly, feeling all freaked and upset that she told him about my plans, because I really don't need a whole bunch of people to know about it before it's even had a chance to happen. But she just shrugged and shook her head, and motioned to me to go ahead and take 'em.

So then I looked at him, but he just laughed and said, "Pretty girl like you, avoiding the appetizers and beer and settling for just water, I figure you're just trying to stay pretty."

Okay, trying to pretend that smashed-up pieces of BBQ potato chips are actually appetizers is totally pushing it. But still, I took the bottle from him, and turned it around so I could squint at the back. Because let's face it, it's no secret that this guy is like our hometown version of Scarface, so the last thing I need is to get all hooked on crystal meth or something equally nasty that will make me skinny but leave me with no teeth.

But then he showed me where it says "All natural." And so with everyone watching and egging me on, I popped one in my mouth and chased it down with some water. And for the rest of the night everyone kept joking around and pretending that I was Alice through the Looking Glass, or Wonderland, or whatever (I mean, I really don't know the difference) and that I was getting smaller and smaller, 'til they could no longer see me.

And then, when it finally came time to leave, Jason kissed me on the cheek, his lips moving against my skin as he said, "You can thank me when you're posing on the cover of Maxim."

And even though Maxim isn't my number one goal (because that would be Vogue) it was still kind of cool to know that he thinks I have the potential. But I just smiled, and then the second I heard the door close behind us I rubbed my fingers over my cheek, removing the trace of his lips and wiping it onto my jeans.

Sept 14
So the last few days we've been hanging with Jason more and more after school, mostly because Carly is becoming a total burnout and is now totally hooked on some shit he sells her for cheap. And the only reason I even go along is so she doesn't go by herself, because she's seriously starting to worry me lately.

And then today, when I was walking home from school (by myself because Carly got detention for sneaking off campus and getting caught), he just happened to drive up and offer me a ride.

And I was just about to say no, 'cause I wasn't sure it was such a great idea to be in his truck alone with him, when I realized how totally stupid that was since I've been hanging with him like practically every day, and it's not like he's ever tried anything before. In fact, he's always been really super sweet. But even so, I was still about to say no, when I glanced over just in time to see Marc getting into his car and Shauna climbing in beside him.

So then I turned and looked at Jason, and said, "A ride would be great, thanks!"

And as I climbed up in his truck and closed the door, I glanced out the window just in time to see Marc staring at me. I mean serious, outright gaping. Just like I did when I first saw them. Then the light turned green, and Jason totally punched it, and in a matter of seconds they were left in our dust.

Sept 15

Jason picked me up from school again today, just like yesterday. Only this time he waited right there in the parking lot, instead of out by the corner like usual.

"Carly still on detention?" he asked.

And I just nodded and climbed in beside him.

At first he acted like he was going to drive me straight home, but then we somehow ended up at his apartment. Which even though it's not the first time I'd been there, it was the first time I'd been there on a bright sunny day, which just made it look even more shabby and messy than before. Not that I ever thought it was a palace or anything, but still, with the crappy stained couch and the dirty coffee table, it kinda makes you wonder where all the drug money goes.

So he grabbed a beer for himself and a glass of water for me, and even though he didn't actually make a move or try anything, I still felt kind of nervous to be sitting in the living room, just me and him, with no one else around. I mean, I found myself actually hoping for that retarded Tom guy to drop by, just to cut some of the tension.

I'm not sure why I was feeling like that, because obviously I'm free to do whatever with whoever. Though I think it's pretty obvious how hooking up with Jason would be a really bad idea. I mean, there are bad boys and then there are bad boys.

But since I didn't want him to know just how weirded out he was making me feel, I made a pact with myself that I'd be polite and hang for a half an hour or so, and then fake some excuse so I could bail out of there and make it home way before my parents.

He propped his boot-clad feet right on top of his filthy glass coffee table, then he started talking about a bunch of VIPs he claims to know in New York, L.A., and Vegas, and all kinds of other nonsense that really made me wonder if any of it could possibly be true.

And then for some reason I started to feel really really sleepy, and after like my third yawn in a row, he goes, "Am I boring you?"

And I felt so guilty I said, "No, of course not. I guess I just didn't sleep all that well last night, that's all." Which wasn't at all true, but still, I didn't want to be rude.

So then he said, "Well, why don't you lay down for a while and chill? I can take you home later." Then he smiled in a way that was trying to be more convincing than kind.

But I just shook my head and said, "No, I should probably get going. Do you mind taking me now?"

And right when he smiled and opened his mouth to speak, Carly knocked on the door.

"Hey, you guys. Got out early. Coach Warner got called away on some kind of family emergency, so he had no choice but to let us all go."

She plopped down on the couch, right beside Jason and smiled in a way that clearly showed how she didn't give a shit about the coach or his family. And it's not like I care about him either, I mean, so many times I've wanted to bust him for looking down my top, but still, a family emergency is never a good thing. Though in this case, I guess it was for Carly.

Jason immediately went to hand her his bong, but Carly just as quickly brushed it away. "Forget it. I've got to stop smoking. I'm getting fat, and my jeans are totally starting to strangle me," she said.

But he just laughed. "I got something to help you with that," he told her.

And she went, "What? They invented a Nicorette patch for burnouts?"

He smiled. "Even better."

"What, like those hippie herbal pills you give Zoë? No thanks," she said, shaking her head.

But he just got up and went into the kitchen (which is basically still in the same room, just over on the other side) and when he came back over he had these two pills in his hand. And when he gave them to Carly, she said, "What's this?"

And he smiled and said, "Zero-calorie, feel-good E."

And she goes, "Omigod, this is ecstasy? I've totally been wanting to try it." Then right before she places it on her tongue she squints at him and goes, "Wait, how much?"

But he just smiled and said, "Now baby you know me, the first three's always free."

So she grabbed my bottle of water and started to take them both, but before she could do that he grabbed her wrist and said, "Hold up, only one of those is yours. The other one's for Zoë."

And so she gave me the other one, and since I've always kind of wanted to try it too, and since I knew it would be safer if we did it together, I just popped it in my mouth then washed it down with a big swig of water.

It was only much later, on the way home, when I started to wonder if that was really E.

Sept 16
Okay, I didn't write this earlier because I'm really freaking out, and I'm not sure I even want to actually sit down and think about it, much less write about it. But at the same time I don't feel like I can allow this to just live in my head because it's starting to feel like way too much for me to hold on to. And since Marc's not around (not like I could ever tell him anyway) and since no way am I discussing it with Carly since she's partly responsible, I guess I'll just have to settle for here.

So let's just say that by the time Jason dropped me off, I was feeling like shit. I mean, seriously messed up and tired and clammy and nauseous, and just basically like total crap. And just as I was making my way up the drive, Marc stepped out from where he was waiting by the tree and said, "Did you have a good time?"

But I wasn't up for any of that. I was seriously upset, and all I wanted was to take a megahot long shower then go straight to bed. So I just shook my head and moved past him, intent on getting to the door without any more hassles, noticing how my mouth still tasted like vomit from when I got sick.

"I want to know if you had a good time with Jason," he said, grabbing my arm now, his fingers squeezing hard and tight.

And just as I was trying to yank my arm away, the

193

porch light went on and my dad opened the door, took one look at me, the way Marc was gripping my arm, and said, "Let go of my daughter."

So of course Marc immediately let go and started backing away. "I'm sorry," he said, both hands raised in surrender. "But you've got it all wrong. It's not what you think."

I just stood there, my forehead pressed against the door, my breath coming slow and weak, listening to my dad's voice, all hard and serious as he said, "I want you to get in your car and go home. And I don't ever want to see you anywhere near my daughter again, understood?"

And even though I wanted to explain how it wasn't at all like he thought, I couldn't. So I made my way upstairs and into my room, where I stripped off my clothes and went straight for the shower.

Great, my mom's knocking. Apparently it's dinnertime, so I guess I'll continue this later.

Later, though still Sept 16

So where was I? Oh yeah, so there are these bruises on my arm that my dad saw the next morning and just naturally assumed were from Marc. And even though I did my best to explain how he had it all wrong and how Marc would never ever do something like that, he still refused to believe me.

He just sat down beside me and gave me some lecture about Those Kinds of Guys. The kind who first charm you, then abuse you. He also told me that if he ever saw him near me again, then he'd . . . but thank G he just left that last part hanging.

And while in a way it was kind of sweet to see my dad get all protective and worked up like that—because let's face it, my family totally sucks at anything remotely emotional—*the fact is, it was all so misguided. Besides, it's not like I had any real faith in my dad's ass-kicking abilities. I mean, he'd seriously be lucky if he could bench-press an encyclopedia.*

Though it's not like I could even try to tell him the real truth. I mean, I'm barely willing to admit it to myself.

Because even though he thinks Marc's to blame, the truth is I know it's from what happened at Jason's. And the horrible things he made me and Carly do.

And even though I was so messed up that a lot of it's still pretty fuzzy, what I do remember really makes me wonder just exactly what it was that he gave us. Because only something really hard-core could get me to do what I did.

Especially in front of a camera.

I shut the diary and stare before me, unable to focus, my mind reeling from the things I'd just read—all the horrible things my sister endured, the secrets she kept that few people knew.

But I don't judge her. And not once while reading that did I shake my head and think, *You should've known better.*

Because Zoë's sweet, trusting nature was the biggest part of her. Her unruly optimism is what drew people to her. And it was unfortunate that not all of those people meant as well as she.

She warned me about Jason though, in her own indirect way. She called me into her room one day and showed me a photo she'd kept on her cell phone of her and Carly and some guy with slick blond hair and a black leather jacket. "You see this creep?" she'd said, stabbing his face with the tip of her fingernail. "Stay far away from him. I'm serious, Echo, promise me that if you ever see him somewhere you'll just turn around and walk the other way, okay? Promise?"

I leaned in and peered at the tiny thumbnail, then

shrugged and turned to leave. But she refused to let me off that easy, so she made me look again. Which is the only reason I recognized him in the park that first day.

Zoë was just trying to protect me, in the way that she failed to protect herself. She was always telling me to look out, to not be so trusting, to run away if my instincts suggested it, to act in a way that she didn't.

And it makes me wonder if maybe I'd been a year or so older, or even just acted a little more mature, if she would've eventually felt safe enough to confide in me.

But then again, probably not. Zoë always made it her job to protect me, even if it meant protecting me from herself.

I close my eyes, afraid of what else I might read, but knowing I need to continue. Then I think about Teresa and her infatuation with Jason, and grab my cell, knowing I have to try to warn her, even if she doesn't want to listen.

When she doesn't pick up, I leave a message. Then I chase it with a text, asking her to call me, explaining that it's urgent.

Thirty-one

Sept 17

For the last two days I've done my best to avoid Carly,
which believe me, has not gone over so well. Especially after the bell rang and it was time to walk home and both
times I didn't want to be anywhere near her. I mean, I'm
sorry but I just can't go acting like everything's all fine and
normal and like that whole disgusting day in Jason's filthy
apartment never even happened. And the fact that she can
just makes me want to avoid her even more.

So just when I thought it was safe, she saw me and was
all, "Hey, wait up! Zoë, jeez! Are you avoiding me?" she
asked as she ran to catch up with me.

I just took a deep breath and looked at her, having
made up my mind not to lie. "Yes," I said, my eyes right on
hers the whole time.

"And can I ask why?" She stood there, hands on hips, looking all mad and indignant and bitchy.

"Do I really need to explain?" I picked up the pace.

"Well, I guess not. But I really don't get why you're so freaked. I mean, what's the big deal? It's not like anyone will ever know."

I just looked at her and rolled my eyes, thinking she was so frustratingly lame, and wondering how we ever became friends. Then I said, "Well, you know what, Carly? I know. And you know. And Jason knows. And since he got it all on tape, it's just a matter of time before the whole freaking world knows! Don't you get it?"

But she just shrugged, like it's not a big deal, which made me even madder.

So I said, "I can't believe you did this to me. I can't believe you put me in that position!"

But she just goes, "It's not like anyone held a gun to your head, so stop acting like such a little effin baby. And let's just get one thing straight. Nobody made anyone do anything they weren't willing to do, okay? You were there of your own free will. Which means you also participated of your own free will."

But no way was I letting her off that easy, so I said, "Oh really, is it still free will if I'm all messed up on something he gave me? Something that I'm really starting to doubt was E? Because I think he gave us something else, Carly. I think he gave us something way worse."

But she just looked away and rolled her eyes, making it perfectly clear she thought I was overreacting. "Yeah? Well, it's not like he slipped it in your drink or anything. You took it right out of my hand, and nobody forced you to do that, Zoë."

And hearing her say that made me so mad I started to shake, probably because I knew in a way it was true. But also because I couldn't stop thinking about that glass of water he gave me, and how tired I felt after just a few sips. Though it's not like I could prove anything, and it's not like Carly would even care. So I just shook my head and said, "But still, don't you realize how messed up this all is? Don't you realize how this will all come back to haunt us? Stuff like this always does, there's just no avoiding it."

But she just rolled her eyes and went, "Relax, already. It's not like it hurt Paris Hilton's career. Or Pamela Anderson's. Or half of Hollywo—

But before she could finish that, I was already gone. And when I got to the parking lot, I saw Shauna kissing Marc.

And seeing them together like that made me burst into tears, and I took off running, just as fast as I could, wishing I could just keep going, just run without stopping 'til I reached the other side of the world.

Sept 19

My dreams are getting worse, and all the stress and lack of sleep is starting to make me look totally haggard. Seriously. I mean, my skin looks so bad I actually considered canceling the photo shoot. But then I realized how now more than ever I need to do whatever it takes to get the hell out of here so I never have to see Carly, or Jason, or anyone else in this stupid fucking town ever again.

I need to go somewhere new, someplace where I can start fresh. And then someday when I'm rich and famous, I'll get hold of that tape and destroy it.

Marc came up to me today at school, when I was standing at my locker, between classes. I was just switching out my books, when he leaned in and said, "Zoë."

That's it. All he said was my name, and I totally crumbled. Started bawling like a big pathetic baby. All of my worry, fear, and anxiety, all of my despair over the tape and my heartache over missing him and seeing how he'd already moved on to someone else, it all got mixed together and just came pouring out in a tsunami of emotion.

But he just held me close, keeping me tight against his chest as he stroked my hair and whispered in my ear. And when I still couldn't stop, he said, "Come on. Let's get out of here." Then he grabbed my hand and led me away.

We went to the park to feed our ducks. And at first we didn't speak much, but then once we got started, we could hardly stop. And I apologized for snooping in his file, and for getting so upset, and he apologized for getting so mad and avoiding me like that. Then just as I was feeling really really close to him, close enough to confide about the whole mess with Jason, he mentioned Shauna. Telling me how it didn't mean anything, how she was a nice girl and all, but still, a very poor substitute for me.

So I held my tongue, and didn't say a word. Reminding myself how he wouldn't really want to know, and how it was far better to just keep quiet.

Though I did say that if he wanted to be back together with me, then he was never allowed to call Shauna again. And he agreed.

Then he told me all about Dr. Kenner, and how he started seeing him way back when his dad first went to jail and his mom started boozing and sleeping around on a regular basis, and how he was so full of rage and anger that he basically went kind of nuts and ended up vandalizing one of the buildings at his private school. At first his mom was able to keep it quiet by paying for the damage, pulling him out, and enrolling him somewhere else, but at the next school it was basically the exact same thing, and it pretty much went on like that until they ran out of expensive schools. So I guess Bella Vista and Dr. Kenner were pretty much his last great hope, since if he messed up again he'd be headed straight to juvie, no matter how much money his mom threw at the courts.

He said it all worked out for the best though, since Dr. Kenner really helped him find his way through all the really bad stuff, and he learned how to control his anger and channel it into other things, like fixing cars and music and books and stuff like that. It's also part of the reason why he doesn't like to drink. He said now that he knows what it's like to be in control, he doesn't ever want to risk losing that again.

So I went, "But why didn't you tell me all this before? Why'd you keep it a secret?"

And he said, "I was about to tell you when I found out where you worked, but the way you made fun of the patients, well, I didn't want you to see me like that."

I just nodded, feeling so incredibly awful for being so insensitive and making him feel bad. And I also felt so guilty when I realized how he'd confided all of his secrets, but I was still keeping mine.

But then he said, "The only thing that could ever make me fly off the handle again is to see you anywhere near Jason. That guy is total trash, and I want you to stay away from him, okay?"

Then he held my chin, and made me face him. And his eyes were so dark and severe, I just nodded, and quickly looked away.

Later, when Marc drove me home, all the cars were gone so I invited him inside, and I found a note from my mom telling how she and my dad and Echo went for pizza and a movie and how they'd all be back later.

So it didn't take long for Marc to coax me upstairs, obviously looking forward to a little make-up sex. And even though at first I thought I wanted it too, once he started kissing me, I just couldn't go through with it.

But when I tried to roll over and push him away, wanting for him to just hold me and love me and keep me safe, he got upset.

"C'mon Zoë, I've missed you so much," he whispered.

But I ignored him and just closed my eyes, trying not to think about Carly and me and Jason's camera. Not to mention Shauna and Marc and what they might've done together.

"What gives?" he asked, kissing the back of my neck and reaching around for my breasts.

But I just pulled the covers over me, and said, "Nothing, jeez." Then I rolled my eyes, but it's not like he could see.

"Then why are you covering yourself?" he asked, refusing to just hold me and let the rest go.

"'Cause I'm cold," I said, going right back to lying again.

But it was clear he didn't believe me. "Does this have anything to do with Jason?" he asked. "Is there something I need to know?"

And even though every part of me was screaming YES, desperate to finally unload this burden so I wouldn't have to carry it alone, I knew that I couldn't. Because when I finally turned to face him, feeling ready and willing to talk, I saw that his eyes were dark and angry for the second time today.

And suddenly I understood how someone as sweet and mellow as he could set fires, break windows, and tear things apart. And all I wanted was for him to leave.

I turned so we were no longer facing each other, then I closed my eyes and said, "What's the matter, Marc, Shauna left you hanging too?"

Then he grabbed hold of my arms, but released them just as quickly. Then he got up from the bed, grabbed his clothes, and fled.

And I lay there like that, 'til long after he left, wondering who I should fear more, Jason or Marc?

I'm almost at the end. The end of the diary, the end of Zoë. And even though I'm desperate to finish, I'm just as reluctant to say good-bye. I gaze over at the clock, seeing how it's well past two, and wonder if Abby and Jenay will talk about me on the way home, or if they're so glad to be rid of me they've already moved on.

I still have time to burn before my mom comes home, and you can pretty much double that for my dad. And wanting to just take my time with the last few pages, I set it on the coffee table and go outside.

Winter has already edged out fall, having moved in quickly with its crisp cold air and warm clean scent of wood fireplace logs—two things I always look forward to. And as I walk around my mom's formerly well-tended but now much-neglected garden, I notice how the spring blooms, having gone completely ignored, are now either all shriveled up and hanging by a sliver or rotting away on the ground, their stalks bent down by their sides. And I wonder if my mom will ever put on her hat and gloves and venture back out here, redis-covering the things that once brought her such joy. Or if this is how we'll always live now, just barely cared for but mostly untended.

I shiver against the wind, my worn sweatpants, thin T-shirt, and thick socks with the big gaping hole in the heel providing a pretty pathetic shield. But still, it's not like I move for cover, or even think about going inside. Instead I just stand there, rubbing my arms for warmth, feeling grateful to have a prob-lem with such an obvious solution.

Reading Zoë's diary has left me on shaky emotional ground, and I feel like I'm living on a fault line, where my moods rise and fall with every slight shift, while the world I'd once known quakes precariously around me.

So compared to all that, Old Lady Winter is pretty much a wimp.

I stay out a while longer, watching my neighbor's black cat delicately pick his way across the top of our fence before jumping down to the other side. Then I head for the door, closing it quickly behind me when I hear my phone beeping in the den, and someone banging hard against the front door.

Thirty-two

You'd think that at some point during my parents' marathon of paranoia, somewhere around the time when they were installing the third dead bolt, they would've noticed how the front door is surrounded by glass. And not stained glass, or bathroom glass, or any other kind of glass that has bumps and colors that do a fine job of distorting an image. Nope, I'm talking plain, old, clear glass, the kind you can see right through.

But somehow they missed that.

Which leaves me face-to-face with Marc.

"Hey," he says, waving from the other side. "It took you forever to answer and I was worried. Let me in."

I watch him standing there waving, part of me about to obey, while the other part freezes. And suddenly I wish I'd skipped the little backyard field trip and just finished that diary once and for all.

"Whose car is that?" I ask, gazing at a bright red, vintage MG now parked on my driveway.

"Let me in and I'll tell you," he says, nodding and smiling, so sure that I will.

But I just shake my head and turn away, moving back toward the den where I sit on the couch, listening as he bangs on the door, saying things like, "Echo, please. I can explain. I want to explain. But you have to let me in."

But I just pick up my cell to check my voice mail, breathing a sigh of relief when I hear Marc finally drive away.

"Echo, hey, it's so weird you called me and said that it's urgent and all, because I really need to talk to you too. So if you could, oh shit, here comes Ms. Jenkins." Then I listen as Teresa says in her sweet, obedient voice, "It's off! I swear, look!" And then she whispers, "Jeez, okay, anyway, it's about—hey, give it ba—!"

And even though her phone is most likely in Ms. Jenkins's possession, I dial her number anyway. But when she doesn't answer, I know the next move is hers.

Sept 21

I don't know what I was thinking when I scheduled this appointment, because if I thought I could just stroll off campus with a duffel bag full of makeup and clothes that I'd managed to hide all day from Marc by keeping it stashed in my gym locker, then shame on me because that was one stupid, not-so-well-thought-out plan.

And since I'm no longer talking to Carly, which means I'm not talking to Paula all that much either (since they're always together now), it's not like I had anyone left to help me pull this off. So I just figured that the second the final bell rang, I'd try to grab all my stuff and skip out.

But guess who was already there, standing by my locker, waiting?

Okay, I know I didn't write yesterday, cuz I was just way too busy getting everything organized, so let me just say that a couple hours after Marc left, he called to apologize, and then way later he came back over and I snuck him into my room and he just held me while I slept. And when I woke up in the middle of the night he was already gone, and then yesterday at school we both acted like none of the bad stuff ever happened, that I never said that shit about Shauna, and that he never got angry about Jason, and that we were never really broken up to begin with. And since that's the way I actually wanted things to be, it was pretty easy to play along and pretend.

And then late last night I snuck out and went to his place since his mom and stepdad are out of town, and we went skinny-dipping, hung in the Jacuzzi, then slept together in the bed in the pool house. Then just before the sun came up, he drove me home. And right before climbing back up the tree, I kissed him good-bye. And at that moment I knew I was being given a second chance, that we really could start over. I just hoped I would be smart enough not to blow it.

So anyway, this is the first time I've ever carried my diary with me, the first time I ever took it out of the house, and even though I keep kind of freaking out and double-checking to make sure I didn't lose it (I mean, can you even imagine?), today is such a humongo big day that I just feel like I should document every single second of it, since it's the first day of taking the first step toward changing my entire life! Not to mention how when I become really rich and famous, they'll probably ask me to write my memoirs, and I can use this as a guide.

Anyway, I feel so incredibly good about this meeting—I've lost six pounds, not that I even needed to, but since the camera does add ten, I figure it can't hurt—and I even found this amazing new cover stick that is totally working at hiding the dark circles and all the other signs of worry, stress, and major lack of sleep. And it's just so amazing how it's all falling so smoothly into place. I mean, before all this came together, I was never all that big on destiny. I mean, yeah, I would joke about it and stuff, but that doesn't mean I actually really believed in it. I just always figured that you get to where you want to go by working hard and totally going for it—not by any kind of cosmic energy, or whatever. But now, with the way it's all moving forward, I just know deep down inside that it's totally meant to be.

So anyway, when Marc saw me at my locker with my overstuffed bag, he just looked at me, and said, "What's that?"

Well, at first I tried to lie and tell him I was getting a bunch of clothes taken in since I'd lost all that weight. But when it was clear he wasn't buying it, I told him I was auditioning for a play, and that I was too freaked out, nervous, and superstitious to say anything more about it.

"Just a community theater thing, no biggie. I'm just doing it for the experience," I said.

"Can I come?" he asked.

But I told him no. Told him that he'd make me too nervous, and that I didn't even want him to drive me. I'd just planned to take the bus, which meant I needed to leave right away, since it'd take me a whole lot longer to get there like that (which isn't even a full lie, because I had planned to take the bus to the photo shoot).

So he just looked at me and said, "How 'bout I drive you and pick you up after?"

And I said, "No way, Jose. In fact, I don't even want to talk about it afterward, unless of course they cast me, then I'll bore you to death with all the details."

So he goes, "Well then how 'bout this—we go to the

park, hang for a while, and then you take my car and come pick me up when you're done?"

"But I don't know how long it will take! I mean, you're just gonna sit there that whole time?" I asked, part of me really wanting the car since it would make everything so much easier, but the other part not wanting to be responsible for picking him up. I mean, what if it runs late? But still, having the car will really help, so I agreed.

Okay, so I just wrote all that in the parking lot of the Circle K, where he just went in to get us some snacks and waters and cigarettes and bread for our pet ducks. And now he's back so—

"Thank you darling," I say, wanting a ciggie big-time but knowing I can't write and open the pack at the same time. But really, what's more important, smoking or recording all the little mundane things that happen to me while I'm still anonymous?

So he goes, "What are you writing about that's making you so happy?"

Then he acts like he's trying to peek over my shoulder, so I pull it away and say, "You have no idea."

So we're at the park now, and I'm feeding the ducks while Marc starts on his homework and then he looks at me and goes, "So what play are you trying out for?"

And since I'm more into movies, and don't really know any plays, I go, "Phantom of the Opera." And believe me, the second it's out, I regret it.

So he looks at me and goes, "I didn't know you could sing opera." Then he gives me this suspicious squinty kind of look.

But I think I pulled it off, cuz I just said, "I don't, silly. It's for a nonsinging part. A really small part, in fact, and *it's really no big deal. I just think it will be good experience to go to an audition and see what it's like to be onstage with everyone watching you and stuff."* And since it seems like he might actually believe that I add, *"But what about you? Are you really just gonna sit here and wait?"*

And he smiles and goes, *"Yup."*

And I go, *"But what if you get bored, or need to go home or something?"*

But he just shakes his head and says, *"No worries, I'll handle it. Just don't forget to come back for me."* Then he jangles his car keys as he starts to hand them over.

And I go, *"Please, I could never forget you,"* then I lean in and kiss him, and reach for the keys.

But then he goes, *"Wait, I want something in return."*

I just looked at him, thinking I should've known better, 'cause there's always a catch. *"What?"* I ask.

"Your diary," he says. *"Leave me your diary just to make sure."*

"Make sure of what?"

"To make sure you come back to me. You know, like collateral?" He smiles.

"You're not gonna read it, are you?" I ask, still wanting those keys but not liking the trade, and wondering if I can trust him to really not read it.

But he just gives me a serious look, and says, *"Only if you don't come back."* Then he leans in and kisses me, and says, *"And when you return, I have a major surprise for you. Something you're gonna love, that will also explain everything, everything you've been wondering about where I was those times when you couldn't reach me. I just want us to rewind, to get back to where we were. I really love you, Zoë."*

So I say, *"And I really love you, Marc."*

Then he smiles and says, "Are you ever going to stop writing so I can kiss you and tell you good-bye?"

And I smile and say, "Yes!"

I turn the page but that's it. And every page that follows is as blank as the one before it, nothing but blue lines on white background, Zoë's loopy handwriting coming to its final rest.

I close my eyes and lean back against the cushions, tears pouring down my cheeks, thinking how strange it is that her diary ended on "Yes!" When her life probably ended on "No!"

I sit there, holding her book in my lap, unwilling to look at it, unable to let go.

And when my cell phone rings, I hit *speaker*, wiping my eyes as Teresa says, "Echo, I'm on my way over. We really need to talk."

Thirty-three

Seconds later when the doorbell rings, I assume Teresa was a lot closer than I'd thought. But when I peek through the glass and see Abby, my stomach drops so fast and hard it takes me a moment to realize that she's smiling as though yesterday never happened.

"Jeez, you really are sick. You look awful," she says, giving me a concerned once-over while maintaining a safe distance from any potential infectious disease.

"Relax, I'm fine," I tell her. "Seriously, it's safe to come in."

She gives me a hesitant look then steps inside, following me into the den, where she flops down on my dad's favorite chair, and goes, "So, what gives?"

But I just shake my head and sit on the couch, pulling the afghan around me, hugging my knees tight to my chest. "I've been going through some stuff," I finally say, knowing I owe her much more than that, but feeling unsure just how far I should go.

"I know." She nods.

"You know?" I ask, looking at her and wondering just how much she knows.

"Well, for starters, you've been acting pretty freaky since the first day of school. And then all that stuff yesterday, well, that was pretty much the pinnacle of your freakiness."

"Does Jenay hate me?" I ask.

She laughs. "Jenay's incapable of hate. She's all about love, pep rallies, and cheerleading tryouts."

"Seriously?"

"'Fraid so." Abby nods. "Tryouts are months away, but she's already talking about it. She wants to be able to cheer for Chess at all of his football games."

"Can't she do that from the stands?"

"Not like a professional." She smiles.

"So, do *you* hate me?" I ask, holding my breath.

"Honestly? I did. But then I got over it." She shrugs. "Because I know what you're going through. Okay, backtrack. Maybe I don't know *exactly* what you're going through. But sometimes I try to imagine it, you know? Like when Aaron's driving me nuts and I'm fantasizing about totally throttling him. Well, sometimes I make myself stop and imagine how I'd feel if he was no longer around for me to hate. And the truth is, as much as he annoys me, I know it would be a whole lot worse without him. And then that makes me think how bad it must suck for you to have to deal with all that, not to mention the way people stare and the things they say. And I don't mean like I pity you," she says quickly, knowing full well just how much I hate to be pitied. "It's just, I don't know, I guess I just want you to know that I care, and that I'm here, and that no matter how hard you try, you can't push me away. Or maybe

you can, but you're gonna have to try a lot harder than that."
She smiles, but her bottom lip is trembling. And seeing that
makes me feel unbelievably sad, especially when I realize how
willing I was to discard her.

"So where is Jenay?" I ask, anxious to change the subject.

"Pep club," she says, rolling her eyes. "But one more thing,
Echo, and then I promise to let it go. I just want you to know
that you can totally confide in me if you need to. Seriously, you
can tell me anything you want and I promise not to judge or
ever repeat a single word of it to anyone, including Jenay.
Scout's honor." She holds up her hand, palm facing forward,
even though we were never Scouts.

And when I look at her, I'm tempted, thinking how nice it
would be to get some of this burden off my chest, not to have
to bear all this weight on my own. But when I start to speak, I
realize there's still a few missing links, and I know I should
wait 'til I've gathered all the pieces.

So instead, I just shrug. "Rain check?" I ask, smiling as she
nods.

When the doorbell rings a few minutes later, this time it really
is Teresa. And when she comes in the den and sees Abby still
sitting in the chair she gives me a quick, worried look.

"I should probably go," Abby says, rising from her seat in
a rare display of submission.

I glance at Terersa, wondering if she'll insist on it, but she
just shrugs and sits on the floor.

"Oh my God." She drops her head in her hands and rubs
her eyes with the pads of her fingers. "I've been so fucking stupid and I owe you the hugest apology," she says, finally looking up at me, her eyes red and worried.

I glance at Abby, who's clearly wondering what this is

about, then I gaze back at Teresa when she says, "I need to talk to you about Jason."

"Who's Jason?" Abby asks, but when I look at her and shake my head, she goes quiet and leans back in her chair.

"Jason is a creep," Teresa says, gazing at Abby and shaking her head. "A total freaking psychotic creep. Echo tried to warn me, but I was too stupid to listen. I thought he was some sexy, exciting, bad boy. Turns out he's just bad."

"Are you okay? I mean, did he hurt you?" I ask, remembering what happened to Zoë and Carly, and hoping that didn't happen to her.

But she just shakes her head and closes her eyes, and when I glance over at Abby I can tell she's confused. "Well, you know how normally we just meet up at the park and hang out and stuff? Like we did that one day? And how every now and then he'd stop by my house and we'd party when my parents weren't home? Well, we did fool around, but only a few times, nothing major, basically because asshole Tom was usually there."

I glance at Abby when she starts to say, "Who's asshole To—" But then she looks at me and shakes her head, motioning for Teresa to continue.

"So yesterday, I was on my way home from school when he drove up and offered me a ride. And since no one was around to see me, I opened the door and got in."

"Did you go to his place?" I ask, remembering Zoë and how he used the same M.O. on her.

She rolls her eyes and nods. "Jeez, you should see it, I mean, it's a total freaking dump. I mean a filthy, cheap, disgusting mess."

And just as I start to say, "I know," I remember how I do know, and not wanting to share that with them, I don't say anything.

"So he offers me a beer, and like the idiot I am, I'm all excited that we're finally gonna hook up, since we're all alone and stuff. So, thinking I should go freshen up a little first, I head for his bathroom as he heads for the fridge, and then I notice how the bathroom door is like right across from his bedroom, and I'm really tempted to open the door and take a look, but I'm also afraid of getting caught. So instead I just go inside and do my thing and right as I come out, I see him sitting on the couch with his index finger all shoved down the neck of my beer bottle. And I think, *what the heck is he doing?* And I start to feel all creeped out, wondering if he's trying to poison me or drug me or something. So then I get all panicked, wondering what I should do. But then I decide to just act all smiley and calm until I can eventually find a way out of there." Then she stops and looks at Abby and goes, "Do you think you can get me some water?"

And before I can even say anything, Abby is already up and heading for the kitchen. Teresa turns to me and whispers, "So anyway, I just try to act all normal, tapping my bottle against his, taking fake sips, and then right when I'm about to make an excuse to get out of there, his beeper goes off. So he goes, 'I have to run out for a sec, so sit tight and don't go snooping around.' And when he gives me this threatening look, I just smile and nod and take another fake sip, and then like the second he leaves I'm about to bail, but then I wonder if maybe I'm overreacting. I mean, maybe he was just fishing a bug out of my beer, which is still pretty bad, though it's not the same as drugging someone, right?"

Abby comes back with the water, and after taking a quick sip, Teresa looks at me and hesitates. "Should I continue?"

And since I have no idea where this is going, I really don't know how to answer. But I also don't feel like I can just kick Abby out, not after the way I've treated her. So I just shrug, letting Teresa decide. Then she takes another sip and goes,

"Okay, so anyway, I decided to check out his bedroom, since the fact that he warned me not to snoop just made me want to do it even more. But then the second I open the bedroom door, I know where all of his money goes." She looks at us and rolls her eyes. "He's got this huge, four-poster bed, with these serious-looking, black leather restraints attached to all the posts, and there're these two video cameras on tripods, and they're both pointing right at the bed. I mean, there's got to be like thousands of dollars' worth of video equipment in there, like he's making home porn or something. Anyway, I got so freaked out, and I knew I had to get out of there while I still could, and just as I was about to leave I noticed this huge stack of videos all lined up on a shelf, each one labeled with different girls' names." She looks at Abby, then me, and takes a deep breath. "And when I saw the one labeled 'Zoë/Carly,' well, I just grabbed it and ran."

She shakes her head and looks at me. "I didn't sleep the entire night cuz I was so scared about everything that happened, and everything that could've happened, and what he might try to do to me if he notices the missing video. And I really needed to see you, but then when you didn't come to school today . . ." She shrugs, looking back and forth between me and Abby.

I glance at Abby, who's sitting there completely still, her eyes wide, her mouth hanging open, then I look at Teresa and say, "What'd you do with the tape?" And I watch as she reaches into her big green tote bag, then hands it to me.

"You should burn it," she says. "You should get rid of it so no one will ever find it."

I turn it over in my hands, wondering if I will.

"I'm so freaking scared," she says, starting to cry now. "I mean, what if he notices it's missing, then tries to come after me and retaliate or something?"

I close my fingers around the tape, pressing it hard into

my palm. Then I look at her and say, "You have to call the cops. You have to make sure he pays."

"I know," she whispers, nodding her head, her eyes filled with tears.

"But then everyone's gonna know your business, and everyone's gonna talk."

But she just shrugs. "I know that too."

Thirty-four

The second Abby and Teresa leave, I run up to my room and shove the diary and tape between my mattress and box spring, placing them side by side, having no idea what to do with them but wanting them out of my sight. Then I pace back and forth between my bed and the french doors, wondering what I should do.

On the one hand, I know they contain evidence of yet another horrible crime against Zoë. Something she felt not only responsible for, but terribly ashamed of. And it makes me so sad to know that she viewed it that way, because even though he didn't hold a gun to her head, Jason still drugged her and tricked her into doing something she never would've otherwise done. Not to mention that he's an adult, one who was well aware of the fact that Zoë and Carly weren't.

But I also think my sister had been through enough. And

I'm not sure I can drag her memory—not to mention my parents—through all of this too.

"I'm gonna go to the cops and tell them everything," Teresa had said as she stood on my porch, right before leaving. "But I won't say a word about Zoë. I swear. I mean, there's probably plenty of evidence to convict him, so I doubt they'll even need it. Besides, I feel like I owe you, I mean you did try to warn me and all."

"What do you think I should do?" I asked, looking from her to Abby, who for practically the first time ever had no advice to give.

"Forget it," she'd said, raising her hands in surrender. "I'm out. This stuff is way over my head. I had no idea you guys were living these dangerous, top-secret lives."

I looked at Teresa, but she just shrugged. "Up to you. But I promise not to say anything you don't want me to."

And as I closed the door behind them, I remembered Marc, and I knew I had to find him.

I flip open my cell and dial his number, listening to it ring so many times, I'm about to give up. But when he finally does answer, I get straight to the point. "I'm sorry," I say. "For so many things. But I really need to see you now, and it's actually pretty urgent. Do you think you can come by?"

He tells me he will, without once asking why.

I throw my peacoat over my ratty old sweats, shove my feet into some boots, pull a beanie onto my head, wrap a long, wool scarf twice around my neck, then reach under the mattress and grab the video, slipping it deep into my coat pocket. Then I purposely avoid looking in the mirror as I unlock my french doors and reach for the tree.

Obviously, I'm not trying to look cute for Marc. Because whatever weird attraction passed between us is now clearly over. At least it is for me. And I'm pretty willing to bet that it is for him too.

Because I think I finally get how my trying to be like Zoë—and Marc and I trying to be together—was just one more failed attempt to save her. And the truth is, Zoë is dead. And even though it's almost unbearable to finally admit to the "D" word, if I truly want to move on then I can no longer avoid it.

But now I'm wondering if there might be another way to save her. Now I'm wondering if I should just burn this tape and save her from yet another starring role as the poster child for bad choices. Or if maybe I should turn it in, so they can add it to the stack of evidence and make sure Jason pays.

But the weirdest thing is, I feel like it's Marc who can finally help me. Out of all the people I know, he's the only one who can help me decide.

I reach for the thickest branch, grabbing hold of it with both hands even though it would be a whole lot easier just to go downstairs and use the front door. But I know this is probably the last time I'll ever do this. And because of that, I want to get it just right.

I swing my body toward the trunk, gripping it between my knees and hugging it firmly as I shimmy all the way down to the ground, so quickly and effortlessly it's as though Zoë's right there beside me, nodding encouragingly and cheering me on.

Then I run to the corner and wait, blowing on my hands since I forgot to wear my gloves, and jumping from foot to foot in an attempt to stay warm. And when a bright red MG pulls up and brakes right beside me, it's a moment before I remember it's Marc's.

"Hey," he says, leaning over and opening the door. "You okay?"

I nod my head and climb inside, grateful for the warmth of the car and the strange comfort he provides. "I'm sorry about earlier, I just—"

But he just shakes his head and lifts his hand to stop me. "No worries," he says, pulling away from the curb and turning onto the next street.

But I don't want to be cut off like that. I mean, I owe him an apology. Lots of people owe him an apology. But I can only speak for me. "I finished her diary," I tell him, forcing myself to look right at him, even though it makes me feel a little uncomfortable. "I guess I got a little caught up along the way, and I'm sorry about that. I'm sorry I doubted you, and I'm sorry my sister doubted you, and I'm sorry this whole stupid town doubts you. But right now I need your advice, and you're the only one I can trust."

He parks in a spot that faces the lake, and we remain in the car, gazing quietly at the water before us until I take a deep breath and remove the tape from my pocket, presenting it in the palm of my outstretched hand.

"Where'd you get that?" he asks, his eyes turning dark, just like the other day.

"From Teresa," I say, my voice steady and sure, despite the erratic beating of my heart. "She swiped it from Jason's."

He grabs it, surrounding it with his fist and lifting his arm as though he's gonna toss it out the window or something. But just as quickly his body crumbles, his back hunched over in despair and defeat. "I should've known," he finally says, his head against his hands, his knuckles pressed to his forehead. "I should've fucking known."

"Known what?" I ask, my voice almost a whisper.

"That he kept a copy." He raises his head and stares at the lake. "I have now truly failed her in every single way."

"Don't," I say, reaching toward him, my hands fumbling, unsure, watching as he drops the tape onto his lap, his hands rubbing his eyes so roughly it scares me. "Don't say things like that. No one could have saved her, and it's time we all realized that. You read the diary, you know what I'm talking about."

But he just turns to me, his face red and raw, his eyes filled with pain. "That day at Teresa's?" he says. "When you were wondering what Jason gave me? What I had in my pocket? It was this. It was another copy of *this*." He picks up the tape and shakes his head. "I *knew* something happened that day, but Zoë refused to tell me. Then about six months after her funeral, when the guy's finally caught and the whole media circus is getting a second wind, he calls me up to tell me that he's got something I might want, and how he's willing to sell it for just the right price. Only the price kept changing. And every time we'd meet he kept dicking me around for more and more money. Just naturally assuming that my parents' wealth had anything to do with me. I had to sell off all the bonds my grandparents gave me, using up all the money I was saving for Zoë's memorial. But that day at Teresa's, he finally settled. And I just kept telling myself the whole entire time that even though it may not be the memorial I'd planned, I was still preserving her memory." He laughs then, but it's not a funny laugh. It's more the cynical kind. The world-just-keeps-getting-worse-and-worse kind.

"Why didn't you just go to the police? They could've handled it for you," I say.

"Maybe I should've." He sighs. "But at the time, I just couldn't risk it. I mean, for Zoë, not me. You hear what people say, and I couldn't stand to put her through that again. Believe me, my life isn't all that important anymore. I only wanted to protect her."

"Don't say that," I urge, gripping his arm, but he won't look at me, he's back to facing the window again. "Zoë would've hated to hear you talk like that," I add. "You know it wasn't her fault, you know she never consented."

"Doesn't matter." He shrugs. "People believe what they want, and I just couldn't put her through that again." He turns to me, his eyes clouded with anguish.

"How much did you give him?"

He closes his eyes and shakes his head. "You don't want to know. Let's just say it was enough to wipe me out until I turn twenty-one and take control of my trust."

"What kind of memorial were you planning?"

He looks at me and smiles. And it's so nice to see his face like that I wish it could last. "A little bench. Placed right over there," he says, pointing toward the lake. "Right in front of the water, where we always used to sit. So that people can come and relax and feed all of her ducks for her."

I reach toward him then, cupping my hands around his cheeks, bringing his face toward mine. Then I close my eyes and kiss him. But not the same kind of kiss as before, not like I'm trying to claim something that was never meant to be mine. I kiss him lightly and quickly and briefly, because he loved my sister. And because he's paid such a high price for it.

When he drops me back at my house, he looks at me and says, "So what should we do with the tapes?"

I take a deep breath. "You know, there could be other copies," I say. Then I tell him about Jason and Teresa.

"Oh, God." He shakes his head and looks away.

"But I still think I should hand it over." And when I say that, I realize how I suddenly feel sure of myself for the very first time since I got involved in any of this. "Because what happened to Zoë isn't her fault. The only thing she's guilty of is having a dream. And I think we owe it to her to believe that."

He nods, then hands me the tape, and as I open the door and crawl out of the car, I say, "But last night, when you said that about 'hurting me too'? What did you mean?"

He looks at me, his eyes wet with tears. "I failed her, plain and simple. And by allowing myself to get involved with you, I failed you too." He gazes down at his hands, balling them into tight fists before letting them release and relax. "I still love her, Echo. And I miss her so much. I'm sorry I let things progress like I did. I should've known better." He wipes his eyes with the back of his hand and stares off into the distance.

"Thanks for sharing her," I say, smiling as he turns toward me, his eyes full of questions. "You were right, I didn't really know her. But now I do."

He presses his lips together and nods, and as I shut the door and turn away, I remember how there's still one last thing. So I knock on the window, and as he rolls it down, I say, "Hey, what was the surprise? You know, the thing you were holding for Zoë? For when she came back?"

He looks at me and smiles. "You're leaning on it," he says. Then seeing my confusion he goes, "All those days when I was unavailable and not answering her calls? I was actually holed up in my garage, working on this car. I bought it off my uncle, cheap, just so I could fix it up for Zoë. I thought a girl like her deserved something special, something nobody else had."

"It's beautiful," I say, standing back to admire it, taking in the spoke wheels, the wood dash, the cherry red paint job, and black, convertible cloth top. "She would've loved it." I smile.

But he just shrugs.

"So what are you gonna do with it?"

He shakes his head. "It mostly just sits in my garage, I barely ever drive it. Yet I've been unable to part with it, though I guess it's finally time. You want it?"

I gaze at the car, part of me wanting to claim it, knowing I may never own a car as amazing as this. But the other part knows it can be put to much better use. "Why don't you sell it and buy her that bench?" I say.

And when he looks at me he smiles. And he's still smiling as he drives away.

Thirty-five

Jan 10

Today the bench was finally unveiled, so we held a big party for Zoë. And even though some people still insisted on calling it a memorial, I refused to see it that way. We did that already, over a year and a half ago. So this was more like a celebration of her life, not another remembrance of her death.

At first my parents acted all weird around Marc, but probably just out of habit. Because now they finally get that no matter how much he loved her, he just couldn't save her. None of us could. And trying to blame anyone other than her killer is just a total waste of time.

So after a few awkward moments, my dad grasped

Marc's hand, his jaw going all tight and determined as he struggled not to cry. And my mom, off the happy pills for almost three months now and no longer scared or enslaved by her tears, hugged him tight to her chest while she smoothed his hair and whispered into his ear that it will all be all right.

Then my mom wiped her face and my dad nodded his head, and they reached for each other, holding hands and leaning together, finally finding strength in the one place it'd been waiting all this time.

And as I watched them standing there, looking so complete, I realized our family sessions with the Dr. Phil wannabe probably weren't as stupid as they seemed.

That day, right after I said good-bye to Marc, I walked into the house, only to find both my parents sitting in the living room, totally hysterically panicked, with the cops well on their way.

Apparently my mom called a bunch of times, just wanting to check in and see how I was feeling. But when I failed to answer she grew concerned and came straight home to find an empty house and no note.

Well, naturally she assumed something horrible had happened, since Zoë's murder pretty much guaranteed that we'll never reside in that safe, protective bubble again. And so she called my dad, and he notified the police, and then they both sat in the den, waiting for the other shoe to drop.

I felt awful that I'd put them into such a panic, and it took me awhile to calm them down, but when I did finally get a chance to explain, I made sure to tell them only what they needed to know, while preserving the rest for Marc, Zoë, and me.

Then I reached into my pocket and handed over the tape (making no mention of the diary), while cautioning them about what it most likely contained. Then I sank onto the couch in total exhaustion, relieved to let them take over and handle these things for a change.

I also explained how the way we were living was no longer working, and how I needed them to finally figure things out. Because while all the late nights and fights would never bring Zoë back, they would eventually destroy what little we had left.

Zoë's killer was recently convicted. Apparently he'd made a longtime habit of targeting small-town girls with big dreams, promising the moon before taking their lives. Seven victims later and the creep still didn't even own a camera. And the Web page he'd set up was a total fake.

But the good news is he'll never see daylight again. He'll never be able to betray someone's faith, the way he did with Zoë.

And as for Jason? Well, the charges are all lined up, with separate trials for the drugs, the videos, and the underage girls. And with such a strong case against him, they won't have to rely on Carly and Zoë to convict him.

Still, pretty much everybody around here knows, and the gossip is worse than ever. But I no longer care. I'm just glad I didn't lose my best friends, Abby and Jenay, and was even lucky enough to find some new ones in Marc and Teresa.

Jenay showed up at Zoë's party with Chess. And Abby, having decided that her nerves and self-consciousness were solely to blame for their awkward first kiss, showed up with Jax. And after seeing how good they are together, how truly well matched they are, I'm glad she ignored my bad advice and decided to give him another chance.

Parker came too, only he brought his new girlfriend, Heidi. And even though things are still a little uncomfortable between us, I was glad he made it.

And when Teresa walked up alone, everyone turned and stared. But since I know full well what it's like to be the center of unwanted attention, I waved her over and told her to join us.

She and Sean broke up, like the second the story broke. And her parents were so angry at what she'd done and the danger she'd put herself in, and yet hugely relieved that she'd made it out basically unharmed, that they went out and bought her a brand-new car—a black BMW, loaded with the most modern GPS tracking system so they can monitor her every move. Even though, technically, she's not even old enough to drive it yet.

And after Paula passed out little Baggies full of Wonder bread, and Abby and Jenay lit the candles, Carly tried to read a poem she wrote especially for my sister, only she had to stop halfway through when she broke down in tears.

Just a few days after the whole Jason story leaked, she showed up at our house, begging our forgiveness, unwilling to leave until she was convinced that she had it. But she and I are okay now. I mean, we're not exactly friends, but now we can at least say hey when we see each other at school.

Then Marc docked his iPod and turned up the sound, and everyone gathered around the new bench, Marc on my left, my parents on my right, as we listened to Coltrane, tossed crumbs to those fat, greedy ducks, and remembered Zoë.